I0646469

Slaphappy

novel by

dug brown

This book is dedicated to anyone that's ever tried to love me...

Slaphappy

Copyright © by dug brown

All rights reserved. No part of this book may be reproduced, stored in a retrieval system, or transmitted in any form or any means—electronic, machinal, photocopy, recording, or any other—except for brief quotations in printed reviews, without the prior written permission of the author.

This is a work of fiction. All characters are fictitious. People, events, incidents descriptions, dialogue, and opinions expressed in this work are products of the author's imagination and are not to be construed as real.

First Edition July 2022

ISBN: 979-8-218-56504-6

Library of Congress Control Number: TXu 2-131-897

Cover Art: J. Oglesby

Editor: Ernesto Mestre-Reed

Pidgin Fresh Press

Content

Synthesizer

It was the birth of a new millennium and the end of a twenty-six-thousand-year cycle as our solar system gravitated haplessly around a black hole. The poles had flipped, unbeknownst to the civilians, and technology was still cute and furry; like in any new relationship, it had not yet shown its filed teeth. Our sun screamed, demanding a jump in evolution as humanity stood atop a spiritual precipice debating whether we had the ability to soar into a new existence, or would we just plummet to the pool of viruses from where we spawned.

A voice beckoned through the darkness, but there was no response, and as we waited our souls grew atrophied. We'd forgotten about the resistance, and what we'd been through just to get to our level of complacent mediocrity. No one had the gumption to fight, as they had started manipulating us a long time ago to keep us docile while they pulled us deeper into their nest of shadows. And sadly, as we drifted deeper into the darkness, and nodded off into our spiritual slumber; the only question being asked was "Where are we going and who's going to be there?" None of that mattered though, they came here long before us with an agenda to enslave a budding humanity and turn this amusement park into a museum of tolerance.

Now as they hold the reins and walk us toward extinction, harnessing our power for their own gain, unaware of the limitless energy that could warm their cold hearts when given not taken, our eyes open as fate has intervened; and we can see there is nothing to return to. The security that we built in our slave quarters is gone, and we are free. Truly free to plummet at whatever speed we find enjoyable while we wait for the next wave of injustice and watch as they take more and more and more. Do we have what it takes to embrace the shift? Can we use it to plow the earth, so that we may plant the seeds that will birth an energetic reciprocity they can't take from us?

Rake

Bruiser, your average six-foot something, bearded, flaxen haired, Gen X talk show host, finds himself in an alley behind a rundown strip mall, bent over and greeting his followers from between his legs. "What up my beloved miscreants, whatnots, and whatchamacallits? Welcome back for another egregious episode of Greed, a reality gameshow built to spill in the hopes of giving the world a break from its mundane existence. I'm your unrequited host Bruiser, and I'm here with my new friend Tiffany!"

"Bethany!" shouts the girl, on bended knee with her hands rested on both of Bruiser's bare ass cheeks.

"So… Bethany, are you going to eat that powdered doughnut or what?" asks Bruiser as his legs shake ardently.

"Or what? You're disgusting if you think I'm going to eat some mirky Georgia pow-pow off your compromised asshole for five-hundred dollars," she yelps.

"What about for a thousand?" he asks, losing his balance and pushing his orifice directly onto her nose.

"Fuck no," she says as she combat rolls out of this anal embrace. She takes her breath back and smacks him on the butt.

Upon contact, Bruiser returns to an upright position, lifting his Dickies. The motion brings fervent sensations to a place long forgotten. "A thousand dollars isn't enough to eat my asshole. It's not like anyone's going to see it." As he says that, another sensation rolls across his being that leaves him with an awkward grimace that he forces into a cunning smile.

Bethany, confronted by his persuasive glare, retorts with, "There's no fucking way I'm licking some shitty blow off of your dirty, defeated asshole."

"This shit's A1 perico, love," he says with a hint of arrogance, shaking the baggie just out of her grasp.

"I'll be the judge of that," she says, snatching the baggie from him and turning her back on him.

It makes you wonder what went wrong, Bruiser thinks. *How'd a vanilla bean, white bread, upper crust, dime piece end up in front of me with the question of a booger-sugar coated rim job on the table? Was it a series of bad decisions, or just the one made by a dark soul that lingered over her induction to this life? The life we all so covet and cling onto blindly assuming there's no better place than …*

"Oh, that's nice," she moans, interrupting his thoughts. "It's not pure, but close." Bruiser grabs Bethany by the back of the neck and pulls her toward him expecting a fight, but she collapses into him, and they connect. Her lips move robotically without direction, and as she regains clarity, she pushes away from him, asking, "What the fuck? You think kissing me is going to help lube up the concept of me licking anything off that sewage pipe?"

"Not for a second, but I thought we'd get the first dare out of the way and move on to you tongue-jacking my freshly dusted balloon knot. So … Tiffany."

"Bethany!" she demands.

"Sure, Bethany, for another thousand dollars, would you like the pleasure of being the first," he laughs childishly, "the first … to eat this … powdered … doughnut?" You can hear the sounds similar to that of an archaic computer from the seventies at work. They always say yes: for a stack of temporary freedom, for the fame that comes with an appearance on the show, for the actual moment that comes with letting go and completing the deviant act. And as much as he wants them to be the one, the one that has the strength to endure his decadent demands, he knows he could never love a girl that could sell herself to a piece of fecal matter like himself on the internet. But that's not what this is about — love.

"Just do it, B nanny!" shouts Bethany's friend from the sidelines. Bethany's friend, Jenny, is a sultry brunette that avoided his original invitation to play. "I've seen you drink sangria off of the bathroom floor."

"I can't, Jenny," she says, kicking a rock.

"I double dare you," says Bruiser. While Bethany is processing the depths of her immoral fortitude, he turns to Jenny and asks, "You want in on this, Jenny?"

Jenny stands up, entertaining the offer, and says with a gaping smile, "For two grand! Shit yeah, I'm in!"

Bruiser holds up a fresh bag of chemicals, saying, "Last chance Bethany, or Jenny gets to have all the fun."

"As if, I'll do it," says Bethany, pushing Jenny out of the way and blowing a snot rocket, making room for her punishment.

He hands the bag to Bethany as he drops trow and bends over, grabs his balls, removing their ominous presence from the shot, and asks, "Unless you two want to double down and split it?"

"You've got some issues, my dude," says Less, the cameraman, as he tightens up the shot of Bethany diving into the bag of coke face first. "There's so many other things you could've gotten her to do for less."

"Are you saying you want in on this?" asks Bruiser.

2

"They do say Less is more, but that's not what I was saying," says Less, swallowing a smirk.

"Well, can you make sure she gets a nice heaping pile on there?" asks Bruiser.

"Sure," says Less, watching Bethany as she tries her best to empty the bag, "And look, we all know the last dare is going to be you asking her to let you bang her in the dumpster for thirty-five hundo."

"Oh, I don't do anal," says Bethany without looking up.

Less looks over the camera at Bruiser and says, "Dick and I just want you to know that you could've gotten a way better looking hooker that would've done completely weirder stuff for less than six grand." He turns to Bethany and says, "No offense."

"None taken. I'm about to do a pile of blow out of his ass for two grand. I know exactly where I stand," says Bethany.

"I just think the viewers are tired of the same repetitious self-gratifying bullshit," says Less. "So, can you come up with something you think maybe she won't do — besides anal."

"Says the cameraman," says Bruiser, "I'm pretty sure she's a dead lay anyway. She kisses like a robot, so I assume she has no knack for uninhibited passion. And I'll have you know we have something special in store for Tiffany."

"Bethany, for fuck's sake, and I'm submissive."

"Bethany, the lazy white girl that won't do anal, has a true test in store for her third and final dare," says Bruiser, pointing through his legs to his producer, Dick, who stands in a dumpster dressed like a homeless person.

"Sorry, boss, I didn't mean to interrupt your process," says Less.

"Bethany! You ready?" asks Bruiser as his knees return to shaking vigorously. "I can't feel anything happening anywhere." Bethany kneels and analyzes the moment from a reasonable distance. She leans in hesitantly as she toys with the thought of bathing his crack with her tongue. Giving up on the moral debate, she dumps out what little coke is left and pauses, and then buries her face into his better half and takes in his condensed essence. As the substance takes over his nether, Bruiser releases a sulfurous, "Yeah, that's the spot."

"Fuck, that's disgusting," says one of Bruiser's guests. The guest, a well-put-together kid sweating through his hundred-dollar, tropical print T-shirt is pointing at an episode of Greed that's being projected on the wall of Bruiser's loft during an assemblage of randoms gone awry. Bruiser is passed out, face down on an old corner booth confiscated from the bar next door that was decoupaged with vintage porn. The kid looks at Bruiser, shakes the table attempting to wake him. "What a clown. I guess that's what it takes to get money though."

"That's why they call it Greed, kid," mumbles Bruiser as he tries to return to his upright position. His pupils dilate and he finds himself surrounded by nouveau-chic, tragically-hip millennials. As interest dissipates, his eyes shut and he returns to his prior state of ruminating semi-consciousness with this thought in the forefront, *They're all trying to impress themselves with how much they impress each other. The truth is: they're too busy being controlled by the technology they love, which was created by the society power brokers they hate. They're too disenfranchised to realize those two things that confine them and keep them docile, far away from a true revolution, are the two things that could set them free: a life without hatred and technology. There's a freedom buried somewhere underneath the environmental landslide of lies they've come to believe. If only they knew their masters; the ones hiding in the shadows.*

And it sucks, they never had the freedom of times past. The freedom to get lost in a world spinning at a slower speed. Not that there wasn't a mass of fear back in my formative years. We had Russia and AIDS, but that was when it was easier to get away from the powers-that-be. Not like now, you ingest fear every time you pick up your phone or go near any sort of electronic screen. There wasn't an online universe that saved every noted moment. When you got your ass kicked, it was for a select group of people, not for the whole world to witness. What was my point? The Mark of the Beast, it was an old conspiracy theory involving the New World Order implanting chips into humans to keep infinite tabs on the coveted taxpayers. We've been asleep so long, no one noticed that we paid to have it done. The chips are in our hands, and we never let go. I generally fall asleep clinging tightly to mine every night. Tonight, the device is in the upstairs section of my warehouse loft, where I'm apparently passed out at my own party (no breaking news there). I like to get fucked up because it takes me to a place I just can't get to sober."

"Bruiser, pick your head up," beckons a voice from beyond. "You're using a grand worth of yack for a pellow." This is Bruiser's long-time friend and producer, Dick Allen. Dick's a Grady baby, not that it matters, the person in Bruiser's life that pushes him to the edge and holds onto him while he teeters on it, staring into the abyss.

"Cool, it's pronounced pillow, Dick, and what do you care?" mutters Bruiser, blowing granules of fluffy white despair all over the table. "Right, fuck off then," he barks as he tries to return to the darkness.

"Because, I paid for it," says Dick, lifting Bruiser's head as he tries to extract a piece of Bruiser's content. "Give him a minute," says Dick, receiving ravenous stares from the ubiquitous followers that surround him, waiting for their toxic offerings. "He's going through a lot right now," says Dick as he returns Bruiser's face forcefully to the pile of temporary delight.

"This is it. Somebody turn this shit up! I need DBs! I want… I want my ears bleeding!" yells some random guy.

"Seriously?" mumbles Bruiser as he returns to the moment, pulling his face out of a heaping pile of dust, to find his trustees have their phones out, apparently trying to ruin him with their technology, not that they could Polish the turd that is Bruiser's rep, but the fact that they're trying agitates him.

"Bruiser, you all right? You were out for a minute," says Dick, nudging him.

"Yeah, yeah, just a little fuster clucked, got trapped in my head for a sec."

"It's been a half-hour, at least. Wipe your face off. You look like a fucking clown."

Bruiser does a mime trapped in a box, wipes a tear from his eye, and gestures an imaginary Jack in the Box middle finger. "Either way, can you turn this shit up for Chuck, so he'll shut-tha-fuck up? I'm going to grab a drink," says Bruiser, propelling himself back into the party.

Dick pulls him back into the vortex of the booth with one finger, turns to the leggy blonde next to him, and says, "Stacey, be a doll and grab a bottle and some beers for the table, please."

"As if," says Stacey, walking away from the table.

"Whatever happened with you two?" Dick asks Bruiser.

Bruiser wipes the drugs off his face and does a bump out of his palm, staring off into the far side of the room silently, thinking, *Stacey's a model maybe. She's definitely beautiful, insecure, skinny with at least a half a million followers. What they would call an influencer. One of the first contestants on the show. I had her chugging Everclear. Actually, I might have found her that way. Either way, I'd never seen anyone handle pure grain alcohol out of the bottle like she did. I figured at that point; I could do whatever I wanted with her. So, I throw some kink at her, thinking there's no way she's going to let me tickle the finish line of her alimentary canal without at least taking her out first, but I really didn't take into consideration the combination of a bottle of Everclear and five-grand on the line. And don't get me wrong, I don't get off on butt play. Honestly, I was more aroused watching her finish the bottle of Everclear than when I was second knuckle-deep in her mouth's evil twin. Anyway, she took the money and slapped me, and I believe that's when my relationship with humanity began to sour.*

"Dude, what?" Dick snaps his fingers in Bruiser's face shouting, "Bruiser!"

"Huh?" asks Bruiser.

"You were mumbling. I have no idea what-tha-fuck you were talking about." Dick scrapes the dust from Bruiser's beard and stares into his decaying resolution.

Bruiser smacks Dick's hand away from his face playfully as a girl from across the table points at the pile of dust and asks, "You sure that's coke?"

"There's honestly no telling at this point," says Dick.

"Maybe it's the psilocybin talking," mumbles Bruiser, cutting out a line from the pile of various powders he was napping on with his hand, "but they all look so worn out: dark circles around their eyes, pale splotchy skin almost like zombies, but more so just patches of dead skin held together by hope, clinging to a flickering light." He spins the tabletop, forming a spiral line that reaches the variety of stragglers that surround him.

Staring at the thousand-dollar line Bruiser just spun out, Dick asks him, "Can you slow it down, B?"

"I'll slow down when you turn this shit off! What'd I tell you about watching this shit here, especially this episode! It's by far my least favorite," demands Bruiser. He watches his following consume their offerings, and this random guy pops up from his line, shining like a seventies game show host: his hair perfect, eyes sharp, teeth a glaring white, and there's a glow around him.

The seventies game show host points to the wall and says, "No man, this is my favorite episode because you had those two girls go down on a homeless guy in a dumpster, so they could buy a new clutch and get a nose job. They're disgusting. Just tell me they were pros and that they weren't next door girls."

Bruiser looks up at the show on the wall and says, "Well, Steve, Dick was the only pro in that shot. He played the homeless guy."

"Oh, well, that's boring," says the kid, returning to his offerings.

The rest of the table hears the word "boring" and pops up like a pack of hyenas going down on a carcass when they hear a threat in the distance. They all survey the room searching for the threat and then stop, focusing their attention on Bruiser. As he returns the silent gaze, the room starts to sparkle and glow behind them. Their faces morph from their zombielike appearance to a perfection meant for a daytime soap opera. Everyone seems open and unguarded. As their auras light up, they stare with a silent confidence, and their best selves are presented. The silence grows, pushing Bruiser into a pensive, self-monitoring moment. He imbibes another face full of his concoction, hoping to remove the hallucination and get back to the comfortably low vibration he prefers to wade in.

As Bruiser pulls his face out of the emptiness, he hears another one of his guests dogging out his show, talking about how superficial and demeaning it is. He looks around the room, but can't seem to locate the culprit, so he looks at the kid in front of him and says, "You know, it's not like I make these people — that's the government's doing. They have their foot on our heads, keeping us in and out of the water with just enough air to gasp but with no way to get out of the water, and we're too tired to just swim away, so we let them enslave us with their rules and regulations. I'm just trying to help by giving them a break from their financial woes. They can say no, but they rarely ever do. You know?"

Bruiser zones out as he looks down at the tabletop, and there's a loud pop as some kid throws a bottle at the wall. The sound of shattering glass resets Bruiser's perspective. He finds the table staring back at him silently waiting for his reaction. He shakes his head, and when he reopens his eyes, the table has returned to their prior darker gray, zombie-like selves, open wounds, and lost looks in their eyes.

Dick stands up and barks, "C'mon, man, does this look like a hobo frat house?"

The kid looks over at Bruiser and shouts, "Kind of, but without the super easy sorority bag-ladies."

Dick tries to make his way out of the booth, but Bruiser stops him and says, "It's cool, man. I got it."

"It's not cool, B. It's disrespect, and you should slap his ass down to the ground." Dick sits back down as Stacey walks up to Bruiser and hands him a beer. Stacey tries to sit on Bruiser's lap, but he pushes her into the booth next to Dick. She returns to Bruiser like she needs the rejection to be whole, and as she puts her hand on his leg staring into his being, he stands up and retreats from his favorite place looking for the impossible — solace.

As he walks through the crowd, he's confronted by the bottle breaker, saying, "I dare you to slap me, Bruiser. C'mon, I double dare you."

Bruiser gives him a light tap on the cheek and says, "I would hit you harder, but I'd be giving you a story to tell your friends at the D&D table, and that would reward your blatant disregard for my home. Clean up the glass, and we'll call it even. Leave it there, and I'll find you and—"

"What? Do what?" asks the kid, bucking up.

"Nothing, nothing at all. I'm going to let you continue to live your meaningless existence, hoping for a chance to achieve something more memorable than the moment when I let you walk away without fucking you up." Bruiser pushes the kid out of the way with his finger and walks off towards a velvet curtain in the corner of the room. He slides behind it and climbs a ladder that leads to the roof, far away from the turbulent buzz of the party. He pops his head out of the portal and surveys the current situation on his rooftop. It's hard to see through his chemically enhanced visions, but he makes out a small group of people sitting on his couch around a flickering candlelight. He tries to focus, but only sees dark shadows dancing around the flame on the coffee table.

"Bruiser!" beckons a girl.

"Who dat?" he asks.

"Don't worry, none of your fans up here," she responds.

"Definitely," states another female voice.

Bruiser climbs out of the hole, stumbling to the group hesitantly, and asks, "What up, nerds?" He climbs over to the couch and plops down next to Desiree. She's got long blonde hair, the body of a swimsuit model, a heart of gold, and a personality that most dudes just can't keep up with. She's one of his broken mirrors, to say the least. If he ever were to give up, settle down, and breed — it'd have to be with her. If it weren't for the fact that she hates him and barely tolerates him because they have the same friends. So, for now, she's hidden in the darker neighborhood of his heart, that place where he's not comfortable walking alone at night. On the other side is Leslie, his editor. She's built like a hairless ferret and carries herself like a stoned tarsier, cute and creepy at the same time. Bruiser loves her banter, but he's always worked hard to avoid spending time in her as he knows her twin, Less, would destroy him somehow, or the show, or both. Probably both.

"Sure, get comfortable," says Desiree as she tries to readjust her seating so that she isn't touching him. Bruiser leans back and the couch swallows him, settling him into a meditative state staring up at the sky. "Don't you get tired of this?" Desiree asks Bruiser. "You don't even know anybody down there trashing your place, do you?"

Bruiser lights a cigarette, saying, "That's what's great about parties, you meet new people. Not like you guys, up here holding hands, staring at your phones while listening to Less recite Reddit posts."

Less, the blatantly recessive twin, who loves sludge metal, video games, and anything that involves technology, puts his phone down on the arm of his chair and leans forward. "I thought you liked it when I read the internet to you?"

Bruiser laughs and says, "No one likes it when anyone reads the internet to them, Less. No offense: I let you talk because it seems like you don't get the chance too often."

Less leans back in his chair and says, "I'm always talking to someone basically all day."

"Who? Your friends on the internet don't count," says Bruiser in a snarky tone, "they're not real."

"They're real." Less jumps back in his phone, digging around for virtual proof of life.

"Yeah, but it's not the same as face-to-face," says Bruiser.

"Leave him alone, Bruiser. You're being a dick," says Desiree as she attempts to get up and away from him.

Bruiser grabs her thigh and pulls her back into the couch, saying, "I remember a time when you loved dicks."

"You're poking at him," says Desiree. "He talks to people all over the world; about what I'm sure are thought-provoking conversations."

Bruiser leans forward and starts digging through the ashtray in search of a sizable roach. "Sure, but he can log off at any moment and just disappear from the conversation. Unlike right now, where he's trapped, forced to fight his way to the escape hatch." Leslie pulls Bruiser by the shirt back into the couch, hands him a fresh joint, and lights it for him.

Desiree grabs the joint out of Bruiser's mouth and says, "But unlike you, and the tiny little bubble you live in, that's filled with the same empty *existential* conversations you have with every random chick you're trying to park your dick in, while your girlfriend's at home pulling her hair out one by one while she tries to figure out why you won't give in and let her love you, he's a good person."

"Okay, now who's being a dick? That's not even relevant to the conversation." Bruiser leans back into the couch and says, "What's it matter to you, how I treat my … Janeuh? We have an … understanding."

"You can't even say it," mumbles Desiree.

"Girlfriend sounds so fucking serious," says Bruiser. "We have an open relationship. There should be a different name for what we have like—"

"Like concubine! It's irrelevant what you call her because you treat everyone like shit. You're always pressing buttons, manipulating psyches for fun. Fuck! You do it for a living. Doesn't it get old?" Desiree stands up, walks the joint to Less, and sits down on the arm of his chair.

"I don't mind, Des," says Less, spinelessly.

"What do you want to hear, Des?" asks Bruiser. "Conflict is all I know. It's my love language. I grew up in a warzone, and the combatants were my family. The only way I could get any attention was by acting out and hurting myself. That I'm miserable, and want everyone around me to feel that pain?"

"Yeah, kind of," she says. "I didn't think you could see it, but—"

"I'm not finished. That I'm surrounded by people that love me, but I can't feel anything. In a room full of people, I'm completely alone because I think people only like me when I'm fucked up. I'm a pair of fucking clown shoes, big red floppy fucking clown shoes."

"No, that's good. We'll say you stopped at your love language. Look, we love you, and you're safe here. Throw down your weapons," pleads Desiree.

"Look, I'm just messing around. Can we start over?" begs Bruiser. He rolls over the back of the couch and disappears, and then motions as if he were walking up the stairs out of an imaginary basement and shuffles over to Desiree, gives her a giant bear hug, shakes her lovingly, and places her back on the arm of Less's chair. Bruiser drops into Less's lap, grabs his chin, and shakes it, asking, "How are you doing, lil' buddy? I missed you. Can we just do this all night long?" Bruiser spreads his arms out, pushing Desiree off the chair onto the floor. She crawls back over to the couch as Bruiser stares deep into Less's eyes and says, "Just hold me. I feel so safe in your arms."

Less puts the joint in Bruiser's mouth, pushes him out of his lap, and kicks him toward Leslie and Desiree on the couch. Bruiser crawls on his hands and knees toward Leslie and climbs in her lap like a dog. He rests his head in Leslie's lap and starts twirling her scarlet locks in his fingers. Leslie leans in and attempts to takes the joint from him, but he flips it around in his mouth and starts blowing smoke into her face until she coughs. "How was your day, Leslie? Did you meet any fresh snacks today?" he asks as he pulls the joint out of his mouth and hands it to her.

"Snacks?" she asks as she gasps for fresh air.

"Chickens?" he asks, volleying her question.

"Chickens?" she asks.

"Disposable dicks? Guys just for fun? Or girls? Whatever you're into or whatever's into you, I guess."

"I was with you all day, silly. We came here straight after work," says Leslie. She scrounges up a thick loogie and hangs it over Bruiser's face.

Desiree, nauseated by Leslie's adoration, pushes Bruiser's feet onto the floor, asking, "See, was that so hard?"

Bruiser sits up, puts his arms around the girls, and says, "No, but that's not me. Maybe it was the stint in the crack house, or those few times I was homeless. It could've been every woman that abused my heart, or maybe it was watching my mom suffer from depression as she was beaten physically or emotionally by every man that tried to love her — ever. This life has been so dark for me; I can't find the light switch."

"That old card, Bruiser," says Desiree, watching him continue to toy with Leslie. "When are you going to let go of your trauma?"

Bruiser pauses and turns to Desiree. "I suppose I should just throw away my paycheck on various mystics and healers so that I can be good?"

"Feel good. Be happy." Desiree punches him in the arm. "And that's not fair. It's not throwing it away if it goes toward healing and happiness. How much do you throw away self-medicating all the while trying to surround yourself with people to hate? I'm so close to booking a show and getting—"

"Paid," he says.

"More like getting; THE fuck out of here!"

"And you think that's because of some ten-day yoga retreat or an energetic cleansing from some old wannabe Wavy Gravy?"

"Yes!" she says boldly as she loses her cool.

Bruiser hands the joint to Desiree, saying, "Calm down, Des. You're safe here." He grabs the girls and brings them in for a group hug. "Love you guys," he says and then pushes their faces into his lap.

"Bruiser!" They scream together.

"What show?" asks Bruiser.

"Where's Dick?" asks Desiree as she fights her way out of Bruiser's nether region.

"I was just trying to show you," he laughs.

Leslie, quite comfortable with her head in Bruiser's lap, says, "I think I found him."

"Leslie! You'll catch FacePV," says Desiree, trying to push Leslie out of Bruiser's lap. Leslie doesn't budge. "No, Dick can tell you. He got me the gig. I mean, I have to audition, but it's just a technicality."

"Audition for what?" asks Less.

"A show out in LA," says Desiree.

"And Dick got you set up?" asks Less.

"Yeah, where is he? Less, get him up here," demands Desiree.

The hatch to the roof pops open and everyone's heads turn.

"Speak of the damn devil," says Bruiser.

Dick laughs as he pulls two tall, blonde, and curvy girls out of the hatch, asking, "Would the devil bring you two angels like this?"

"Yes," replies Desiree.

"Well girls, here he is. Bruiser, this is Stephanie and Sydney. They're up-and-coming actresses, and they want to talk to you about getting some exposure."

"To what? Herpes?" asks Leslie as she high-fives Desiree.

Bruiser pushes Leslie off him and tries to clean himself up and get erect. "What would two works of art like yourselves want with an appearance on Greed?"

Desiree mumbles, "Probably looking to fuck their way to the bottom."

Leslie is the only one who laughs. The two girls sit down on either side of Bruiser, pushing Leslie and Desiree down the couch. Less leans over, trying to get in on the action and asks, "Girls, how we doing? I'm Less and this is my sister, Leslie. We work with Bruiser. I run the camera. Leslie does all the editing."

"Cute," says Sydney.

"Not really," says Stephanie.

"Sarcasm," retorts Sydney.

Less backs away gracelessly tripping over the coffee table.

"Ladies, play nice," says Bruiser as he puts his hands on the girls' thighs. "Less is actually the guy that's gonna' make your worst decisions look like it was worth it."

"We don't have to sleep with him to get on the show; do we?" asks Sydney as she rubs Bruiser's hand.

"You don't have to do anything you don't want to do," imparts Dick.

"Oh, good. I don't think I could have done it," says Stephanie, "he's just so little."

Desiree and Leslie look at each other and Leslie asks, "Less, you ready to go? We've got an early day tomorrow."

Desiree stands up and says, "Me too."

Less starts to stand up, and Bruiser stops him saying, "Less, sure you don't want to stay and hang out? We could get weird and shoot an episode with these two."

Desiree looks over at Less, drooling over the girls as they ignore him. "C'mon, Less, let's leave these not-so-gentle men to their business."

Less stutters, "But—"

Leslie snips, "Less, let's go before you catch the Herp."

Less walks over to shake the girls' hands, and they scoff at him, and immediately start kissing Bruiser's neck.

Desiree grabs Less by the hand and says, "C'mon. G'night, loser, I mean boozer, sorry … Bruiser." Desiree, and Leslie give Dick hugs and make their way to the hatch with Less.

Bruiser goes to hand the joint to the girls, and not wanting to offend either of them, puts it directly in the middle of the two. The girls reach for it at the same time. He smirks and says, "Girls, no need to fight over it. There's enough to go around."

"Game on," the girls say together. Sydney takes control of the joint, and Stephanie slithers over Bruiser's lap onto her. Sydney goes in for a kiss and slides her hand up Stephanie's skirt.

Dick tries to slide into the action, and Bruiser gets up and pulls him away from the couch. "Girls, can you give me a minute with my associate?"

"You can't have them both," says Dick.

Bruiser and Dick set their gaze on their new friends and the two watch as the girls entertain one another. "I don't think you have much say in it," says Bruiser.

"What do you mean? I found 'em."

"Means nothing. They're here for the talent. You can watch," says Bruiser, laughing.

Dick pulls a blunt from behind his ear and lights it, asking him, "Are you still mad about last time? Dude, it won't get weird, I promise!"

Bruiser takes the blunt from him and snarks, "Our balls touched, Dick! That's something that never should've happened."

"It was a miscalculation. I thought I had it," says Dick.

"Well, you didn't, and you're grounded. No more fun time for you." Bruiser hands Dick the blunt back and returns his attention to the girls, asking, "You got Desiree on a show?"

"Yeah. I got her a part on a sitcom in LA. It's like a revamp of Cheers but in a reality format."

"In LA? What show?" asks Bruiser.

"Well, it's a pilot, a quasi-reality show that takes place in and around a bar. All actors and comedians in a real restaurant, with real patrons, but they film the relationships of the employees in and outside of work. Nothing pretentious like Vanderpumps. It's more of a dive bar scenario."

"So, you sold our show?"

"Wasn't me. I'd forgotten about that whole concept." Dick spaces out, watching the girls go at it. "Needameyer asked if I knew any sexy bartenders that wanted to be on TV. I had no idea what for."

"Needledick? He sold our idea. I want a piece of it." Bruiser walks off with the blunt and starts pacing in a circle.

"I didn't even ask. I believe he said it was a friend in LA," says Dick.

"You know what's funny? Des books a show, but she's still stuck in a restaurant. Fuck. I can't believe you," says Bruiser.

"What?"

"Reality is going to ruin her non-existent career."

"Dude, she'll be making money out in LA. How is that bad?"

"Because it's a dead end. Besides, all the serious film gigs are here in Atlanta now. LA is a ghost town."

"Anything can happen in LA. You know that. You just don't want her to go, do you?" Bruiser is unresponsive. "Just be happy with her being the one that got away; and try to focus on the avalanche of puss that's still crushing you as we speak."

"She's different."

"And that's why you're never gonna' get in that," says Dick, laughing. "She knows what you're capable of, Bruiser."

"What's that supposed to mean? And I've been in her delightful little unicorn pussy."

"When?" asks Dick.

"It doesn't matter." Bruiser returns his gaze to the girls and finds them on the floor fighting for pole position.

"When?" asks Dick. "I don't believe you."

Bruiser stares Dick down. "Look, I love you like a brother, and I've been wanting to get this out for a while now because the guilt is turning into a tumor."

"Desiree and I haven't dated since high school. Why would I care?"

"Look, you can hit me, but I'm gonna' say it," says Bruiser, tapping his cheek.

Dick cracks his knuckles and says, "This should be good."

Bruiser steps back, hoping to get out of his reach, and asks him, "Remember when your mom kicked you out and you went to stay with your dad in Charlotte for a minute?"

"Wait, fuck you, B! Seriously."

Bruiser puts his hands up, covering his face, and says, "It wasn't me bro, she—"

"Raped you, Bruiser? C'mon."

"No, not exactly. Me and Stew-balls were over there, trying to get at her sisters. I hadn't even thought about Des as an option. I mean, me and you weren't really tight at that point."

"I brought you into the circle on your first day, showed you around, and introduced you to everyone. That didn't mean anything?"

"She was so upset you were gone. I don't know what you were doing to her, but she was about to overheat."

"So, you were just trying to help?"

"Who would say no to that girl?"

"I still have to hit you."

"Dude, not in the face, please. You can have both the girls."

"I'd rather hit you than hit that," Dick says, pointing at the girls as they stare back with lost looks in their eyes. "Plus, I already tried."

"I think all you need is a dick, bruh," says Bruiser, pointing at the two girls as they force themselves inside one another. "Apparently you don't even need that," he says, patting Dick on the back aggressively. "Fuck it. I probably won't feel it anyway."

"I can't believe you've been sitting on that one for almost twenty years," says Dick, throwing a playful jab at Bruiser.

Bruiser flinches and says, "I'm not proud of it, but I'm glad it's out there now."

"Come here," says Dick as he tries to pull Bruiser into his embrace. Bruiser flinches. Dick laughs and says, "I love you, buddy, but you owe me dibs whenever I want it."

"Are things that bad? You going through a dry spell?"

"Please, I've thrown away more pussy than you'll ever get! I just want to cock-block you for fun at this point."

Bruiser looks back at the girls, trying to determine his point of entry, and says, "Fair enough. For how long?"

"At least a year. Oh, and Bruiser—"

Bruiser turns his attention back to Dick and asks him adamantly, "What?"

Dick punches him in the gut, dropping him to his knees, and says, "I can't blame you for fucking Desiree. That's for not telling me."

"Won't happen again, sir." Bruiser crawls to the end of the couch and perches on the arm like Batman hovering over Gotham. Holding his abdomen as he overlooks the girls, he asks them, "Girls, are we thirsty? I believe I have some champagne in the cellar."

Stephanie squeaks, "We love the champs!"

"Dick, do us a favor? Go grab a couple of bottles and some cheese out of the fridge. I'm starving."

"Seriously, bro?"

"C'mon, Dicky poo. We're parched. Save us!" says Sydney in a seductive baby voice.

Bruiser laughs and mimics Sydney, saying, "C'mon, Dickie poo, pwease?"

"Okay, but lock me out like you did last time, and I'm firing you!"

"Fair enough. We'll just be going over the girls' hobbies, strengths, weaknesses, and such. Take your time." The girls traverse the arm of the couch, climbing onto Bruiser and dragging him back to the couch. They start licking his ears and neck while rubbing on his stomach and then move toward his favorite party trick. Bruiser leans back, unzips his pants, and looks up at the sky, saying, "You two get comfortable, make yourselves at home."

The stars become his transcendental desktop as he removes himself from the moment, thinking, *I don't have any savings really. No retirement, no health insurance, and honestly, I don't even remember where I parked my car. Haven't seen it in weeks, but for some odd reason, these two beautiful girls are totally comfortable with me because they think they know me from the show; the show that feeds my voracious libido. Don't get me wrong, they're generally worse off than I am when it comes to the whole sex drive thing: like cats in heat, clawing at the couch, moaning for relief from their suffering. But I think what really does them in is the incurable pursuit of the ego to find its personal worth in the shimmering reflection of someone else's eyes.*

Sydney finds her way to the floor on her knees between Bruiser's legs, sticks her hand in his pants, and pulls his dick out. She licks her lips and kisses the tip. He looks over at Stephanie and smiles, grabs her waist, stands her up on the couch over his chest, and looks up her skirt. "You from Florida?"

"Yeah, how'd you know?" asks Stephanie.

"Lucky guess," he says and forces her already moist little snatch onto his face. He goes up on her, lapping away, like the cure is in there. Somewhere. He stops Sydney before she gets carried away with the task at hand and asks her, "Can you go lock the hatch?"

Sydney wipes her mouth. "What about the champ and cheese?"

"The champ's right here, and I think we can do without the cheese. I'm pretty sure Dick would just slow us down."

"But he said he'd fire you," Sydney says.

"He said he'd fire *me* if I locked him out. He can't fire you, cute stuff," snickers Bruiser. Sydney gets up to go lock the hatch as Bruiser slides Stephanie down his chest right onto his other best friend. He slides her blouse off to find she has a perfect rack — torpedoes: young, firm, and always appreciated. "You can have whatever you want," he mumbles.

"I just want to cum," she whispers in his ear.

"That shouldn't be a problem. I'm squirtified in the art of female ejaculation."

Stephanie closes her eyes and faces the night sky without challenging his boast. Sydney starts to walk back to the couch and stops, lights a cigarette, and watches as her friend is fulfilled. "Save me some," she says, walking over to Bruiser and staring him down. She pushes Stephanie off Bruiser and puts her cigarette in his mouth. She looks down at his member, covered in her friend's freshly squeezed juices, and says, "Yumm … meee."

"I was so close. You suck," says Stephanie.

Bruiser climbs over the back of the couch onto a mattress resting behind it. The two girls follow him, jumping over the couch as they strip down. He lays them on their backs and starts making out with them at the same time. He proceeds to play with their openings, holding them like bowling balls, working the G-spot and the clitoris at the same time as they intertwine. They're starting to twitch, and he can feel the energy running up their spines as it tries to escape their bodies. The harder he works to get them off, the more they get into each other. The energy rolls between them. They squirm vigorously, almost as if they want to get away from him, but he won't let go. The girls release at the same time and collapse onto the bed next to him quivering. He gets up on his knees, and staring down at the girls, asks boldly, "What's next?"

"Whatever you want, daddy," purrs Sydney as she rolls over, pointing her dripping wet peach at him. He pulls her up by her hips and starts going at her from behind. Stephanie slides underneath Sydney and throws her legs over her friend's shoulders. Bruiser grabs Sydney by her haunches and proceeds to pound away at her back end. Sydney loses focus and stops entertaining Stephanie. She arches her back as Bruiser puts in his best effort to not get thrown. Stephanie, filled with greed, pushes Bruiser off Sydney onto his back and mounts him. Sydney, bewildered by what just happened, decides to take Bruiser's face for a spin.

Stephanie grabs Sydney's waist and pulls her in for a long sultry make out session. Her body starts to convulse, and she grabs Bruiser's balls, screaming, "I want you to cum! Cum for me, Bruiser!"

"I won't, and you can't make me," he says confidently as he pushes Stephanie off onto her friend. She retreats contentedly from the gathering having taken what she wanted from the night. Bruiser flips Sydney over on her back and folds her up like a lawn chair. He revisits her nexus with his tongue, hoping to lick his way to her center, that place of truth that no one else knows. His jaw pops out of place, and he waits for her to beg him to infiltrate her. He looks over at Stephanie, lying there, touching her pussy gently, caressing it like a friend that had been through a great trauma, and then returns to Sydney's warm loving hole.

She starts to shake until she erupts with a blast of warm female secretion and collapses into the bed, screaming, "Again! Again!"

"I give up," he says as Sydney's contents drip down his face.

"I got you," says Stephanie as she rolls him over and then puts her new bestie in her mouth.

"What's missing?" he mumbles, lying in a puddle of fluids, staring up at the stars while Stephanie tries her hardest to return him to his formidable state. *Every man dreams of being loved momentarily by two beautiful women,* he thinks.

Stephanie backs up off his member and states, "A glass of champagne and some Manchego would be perfect."

Love, he thinks, and at that moment a shooting star crosses the sky. "Thank you," he says out loud.

"For what?" asks Stephanie.

"I saw a shooting star, Sarah," he says.

"It's Stephanie, and I believe I get your wish for that."

"Fair enough," he says. "What would you like?"

"World peace," she responds.

"Well, wouldn't want to waste a wish on that fairy tale."

"It's my wish!" she belts out.

"World peace it is."

"What are you two going on about?" asks Sydney.

"I saw a shooting star," he says.

"What are you going to wish for?" asks Sydney.

"What would you wish for?" he asks.

"Other than an ice-cold bottle of champs? World peace."

"Really? That's what Stephanie wished for," he says.

"Couldn't hurt — this place is a mess," says Sydney.

"You might as well go for intergalactic peace while you're wasting wishes," he says as he lays back.

"Intergalactic peace it is," says Stephanie.

"What would you wish for?" Sydney asks him.

"Another shooting star," he says, and retreats to his own thoughts, filing through all his lost loves as they appear in the foreground of the cosmos. Many without names, just little things like mole placement, scars, or other personal nuances.

The last face he sees is Janeuh, and her ghostly image starts yelling at him immediately, "What-the-fuck are you doing, you worthless piece of shit? You're never going to love me, are you? You're just like my dad."

"And you couldn't be more like my mom," he says aloud.

"What?" Stephanie grabs his dick tightly.

Bruiser flinches and says, "Nothing. I said your cock work is exemplary." Stephanie swallows his dick and puts it deep in the back of her throat, smashing her uvula. Bruiser cums, and as he does, he sees another shooting star, saying, "Thank you," as it crosses the sky.

She coughs a little, spits his blueprints over the side of the bed, and rolls over onto him, saying, "You're welcome."

"You were amazing, but I was talking to the sky and whoever imagined it."

Bruiser, finally alone, lies there staring at the sky, and it seems like only a moment passes as his eyes shut and then open to daylight. He looks over the two mistakes he made from last night, and the light reveals their true selves, free of the makeup and garments used to hide their flaws. He looks them over, noticing how very far from perfect they are, and realizes that he must sneak away to avoid an awkward confrontation.

He looks for the clearest path out, one that that won't wake the trolls that guard his freedom. He sits up and slides to the edge of the bed while he rehashes his night in search of his phone, hoping to get a bearing on how far behind he is on this new day. He finds his phone, but it's dead — a useless paperweight. He rubs his face and scans the rooftop looking for a fluid, hoping to find a sandbag he can use to remove the skank taste from his mouth but finds only empty beers.

He looks back at the bed, wanting to crawl back in, and is startled by one of the girl's crusty, corn-infested hoofs. He jumps up out of bed and feels something hit his foot. He looks down and sees his best friend flopping around like a fish out of water. He grabs his pelvis and finds he has nothing with which to protect himself.

Bruiser's eyes burst open with the thought, and he screams, "I'm a FUCKING EUNUCH, my dick, my FUCKING DICK!" as he's pulled from his nightmare. He awakes to a banging on the hatch, that's paired with his throbbing head. He walks over to it, opens it, and Dick pops his head through, screaming, "Yeah, its fucking Dick, Dick Allen. Let's go, we're running late!

Ouroborous

The ardent Georgia sun pushes down on Bruiser awakening a well-deserved but vicious hangover he was hoping he'd left at home. He makes his way to the production van. His phone, in hand, connected to a portable charger, comes to life, and then starts vibrating vigorously. "Heyyyyyyy, Janeuh, I know, my phone died. How are you?" he asks as he climbs in the van and lights his first cigarette of the day, unconcerned with the silence he just corrupted.

"I won't accept that one anymore," screams Janeuh through the phone, "You're a grown-ass man!"

Bruiser pulls the phone away from his ear, puts it on speaker, and says, "I passed out on the roof."

"That's not a valid excuse, either. I'm coming over there right now. I swear, if that deee-scusting rooftop mattress is covered in more whore secretions, I'll—"

"What, psycho? You'll follow me around in that terrible Paris Hilton disguise, sneaking around in back alleys, and haunting my parties via social media," he says belligerently.

"You're the one that said you preferred blondes. I was just trying to mix it up. I wasn't creeping. It was a stalker fantasy thing," she says laughing.

"It was kind of sexy, but look—"

"We had plans!" she says adamantly.

"I know, I got fucked up!" he yells into the phone.

"You're always fucked up!"

"How many times have you ghosted me for work when we had plans?" he asks. And then there's that silence that comes right before the gasping of air that's followed with tears.

"Look, booger, the house filled up with randoms. I couldn't leave. I got lost in the moment." He fakes throwing the phone, wishing he could.

Dick hits the gas wishing he could outrun Bruiser's conversation, asking, "You in trouble?"

"Always," whispers Bruiser, as he puts his hand out like a Jedi using the force trying to silence his friend. "Look, bunny farts,

I've got to do the work thing. Let me make it up to you tonight? We'll go check out a band maybe, grab some yum-yum."

Mocking Bruiser, Dick says, "C'mon, bunny farts, let's grab some yum-yum."

"I gotta' go!" Bruiser says.

"I love you. Don't fuck up, or you won't get to fuck it up," Janeuh barks through the phone and then lets out a sigh filled with disdain and clicks off.

"I won't. You're the best…"

"No, you're the best," says Less, poking the morning bear.

"Less, get in the back!" shouts Bruiser.

"What's going on, mein? You all right?" asks Dick, noticing Bruiser's face has turned a rather greenish hue.

"Yeah, same old, you know," says Bruiser.

"I do know, but there's something I want you to know."

"What?" asks Bruiser blindly.

"I love you," Dick starts laughing, "and I just don't think I can take it, if you fuck up … before you get to fuck it up."

"Thanks, I needed to hear that. I didn't think you could say it," says Bruiser. Less leans back into the front seat with Dick and Bruiser wearing a pair of Buddy Holly glasses. "Nice glasses. It's about time you finally committed to full-on nerd." Less hands Bruiser his tablet. Bruiser looks at a live shot of the dashboard and then looks back at Less and then back at the tablet. He grabs the glasses from Less, puts them on, and looks at the tablet while looking ahead, creating an endless image. "Sick! Did you make these, Less?"

"I found 'em on a spy supply website and altered them. The quality on the lens was lacking, so I souped them up a little."

"Do they have audio?"

"For sure, not the best, but we can work around it."

"Little buddy, I love it. I don't know where we'd be without you."

Leslie yells from the back of the van, "Probably still bartending at Chili's on exit 272."

"Those were the days, all you could eat awesome blossoms," says Bruiser playfully, as he gets lost in the bottomless tablet.

"What happened with those two girls last night, Bruiser?" asks Less.

"Yeah, and fuck you very much by the way," interjects Dick. "I told you I'd fire you, if you locked me out!"

"It wasn't me, Stephanie, or Sarah, one of the two. It was their idea," says Bruiser.

Dick scoffs at him, saying, "You mean Stephanie and Sydney?"

"Whatever. I thought you said they weren't into you," states Bruiser.

"I climbed all the way up that dumb ladder with a bottle and a cheese tray. The least you could have done—"

"You wanted to watch, didn't you? Take some notes?" asks Bruiser as he pokes Dick in the ribs playfully.

Dick turns to Bruiser, laughing confidently and says in an alpha tone, "I taught you everything you know."

"That was everything? I used it as a foundation. You wanted to see those torpedoes on Sydney, didn't you?" Bruiser motions like he's holding some large pointy breasts.

"They were great, from what I could tell," says Dick as he tries to grab Bruiser's imaginary tit.

"Torpedoes?" Leslie asks, as she looks down at her chest, and then her head turns sideways like a dog contemplating life.

"Uh, biggens that hang low, but shoot out like torpedo tips," says Bruiser.

"I love whorepedos," says Less. "They're almost vintage at this point with all the fake ones out there. I knew I should have stayed. How were they?"

"The girls? You didn't miss anything. We just talked all night and then passed out in a snuggle pile," says Bruiser, trying to hold a straight face.

Dick starts laughing. "Good, because I was trying to tell you that one of them had herpes. Can't remember which one though."

Bruiser turns to Dick and pushes up his glasses. "Fuck, dude, isn't that something you should have mentioned?"

"Like that time we were smoking a bowl in that hacky-sack circle with those randoms at Lollapalooza and that dude put PCP in it, and you never mentioned it to me?" asks Dick.

"Yeah, like that," says Bruiser as he leans back in his seat, staring out the window, smoking.

"After you locked me out, I texted you and tried to warn you. You didn't get it?"

"No, my phone died." Bruiser digs through his phone looking for verification. "I really need to start checking my ho-faxes."

"What's a ho-fax?" asks Less.

Dick says, "It's like Carfax but for—"

Leslie jumps into the convo stating, "Whores like Bruiser. And I believe there's a window. Without an actual outbreak, you should be safe. Besides, you can't get it twice."

"I'm not going to say it again — I'm spotless. You know that's my superpower, avoiding girls with the dirty vag. I can see it in their eyes, and there's this voice that whispers 'I've got a dirty vag,' but it's in this creepy old woman's voice," says Bruiser in his attempt to recreate an ancient witch's voice.

"Where do you want to shoot today, Bruiser?" asks Dick.

"I don't know. Little Five, I guess. There's always a willing crowd there," he says, looking into the rearview mirror.

Dick looks over at him and says, "Speaking of willing crowds, don't forget you owe me dibs."

Bruiser looks at him and asks, "You still crying over that? You can have dibs for life. I already hit my number anyway. Maybe I'll hang up my jersey and take up crocheting."

"Shit, you retire and Less might actually get out of the single digits," says Dick lightheartedly.

"Does zero count as a single digit?" asks Leslie from the back of the van, laughing.

"I'm not a—" starts Less.

"Yeah, we should get started on that today," says Bruiser.

"Let's not and say we did!" snarks Leslie.

Bruiser turns back to Leslie and asks, "Why do you care?"

"I don't want him catching anything, trying to keep up with your slag-slaying egos."

"Those girls weren't slags. They were more like trolls, horny little trolls," he says, scratching his junk and staring Leslie down.

Dick's phone starts ringing, and he picks up asking, "What's up, Boss?"

"Tell that greedy fart I want a cut of the restaurant reality show, an executive producer credit," says Bruiser.

Dick puts his hand in Bruiser's face, trying to silence him. "No, he's up. We're pulling up to the location now."

"You totally banged those chicks," says Less.

"I did. And I'll tell you how; when you're ready."

The production van pulls into the square at Little Five Points, a southern bazaar of alternate culture: head shops, cutting edge haberdashery, and miscellaneous debris. Bruiser jumps out of the van wearing his new glasses, with a gold mic in his back pocket. He puts his cigarette out and starts scanning the crowd.

The first thing he sees is a group of train kids sitting with their dogs, sporting backpacks and bad face tattoos. They're always interested, but being so hard to shock, they always win. He walks by a group of older homeless dudes with their hats out, cussing everyone who walks by without acknowledging them. A younger hip millennial couple strolls by, turning Bruiser's head with interest. The girl's hot. She's dolled up to the nines, pin-up style. The way she walks without swing gives him the feeling she's never been given it properly. The dude with her looks more on the intellectual side and seems to be trying too hard to be accepted, rather than beat up.

"Excuse me, sir, do you have an extra cigarette?" asks the dude.

"I've never had an extra cigarette," says Bruiser playfully. "I generally smoke them all, part of the addiction. If you give me two minutes and stop calling me 'sir,' I'll explain to you how you can make a pile of cash and buy your own." Bruiser looks to the gangly, ravenous girl, wearing her ironically chic vintage garbage, covered in bad tattoos. She has the try-hard check list: chandelier cleavage-piece, thigh and cankle tattoos, Mary Jane foot tattoo, Friday the thirteenth freebies, and the infamous generic library of kitties, skulls, kitty skulls, and a cat on a sewing machine.

"Fuck off, scientologist!" says the girl.

"Ha, not even close. Buddhist," says Bruiser.

"I'm sure it's a pyramid scheme," she fires back at him. "My mother told me about that scam, and I don't have enough friends to get rich. Finn, tell him no one likes us."

"I believe you," says Bruiser dryly.

Finn, with the ranger hat, beard, flannel, tight pants, girl's Keds, and what seems to be his own bad artwork, places himself between his girl and Bruiser as if something of a violent nature were about to happen. "No, Dot, I believe he's the host of that internet game show, and he's definitely no Buddhist. Something demoralizing and cliché … 'Greed,' I think. Bruiser, right?"

Bruiser flashes a bill at them. "Sir Bruiser of Greed, and a hundred bucks if you let me make out with your girlfriend." Finn looks at Dot, analyzing whether or not she'll do it, and says, "She's not mine to barter. You'll have to ask her."

Bruiser grabs Dot's hand gently, stares deeply into her, and asks her, "Well, Dot, you think you can handle a real man?"

She pulls away quickly without thought and says, "Let's go, Finn. We've got to get to our crumping class at the Goat Farm. I can't stand to miss it again."

The couple starts to walk away.

"You still need a cigarette?" asks Bruiser.

Finn stops, turns to Bruiser smiling, and says, "That'd be rather human of you."

"Get a job. You're taking up space, creating mountains of trash, and contributing nothing to society," laughs Bruiser.

"Sorry, we don't live up to your standards, internet creep show," says Dot and drags Finn off by the arm.

Bruiser looks to Less and asks, "Did you get that?"

Less looks down at his tablet. "Yeah, it was perfect. It's crazy how the presence of a camera retards people. Those glasses really free the human interaction while capturing something closer to reality."

"Yeah, but how do they look on me?" asks Bruiser.

"I think they pair nicely with the hobo beard and the hippie hair, B." Less starts laughing, acting like he's pushing his glasses up his nose.

"Dick, go get signed releases," says Bruiser. He pulls the gold mic out of his back pocket and turns it on. "Less, go get your camera. I feel a segment coming." Bruiser kicks Less in the butt playfully, pushing him toward the van as an older man, well-dressed for a homeless person, approaches. His clothes match and seem to be up to date, but they're torn as if he's ripped pieces off them to huff some sort of solvent.

The man walks directly up to Bruiser and asks, "Brother, where you been? I been looking for you."

"Yeah?"

"Yeah, brother, you're always so good to me." The guy goes in for a hug. Bruiser stiff arms him, trying to avoid being covered in his vagrant fragrance.

"You always bless me. How long we known each other?"

"C'mon, Fly. I told you, they're tired of seeing you on the show."

Fly responds, "That's good because I can't take being on your show no mo'. I gotta' get some sleep. I just need twelve dollars for a place to stay."

"Do I look like your dad?" asks Bruiser. "Cause' I don't remember having any kids."

"If you were my dad, your dick would be twice the size and your credit would be half the number," laughs Fly.

"If that's possible," says Bruiser.

"Your dick?"

"No, man, my credit. It's so bad, it couldn't get any lower. Go find me someone for the show, and I'll take care of you." Bruiser looks at Dick and shrugs.

Fly puts his palm out, expecting payment, and says, "I'll be right back. I've got the guy for you."

"When you bring me back someone I can work with."

Fly shuffles off around the corner.

Bruiser looks down at his phone.

"You've got Fly doing casting now?" asks Dick.

Bruiser doesn't even look up from his phone. "I mean, call the girls from last night. They were down for whatever."

"I'm not trying to hand out a pile of cash today. Needameyer says we're over budget. You're handing out money like it was bottled water from the Red Cross. Ted wants you to make the dares more challenging. He said we're not your personal escort service, paying for all your extravagant sexual relations while feeding your need to perform in front of the world."

"He said that shit?" asks Bruiser as he lights up.

"Na, you know he doesn't care. We make so much off ads it's ridiculous." Dick takes the cigarette from Bruiser.

"What'd he say about getting us on Desiree's show as producers?" asks Bruiser as he lights another cigarette.

24

"I'm pretty sure he wants to keep us on Greed," says Dick as he scans the crowd. "You'd leave all this?"

"Anything to get back to LA; Atlanta's beat," he says, as he looks across the square for broken souls.

"We could take the show on the road," suggests Dick.

Bruiser's eyes light up. "Fresh meat! We can start in Miami, then New York, and then go kick it with Des in LA."

"You're still on that whole Desiree thing? Maybe she's trying to get away from you," says Dick with a smirk.

"She said that?" asks Bruiser slightly butt hurt.

"You're a little slow, aren't you?"

Less walks up with his Steadicam rig and says, "Bruiser, yeah, a little."

"I've got a bad feeling about her going to LA for this show," says Bruiser, scratching his arm.

"You just don't want her to leave because you'd no longer have your unobtainable goal."

"It's not that, Dick," says Bruiser with a serious look. "It's reality TV, and it's going to ruin her career."

"You know how bad she wants to act, even if it is reality? Do you know how hard it's been for her to watch all her friends working in the industry while she's stuck behind the stick at some hipster gastro pub?"

"I thought she hated our show," says Bruiser. "It's the main reason she thinks I'm such a scumbag."

"Yeah, but as sad as it is, she still works in a bar, and you're doing what you want."

"Ruining the internet one webisode at a time is exactly what I wanted to do with my life." Bruiser smiles as he surveys the crowd growing rapidly around him.

Dick starts laughing, covers his face, and asks, "What's it feel like to have a purpose in this crazy pointless existence?"

Fly walks up, dragging a dirty, piss-stained hobo on a rusty, old Radio Flyer.

Less elbows Bruiser in the ribs and says, "Yo, Bruiser, looks like Fly found your dad."

Dick inspects the body. "There's definitely a resemblance."

"What-the-fuck, Fly? Is that guy even alive?" asks Bruiser.

"He smells like he got trapped underneath a hobo soup kitchen in the back of a garbage truck. Is he even breathing?" asks Dick.

Fly shrugs and asks, "What do you want me to do with him?"

"About all this guy is good for is a dirty, dirty, bench or maybe a lawn dart board," says Bruiser.

Fly dumps him in front of Bruiser. When he hits the ground there is a series of noises: pocket full of change, his head bouncing off the sidewalk, a moan following, creaking of bones, and a deep hollow fart that leaves the eye twitching and the nose running from the smell of something like the first time in many millennia an ancient catacomb was opened. Bruiser kneels and starts slapping the vagrant. He stops and looks up at Dick.

"Can you use him?" asks Dick.

"Not like this. Fly, figure out what he's on and get me some. Then go get something to wake him up, a Cuban coffee for now or some coke if you can find some," says Bruiser.

"What do you want to do?" asks Dick.

"Eh, I'm sure I can get someone to fondle his lifeless chariot," says Bruiser, checking out the crowd for applicants. The sun catches Bruiser's line of sight, and all he can see is the silhouette of a portly couple walking up to the square hand in hand. As they get closer, it becomes clear they are graced with all the ingredients of a great episode: jorts, jeggings, sandals with socks, big hair, wife beaters covered in sauce, forty-ounce Slurpees, and racing hats — stock car that is — obviously.

"This should be fun. You rolling?" asks Dick.

Bruiser belts out, "Free hot dogs, get your free hot dogs!" The couple stops dead in their tracks and turns in slow motion, trying to find the source of the offerings.

Dick acts like he just hooked a tarpon. "Just reel them in, nice and slow."

The couple approaches slowly, sniffing around like a German Shepherd in baggage claim. They almost run into Bruiser, as they are blinded by their gullets' desire to be filled with the divine swine.

"Sorry, folks, no hot dogs here," says Bruiser.

The rotund man says, "That's not funny." Their heads drop, fixated on the ground, and their tails tuck as they start to walk away from the camera.

Bruiser grabs the dude and says, "But give me two minutes, and I'll explain how you can make enough to buy all the wieners you can fit inside of you, and then some!"

The portly gentleman looks at his overweight lover, grabs his hat, and wipes his greasy brow. "What do you think, Arlene?"

"How many wieners we talking about?" asks Arlene.

"Depends on how adventurous you are. Five grand, if you complete three dares," says Bruiser, pulling a fat roll out of his pocket.

Her beau turns to her and says, "Come on, honey, these guys look like scoundrels. Nothing personal."

"It'd be personal if you knew us, and you're not wrong. We've got a pile of cash we're trying to give you, if you'd only entertain us by unsheathing your fortitude."

"What do you think, baby?" asks Arlene's beau, clearly intrigued. "We could use the money."

Arlene laughs. "Jon hasn't worked in over a year, and Big Lots isn't cutting it for the both of us."

"Damn it, Arlene, way to tell the whole world. I'll get you your rent. You've got two minutes, grifter."

"Welcome to Greed. I'm Bruiser, your host, and today we're going to tempt you to expand your moral boundaries for money. Money for stuff, shiny stuff, or the money to make your old stuff shiny again."

Bruiser extends his hand.

Jon shakes it and says, "Jon, and this is Arlene."

"Great, here are the rules. First dare is worth five hundred dollars, second a thousand, and the third thirty-five hundred. If you don't complete all three dares, I get to slap you. If you finish all three, you get the money and you get to slap me. If I double dare you, it means we really want to see the dare completed, and it doubles the value of the bet. All right? Anything goes."

"Anything?" asks Jon.

"Anything." Bruiser points to the homeless body lying on the ground and says, "For the first dare, Arlene, I want you to make out with that homeless guy."

"You want me to make out with a dead guy? Is that even legal?" she asks and returns to sucking on her Slurpee.

"Hah, he's not dead, Arlene, close, but not yet. If he was, that would definitely be illegal and would also make us, officially, the dirtiest thing on the internet. Think you can do it?" Bruiser asks as he kicks the homeless man lightly.

Arlene licks her lips and straightens her jeggings. "I don't know. Five hundred dollars is a lot of money. I reckon we've got to do this one to get the whole five thousand."

"Correct, Arlene." says Bruiser, rubbing his gold mic on one of her many chins.

"I've never cheated on Jon before," says Arlene, pushing the mic away from her face with her Slurpee.

"It's all right, it's just a game. It's not like you're going to run off with the bum," says Jon.

"Good point," says Bruiser.

"Heavens no!" Arlene looks at the homeless guy sprawled out on the ground and fakes like she's throwing up in her mouth.

Bruiser kicks him, trying to wake him. "Hey, shit stain!" The homeless man groans. "See, I told you he was alive."

Fly jumps in, "His name is Bootleg, Bootleg Johnson."

Bruiser crouches down to Bootleg's level. "Of course. Bootleg, if I could get you back in this realm just for a moment. There's a beautiful lady that would like to give you a kiss." Bruiser shakes him, and he doesn't flinch. He hands Fly a twenty. "Get him an energy drink or some Adderall. Shit, make it a bag of crank, and you guys can split it."

Fly shuffles off.

"It might be easier, if he doesn't wake up, Arlene. It'll be just like kissing grandpa Larry," says Jon.

"Damn. You used to French your grandpa?" asks Bruiser.

"You didn't say anything about tongue," squeals Arlene.

"Yeah, sorry, for five hundo I definitely want to see tongue, and it has to be for at least a minute."

Bootleg's eyes open abruptly. "Five easy. I'm in."

"Well, Mr. Bruiser, it's been a pleasure, but there ain't no way in hell I'm making out with that vagrant," says Arlene, stepping back, startled by Bootleg's resuscitating.

"Bootleg is his name, and I'm sure he's a nice guy. Probably just wasn't held enough as a child." Bruiser lights a cigarette and hands it to Bootleg. Bootleg, still lying on the ground, smiles, revealing the few teeth he has left, and winks at Arlene.

"I can't do it, honey!" demands Arlene.

"Arlene, you have to do it," begs Jon. "That's our mortgage payment. If we don't do this, we're going to be living next to this guy."

"Well, I guess *we* better do something or *we're* gonna' be homeless. I've got the next one," says Arlene, establishing dominance over her lover.

"I'd do a shot first, Jon, and then it'll be exactly like kissing your grandpa Larry," says Bruiser.

"For the record, it was Arlene that made out with my grandpa Larry. It was around the holidays, we'd been drinking moonshine, and he was passed out. It was just for laughs, you know?"

"It's still weird, but who am I to Mike Judge you?" asks Bruiser.

Jon paces around for a moment, nervously rubbing his hands together. He looks over at Bootleg. Fly is on top of him trying to blow illicit powders through a Slurpee straw into his nose. Bootleg jumps up screaming, "SHIT IN MY MOUTH AND CALL ME JOHN!" and starts dancing a jig.

"Oh God, you have a sick sense of humor." Jon looks over at Bruiser, and then at his wife and says, "I can't do it, baby."

Bruiser pulls out a wad of money, saying, "Ok. You got me, Jon. We've all been laid off — it sucks. You lose your masculinity, and I really want to help you get that back."

"By getting Jon to make out with an old homeless dude?" asks Arlene.

Bruiser shakes his wad of money at them and says, "Yep, for a thousand dollars. That's two month's rent, Jon. I double dare you to make out with our good friend, Bootleg."

Jon pulls up his jorts and tries to embrace Bootleg, saying, "This would've been easier when he was passed out."

Bootleg turns to Bruiser and starts bitching and spitting a milky foam. "Now what makes you think that … just 'cause … I've got no home … and I smell like piss … that you can just force me … to make out with this … inbred, Twinkie eating hillbilly … No offense."

"None taken," says Jon, sneering at Bootleg. "Can you get gingivitis from someone else?"

"I hope not," laughs Bruiser. "Bootleg, obviously we're going to pay you." Bruiser waves his knot of money at him.

Bootleg swats at the knot and says, "Sweet, sweaty balls, the people I can buy with a thousand dollars."

"Nope, I assumed that Fly had mentioned to you that it's twenty dollars for you people," he says as he pulls his wad back.

Fly jumps in, "You people!"

"Sorry, domestically challenged. You didn't tell him, Fly?"

"Didn't have the chance," says Fly, scratching his head.

Bootleg gets in Bruiser's face and barks, "So … because I smell like the dumpster behind Gladys Knight's Chicken and Waffles … over on Cascade, I don't deserve the same amount of money for making out with a dude … for the first time?"

Fly laughs, "The first time!"

"Who do you think needs the money more?" asks Bootleg.

"A thousand dollars and you'll be dead tomorrow. Have you ever tried to smoke that much crack?" asks Bruiser.

Bootleg responds dryly, "Yeah."

"The last time I gave one of you guys that much money; you gold plated your shopping carts and put rims on 'em. There's a reason you don't have any money," laughs Bruiser.

"How do you know I won't use it … to reform my life … and others around me … stuck in the never-ending battle between the free and the controlling?"

"Right, the free?" Bruiser scratches his head.

"You'd be the one to help bring that change into my life. The change that I've always needed."

"I've got a whole handful of change for you," says Bruiser, pulling a crumpled-up ball of ones out of his pocket. Bootleg swiftly snatches the ones from him. Bruiser pulls away quickly, hoping to avoid infection. "I used to see the world that way. Now, I know that we are here to suffer, and we'll do anything we can to avoid that feeling. If I give you a thousand dollars, you'll end up dead. I'll give you a hundred."

Bootleg laughs and stares deep into Bruiser, asking, "Who broke your heart, and why didn't you do anything about it?"

Bruiser stops and stares back into Bootleg's eyes. There's a familiarity there that he can't explain. His eyes look like they've seen hell, walked though it barefoot, asking where the party was. Bootleg smiles and throws up a peace sign.

"Two hundred," says Bruiser with a lack of confidence.

"Deal." Bootleg puts his wretched hand out for confirmation.

Bruiser grabs his dumpster claw reluctantly. "All right, you guys want to make out that bad, two minutes, let's go, but no holding hands or anything romantic. I want tongue flicking action," says Bruiser, as he sets the stopwatch on his phone. The two men look at each other, they both gag a little, and then interlock like Greco-Roman wrestlers grappling for their lives.

"I think I'm gonna' be sick," says Dick, looking to Arlene who has her eyes covered.

And this is the part about humanity that has taken any molecule of hope from the center of my soul and punted it off into the abyss of darkness from where we came. No matter what, if they have no money, down on their luck or whatever, they do it. No matter what 'it' is. We all know that there are things you do in life that you can't ever erase from the hard drive. No matter what we do to forget, the hole that these tests burn through us takes something worth more than the pieces of paper or shiny trinkets to refill it. It's never enough. I personally have never had extra money, ever, but I at least know I'm creating a larger hole, trying to be whole, just by returning to this job every day, thinks Bruiser as he looks up to find Dick staring heavily at him.

"Dude, it's been over two minutes," says Dick, jarring Bruiser.

The two are still interlocked at the mouth, tongue fucking.

"Hey, you two, times been up. Break it up," Bruiser says, pulling them apart.

"What-the-fuck, Jon? Is there something you wanna' tell us?" asks Arlene.

"Yep, we're eating Sizzler tonight, baby, surf and turf." Jon goes for the high-five and Arlene leaves him hanging. "Woo!" screams Jon, and then spits and wipes his mouth.

"What happened there, B?" asks Dick. "I've never seen two straight men so happy to be inside of each other."

"Yeah, that was fucking weird. Definitely a new one for me and the show," says Bruiser as he turns to Arlene. She's standing next to Jon with her lower lip resting on her front butt. "Let's move on to the next dare," says Bruiser, as he tugs at Arlene. She's frozen in fear. Jon has a gaping smile on his face and has gone completely catatonic. Arlene returns, starts snapping her fingers at him, and then throws her giant Slurpee at him, covering him in blue.

Jon's eyes lock back into the moment, and he laughs like a child. "Arlene, you're up. Get that money, baby!" Jon yells as his eyes light up, and he starts jumping around like he's the next contestant on the Price is Right.

Bruiser takes off his glasses and goes to hand them to Jon. "For this next dare, Jon, I'm going to need your help."

Jon pushes away the glasses and yells frantically, "I'm done! It's Arlene's turn! I can still taste that man in my mouth. It's like malt liquor and what I imagine baby shit tastes like."

Bruiser pushes the glasses back at him, saying, "Sorry, Jon, this one involves the both of you, but I'm going to be nice. You've earned my respect, and I'm a little intrigued by what we found lurking inside of you. This one's called 'Hide and Freak.' Hand me your cell phones. I'm going to give Arlene a five-minute head start. All you have to do is catch her, and I'll give you both another thousand."

"Two thousand?" Jon and Arlene both nod their heads.

"But wait, here's the catch; I'm sending my cameraman, Less, to make sure she doesn't stop. The only clues you'll get are articles of clothing she leaves behind. Every time you find one, you lose one. So, I'm assuming by the time you find her, you'll both be baby-naked. Now here's the weird part, those glasses I gave you?"

"Yeah?" asks Jon.

"They've got a built-in camera. We want to look into her eyes as you make sweet love to her. Arlene, you in? Arlene?" Arlene has already ripped off her shirt and now runs through Little Five Points, jiggling towards Candler Park.

"Shots?" asks Jon, looking to Bruiser.

"Shot and a beer?" asks Bruiser, looking to Dick.

The gentlemen walk into the bar behind them. Bruiser orders a round, and they pound the shots and chug the beers. Bruiser pats Jon on the back, saying, "Fuck off, and don't take the glasses off. We want to see everything. You gonna' be able to do this?"

"I just made out with a vagrant. I'm pretty sure I can boink my wife on camera." Jon heads for the door in a hurry.

"Jon, if she comes before you do, we'll throw in a grand for you on the side."

Jon runs out the door screaming, "Woohoo!"

"You think he'll even find her?" asks Dick.

Bruiser looks down the bar to find Bootleg's toothless smile pointing at him. Bootleg waves at him like a five-year old kid, all happy and high-energy. "She couldn't have gotten too far, you know," he says as he tries to get eye contact from the bartender. "Barkeep, get that man a really tall cheap beer, a straw, and another round for us."

The bartender replies, "That's fine if he drinks it outside. I thought somebody shit themselves until I realized Bootleg snuck in."

"You're right, she couldn't have gotten too far," says Dick. "That's a big girl."

"You think he'll get her to come?" asks Bruiser.

"I'll lick Bootleg's asshole clean if he does," says Dick, laughing as they put down two more shots.

"As much as I'd like to see that—" Bruiser stops mid-sentence to check a banner on his phone.

"So, what was the Janeuh going on about earlier?" asks Dick as he watches Bruiser analyze the text.

Bruiser ignores Dick and grabs the bartender, asking him, "Hey, bub, Jesse around?"

"Nobody here with that name," says the bartender. "Can I get you something?"

"Two more, I guess." Bruiser turns to Dick and says, "There's so many things I'd rather do than talk about her and me; like go watch the live feed of those two hillbillies fucking."

"Just saying, I don't ever see her around anymore, and every time you're on the phone, you're arguing."

"That's pretty much it. She comes around when she needs her oil changed, otherwise she works all the time, and I'm always completely fucked up. Our relationship has become an endless battle to create a space where we're both in the same room, naked, and not set on destroying one another."

"Sounds like every relationship I've ever been in," says Dick, patting Bruiser on the back.

"Good, I was starting to think it was me," says Bruiser.

"Well, I'm sure it is. You've always had it easy when it comes to getting girls. You're shit when it comes to knowing when to get rid of them," says Dick.

"Yeah. It always starts out roses and turns to shit right around three or four months in," he says as he lights a cigarette.

"About the time they get to know you. You think it's got something to do with you entertaining every girl you scrape up on the show?" asks Dick.

The bartender walks up and pulls the cigarette out of Bruiser's hand, hits it a couple times and extinguishes it.

"Na, it's not that. That's why we kept it open. I know who I am, and it only gets worse the more they try to domesticate me."

"Why do you even try?" Dick looks toward the door and then at his phone.

"Same reason you don't. When's the last time you had a girlfriend?"

"I'm not one to mount my kill on the wall. I'm more of a fisherman."

"How so?" asks Bruiser.

"Catch and release. I like sitting in the boat all day floating around in the sun drinking beer. I catch a big one, pull it in, take a look, smack it on the ass, and throw it back in the water. That love thing is all ego-stroking parasitism. I had some girls I kept around, but it wasn't worth the trouble. They all just wanted money or wanted me to do shit for 'em. At the end of the day, they were just using me and fucking somebody else."

"Love — that old hustle," says Bruiser.

"Why do you keep her around?"

"She's beautiful, her family has piles of money, she works in a lab that researches stem cells, and I'm pretty sure I'm going to need another injection in the near future," says Bruiser, trying to light another cigarette.

Dick snatches Bruiser's cigarette from him. "Another injection?"

"Yeah, my sister shot me up in Tijuana when I was running people across the border for her," says Bruiser.

"That's right. Do you think the government will ever pull their heads out of their assess and approve them?"

"You saw what happened with my sister. There's too much money in being sick, Dick," Bruiser says adamantly.

"Right: The Illuminati, Free Masons, total control, slavery, the weather machine. Who's in charge, Bruiser? Aliens? Is it the Grays or the Reptilians?"

"They're working together to create the perfect slave. I'm just saying, our sickness is their wealth. Cancer alone keeps the insurance companies, pharmaceuticals, and hospitals in business. It's a racket. I mean tobacco, the same people that grow it are the ones that put the chemicals in it to get us addicted, and then raise the taxes to fill their own pockets," he says, irritated.

"Right, why haven't they put aspartame in these things yet? I could fit another pack in my day for sure." Dick looks at the tab in front of him. "Can't even enjoy dying." The two sigh together and Dick says, "You want to go smoke one and check the feed in the van?"

"Sure." Bruiser gets up and walks out the door without even thinking about paying.

Dick settles the tab and catches up with Bruiser at the door. "So, what really happened with those girls last night?"

"Honestly, that shit fucked me up. Maybe it was the mushrooms, but when I was all knotted up in them, I couldn't even enjoy it," he says.

"I'm pretty sure you're just bored. You probably need to move on to orgies, furry orgies, or maybe something challenging like loving yourself," laughs Dick.

"It's definitely not that; something changed in me. It's fucked up, but I didn't think of it until you mentioned Janeuh. She shuts me down, like my mom. This might sound weird, but I envy that stripper from the other night, Laura Lee. She's buck naked on display and totally comfortable."

"What do you mean?" asks Dick.

"Her heart was wide open, like she had nothing to hide," says Bruiser as he opens the door to the van to find Leslie watching the feed through her fingers. "I wouldn't even know where to start looking for my heart."

"Have you checked the dumpster behind the Claremont Lounge?" asks Leslie.

Dick and Bruiser stop talking and both their jaws drop. On the screen, Arlene and Jon are butt-naked, rolled up in a ball like a mongoose and a cobra meeting for the first time. Dick's first instinct is to cover his eyes like Leslie. "Well, fuck, Bruiser. How you gonna' wrap this one up? We can't afford to let this one turn into a ten-thousand-dollar episode."

Bruiser laughs heartily and says, "You also can't afford Arlene cumming, 'cause you're going to be cleaning Bootleg's turd cutter like a whisk fresh out of some cake mix."

Leslie motions like she's puking, and says, "That's disgusting."

"A grand says he cums on her tits," says Bruiser.

"Bet. He looks like he cums inside. They're probably trying to replicate their species. You gonna' add that grand to what you already owe me?" asks Dick.

"Sure, it's not a rational number at this point anyway," replies Bruiser.

"There's something deeply wrong with you two. If this job didn't pay so well—" says Leslie.

"You'd what, Leslie?" asks Dick.

"I'd ask for a raise, and it looks like you're tongue jacking hobo butthole. Arlene just came," says Leslie.

"No, that's impossible!" shouts Dick.

"I can run it back for you," says Leslie.

"My dude," says Bruiser as he flicks his tongue out like a cobra.

Leslie loops the moment on the monitor and says, "Watch how she shakes, her eyes close like she doesn't want to leave that feeling, and then open wide with a look of confusion like she has no idea where she is."

"Fuck." Dick punches the roof of the van. "We never shook on it." Leslie cuts back to the live feed to find Jon still pumping away at Arlene. He stops and collapses atop her. At least he tries to, but instead rolls off to the side. "Well, at least I made a grand off of this mishap," states Dick, bursting out of the van.

"You want cash, or will you take a check?" asks Bruiser.

"Look, make sure they don't win any more money off us, and we'll forget about both bets."

"I'd rather pay a grand to see you toss that Better Homeless Garden's salad; besides there's no way they'll make it through the last dare."

Bruiser jumps out of the van and finds Fly talking to some tourists. Fly has them mesmerized. "You see this twenty-dollar bill,

I'll show you how it tells the story of humanity before this planet—"

Bruiser interrupts his hustle. "Hey, Fly, you seen Bootleg? I need one more favor for the cash we're giving him."

Fly turns his back on his meal tickets, saying, "I saw him walking that way with a huge mug of beer. I believe he's already spent it. I heard he's throwing a party downtown at the Hyatt."

"He couldn't have gone that far. We haven't paid him yet. Find him!" Fly puts his hand out, gesturing for a tip, but Bruiser pushes his hand away, saying, "I'll take care of you when you come back with him."

Bruiser lights up a cigarette and fades out of the moment staring at a young couple with their child. They're sitting in front of the bar, drinks in hand, menthol cigarettes lit, and a kid on a leash. The kid's digging through a large flowerpot. He eats a handful of dirt and cigarette butts, and his creators look at each other, smile, and then kiss. His mother leans her head on her man's shoulder, and they pause. The kid goes to grab another handful of dirt, and his mom yanks his leash and lands him on his butt. He starts to cry, looks around, realizes no one cares, and stops himself. "If that isn't love." Bruiser looks down at his cigarette, takes a hit, and then looks off into the distance to find Less, Jon, and Arlene walking up in the horizon.

"How'd it look?" asks Less.

"Hard to watch, even for me." Bruiser scratches his head and Jon rushes into Bruiser's personal space, grabs his hand, and starts shaking it vigorously. "Take it easy there, Jonny, I know where that hand's been."

"I'm sure your hand's been worse places, but damn it, I want to thank you, Bruiser!" Jon goes in for a hug. Bruiser tries to fight it, but Jon overpowers him. "You gave me the best day of my life. You just paid me to make love to my wife in the middle of the park! Something I never would have even thought to try, and she loved it."

"I know, I saw that. It cost me a grand," laughs Bruiser.

"You gave us a break from our lives and got us caught up on the mortgage. You're a saint!"

"That's a first, Jon," says Bruiser.

"Seriously!" Jon insists.

Arlene walks up. "What are you two talking about?"

"He said he'd give me another grand if you came first."

"And what makes you think I did?" asks Arlene.

"I know the face. It's the same as your poop face," he says, laughing.

"Shu-tup!" Arlene reaches in, gives Jon a titty slap and then hugs him.

Bruiser stares at the two, confused, as he tries to comprehend what's going on between them.

"What's the last dare?" asks Jon.

"We're waiting on your BF Bootleg. As soon as he shows up, we can get started," says Bruiser, looking around the square.

Jon wipes his brow with his NASCAR hat and says, "I don't know where this is going, but I want you to know I'm not gonna' suck his dick or anything 'gay' like that."

"Nobody mentioned it, but it's funny that was the first thing that popped up in your mind," says Bruiser, smiling.

"Fuck! I might if the money's right," says Arlene, also smiling. "Bootleg really woke something up in Jon. He's never plowed the field like that before."

Bruiser laughs as he takes his glasses back from Jon.

"It's true, kissing Bootleg was like making out with an angel: soft, gentle, endearing," says Jon, reenacting the moment.

Arlene slaps him in the back of the head, screeching, "I'm right here, Jon!"

Bruiser gets his mic out and says, "And here he is, the man of the hour. BOOTLEG JOHNSON everybody!" Fly and Bootleg begrudgingly walk up to Bruiser, biding their time as they split a hand-rolled cigarette and chugging twenty-twos of Steel Reserve. Bruiser puts his arm around Bootleg. "How we doing, brother?" he asks as he grabs Bootleg and shakes him like an old friend, walking him away from the couple.

"You got my money?" asks Bootleg.

"Where'd you get the name Bootleg? You runnin' hooch during prohibition?"

Bootleg laughs, "I was born in nineteen forty-fucking-two, you ninny. You ever been to a Dead show, or I guess Phish in your case?"

"I've seen the Dead, right before Jerry passed," says Bruiser. He takes a second and asks, "You used to make illegal copies of the shows?"

"Somethin' like that." Bootleg grabs Bruiser's hand, pulling him within three inches of his face, and spits while saying, "Listen here, son. Do you think you could spare some change?"

"Bootleg, I already gave you a handful, and you've got your retirement plan coming if you help me with this next dare," says Bruiser adamantly.

"No, this world's changing … and we must be ready. We need you to change. We need you to light this place up. We must strengthen the people, or they'll cease to exist."

"Okay?" Bruiser tries to pull away, but Bootleg's malt liquor fueled hobo strength is too much, and he pulls him closer.

"We need you, and you're not ready!" he says, spitting in Bruiser's face excitedly.

Bruiser tries to pull away again, but Bootleg won't let go. "Ready for what?" asks Bruiser.

"Change," says Bootleg, looking deeply into Bruiser's eyes.

Bruiser nudges Bootleg back a smidge and asks him begrudgingly, "Look, you want your money?"

Bootleg nods.

"Are you going to help me?" asks Bruiser.

Bootleg locks eyes with Bruiser and says, "I'm going to help you. Are you going to help us?"

"Sure." Bruiser pulls from his embrace, putting his arm over Bootleg's shoulder, and walks him toward Jon and Arlene. He leans in and whispers in Bootleg's ear.

Bootleg pushes Bruiser off him, shouting, "HELL NAW!"

"C'mon, Bootleg, I'm giving you two hundred, and that's going to help you. Now help me." Bruiser pulls Bootleg in close and says quietly, "There's no way they'll do it."

"Ah, fuck it. Let's go," says Bootleg.

"Less, set up the shot in the courtyard and grab Dick." Bruiser walks Bootleg over to the couple and says, "All right, kids, it's our third and final dare. So far, you've won four grand. Not a bad day, right?"

"One of our best!" says Jon.

Arlene smiles. "What's next?"

"The third dare is for thirty-five hundred dollars. That puts you at seven-point-five grand for the day, and you get to slap the shit out of me," says Bruiser. Jon and Arlene high-five each other and act like they are going to slap Bruiser. "Should this dare be more daring than you'd like to be today, I get to slap you, and you walk away with four thousand dollars. Deal?"

"DEAL!" they say together.

"So, this dare's called 'Truck Stop Shower/Bath.' Bootleg, when's the last time you had a shower or a bath?"

Bootleg starts counting on his fingers. "Well, Mr. B, I'd have to say six months at least."

"And have you shit or pissed yourself since then?"

"Oh, at least once a week. Never trust a fart, that's what I say. They're all liars." Bootleg laughs at his own joke.

"You're up, shewg," says Jon, as he pushes Arlene towards Bootleg.

Arlene groans, and asks, "You want us to give him a bath? Like a sponge bath?"

"Yeah, Bruiser, where are we going with this one?" asks Dick. "We don't have a bathtub nearby."

Bruiser cringes at his own words, saying, "For thirty-five hundred dollars, if you can stomach it … all you have to do … is lick Bootleg from ball sack to the top of his butt crack."

"Tongue bathe the sand trap?" asks Jon.

"Nice and slow. I want to see all three of Bootleg's teeth," says Bruiser.

Dick starts laughing and says, "That's fucked up!"

"Well, I was gonna' let them prep it for you, but if you want to go first," says Bruiser.

Jon pushes Arlene toward Bootleg, saying, "All right, baby, you got this. Seventy-five hundred dollars. That's a lot of scratchers!"

Arlene stands there for a second, trying to wrap her mind around licking Bootleg anywhere, let alone from hole to pole. She walks over to Bruiser and puts her cheek out, saying, "Well, Bruiser, it's been fun. Thank you for the help with our mortgage and our relationship. You're welcome at the house anytime. The seventy-five hundred would be nice, but I wouldn't do it for ten. I'm used to being poor. Jon might, but he knows I'd never kiss him again."

"There's no double dare on this one, Arlene. Jon, you in?" asks Bruiser.

Jon's eyes bulge and he says, "There's no way I'm getting near that vagrant's—"

"Hey, vagrant? Easy, I thought we connected earlier. Keep your money. No one's licking my sand trap today. I've worked hard to acquire this delightful aroma." Bootleg reaches in his polyester pants, scrapes a sample, and puts it to his nose. The smell startles him, and he runs around in circles with his finger out, looking for somewhere to wipe the dead cells.

Jon steps back in fear of being near whatever is on Bootleg's finger and says, "Look, there's no one on this planet with the lack of self-respect that would even try to lick Bootleg's asshole. His mouth tasted worse than any butthole I've ever licked, and I know you gave us that dare so you could keep your money. I get it."

"So, that's a no?" Bruiser shrugs and pulls back to slap them.

"You're still going to slap us?" asks Jon.

Bruiser reaches back and says, "That's the game. Don't make this weird."

"Wait a minute!" yelps Dick, as he steps in the shot. "I know someone with absolutely no self-respect that'll do it."

"Dick Allen, everybody, the producer of Greed," interjects Bruiser.

Dick turns to Bruiser and takes his mic from him, asking, "You remember that nine, ten grand you owe me?"

"Sure," says Bruiser, waiting for the other shoe.

"I dare you to Truck Stop Shower/Bath Bootleg's chode, and we're even. Nine grand paid in full by the show, a grand for Bootleg, and I'll even let you slap me."

"You're such a dick," says Bruiser, motioning to Less to cut the camera. He pulls Dick in and whispers in his ear, "First of all, fuck you for putting me on the spot in front of my fans. Secondly, this is your forfeit, not mine."

"That's why I'm clearing your debt," says Dick, smiling.

"Why would you want to see this?" asks Bruiser. "Is this about the whole Desiree thing?"

"Believe me, I don't want to see it. I told you; we're cool." Dick points to the crowd gathered around them. "This is about them. I want the world to see it, and why not? All the shit you've made other people do. And fuck you, you owe me nine grand for drugs and hookers. This way, I get my money, and I get to enjoy watching you lick a hobo's crease. Let's go." Dick claps his hands. Bruiser looks around at the crowd. They're salivating. Then he looks over at Bootleg still sniffing his finger like he was getting high off it. Dick steps back to the edge of the crowd and asks, "What are you gonna' do, Bruiser? You can't let down your people, can you?"

John and Arlene start chanting his name, and the crowd follows, "BRUISER! BRUISER!"

"What kind of person would I be?" Bruiser closes his eyes. "What's the worst thing that could happen? Less, set up the shot."

"I never stopped filming," says Less. "We're waiting on you."

"Bootleg, you in?" asks Bruiser.

Bootleg walks to the center of the crowd, drops his dingy drawers to the ground, and lets his cock and balls swing free like a corroded pendulum. The crowd groans with disgust. Bootleg grabs his sack, leans forward, spreads his cheeks, and points his brown recluse at the audience. The crowd screams with an ostentatious revel. Bruiser looks Dick in the eyes and asks him, "Zero balance?" Dick puts his hand out, and they shake. Bruiser walks through the inner ring of the crowd, slapping people lightly, and then slaps Bootleg on the ass. The crowd goes wild. Bootleg pulls up his pants and shakes his finger at Bruiser. Bruiser puts his hands together and bows in submission as Bootleg returns to his ninety-degree angle.

Bruiser gets on his knees, eye to crusted brown eye, and finds a heat emanating from Bootleg that forces him to pinch his nose. The crowd boos, and he releases his nostrils, spreads Bootleg's cheeks, and sticks his tongue out in an attempt to go down Bootleg's rabid hole. Bruiser pauses and backs up, asking, "Can I get a shot?"

Dick laughs. "I'm pretty sure you're good and drunk."

"It's not for me, it's for his wasteland of a nether region. His ass is just screaming experimental virus."

"Your girl works at the CDC. I'm pretty sure she can help you *patient zero balance*," says Dick.

"Fuck." Bruiser looks up to the clouds as the crowd starts chanting his name again, but louder. He leans in, trying to force himself into the abandoned nook. The stench chokes him, and as the natural gasses cloud his thoughts, he thinks, *Does anyone ever win the cool game? Do these people's opinions matter? Do they even exist? Why would anyone even consider taking on the series of consequences that will come from this demented action. Because we're too proud of the mask we've made to wear in public and we won't accept one bad review. There's no way to win this one: Move forward and be disgusted with yourself endlessly or submit to humility, take the boos, kill your creation, shake Bootleg's hand, and walk away.*

Bootleg looks back at him and says, "Please forgive me?"

"What?" asks Bruiser. And just as his tongue is about to hit Bootleg's asshole, Bootleg rips one, farts right on his tongue. And as the minuscule fecal matter slides down his throat like a fat kid on a water slide, Bruiser starts vomiting all over Bootleg's asshole, pants, balls, and bare feet.

The whole crowd starts laughing. Bootleg jumps up and tries to put his pants on, even though they're filled with last night's gatherings. Bootleg looks down at Bruiser, dazed by the interaction, and says in a snarky tone, "Can't do it? You know what that means?" He pulls back and slaps Bruiser across the face as hard as he can with all his drunken hobo rage, knocking Bruiser on the ground into his own vomit.

Bruiser immediately pushes himself up and starts vomiting again, but this time it's a bright green, like an energy drink, and then collapses back onto the ground. Bruiser looks up at Bootleg standing over him, shadowed with a halo around his head the sun created. Bootleg's eyes light up an alluring indigo blue, and Bruiser hears a whispered thought from Bootleg, *How's that for a handful of change*? as his head hits the cement and he leaves this celestial maze.

Breaking the Girl

Bruiser's eyes open to Janeuh, his quasi-girlfriend, straddling him, pounding on his chest with a balled-up pair of pink panties in her hand. The thought of returning to the trials and tribulations of this waking life leaves him yearning for another realm, and he shuts his eyes in hopes of deflecting whatever inevitable drama that awaits him. "No, no, no, Scott! You're not going back to sleep. Wake up, you fuck show!" Janeuh collapses on top of him, crying while still beating on his chest.

Janeuh's tears spill into his beard, and he pops up, grabbing her by her wrists. As he pushes his fragile attacker back, his eyes catch the neon pink panties in her hand. "What did I tell you about calling me Scott?" he asks, stalling for time while he tries with all his gray matter to place the origin of the incriminating garment.

Her sanity returns to the room as she realizes she's not alone anymore. She wipes her tears with the panties and says in a childlike tone, "Never. I can never call you Scott because that name reminds you of a place you'd prefer not to remember."

As her emotional outburst degrades to a pensive stare, he releases her, asking, "Can you please just get off me?" His eyes shut as he tries again to retreat to the dream from whence he emerged.

And just as his consciousness is about to return home, Janeuh slaps him and shouts, "Dude, you're not passing out again! I've been here two days watching over you, protecting you while you were trapped in your hobo-induced coma."

His eyes open abruptly. "Fuck! It's Saturday!" He rubs his cheek, saying, "I totally forgot about that. Wait, you've been watching me sleep for two days? That's not weird — at all."

Janeuh collapses into him and tries to burrow into the pit of his arm, but she can't get him to open up. "Try Monday, you silly little time traveler." She pauses and starts walking her fingers across his belly towards his junk. "There's my special boy," she says as she grabs a handful. He lowers his guard as she strokes him, letting her in, hoping that some good ol' fashion dick will subdue her insanity. "I might have raped you one or two times while you were out. I hope you don't think that's too weird," she whispers.

"As long as you pulled out or off or whatever. Wait," he says, pushing her hand off his member. "Why the fuck were you pounding on my chest?"

"I missed you. You were in some weird fairytale coma. I found those panties in your bed, and I freaked out," she says, nuzzling up into his embrace, waiting for his acceptance.

Bruiser tries to roll away from her onto his back, but she's pinned his arm and is holding onto it with all ninety-five of her pounds. He rubs his eyes and looks out the window to find the sun staring back at him. "What time is it?" he asks.

Janeuh stares at the ceiling, wondering where he would go if she released him, "Ten-thirty, eleven maybe," she says, rolling into him, pinning him and whispers, "Bruiser?" She waits out the silence, expecting some sort of a gruff response.

"What?" he groans, pushing her off as he tries to escape her clutches in pursuit of his tracking device.

"I love you," she says as his feet hit the concrete floor.

"I've gotta' piss," he says.

Janeuh grabs his hand and asks, "Why can't you say it?"

There's a buzzing from underneath a heaping pile of clothes that distracts him from the inevitable. He pulls away from her as he knows refuting her last statement is going to unleash her verbal quills. "How do you have any love left for me anyway?" he asks her as he pulls his phone out of the pile to find he has fifty-five texts from Dick, the last one being:

You alive, my guy? We shooting today?

"Please don't," she begs, grabbing his phone from him and throwing it back in the pile of unmentionables.

Bruiser digs his phone back out of the discarded garments and walks off to the pisser, phone in hand and responds to Dick:

Yeah, for sure.

"Don't you run away from me!" she shouts.

He returns to a new text from Dick:

Less and Leslie are out front.

"The vans out front waiting on me. I gotta' go," he says from the bathroom, smirking into the mirror.

"Do you have to?" she asks, waving the pink panties like a flag. "You're not going anywhere, not until you tell me you love me, or you tell me whose pink panties these are?"

42

"That's cute, tell me what else I can't do for you," he laughs as he returns from the bathroom and throws on a pair of jeans from the pile. He grabs the panties from her hand, looks her in the eyes, and says, "I assume they're yours. I don't generally bang chicks that wear panties."

She laughs and says, "Thanks for making an exception, but have you ever seen me wear anything other than black; especially pink?" She stands up on the bed, hovering over him aggressively with lasers in her eyes. "AND when's the last time we even fucked — let alone, in your bed?"

Bruiser turns his back on her and begins searching for his cigarettes. "Other than the time when you raped me?" She doesn't respond to him, and he gives up his quest, turning to her and saying, "Besides, we have an open relationship, so this whole conversation is silly." He stares deeply into her as she processes the thought. "What do you want from me?"

Janeuh drops to the floor at his feet and curls up into a ball. She grabs hold of his legs and starts weeping. She looks up at him, tears running down her porcelain cheeks. "Tell me you love me. Even if you don't mean it. Fuck, Bruiser!"

There's a long silence. Bruiser can feel the vibration of her gears. And just as she's about to start back up, he loses his cool. "I've been out for daze! I wake up to you swinging on me and then you tell me you raped me! Hovering over me while I sleep isn't in our contract, and you can't be mad about panties in my bed because you don't have that right! You're the one that wanted open because you were afraid!"

"Well, maybe I'm ready for closed," she whispers.

"What do you expect to happen with us, after everything and everyone we've been through? Love? A happy ending?" he asks, pulling her to her feet and placing her back on the bed ever so gently.

"I'm just trying to love you, you asshole, but you put up such a fight. You know I've wanted something real, eventually, but you've kept me at a distance because you think love will kill your show. I honestly feel like, deep down in there somewhere, you don't feel like you deserve it."

He pauses and stares at her blankly while he processes the thought. She smiles at him, using her glimmer as a weapon, and he defends himself with, "I don't … I don't deserve to be happy. Every time I smile, someone tries to take it from me, and it's the same with love. I feel sorry for—" Janeuh lets a cute little girly fart sneak by in the middle of his episode and giggles, rendering him helpless. Bruiser pauses and turns away from her saying, "Anyone that tries." As the words fall gracelessly out of his mouth, he realizes what a mess he truly is and crawls back into bed with her.

She stops fighting the moment with his embrace, and Bruiser hears what he believes is another whisper from her, *Just fuck me, you dolt.*

"What?" he asks.

"I didn't say anything, love. Just hold me," she says, burrowing into him. Janeuh starts gyrating her butt gently against him and reaches for his totem.

She caresses him slowly, his defense mechanisms start to fail, and his failsafe kicks in, saying, "I could've sworn I heard you beg me to fuck you."

She slithers underneath the sheets mumbling, "I was thinking about it, but I didn't figure I needed to say it out loud."

Bruiser pulls her back up to sea level by her arm and asks her, "Why would you even want to love me?"

She wipes her mouth seductively, and there's a long silence filled with her trying to distract all the blood from his processor as she grabs a hold of him. "There's something truly amazing trapped in your deepest, darkest, most hidden place. Every now and then I see a flicker of it, and I want to help you release that person," she says, stroking him in multiple ways. "And I don't want anyone else to have you. What do *they* have that I can't give you?" she asks disparagingly.

"Free time! They're just there." Bruiser pushes Janeuh's hand off his rig and starts yelling, "Maybe if you were around, instead of playing with your fucking bunnies down at the CDC, you could have that person, and I wouldn't be wasting my strokes on meaningless fuck bunnies in back alleys."

He tries to pull away, but Janeuh gets back on top of him and asks, "So, it's my fault you're a dumb whore that fucks chicks that wear pink panties? Because I have a driving passion that will affect the curve of humanity!"

"And I'm just a dumb dick!" He pushes her off him onto the floor and says, "You're a workaholic, I'm an alcoholic. I'm a fixer upper, and you're a beach house."

She starts to crawl submissively back onto the bed and says, "That might be the nicest thing you ever said to me."

Bruiser tries to offer her a hand up as she's climbing toward him, and she flinches. "You're never going to trust me," he says as she hides behind the horizon of the mattress.

Janeuh starts crying — again. "Why would I trust you? You're a philandering drug-addled miscreant and—" Her tears quickly turn to rage, and she jumps on the bed, standing over him, yelling, "And you fuck girls for a living!"

He rolls out of bed, avoiding her rage, and responds, "WE'RE IN AN OPEN RELATIONSHIP!"

She jumps off the bed toward him, pushing him against the wall, and starts pounding on his chest. "I fucking love you, and I won't stop until it kills me!" she screams as she slaps him repeatedly. Bruiser, mindlessly filled with an emotion he thought he'd caged, grabs her by the throat. As he holds her delicate breath, he hears another whisper from her motionless lips, *Why don't you love me, daddy?* With those words, he drops her like a red-hot skillet, and as a new self-awareness takes over, he shuts his eyes hard and mumbles, "You're not going to turn me into him."

"Who?" she asks as she caresses her neck.

"Your father," he says stepping back from her.

"Oh, an alcoholic, abusive, philandering bum. You don't need my help with that. It's why I fell for you," she says, piercing him with her words.

"Funny that's what my mom used to call me when she wanted to be closer to her father. I'm not going to jail today just so you can feel something familiar. I just woke up from a coma after a homeless dude took a shit in my mouth. I need a drink, and I've got to go to work. Don't you have somewhere to be?" he asks as he gathers his possessions, aiming to bail himself out of this daytime soap opera.

"They gave me the day off — kind of. I told them you were dying, and we figured you had some rare disease you'd acquired from one of your whores or maybe a dead body or something." Bruiser turns to walk away. Janeuh drops to the floor, returning to a ball, and starts laughing maniacally. Between tears and screams, she says, "I love you. Why doesn't that mean anything to you?"

Bruiser walks away from her quietly and says, "Because I can't feel it." He makes his way to the steps of the loft, yearning for a freedom that will come from passing through the front door. He stops, looking down the stairs, and says, "All love ends with tragedy. I thought your life was simple, and I hoped that would rub off on me; but with everything you were given, they took the only thing that matters."

She rubs her throat where he grabbed her, and from underneath her tears she asks him, "And what's that?"

Bruiser starts his descent toward the door and says, "The same thing they took from me."

She prods him with her words, asking, "This is about your sister, isn't it?"

"I'm definitely not going there right now," he says, walking away from her.

"You have to deal with it eventually, Bruiser," she says, gathering her whatnots frantically in hopes of catching him as he crosses a range of debris in the loft, glass breaking under his feet. His hand hits the doorknob and Janeuh screams, "I fucking love you, you stupid piece of shit!"

He opens the door, looks back, and says, "You don't know what love is. You use that word to control people. I'm a thing you play with when you're bored, and you probably have three other dudes lined up right next to me."

Bruiser steps through the threshold, and Janeuh screams, "You're really going to leave me here crying, you fucking loser!"

"There it is," he says, barreling toward his freedom.

As the door slams, Janeuh starts screaming at a decibel that pierces Bruiser's lifeless, paralyzed heart, moving it an eighth of an inch to the left, as she screams, "What about me?"

Bruiser stops, pauses, lights a cigarette, and cringes at the new sensation. "What about you?" he mumbles and walks down the hallway toward the exit sign.

As he walks outside into the unknown, he is greeted by Less, "What's up, fart sniffer?"

"I believe fart sucker would be the more appropriate term as I felt his inner wind hit the back of my throat," says Bruiser in a serious tone. He jumps in the production van and says adamantly, "Can you just step on it. Janeuh's on her way out, and I'd love to leave our conversation where it ended."

There's an unwavering silence that lingers as Less pushes the van toward their future. Leslie, deaf to the silence, pops her head up into the front seat with Less and Bruiser and asks, "How is *the* Janeuh?"

Less and Bruiser ignore Leslie's misdirected concerns, and Less turns to Bruiser, asking, "Where to boss?"

"Shit, it's Monday. Let's hit the mall. Lennox, I guess." Bruiser looks back in the rearview to find Janeuh watching them from the distance. "You ever wake up tired, Less? Like you spent the whole night waiting tables with a full section and no glassware?"

"I guess. Why?"

"I spent the whole night … two … three nights on an island flying around."

"Dick said you've been missing since Bootleg slapped you. Are you okay?" asks Less.

"I guess, I don't really remember anything other than the dream," says Bruiser, watching Janeuh's reflection shrink in the mirror. "It was weird. I was in an office breakroom with all my coworkers, and we were all drinking coffee and eating cornbread."

"That's definitely weird," says Less.

"All of the sudden, I start floating."

"Nice!"

"And when I realized it, I sank just a little bit. Then I have this moment of clarity," he says.

"How so?" asks Less.

"I realize it's a dream. And the next thing I know, I'm floating around doing backstrokes in the breakroom." Bruiser motions like he's floating with his hands behind his head.

"What did your coworkers do?" asks Less.

"No one noticed. They were too busy talking about some miserable reality show."

"I've had dreams about being a warlock on a reality show where I'm always in battle with some evil force, and right when I'm about to defeat my enemy, my powers disappear. I'm defenseless, and I realize I just lost all the money," Less confesses despairingly.

"What do you think that is?" asks Bruiser.

"Sexual impudence that masks blatant homosexuality," snarks Leslie from the back of the van.

"Thanks, sis. Love you," says Less and then returns his focus to Bruiser. "I always figured it's just a lot of caffeine, weed, and video games before bed." Less pulls into a spot on the outskirts of the mall parking lot. "What do you think it is?"

"I think Leslie's right. It's directly linked to your impudence and your failure to leave the nest," says Bruiser, cackling.

"I'm not gay. I'm asexual," says Less defensively.

"Sorry, I didn't know that's what the kids were calling virgins these days," says Bruiser.

"I'm not a …" Less pauses, regroups, and redirects the attack, asking, "You were saying something about your dream?"

"It felt as real as ever. Even when I was flying, I was totally aware. It makes me think dreams are as real as this life; and this life is just another dream we stop by when we want a break from the other fucked up lives we're living."

"So, I'm a warlock?" asks Less.

"On a reality show, and in another life, I can fly," says Bruiser with a straight look on his face.

Bruiser hops out of the van and stretches out.

Less jumps in the back, asking his sister, "Does he seem different?"

"Bruiser?" asks Leslie as she starts hitting switches, activating the digital bay in the back of the van while Less gathers his camera equipment. "He just slept for three days apparently after that homeless dude farted in his mouth. What do you expect?"

Bruiser stands outside the van, staring off into the distance while he tries to enjoy his first cigarette of the day. Less pops out with his camera and Bruiser asks him, "What do you think's different?"

"You could hear that?" asks Less.

"No, well, I felt it. I could hear Janeuh's thoughts earlier when we were arguing," says Bruiser, still staring off into the distance.

"How was that?" asks Less.

"Uncomfortable." There's another awkward silence as the two stare at a desolate parking lot, watching a tumble-weave blow past a pile of half-eaten chicken wings and a dirty diaper.

"You think Bootleg gave you psychic powers when he shit in your mouth?" asks Less with a straight face.

"Yeah, some homeless guy farted in my mouth and triggered my psychic abilities," laughs Bruiser.

"What am I thinking right now?" asks Less, shutting his eyes, trying to block his thoughts.

"You don't think we'll find anybody out here first thing on a Monday?"

"Dude, get out of my head," says Less.

"It's Monday, there'll be those girls that return everything they bought this weekend. Watch." Bruiser takes a long drag from his cigarette and sighs.

"So, how'd your dream end?" asks Less.

"I flew out of the office, as no one noticed me, and I flew around the island, soaking up this unique place, you know? An island with a corporate park. I realized I had no idea how to land. Fear set in and it got turbulent. So, I aimed for a light that felt like a safe beacon on the mountain top in the middle of the island. As I accelerated toward it, I could make out a being that seemed to be meditating. At this point, I had no control over myself at all and gravitated toward the being inevitably. I flew right into them, but it turns out that the person I was flying toward was me. I froze in that meditative position without landing. I've never felt anything so comforting as I sat there hovering, connected to myself." Bruiser looks down at Less, waiting for a reaction.

"Great dream," says Less.

"Yeah, but here's where it gets fucked," Bruiser hits his cigarette and says, "I'm floating on this mountain top, meditating, all Zen and shit, never been so calm, and I hear rustling in the woods behind me. I want to figure out what it is, but I'm so deep in this meditative state, I don't want to lose the feeling. I return to my breath, but the noise gets louder, and I hear moans behind it. I don't want to be pissed, but I am. I know I've already lost all tranquility, so I try to turn my head, but I can't. I'm frozen. I have no control over this form, like I'm trapped in this meditative state and from the noises I'm hearing, there's a crowd of people coming from behind me."

"I thought that was how you liked it?" asks Less, giggling.

"Good one. Seriously though, I'm surrounded by my coworkers, but they're zombies now. The next thing I know, they're all gnawing on me, tearing away at my flesh, and there's nothing I can do. I have to just sit there and feel every bite as I feed these brain-dead, corporate, fucking zombies."

"That's fucked up. What do you think it means?" asks Less.

"What do *you* think it means?"

"It means you can fly in your dreams, I'm a wizard, and people suck," says Less, stroking his imaginary Gandalf beard. "Other than that, dreams are just something to keep your brain occupied while you sleep."

"I wish it was that simple. It felt way too real," says Bruiser.

The two stand there in silence; not an awkward one, but one where two people just enjoy the sunshine and a good breeze. "You look great by the way. That's what's different. You have a glow about you," says Less.

"You trying to fuck me?" he asks sarcastically.

"No. I'd definitely want someone with a heart to be my first." Less kicks a rock, looks up at Bruiser and says, "I was just saying you look very vibrant. I've never seen you so fresh."

Bruiser puts his hand on Less's shoulder and says, "I'd hope so, I just slept for three days. I feel like I'm fresh — fresh out of rehab." He holds out his hand and jestingly checks for the shakes.

A little white on black Lexus 200h with tinted windows pulls up a few lanes over from the van, bumping some trashy disco EDM. Bruiser flicks his cigarette across the parking lot. "Here we go. Fly in my web and what not." He starts walking toward the Lexus, and this smoking hot OTP college girl pops out of the car wearing short shorts, a flannel that's been butchered, and a Megadeth shirt. She's covered in tattoos and hiding from the sun with a pair of large bug-eyed shades. The girl pops her back-hatch and starts rummaging through a pile of dresses with tags on them. She crams them into the appropriate shopping bags as Bruiser approaches her with a stealth like movement.

"What would you do if I told you that you didn't have to return any of those?"

Startled, the girl turns around with her fist out, screaming, "Fuck off, creep!"

"Bruiser is what my friends call me, but creep's good," he says without flinching.

She stops mid-punch and returns to rummaging through her trunk. "I know who you are."

Bruiser leans against her car and asks, "You're a fan?"

Leslie pops out of the van with a camera and startles Less while he's checking his batteries. "You think she's gonna' fuck him?"

"College girl, bleach blonde, covered in tattoos, guaranteed low self-esteem, and for-sure daddy issues. She wouldn't have a chance with the old Bruiser. There's no telling with this new version."

"What are you talking about?" asks Leslie.

"Something's off with him." Less hits record and heads towards Bruiser with Leslie in tow.

The girl looks at Bruiser and then at her return items, saying, "I always wondered what I would do if we crossed paths. My boyfriend, Drew, would have a panic attack if he knew you were even talking to me."

Bruiser leans in and whispers in her ear, "He doesn't have to know."

The girl laughs and says, "We've seen every webisode. He loves you. I can't, but—"

"But you'd really like to keep those dresses and maybe get a new pair of shoes," he says, while analyzing her physique.

"Can I keep my shades on?" she asks.

"We'd prefer you didn't," he says and then screams, "LESS!" He turns around to find his camera crew behind him, already filming. Bruiser puts his hand out and says, "Well, you already know my name."

"Alex," she says.

Bruiser snares her with an overly confident grin. "All right, Alex. I assume you know the rules?"

Alex, locked in the tractor beam that is his gaze, says, "I do, I do. Now, promise me you're going to play nice; or I'll go ahead and let you slap me now, and we can both walk away unsatisfied."

"Ok, first dare," he says and is interrupted by a full-on hug attack from Alex. He tries to push her off his person and break free from her overzealous affection, but she climbs up him like a squirrel on a telephone pole and starts making out with him. He gently sets her back down to the ground and asks, "What was that?"

"The first dare. You always make out with cute girls. No?" she asks, staring up at him in awe.

"Fair enough, I'll give you that one. For the second dare, I want you to tell me your deepest darkest secret," he says, shutting down her gaze with the question.

Alex pauses and looks at the pile of clothing in her trunk. "I … like to pick my nose … and eat it,"

"Deepest and darkest. That, if anything, is a trust fall for lovers. I know we can go deeper than that."

"I just told the whole damn internet I eat boogers. What do you want from me?"

"Who doesn't eat boogers? For a grand, I need something that makes the whole world shudder just for a second and then reevaluate their own levels of happiness. We all have at least one stomach-wrenching godawful truth: the one that's burned into the back of our retinas. The one that only gets worse when we close our eyes." Alex walks off and starts pacing around in circles through the parking lot. "A thousand dollars, Alex. Give me something bad! I know it's in there," he says.

"For the whole world to digest? You know my boyfriend is going to leave me over this," she says.

Bruiser points at Less and says, "My cameraman's single."

"Thanks. Okay, sure. One time when I was younger, maybe ten or eleven, I let my uncle stick his finger in my butt. He said that he had to check my poop distributor to make sure everything was running smoothly. I didn't mind it much, but I didn't see him after that," she says smiling awkwardly.

"I'm not buying it, not for a grand. Did that really happen?" he asks.

"No, but I used to fantasize about it," she laughs.

"We're close, but give me something real, truthful, and stomach-turning. I double dare you."

"Two grand, shit." Alex fidgets nervously, scratching her arm, and covers up her trashy flesh art, as she gets trapped in his discerning gaze. She hesitantly pushes her shades to the top of her head, revealing that her eyes don't get along. Bruiser is left speechless by her visual impairment. She stammers at his response, and then releases, "I guess … I guess I've always felt like an amazing person that deserves love, but because of my wandering eye … I don't think anyone will ever truly love me."

"I'm sure people love you," he says delicately.

"No one that I'd want to love me. Look at me, I'm the Beauty … and the fucking Beast." She presents herself with a spin and caresses herself gently while gyrating.

"What about your boyfriend?" he asks.

"He's a weasel. I want a man. A real man. A real handsome man like you, Bruiser." She grabs his hand. "The things we could do together."

Bruiser steps back from her and at a loss for words says, "I, uh … um er uh."

Alex starts crying. She puts her sunglasses back on and screams, "Seriously! Because of my eye, right?" She lifts her shirt and flashes him saying, "Look at these tits. They're perfect."

Bruiser goes to grab her boob, stops himself, looks back at the camera, and says, "They are, but I'm a mess right now. I'd break you."

"I'd like to see you try," she laughs, while almost choking on her snotty tears.

"I'm sure you're super sweet — out of context. I'm also sure you'd be a real bitch, if it weren't for the whole eye thing, because you'd be perfect."

He pulls her in for a sincere hug and hears a whisper from her heart, *No one's ever going to love me. Why don't you just fuck me in the ass and throw me back in the fucking trash?* Alex pushes him away and starts fidgeting with her feet. "So, what's number three?" she asks, staring up at him while wiping away the tears from underneath her sunglasses.

"Number three. Let's see … I mean, I'm going to need to check out your poop distributor. Just to make sure your shit bearings are all in place. I've got the perfect tool to get it straightened out and running smoothly," he says confidently.

Alex takes off her sunglasses and throws them on the pavement, shouting, "Seriously, Bruiser? I'm over here crying, and you want to stick it in my ass! On the internet, tears dripping on my feet while my little brother watches. I asked you to play fair."

"I thought you wanted me to. What's not fair when you're talking about thirty-five hundred? I can't just walk around handing out money. That's what makes it a … game … show."

Alex sticks out her chin, so that Bruiser can slap her, and says, "Go ahead and slap me, Bruiser. You're not sticking it in my butt — at least not on camera. I would have done anything other than that, anything."

Bruiser turns to the camera as if he were asking permission and says, "I can't slap you."

"Why, my eyes?" she asks.

"No, you're just too cute. I wouldn't want to hurt you," he says as he steps back from her misery.

"What do you care, butt-fucker? I've seen you slap girls ten times hotter than me on your show. Just do it, pussy!" She pokes her chin back out at him aggressively. Bruiser reaches back with his left hand and smacks her like she was family. Alex covers her face and starts crying again. She collapses to the ground, grabs her sunglasses, and returns them to her face.

Leslie drops her camera and jumps on top of Alex, asking, "Bruiser, did you have to hit her that hard?"

"She called me a pussy!" he says.

"She's just a baby," says Leslie, rubbing her back softly, trying to console her. "She's eighteen, right?"

"I don't know," says Bruiser as he starts pacing in a circle. "We didn't make it that far. She's got so many tattoos, I figured … We just started shooting."

Leslie rubs Alex's shoulders, saying exigently, "Fuck, Bruiser, Dick said one more lawsuit and we're off the wire."

"I'm eighteen," she says, sobbing uncontrollably, "and I don't have time for a lawsuit."

Bruiser lights a cigarette and continues pacing. Less grabs Bruiser, stopping him from his frantic wandering, points at Alex, and asks, "Bruiser, do you see that?"

Bruiser takes a hit from his cigarette, and tries to connect to what Less is pointing, and blindly says, "Tell her I'm sorry, Less, and turn the camera off. Nobody wants to see this."

Less zooms in close on her forearms and says, "No, look at her tats. They're disappearing."

"Don't be daft," says Bruiser, stuttering as he connects with her fleeting artwork and is overwhelmed by confusion. At that moment, Dick pulls up in an old five series and jumps out without cutting it off. He finds Alex still being held by Leslie, Bruiser pointing with his mouth agape, and Less still filming. "Dick, come here. You've got to see this," demands Bruiser as he grabs Alex's arm for examination.

"I told you fuckers, no more lawsuits! What's going on here?" asks Dick. No one responds. "Are you all right, miss?"

Alex with her elbows on her knees and her hands covering her face, doesn't respond.

"I think Bruiser broke her," says Leslie.

Bruiser points at Less, motioning for a close-up of him holding her forearm and says, "Quite the opposite, Dick, her whole sleeve just disappeared."

Alex uncovers her face and looks down at her arms as the artwork turns to a psychedelic watercolor and disappears. She pushes everyone off her and starts shaking her arms in hopes of making it stop. "What the fuck is going on, Bruiser?"

"Bruiser, what did you do?" asks Dick.

Bruiser shrugs and says, "You got me, boss."

Alex starts crying harder as she tries to grasp the surreality of what's taking place. She starts bouncing around hysterically, freaking out, and her shades fall off her face. She wipes her tears and stares Leslie down, looking for clarity. Leslie picks up her glasses and goes to hand them to her, making eye contact.

"Bruiser. Bruiser! Bruiser!" shouts Leslie.

"What?" he shouts back.

"Her eyes. They're—" says Leslie, pointing at Alex's face.

Alex covers her eyes in shame and confusion.

"It's all right," says Leslie, pulling at Alex's hands.

Alex drops her hands, looks at everyone staring at her, and stops crying. She looks down at her arms again, shakes them, and then lifts her shirt, looking for her other tattoos. "I don't get it?" says Alex as she spins around like a cat chasing its tail, trying to find her bumper sticker. "It's gone. Well, I won't miss that one." She stops, looks up to the group, and is confronted by looks of astonishment.

Less blurts out, "Dibs!"

"You can't call dibs on a girl," states Leslie.

"Whatever. I was going to ask her out before Bruiser slapped her pussy-eyed," says Less.

"What?" asks Bruiser.

"Whatever the opposite of cockeyed is; normal, straight eyed. I don't know. You've stolen so many girls from me, you owe me. I call trump, dibs, spade tight, she's mine!" demands Less.

"Bruiser, what the fuck's going on?" asks Dick adamantly.

"I believe Bruiser just turned Alex into a ten," says Less.

Bruiser gets his phone out and puts it in selfie mode. He turns the phone around and shows Alex a picture of her face. He hands her his phone, she drops it immediately, and then collapses.

"This is some real chicken-foot voodoo shit. What's really going on?" asks Leslie, shaking Alex.

"Magic," says Less, "Bruiser's a warlock."

Bruiser waves his hands around in a mystical movement.

"You've got to be messing with us?" asks Leslie.

Leslie shows Alex her face in Bruiser's now cracked phone, and she starts crying even harder. She takes a few shallow breaths and looks around the parking lot as if she'd never seen one before.

Alex pops up, shouting, "Holy fuck-nuggets!"

"Are you fucking with us, Alex?" asks Bruiser.

Alex pushes the phone away and asks, "Am I fucking with you? Are you fucking with me?" She grabs the phone back from Leslie, looks at her face again, and asks, "Is this a dream?"

Less responds aptly, "Apparently." Dick pulls Bruiser off to the side, and Less shouts, "Be careful, Dick, he can hear your thoughts."

"What the fuck's going on, Bruiser?" asks Dick.

"I can't say I have a clue," says Bruiser. "I believe I fixed her visual disability and wiped her fleshy slate clean.

"Bruiser!" demands Dick.

"Dude, I slept for three days. When I woke up, I started hearing voices. I slapped her, she started crying, her tats disappeared, and then her eyes made up and they're friends again," says Bruiser as he lights yet another cigarette.

"She was cross-eyed?" asks Dick, looking her over. "Anybody can fake cross-eyed. The tattoos had to have been drawn on, and the tears washed them off or something."

"You think she's fucking with us, go look though," says Bruiser. "There's not even a smudge left. The whole sleeve is gone, and the skin where the tattoos were, looks new."

"You're telling me you slapped her and erased all of her tattoos," says Dick, staring hard at Bruiser, looking for any hint of bullshit. "What am I thinking?"

Bruiser smiles and says, "You're as blank as a fart, dude. I don't know."

Dick and Bruiser walk back over to Alex. Dick examines her, and says, "Bruiser, stay with her! Less, Leslie, back to the van."

Bruiser hands Alex his phone, asking, "So, what are you up to tonight?"

54

Alex pushes his phone back at him, and says, "I thought you said things were complicated right now."

"Na, I mean, they are. I've got my quasi-girlfriend up my butt because I won't tell her I love her. I don't want to say it because I have to; and maybe I don't love her. Who cares? I've gotten around on her so much that I don't think I could ever respect her for loving me," he says.

Alex jumps on top of him and starts making out with him. She pulls back, grabs his face, and says, "I don't need you to love me. You've already changed my life more than I believed anyone could."

Bruiser pauses, embracing her current perfection and asks her, "How's it feel?"

"Amazing, everything was always so wonky and distorted. Do you think it'll stick?" she asks, playing with his beard.

"I hope so, for your sake." He grabs her hand and pushes it away, saying, "I can't. My cameraman has a thing for you."

"That nerd? He probably still lives with his mom," she says in a snarky tone.

Bruiser has a good laugh and says, "He does. You're good, but the second I feel any attachment, I'd split on you faster than a crackhead's heartbeat."

"I don't care. I just want to know what it feels like to be penetrated by a champion like you. Right here in the middle of the parking lot." Alex forces her way back to his mouth and gets him to submit.

He pulls away from her affections, asking, "Right here?"

"Right here," she says and unzips his pants, getting ready to discover his most poignant talent. Her phone rings and she straddles him, as to contain him while she answers her phone. "LISA! You're never going to believe this! I was just on an episode of Greed … I know you told me you never wanted to see me on that shit show … Well, guess what? No, I didn't fuck or suck on camera. I lost for turning down butt sex, and then he slapped the shit out of me. So hard he got my lazy eye off the couch and back to work! Yeah, your princess is perfect now … I don't know how long, but I'm going out tonight and I'm not coming home … Yeah, I'm gonna' get me some premium—" Alex's hand goes back into Bruiser's dungarees.

"Dick!" says Bruiser, grabbing Alex's hand, stopping her.

Dick bypasses Bruiser and hands Alex a contract, saying, "Sign this and I'll give you the five grand."

"What is it?" asks Alex.

Dick hands her a pen, saying, "Releases for the footage. The second states that you weren't harmed in any way and won't sue."

"Quite the opposite," she says as she signs the contract on Bruiser. She takes the money and climbs into Bruiser's lap, asking him, "How do you want to spend it, daddy?"

Dick grabs her hand and pulls her off Bruiser. "Sorry. Can you give us a minute?" He hands her his card and says, "Let us know if anything changes." He pulls Bruiser to his feet and walks him back to the van.

"What's up?" Bruiser asks blindly.

"What's really going on here?" asks Dick.

Bruiser pauses, and then says, "You got me. I mean, when I slapped her, I saw this shadow crawl out of her. Then I have a vision of this creepy old dude on top of a child. It was out of a horror film. The child was screaming something fierce, and I could feel the fear in her bones. It was horrifying."

Dick laughs and says, "Now you know how all those poor girls felt."

"Anyway, the light comes on and you can see his face. He's drooling and covered in sweat, and all I hear is the old dude whisper, *I'm sorry*."

Alex walks up and interrupts the two, asking, "You guys hungry? Food court is on me."

"Sorry, darling, we've gotta' hit the road," says Dick.

"That's no fun. Can I come with you?" she asks.

"Dude, I'm starving," says Bruiser, ogling Alex.

"We can't. We've got a meeting with Needameyer," says Dick.

"Fuck him! What's he want?"

"He didn't say. He just said he wanted to sit down with us today."

"No fun at all. Go enjoy your shopping spree, Alex. Call me, so I've got your number, and maybe we can get up later tonight," says Bruiser.

He goes in to give her a hug and she attacks him with her mouth. She licks his neck and then says, "You changed my life forever. I love you, and you don't have to say it back." She releases him and walks back to her car.

Bruiser and Dick stand there, staring as she walks away. "Slap me," demands Dick, and Bruiser smacks him with a swift right without hesitation. Dick rubs his face, asking, "That's it?"

"You were expecting something more," laughs Bruiser. He turns around and finds Less and Leslie sitting in the van with the door open, staring at him in a way he's never felt before. "What? Both you guys trying to fuck me?"

"That's where you're at, Bruiser? Do you even understand what just happened?" asks Leslie.

"All I know is that I'm shaking from hunger," says Bruiser.

"The shaking is probably from withdrawal," says Leslie, dumbfounded by his lack of seriousness.

Bruiser, pointing his finger at the Atlanta skyline, says, "Well then, the Antidote it is."

D-7

The Anecdote, renamed the Antidote by the westside, is in every way possible a dive bar. It's dark, smokey, smells like piss, with a classic selection on the Wurlitzer, a snarky older bar maiden, a pool table with a bunch of crooked sticks, and if you ask for anything other than a shot, a beer, or a two-part liquor drink, the bartender walks away from you. Not to mention, on any given night, you're drinking with the destitute and celebrity alike.

Bruiser bellies up to the bar and is greeted by Lucy, the bartender: she's in her forties, a little overweight, what one would call voluptuous, with red hair, green eyes, and the personality of an LA vagrant, which she would take as a compliment. Lucy slides Bruiser a Bud heavy with a shot of tequila, and his head instantly starts to swivel in search of a girl he'd like to bone or has already done so and believes he can do so again. But today it resembles a beach bar at happy hour that's hosting a fraternity reunion (if that means anything to you.) If it doesn't: the bar is filled with a rainbow of golf polos, paired with khaki shorts and flip-flops, or khaki shorts and loafers without socks. It's a breed new to this recently gentrified neighborhood, not the standard beat down, upper-lower class crowd one's used to seeing, but more of a post frat, excessively rich for doing nothing, possibly cleared rape-culture, mixed with a few retirement home refugees.

Bruiser looks to his right to find an older man with a gray handlebar mustache and long dwindling beard. He turns to the gentleman, hoping to start a conversation, and asks, "How's it going?"

The guy looks him in the eyes and says nothing. Bruiser notices a dim, sparkling glow around him. He rubs his eyes and then watches the man's face change into something of a devilish nature as he hears the man start talking, but without moving his lips, *I'd smile, but my wife's a whore, and she's fucking my brother!*

Bruiser replies. "We're all whores."

The man responds, but this time in a childish whisper, *I really loved her, but I know she left me because I can't give her what she wants.*

Bruiser shakes his head and responds, "Nice mustache."

In an old raspy voice, the man says, "Thanks, kid."

Bruiser starts to hear more chatter in the same childish whispers, like he's standing in the middle of a daycare center. He looks around and sees no one's lips moving; just a bar full of people staring at their phones. He covers his ears, shuts his eyes hard, opens them, does a shot, and pounds his beer.

"You all right, Boozer?" asks the bartender.

Bruiser's eyes open and he says, "I think I'm losing it, Lucy. I'm pretty sure I can hear people's thoughts." He motions for another round by circling his empties with his pointer finger.

"Oh, yeah … What am I thinking?" she asks playfully.

Bruiser puts his fingers on his temples and closes his eyes as if to focus on her thoughts. "You were just thinking about how you want to take me in the back and fuck me til' I break."

"Honestly, it looks like someone already beat me to it," she laughs and slides him another round.

"I believe that was life that beat you to it; it's been a strange day, for sure," he says, embracing his bottle with his left hand and grabbing Lucy's hand with the other.

He stares at her while he continues to try and breach her psyche. She pulls away from his embrace, and says, "It's a cold dark place in there, Bruiser, you're not gonna like what you find."

"You're waiting to find out if you've got a cancer; breast cancer, maybe?" he says and does his shot.

Rattled, Lucy steps back from him, does a lap around the bar, and then returns to him. She leans in with both elbows on the bar. "Bruiser, how-the-fuck did you do that? I haven't told a single soul."

"I don't know, honestly. Some bum farted in my mouth. I was in a coma for three days, I'm seeing things, and now I can hear people's thoughts. I just slapped a girl, fixed her wonky eye, and removed her tattoos."

Lucy pours two shots and asks, "Do you think you can heal me?"

Bruiser quickly responds, "Yeah, show me your tits and I'll—"

Before he can finish saying it, Lucy throws the shot she was pouring in his face, flashes the bar while he's wiping the tequila out of his eyes, and does the other shot.

The bar applauds, and that's about the time when Dick walks in on his phone. "I don't know, Ted. We're just grabbing a bite, and we'll see you in a few." He ends his call and sits down next to Bruiser, puts a bill on the bar, and tells Lucy, "Nice jugs, Loose. A hundred dollars if you do it again."

"Which part?" she asks.

"Both. Either or," he says.

"I thought we were cool," states Bruiser, as he wipes off his phone with a Bev-nap.

"We are, but who could resist," laughs Dick.

Lucy pours a shot of Dick's favorite Scotch, Johnny Walker Green: usually it's thirty-two a shot, but he's the only one that drinks it, so Lucy gives it to him for twenty. She throws the Scotch in Bruiser's face, turns around, pours a three-finger glass of Johnny Walker Blue, and slides it to Dick, grabs the bill, and throws Bruiser a towel. "Next rounds on me," she says.

Bruiser, wiping his face, says, "Fair enough. I don't think I could take another round on me." He lights a cigarette, squinting, hoping that he doesn't combust, and continues to dab the liquor off himself with a bar rag, asking, "Was that Needameyer?"

"Yeah, he offered us a new show," says Dick.

"For selling our concept and—" says Bruiser.

"Making us rich and getting you laid for a living," interjects Dick, interrupting Bruiser's rant. "Do you have any concepts for a show, Bruiser?"

"What about the one from back in the day? What was it called? The one where we get drunk on the porch all night and when the joggers come out, we heckle them. It starts out like a talk show and spirals out into a blatant disregard for humanity."

"I remember you wanting to call it Human Traffic? Because there are so many obnoxious joggers in your gentrified hood," says Dick, scrolling through his phone.

"That's right, Human Traffic," says Bruiser as he looks around the room at all the drunkards in the bar ignoring one another with their gin blossoms pointed at the TVs or at their phones. Everything gets blurry and he grabs the seat of his stool. The room fills up with the sounds of a playground full of children arguing, which threatens to drown Bruiser in unresolved emotions.

"It's Atlanta; there's no way anyone would buy a show called Human Traffic here or anywhere," says Dick as he watches Bruiser struggle to stay upright. "You alright, bub?"

"It would've been great though," says Bruiser as he slams his beer. "What happened to getting us on producing Desiree's reality show?"

Dick fires back, "They don't want you involved at all."

"But that was our idea," demands Bruiser.

"We can't prove it. I tried to get you on the show with Des, but Ted said, 'they said you're too big for the show.'"

"Too tall?" asks Bruiser dimly.

"No, dummy. You have a fame that surpasses reality. I think it's because they don't want 'you' and your 'dirty dick' on the show."

"What do you mean?" asks Bruiser.

"They think you're a scumbag, and they want to keep it relatively clean," says Dick, trying to return to his phone.

Bruiser asks him humbly, "So … what do we have?"

Dick returns from his thoughts, lights a cigarette, and looks down the bar, checking out Lucy. "I don't know if you're ready for it, but … how do you feel about porn?" asks Dick, trying to hold back his deviant laughter.

Bruiser stares blankly at Dick, challenging his remark with a smirk, puts out his cigarette aggressively, and says snidely, "I mean, nothing new there, my friend, that's basically what Greed is at this point?"

"We definitely pigeon-holed you as a decadent game show host. It's going to be hard for anyone to take us seriously."

Bruiser picks up another cigarette and lights it, asking, "So, what is it?"

"How would you feel about a reverse gangbang?" asks Dick.

"A reverse gangbang?" questions Bruiser as he scratches his head.

"Have you ever seen a dude plow through a room full of chicks on boner pills?" asks Dick.

"No, but it sounds like fun," says Bruiser as he scoots his stool in and relaxes into the bar top.

"Two shots, Lucy!" says Dick.

"Scotch shots, boo?" she asks.

"Tequila," says Dick. "Do you think you can handle a roomful of girls, B?"

Bruiser pops up off the bar and says, "I'd like to think I'd die trying."

"Is Janeuh going to be all right with it?" asks Dick.

"Who?" Bruiser has a good chuckle and says, "After the way she woke me up this morning, I think I'm done with her."

"I'd like to say congratulations; but you could get rid of your herpes before you'll get rid of that chick," laughs Dick.

"I don't have herpes, and I'm done with her. I've been ignoring it the whole time because she's beautiful, smart, and rich, but she's … crazy … as fuck," he says.

"Yeah, you fucked her up pretty good." Dick raises his glass.

Bruiser doesn't raise his glass. Instead, he pulls the pink panties from earlier out of his pocket and puts them on the bar in front of Dick, saying, "I was asking myself that same question earlier when she woke me up pounding on my chest with this pair of pink panties in her fist. She told me she'd been waiting two days for me to wake up, so that she could confront me."

Dick pushes the panties away from his direct personal space, saying, "Definite red … pink flag, but I asked her to look after you.

I figured she could help in case your Hobola took a turn for the worse."

"Hobo Ebola? You were worried about me, weren't you?" Bruiser puts his hand on Dick's sarcastically.

Dick pulls away immediately and says, "Still am, and I'm not ready to make a steak out of my cash cow — that's for sure."

"Do you really think it was me?" asks Bruiser.

"That broke her?" Dick hesitates as he gathers his argument. "You know, there's definitely a pattern forming."

"Whatever. I got her that way. It was just hidden behind her mask, and when she took it off—"

"You didn't like what you saw, and you choked her out?"

"Easy, Dick, it's not like that," says Bruiser, backing up from the truth.

"Listen, I can't have you locked up over some trifling ass bullshit."

"It took everything I had to walk out of there," says Bruiser with a distant look in his eye.

"What? Do you want an award for not beating your girlfriend?" asks Dick aggressively.

"Dude," whimpers Bruiser.

"You used to get into it with your mom like that?"

"All the time. She's bipolar, hates men, and I was the only one left to wail on."

"Clearly you never grew up in a house full of black people. My mom used to beat me for breathing too loud."

"Yeah, but at least your mom backed it up with a strong loving foundation. My mom dumped me in a cycle of psychotic relationships with girls that are always trying to kill me."

"So, it's your mom's fault you've reincarnated her insanity in every girl you've ever tried to love, just so you can have the opportunity to fuck her into complacency?" says Dick.

"No … I guess … Well, since you put it like that, I guess it's my fault," says Bruiser. "For letting them anywhere near my muddled reflection of a heart." As the words leave his mouth, an older gal in the back corner by the pool table, wearing an electric blue dress, catches Bruiser's eye. She's overdressed for the setting, but she has a sparkle that draws in his overheating libido. "You know that girl over there in the blue dress?" he asks Dick without breaking his leer.

"Girl? Lucy's mom?" asks Dick as his eyes cross.

Bruiser points across the bar and says, "Na, the young one in the electric blue dress?"

Dick grabs Bruiser's shoulders and turns him on his stool, saying, "Look at me dude — that's Lucy's mom. She's like sixty-plus."

Bruiser, locked in a seductive trance, turns back to his new obsession. He stands up on his barstool to get a better view of his only option at the moment, AKA Lucy's mom: the woman in the blue dress. Dick pulls him back to his seat on the barstool. "Lucy, cut him off, seriously." He pulls a bill out of his pocket and slides it towards Bruiser saying, "I'll bet you a hundo you can't nail her."

Bruiser looks around the bar. "I'm done gambling with you, this one's for love." He walks away from the bar, laughing as he is pulled mindlessly toward the jukebox. He stares Lucy's mom down with a silent confidence and hits D7 on the juke. "Crazy" by Patsy Cline takes over and he puts his hand out. "Bruiser," he says with an endearing tone.

She doesn't take his hand, rescinding his invitation. "Jean, can I help you?" she asks as she stares back at his selection.

"Depends," he replies.

"On what?" she asks, returning to his hungry eyes.

Bruiser grabs Jean's hand, returns the gaze, and looking into her eyes deeply like he's trying to hypnotize her, says, "Depends on how you feel about love."

He hears a whisper from her motionless lips, *I just want to be handled with pure love, like a woman, until my body convulses, and I explode like a watermelon at a Gallagher show.*

"I'll throw on some galoshes," he says excitedly.

"Excuse me!" she says.

"You have beautiful eyelashes," he says.

"I've been struggling through this life for a long time, and the only thing I know about love is, it shows me exactly who I am and then tears me apart every time." Before he can continue his toxic mating ritual repertoire, she pushes him into the corner and pulls herself into him, forcing his neck into her mouth. She licks it slowly, flicking it with a lifelessly cold touch as if to sniff out her prey; all the while drooling rum and coke down the side of his neck. She whispers into his ear, "You don't get back the love you give."

He tries to pull away as his first reaction, but she holds on to him tight, and he's forced to acknowledge her words. "What do you mean?"

"You don't get it?" she whispers.

"Get what?" he asks as he falls deeply into her coil.

"The love — get it?" she asks with a penetrating hiss. His eyes shut and she continues, "Someone's stealing your love. That's why you always feel empty."

"Who's stealing it?" he asks.

"I don't know, but you're on the path to finding them," she says, sliding her hand down his cheek.

Slaphappy

Desiree walks in wearing skintight jeans, a pair of royal blue half cabs, and a white frilly blouse that shows off her midriff, her shoulders, and her neck. Her neck is accentuated by her flaxen braided pig tails and her lapis blue eyes that pull the whole thing together. She stumbles into the awkward moment and asks Dick, "What's going on over there?"

Dick spins his stool around to greet her and gives her a generous hug. "I bet him a hundo he couldn't nail that chick."

"Lucy's mom?" she asks, still staring directly at Bruiser as Lucy's mom pulls his hand into her and dryly grinds her pelvis on his leg.

"He said he was doing this one for love," says Dick.

"Lucy, you all right with this?" asks Desiree.

Lucy slides Desiree a gin and soda with a lime and a lemon. "Give it five or ten, and then you can try and break it up."

"You'd probably lose a limb trying to break those two up," says Dick.

"At least a finger," says Desiree.

"Well, if you can't break it up; make sure he wraps it up," says Lucy.

"That's your mom," says Desiree.

"So, he should probably double bag it," laughs Dick.

Lucy pours out three shots. They toss 'em down and return to the situational blackhole that opened up in the bar. Lucy walks off as she is being beckoned by another bar guest.

Desiree turns to Dick, asking, "So … have you heard anything?"

Dick stops for a long pause and then asks, "About what?"

Her laughter percolates under a playful guise, and she bursts out, "Did I book the show?"

Dick puts his focus on the floor and says, "Desiree … I don't know what went wrong, but … you … didn't … not … get the part!"

She jumps out of her bar stool and attacks Dick, screaming, "Hell yeah I didn't … not!" Desiree bear-hugs Dick and starts jumping up and down spastically. "You're so fucking awesome, Dick! I love you! I don't even know how to start to repay you."

"You're fucking awesome, and you fucking deserve it," he says and hugs her again, whispering in her ear, "I can't wait to see where it takes you."

She stops completely as her gears start grinding. She pulls out her phone, trying to figure out where to start the wildfire of news. "There's so much I have to do."

"Everything just changed, huh?" asks Dick. Desiree has zoned out on her phone and doesn't respond to Dick, so he pushes her phone away and says, "Worry about that tomorrow. Enjoy a drink with us and don't forget to thank him. The show was his idea: he's all twisted about not getting credit and losing you."

"Losing me?"

Dick puts his hand on her leg and says, "We all love you, and there's going to be a hole when you leave."

She puts her hand on his and says, "Whatever. You guys will all be living in my plush Hollywood mansion before you know it."

"Lucy, two shots of your most expensive tequila!" shouts Dick. "You want one, Loose?"

"I'm good, but can you seriously get him off my mom?" she asks and points to a baffled bar crowd. "It's starting to confuse my regulars."

"Do you have a spatula and some tongs?" asks Desiree.

"I've got a taser in my purse," says Lucy.

"I got it," says Desiree, as she pushes her stool out.

"You want to hit this first?" asks Dick, waving a pen at her.

Desiree takes the pen with her, hitting it as she walks towards the jukebox. She blows her hit out in their faces, in hopes of separating the two, but they're intertwined so tightly in a passionate kiss that it seems as if Jean is about to swallow Bruiser whole. "Scotty. Let's go!" shouts Desiree. "You're done here!" she barks, and hesitantly wedges her way between the two.

An odd hissing noise emits from Lucy's mother that Desiree ignores as she continues to pry her off Bruiser with her butt. Bruiser is trapped in a comatose state, smiling with a distant look in his eyes. Desiree slaps him playfully. He rubs his face, looks her down and up, and says, "Hey you." He looks past Desiree to Lucy's mom, fighting to get back to him, and his perspective of her shifts. She goes from mid-thirties hot to the mid-sixties ragged out, weathered woman that she is: saddle-like skin that rolls over on itself, thinning hair, and a defeated look in her eyes. Desiree tries to pull him away as she sees him acknowledging the mistake he was about to make, but Jean's callused talon retains her presence.

Jean, looking through Desiree to Bruiser, whispers, *I'm sorry, but you must find them.*

"Who?" he asks as Desiree tries to pull him away.

The one that left with your heart, whispers Jean.

The statement leaves Bruiser with an empty confusion as he's dragged away from Jean by Desiree. "What was that all about; and how do you not recognize Lucy's mom?" Desiree asks, pulling at him.

Bruiser pauses while he tries to decipher Jean's words and then asks, "What happened with us?"

Desiree laughs and places Bruiser back on his barstool saying, "I don't even know how to start that conversation with you, Bruiser."

She steps away from him and sits down on the far side of Dick, asking him, "Is he okay?"

Dick looks to Desiree with as serious a face as he can muster and says, "Ever since that hobo farted in his mouth, he's been hearing people's thoughts, and apparently he can heal people."

Desiree breaks the moment with a guffaw and says, "Yeah right, Bruiser… a healer." She looks past Dick and asks Bruiser with a giddy childlike voice, "What am I thinking?"

Bruiser lights a cigarette and says, "You booked the show in LA, you're super stoked, but you know there's no way you can leave us behind."

"Close. You already told him, Dick?" she asks him with a pouty, dumfounded look.

"No, I didn't have a chance," says Dick, staring at Bruiser with Desiree in silence.

Bruiser jumps up, avoiding the conversation, and belts out, "Shots fired, Loose! Desiree booked her first show!"

Lucy walks up with shot glasses and pours out a round. "Here you go, kids. Congratulations, Desiree. What show?"

Desiree's eyes beam with her first taste of success. "It's called 'Public House' or something lame like that. They're still working on it. It's a reality show built around restaurant people and their patrons. I'm still bartending, but it's on camera now. And here's the kicker, it films in LA! Finally getting out of Atlanta!"

"You're leaving us?" asks Lucy. Desiree's head almost pops off, she's shaking it so hard. "Good for you. Do they need any veteran bartenders with a great rack and a dry sense of humor?"

Desiree points to Dick and says, "Talk to this guy."

Lucy points her cleavage at Dick, smiles, and asks Desiree, "When are you leaving?"

"Soon, I'd imagine," says Desiree. "They said they want to start shooting on the first, and I have to find a place, start working on my tan… and furniture. Ah, I can't wait." Desiree claps her hands fast and quietly as she's overwhelmed by all the excitement.

"Well, we have to have an epic going away party for you," says Bruiser.

"I definitely want to have a party, but my place is cramped—" she says softly.

"We can totally throw it at my place, Des," says Bruiser.

Desiree jumps up and wedges her way between Dick and Bruiser. She kisses them both on the cheek, saying, "You guys are the best."

"When were you thinking?" asks Bruiser.

"Will Saturday work? I'd like to be on the road by Monday."

"You're driving? That's bold," says Dick.

"I've always wanted to, and I figured now or never."

"You're driving a moving van across the country?" says Bruiser. "Des, that's not safe."

"I'm leaving it all behind, starting fresh. I've always wanted to drive cross-country."

"The Midwest is a bore. There's not much between coasts," says Bruiser as he lights up.

Desiree waves the smoke out of her face and asks him, "What would you know about it?"

"I toured with that band: the one I was shooting a documentary on," says Bruiser.

"Whatever happened with that?" asks Desiree.

Bruiser puts his arm around Desiree's shoulder and says woefully, "The label collapsed, the band broke up, and all that came from it was one riff on a postdated geriatric pop punk album." He picks up the pink panties and waves them in Desiree's face, asking her, "Are these yours by the way? You're the only one I know that wears pink."

"That's D-scusting!" she squawks, as she pushes the panties away from her face. "Why would I leave undies at your place!"

Dick grabs them from Bruiser and throws them across the bar, hanging them on the moose head that's mounted on the wall behind the bar.

"Nice shot," says Bruiser.

"You know, you really fucked her up," says Desiree as she stares at the dangling pink panties.

"Who?" Bruiser asks naively.

"Your *girlfriend*," she says, staring at him with a derogatory smirk.

"Which one?" he asks, playing coy.

Dick jumps into the conversation. "So, Dez, you do think that was Bruiser?"

"That fucked Janeuh up? Definitely. He's got a pile of broken bitches buried in his backyard. She used to be so sweet," she says confidently. "She said she watched you sleep for two days, and when you woke up, you started a fight with her and choked her out," says Desiree, as she pounds her cocktail.

"First of all, she was hitting me in my sleep which takes me to a place I'd prefer not to go, but since we're here, when people tell me they love me, it's usually followed by them reminding me with their fists. I'm sorry if I acted on impulse by grabbing her by the throat, but she wouldn't stop beating on me. And just because she's a chick, she can wail on me? I'm completely helpless against her psychotic rage and … and she raped me. Did she tell you about that?"

"So, she just took that shit from you and forced herself on you, literally?" asks Dick, trying not to laugh.

Desiree rubs Bruiser on the back, placating him. "It's not funny, Dick. Just tell us how we can help."

"We should probably take him in for a rape kit. The first twenty-four hours are the most important."

"I'm glad you two think rape is funny," says Bruiser as he lights yet another cigarette.

Desiree takes his cigarette from him and hits it, saying, "Rape is never funny, nor is abuse, but c'mon, really? When's the last time you said no?" Dick loses it, and Desiree joins him.

Bruiser takes his cigarette back from Desiree, saying, "I was in a coma, so I didn't have a chance to say no."

Dick's phone lights up and he says, "I gotta' take this. Des, can you make sure no one forces themselves on Bruiser while I'm gone."

"I'll try, but no promises, Dick. It's like he's asking for it with that stupid look on his face," says Desiree.

"Loose, can I get bottle of champagne?" asks Bruiser.

Lucy looks around her bar sarcastically for his request and walks off. She returns seductively stroking a champagne bottle. "J Roget, for special occasions."

"Speaking of special occasions. Was that the first time you've been on the receiving end of a good ol' fashioned rape, Bruiser?" asks Desiree, trying not to smile.

"On either end of it, but that doesn't matter, Des," says Bruiser, raising his glass. "To you booking your first show and moving to LA."

They clink the finely tuned sand, and there is a silence as the two stare into one another. Desiree breaks the silence swiftly as she grows more uncomfortable with what she is truly feeling by saying, "I know, I feel like my hearts about to explode. There are so many blank spots to fill. Like: where am I going to live, do I need a new car, and what if I'm terrible and I get stranded in Los Angeles — alone," she says, as she takes another sip off her champagne nervously.

Bruiser slides down a barstool, placing himself next to Desiree and says, "Definitely treat yourself to a new car. It's LA, you'll be spending a lot of time in it. You're a solid bartender and you're so fucking beautiful the camera's going to love you, not to mention your interaction with people is so natural." Bruiser puts his hand on her thigh.

Desiree looks down at his hand and says, "Well, thanks."

He pulls it back and says, "But you're worried about penetrating Hollywood's facade and getting lost in the dark avalanche of epic egos?"

She catches his retreating digits and grabs hold of his hand, saying, "If you couldn't handle LA, I don't know how I'll survive it."

"It wasn't that I couldn't handle it, and I was being chased by crackheads and scientologist alike. I ended up back in Atlanta on my own accord." He raises his glass and says, "To you and finding the lighter side of Hollywood and being embraced by it."

The two clink glasses and Desiree looks away, toward the door and asks, "Is there a lighter side?"

Bruiser leans back and says, "There's a dark side, it wouldn't leave me alone. So, there must be a lighter side."

"What do you mean?" she asks.

"I don't know. Like, there was an eight-ball lurking around every corner, and a dark shadow behind every eight-ball, watching me, waiting for a vulnerable moment to compromise me and take me under its scaly wing."

Desiree puts her hand on his and asks him, "And why do you think that is?"

"What do you mean?" he asks, returning his focus to her.

"Why do you think the darkness follows you?"

Bruiser says in a child's voice, "The darkness is my friend. It protects me."

"Bruiser, seriously though," moans Desiree.

"Seriously. I feel like it's there to protect me from the complacency that comes with happiness," he says and frowns sarcastically.

"I can't say that watching your life unravel has been easy for any of us," she says and puts her hand back on his leg. "Especially, the last few years."

"What's that supposed mean?" he asks.

"That whole thing with your sister: you gave up," she says.

"That's not fair, Des," he says, pulling away from her grasp, "I can't go there."

"You have to, if you want to heal," she says, chasing down his embrace with a shaky reluctance.

"I loved her more than anything in this life, and she's gone — forever," he says, looking away from Desiree as he tries to turn off the uncomfortable feeling in the center of his chest.

"You don't know that," she says, rubbing his leg and pulling his attention back to the conversation.

He returns to her with condensation in the corner of his eye and says with a dearth of emotion, "I don't. I don't know if she's dead or alive — she's just gone."

Desiree breaks from her attack as she finds the reality in his eyes and says, "Go look for her, bury her, get a tattoo with her name, talk to a counselor, or something. You can't just hide in the dark getting fucked up with your demons."

"What the fuck's that supposed to mean?" he asks.

"You excommunicated your family; your friends are at a distance. You're alone in the dark, trapped in a deadly consumption of narcotics, surrounded by your demons while they egg you on and watch you vengefully plow your way through greater Atlanta," says Desiree, rubbing his back.

"One day, everyone important to me just became a distant voice," he says, pushing another shot towards Desiree.

She refuses the shot and says, "You did that to protect yourself from love and the inevitable pain that comes with it."

"That's not fair. What do you know about it? I haven't seen you with a dude in years, not even a hook-up. We all figured you were banging Leslie," he laughs.

"Maybe I am. What does it matter to you or anyone else? I'm focused on myself. I'm trying to heal old wounds and not create new ones. You've got so much pain attached to your dick that I'm surprised it hasn't fallen off," she laughs.

Bruiser returns her laughter, sighs, and says, "You think I'm disgusting, don't you?"

"No, I'm disgusting because I still believe in the concept of someone loving me. Meanwhile, you guys are out there, putting up numbers while we're binging and purging just so we can maybe, hopefully, be one of those numbers. I go to the gym, get my hair done, cut, colored, waxed, and my nails done. I take birth control, so you can enjoy the thirty seconds to a minute you'll spend inside of me thrusting aimlessly, and I won't have to suffer an eternity with your bastard spawn that you'll hate because it slowed down your race to that magic number; whatever that is. Meanwhile, I starve myself, so that I can fit in that one dress that will get you to stop and say, 'I'd hit that.' The funny part is, the more girls you *bang*, the further you get from love, true love, whatever that is." She stops her rant, waiting for him to process that much truth and gets anxious as she doesn't think he'll respond directly. "Did you ever think the darkness that follows you, might just be your punishment for extensive lifetimes of being a complete dick-bag to everyone you've ever loved or at least tried to love?"

"So, it's my fault? I created these demons?" he asks, playing with an unlit cigarette.

"Yeah, don't you think it's time to start taking care of those people," she asks as she sips her champagne in a seductive manner, taunting him with her eyes, "the ones you've hurt."

"If I knew who they were," he says and looks away from her.

She grabs his chin, returning him to the moment, and says, "They're everywhere." She puts her arm up and points down at her head. "They've surrounded you, and they need your love, but you're so afraid of being hurt again and again that you've turned your heart off and buried it deep in your chest."

"So, you're saying I've built a wall of darkness around myself that protects me from being loved because it's just a chance to let them in, so they can penetrate my chest, rip out my heart, and tear it apart repeatedly?"

"Yeah, basically. Don't you think you'd be less of an asshole if you could remember all your past lives. You could confront your demons, the same people you've broken. The ones that come back in every life to fearlessly teach you the same lesson about love until you collapse with tears and smile from the freedom that comes with forgiveness?" She looks up at him with an endearing smile.

He smirks at her comment and says dryly, "Doubt it. I can't imagine what it would take to expel all my demons."

"It would probably be something like hell on earth," she says and laughs sadistically.

"What would you know about demons anyway?"

"Just because I don't have a stadium full of souls haunting me, doesn't mean I don't fucking know suffering!"

"I'm just saying, your life seems to work out for the better," he says, petting her arm.

She pushes his hand away and growls, "Fuck that, and fuck you! I'm fully aware of my karmic debt, and my biggest fear is being a forty-year-old waitress. I've been in the trenches, sucking dick for pennies way too long, and I'm finally going to be free!" She turns up her glass, looking to the door, planning her escape.

Bruiser refills her glass and says, "I'm just saying, you always seem happy. It confuses me."

"I credit that to meditation, self-awareness, and the balls to confront my shit while it's happening. You should try it."

"Is that what's going on right now?" Bruiser leans into the protective bubble she just made, puts his face as close to hers as he can without touching her, and says ever so softly, "It was a compliment. Life seems easy for you. I envy that."

She leans in, pushing him back, stops at a half-an-inch, and whispers aggressively, "That's what I'm saying, fuck off! I've been through my share of shit. Nowhere near what you've been through, but I've done the work. You have no idea how hard it is to confront yourself, look at the shadowed reflection in the mirror, and sit in the truth of who you are, having the patience to deal with the mess you've made in an effort to bring in as much light from the source and share it with as many people as possible."

Bruiser leans forward and fills the gap, kissing her slowly with hesitance, waiting for her to run away from him; but she doesn't, so he leans into the kiss. He runs his hand gently along her cheek and feels her twinge slightly. Then he hears a silent whisper from her, *Are you gonna' grab me by the throat and slap me too, pussy!*

Bruiser flinches and is taken aback by her thought, saying in his defense, "That's not fair, I could never hurt you, Des."

70

"Again, you'll never hurt me … again!" she says, pulling away and grabbing her clutch in an attempt to run away as she realizes she was just compromised by the moment.

"You're scared of me, aren't you?" he asks.

"No, but I could never love anyone that hits women."

"So, you've thought about it?" he asks and pulls her back in, trying to return to her lips.

She pushes him away, fighting the voice that keeps telling her it'll work itself out, and asks him endearingly, "What do you expect to come from this, Bruiser?"

"I'm hoping you fall in love with me, and that your pure goodness protects me from the world. I'm tired of being fucked with by the gods. I want a family, a dumb job, and a boring house in a silly, little neighborhood."

"You have to be that person for yourself because no one cares. And I'm gone in a week. So, this is pointless because you can barely do any sort of relationship; let alone long-distance. So, why now?" she asks, looking at the door, planning her escape from the moment.

"I'm sorry. I'll stop. I know there's no way you'd ever love me," he says, pulling himself away from a moment of vulnerability.

"I do love you. You have no idea, you never have. You've hurt me so many times. Times I'm sure you don't even remember."

"How so?" he asks.

"Do you really want to know?" she asks and pauses in debate over what can come from the truth.

He blindly says, "Yeah."

Lucy walks up and pours the rest of the champagne out, leans onto the bar top, resting her boobs on it in front of Bruiser, and asks him, "So, are you going to heal me?"

Desiree starts cackling and scoffs, "I'd love to see that."

"He knew about my cancer. There's no way he could have known about that, Des. I haven't told anyone, so I don't see why he couldn't heal me as well," she says, smiling at him and hoping to ensnare his gift.

Desiree, humbled by Lucy's sincerity and threatened by her infatuation with Bruiser, says, "Wake up. He just wants to slap you, Loose. It's gotta' be a joke."

"And I'll let him. It's better than any other option I don't have," says Lucy, challenging Bruiser with her eyes.

Dick walks in, breaking the moment, and wedges his way between Desiree and Bruiser. He throws his card on the bar, saying, "Let's go. We've got a meeting with Needamyer. He's got a pitch meeting set up for us with a bunch of network execs."

"A pitch meeting for what?" asks Bruiser.

"The show about your superhuman intelligence and how you use it to fix the world."

Desiree and Lucy break out in a boisterous chuckle.

Bruiser bows up and asks, "Yeah?"

"No." Dick slaps Bruiser playfully without warning. "We're doing a show about you slapping people and healing them," says Dick, hitting his pen and handing it to Bruiser.

"Dick, seriously," says Desiree. "It's Bruiser. There's no way that he can heal people."

"I saw it, Des. It might not make sense, but it's real," says Dick with a solid conviction.

"I'm not even that sure myself. I'm starting to think it was a hallucination; and even if it is real, what's to say it won't wear off? How can we base a show off a maybe?" asks Bruiser filled with self-doubt.

"I don't think it matters. We have a show, real or fake," says Dick. He puts his hand on Bruiser's shoulder. "Needameyer sent out the clip of you slapping Alex. He scraped together a room full of people that already know what a degenerate you are, and they were still willing to show up based on the concept. I've watched it ten times. When her tats disappear and her eyes straighten up, my heart drops every time."

"Dick, I slapped you and nothing happened," says Bruiser.

Lucy jumps over the bar and says, "You can test it out on me. I've got a shit tittoo of a rose I wish I'd never picked."

"Fine. Whatever. I owe you a good slap anyway," says Bruiser, rubbing his hands together. He reaches back with his right hand and slaps Lucy at about fifty percent. Lucy rubs her face as the group stands around her, staring at her in silence while they wait for their miracle.

Desiree's phone rings, breaking the silence. She looks at the number and declines the call, saying, "Are you happy now, Bruiser? You slapped Lucy."

Bruiser, swaying as the spirits consume him, mumbles, "Maybe it takes longer with some people. It's my first day on the job. Sorry, Loose. Can we revisit this when I've got some sort of grasp on how it works?"

Still rubbing her face, Lucy says, "Sure, Shewg. I'll call you if anything changes. I've got to get back to it."

"Yeah, I've got a new life to plan, guys," says Desiree, gathering her belongings and attempting to pay the tab.

"I've got this one," says Dick, pushing her card back.

"No, Dick. It's the least I can do," says Desiree, pushing her card back and turning to give him a hug.

Bruiser, awestruck by the absence of a miracle, crosses his arms, and walks out the bar, saying, "I don't get it. I mean, I do get it. It makes complete sense, you know. Me, a healer?"

I'm Not

"Dude, you all right?" asks Dick as he follows Bruiser down the hallway toward their production office. "You haven't said a word since we left the Antidote." Bruiser, lackadaisically diddling on his phone, doesn't respond. Dick takes his phone from him and tosses it down the hallway.

"I'm not," says Bruiser with a defeated tone. "I'm nowhere near all right."

"Well, can you pull it together? I'd like to get this pitch tight before we walk into Ted's office."

Bruiser walks down the hallway toward his phone, saying, "It sells itself, Dick. We don't need a pitch. We need to figure out what went wrong with Lucy back at the Anecdote." He leans over to grab his phone, falls into the wall, and slides onto the floor.

"Maybe it didn't work because you're wasted, dude," says Dick as he tries to pick him up off the floor.

Bruiser resists his help, saying, "I'm not even close to wasted." He tries using his own volition and drops his phone.

Dick picks up his phone again and pushes Bruiser up against the wall, asking, "What the fuck happened back there, Bruiser?"

Bruiser burps in his face and then says, "I don't know, my guy. This whole daze making my head spin."

"You should probably try eating something," says Dick, backing off Bruiser. "I really think it could be beneficial in the long run."

"Foods overrated, my friend." Bruiser pushes himself off the wall and says, "I've got some fucked up voices in my head, most of those being from Lucy's mom. I'll be honest with you; I had no idea it was her. It was like she camouflaged her dilapidated meat carriage so that I wouldn't be able to stop her from penetrating me with her whispers. To top it off, I think I'm in love with Desiree." As he says that, he bends over and pukes in a fictitious Ficus plant at the end of the hallway.

"There you go, bub," says Dick as he rubs Bruiser's back, "get it all out."

Bruiser shrugs Dick's hand off his back, stands upright, lights a cigarette, and burps a hiccup. "Yep … I lub … her."

"Yeah, you're def wasted. Can we just focus on pitching this dog and pony show before your '*superpowers*' wear off?"

"Who says I had any to begin with? What if Alex was just fucking with us?" Bruiser straightens up and leans back on the wall. "I mean, Desiree's right. Why would they give a piece of shit like me the power to heal people?"

Dick has a hearty laugh at Bruiser's expense. "You know, I was thinking the same thing."

"Thanks," Bruiser says and starts to walk away from Dick.

Dick grabs him by the shoulder, stopping him, and says, "If anybody knows what a piece of shit you are — it's me. I've watched this life tear you apart. You turned tha-fuck off and shut down, but who wouldn't? They've been coming at you hard your whole life. This is your opportunity to make things right with the universe."

"How so?" asks Bruiser.

"You know, like, maybe there is a reason you've been through so much. Maybe you finally passed some fucked up test, and now's when you get your freedom. Heal as many people as you can while you can, and maybe they'll stop fucking with you," says Dick. He watches Bruiser's processor overheat with the thought. "Can you sober up just enough so that we can sell this show?"

"I can sober up and down, mufucker," slurs Bruiser as he kicks open his boss's door.

"That doesn't make any sense, B," says Dick as he follows Bruiser into Ted's office.

"Needledick, what's going on?" yells Bruiser as he barges into his executive producer's office, speckled with puke, and sporting a pair of busted capillaries.

Ted, a tall, weathered man, wearing what's left of a great suit, laughs. "Bruiser, you look like shit." Bruiser clumsily falls into a chair and puts his cigarette out on Ted's desk, ignoring him. "Cool. Dick, how you doing, buddy?" asks Ted.

"Good, Ted. I'm good," says Dick as he sits down.

"So, you've got a show for me?" asks Ted.

"Yeah, man. You saw the footage," says Dick.

"Before we get into that," states Bruiser, slurring with a straight face, "I want to put something on the table."

Dick wipes the sweat off his forehead, turns to Bruiser, and says, "Don't fuck this up, B."

"I don't think I can. That's why I'm bringing it up." He smiles at Ted and says, "Ted, you fucked us."

"How so?" asks Ted.

"The restaurant show that Desiree just signed on."

"What about it?" asks Ted as he shifts in his seat.

74

Slaphappy

Bruiser leans forward and starts fiddling clumsily with Ted's desk accessories. "Seriously, we pitched that idea to you a while ago. How much are you making off our intellectual property?"

"Bruiser, it's not like that. You've been my highest grossing web series for a few years now. I remember when you two walked in this office and pitched Greed, I didn't think it would work. Honestly, I didn't think you'd get anyone on the show. The only reason I took a chance on you was because of your presence, Bruiser. Today I got a call from Monster. They want to buy time on Greed. That's a huge sponsor," says Ted as he throws a bunch of Monster swag at them. "They said they'd only buy time as long as you're involved; and I'm still offering you a new show."

There's a silence in the room.

"Oh, got it, Ted. You sell our idea, and as a favor to us, you're going to give us an opportunity to make you rich — er by giving you another priceless idea," says Bruiser. Ted stares back at Bruiser blankly. "That was our idea, and you sold it without any accreditation to us!" demands Bruiser adamantly.

"Bruiser, if you're not just fucking with me, that show won't matter. I could sign you on as an executive producer of 'Public House' and you'll have a steady income flow for doing nothing."

"Nothing? That concept was ours," says Bruiser.

"Inconsequential." says Ted.

"Inconsequential?" barks Bruiser.

"Bruiser, the concept already existed. We just tweaked it. If this new show isn't complete and absolute bullshit, you'll never think about money again," says Ted. "Open your eyes."

Bruiser leans back in his seat and says, "My eyes are open, Ted. You sold my show, and I want my cut!"

"Is he fucking with me, Dick?" asks Ted.

"It's hard to tell with him lately. I mean, he's pretty fucked up, but I don't think so," says Dick.

"Ted, if I'm capable of healing people just by slapping them, I can produce the show myself and sell it to any network on the planet. Right?" asks Bruiser.

"If you knew the right people," says Ted as he gets out his checkbook and starts to fill it out. "Bruiser, I sold the restaurant show by accident over lunch. It'd been so long since we talked about it, I truly forgot where it came from. If you aren't just fucking with me, and you really are gifted with a healing hand, this check is yours." Ted folds the check in two and slides it across his desk.

Bruiser unfolds the check, and his eyes fight to jump out of his skull. He regroups and asks, "Do you even have a million dollars?"

Dick aptly snatches the check from Bruiser in disbelief.

"I do, if you can heal my son," says Ted.

The room goes silent.

"I'm not going to slap Tanner. That's completely fucked," says Bruiser.

"Why not? Because it's all bullshit?" asks Ted.

"No. He's got ALS. He's defenseless."

"It's cerebral palsy; and you won't even try for a million dollars. You won't heal my son. Because you can't. Drop the hustle and sell me a real show." Ted hits a button on his intercom and his assistant walks in the door with a tray full of beverages. "You guys remember Sonya?"

Sonya is a young, hip, ladder climber, wearing a tweed pencil skirt pulled up to her belly button, a black silk blouse that accentuates her breasts just enough to where she's stunning not slutty, hair in a bun, and she tops the outfit off with a pair of fifties style butterfly glasses. She walks around the room handing out the coffees, and there isn't an eye in the room that's not on her as she sets down the tray. "Three Shots in the Dark and a glass of water. Anything else, Ted?"

"Actually, yes. We need your help with a new show we're working on," he says as he grabs the glass of water off the tray.

"How can I help?" asks Sonya.

"Just stand there," says Ted as he stands up and takes a sip of the water.

"I can do that," she says as she puts her hands on her hips and arches her back. Ted walks behind Sonya with the glass of water in his hand. Sonya tries to smile and cloak her discomfort as Ted takes another sip and then dumps the rest of the water on her head slowly as if he were watering a succulent plant. She wipes the water off her face frantically and then shakes her hands in a tizzy, shouting, "What the fuck, Ted!"

Dick and Bruiser start laughing.

"It's only water, Sonya," says Dick.

"You'd think she was allergic to it," says Bruiser.

"She kind of is. Sorry, Sonya, I had to do it," says Ted.

Sonya starts scratching her arms and then tears her blouse off.

Dick and Bruiser's jaws drop as she reveals her slender torso and glorious rack. "She's covered in rashes," says Dick, pointing at her. "That's gotta' suck."

"She's really allergic to water, Ted?" asks Bruiser.

"It's called aquagenic urticaria, but yeah."

"That's a thing?" asks Bruiser.

"Are you going to slap her, Bruiser?" asks Ted.

"What kind of freaky shit is going on here, Ted?" asks Sonya as she frantically tears her dress off. She starts to take her bra off, saying, "I need lotion, Ted!"

"B, just slap the girl out of her misery," barks Dick.

"Can we wait 'til she's all the way naked? She's stunning, even in peril," says Bruiser, watching her scratch herself so hard she starts to bleed.

"Just humor me, Bruiser," says Ted. "If you can't get her to stop, I'll assume you were just fucking with me."

Bruiser stands up and grabs Sonya's arm. He pulls back to slap her and says, "Sorry."

Sonya flinches and asks, "Ted, what the fuck?"

"It's okay, Sonya. Just let him slap you," says Ted.

Bruiser slaps her lightly and asks, "You happy, Ted?"

"No. Follow through this time. Hit her like she's been cheating on you with your mom," says Ted.

Bruiser reaches back and slaps her hard with his left hand. Her glasses fly off her face and she collapses on the outdated, shag carpet face down. The three men stand over her like a gaggle of frat boys at an orgy gone wrong and Ted says, "Nice tramp stamp, Sonya. Where'd you get that, Florida?"

"Is that two pigs fucking?" asks Dick.

"They're makin' bacon," whimpers Sonya. "I got it in Myrtle Beach on spring break. I was fifteen." Her irritation gives way to a new feeling, she collapses and starts slowly undulating on the shag carpet.

"It doesn't matter anymore because it's disappearing," says Dick. "The rashes are fading too!"

Ted kneels, staring in awe at her as she heals right in front of him. He pokes at her, saying, "And the scratches."

Sonya finally returns to the moment and stands up. She realizes she's half-naked in a room full of dudes and tries to cover herself. Ted hands her an extra-large Monster shirt to put on, and she walks over to the stand-up mirror. As she looks over her new form, she looks back at Bruiser through the mirror in amazement, and asks, "Is this going to be permanent?"

Bruiser shrugs and says, "I hope so. I'd love to take a long, hot bath with you sometime."

"I feel like I owe you that," says Sonya, giving him the same pensive look, he's been getting all day.

Ted gives her a hug and says, "Sonya, thank you. Take the rest of the day off. Go home, take a long hot bath — by yourself."

"Thanks. Anything else?" asks Sonya.

"Tell them to send Tanner up," says Ted.

Sonya looks back at Bruiser with a look in her eyes.

Bruiser stands up in a trance and starts to follow her.

"Ted, how'd you know that would work?" asks Dick.

"I didn't. When I saw the footage from today, I was pretty sure you guys were fucking with me, you know, turning the show into something else without consulting me," says Ted.

"Bruiser!" shouts Dick in hopes of pulling Bruiser back to the meeting. "What do you think?"

Bruiser stops, turns around, and lights a cigarette, saying, "Well, at least we know it wasn't the booze that fucked things up; but what if it doesn't last?"

"What do you mean, if it doesn't last?" asks Dick.

"So, I can do tattoo removal and I straightened some girl's eye out with a slap," says Bruiser as he sits back down.

"You just changed Sonya's life infinitely," says Dick.

Bruiser smiles and says, "Yeah, but look what happened with Lucy and you, Dick?"

"What happened?" asks Ted.

"Nothing," says Bruiser.

"Don't worry about it. We're good," says Dick.

"Are you going to tell me what I," Bruiser throws up some air quotes, "fixed with you, dude?"

"It doesn't matter, B. It's kind of personal," says Dick.

"Well, didn't know it was like that," says Bruiser, leaning away from Dick. "I mean, what if this whole thing is a fluke or shit, a dream. What if I'm still trapped in that hobo coma?"

"We don't have time for a fluke," says Ted, "and you're not trapped in a coma. I've got Tanner in the van on the way up here, and every major network exec I could pull last minute to see you heal him. Do you think you can do it?"

"What makes you think I can? And why does it have to be a show? Why can't I just walk the earth healing people?" asks Bruiser.

"It doesn't. It's up to you, Bruiser. You're the big dick in the room, but I don't see why you wouldn't want to make a vault of money off this," says Ted with an unfamiliar glimmer in his eye.

"What happens if this is all bullshit, and we come off as frauds?" asks Bruiser.

"What's up with all the what-ifs, B?" asks Dick.

"None of that matters. We'll fake it, if we have to," says Ted as he dives into an array of texts on his phone.

"I don't want to fake it. I've already ruined my rep as a human with Greed. I don't expect anyone to embrace me as a healer after watching me poop on people for a living."

"Slap me, Bruiser," says Ted.

"Give me a minute. I'm still trying to get Sonya out of my head," he says as he checks his phone for a diversionary thought.

"What's wrong with you?" asks Dick.

"Well, for starters, I've got some bad tattoos from the eighties, a bad back, and I've been smoking for thirty years."

"I'm pretty sure you've got herpes too. How long were you in LA?" asks Dick laughingly.

"I don't know anyone that makes it out of LA without them," says Ted. "It's like a rite of passage in the film industry."

"I guess I should thank the crazy witch in my head." Bruiser leans back in his chair, hits his cigarette a couple times, finishes his coffee, and puts his cigarette out in the cup, saying, "Stand up, Ted." Ted gets out of his chair and walks over to Bruiser. Bruiser puts his hand in Ted's face and says, "I want total control on this, no fuckery, and I want points on 'Public House.'"

"Get rid of my herpes and you can have whatever you want," says Ted as he takes off his glasses and sets them down on his desk.

"I want to take it on the road, cross-country, and I want a backup plan for when it runs out," says Bruiser.

There's a moment of silence. Ted loosens his tie. Bruiser draws back, Ted flinches, and Dick laughs. "I wasn't ready," says Ted.

"You looked ready," says Dick.

"I can't see without my glasses," whimpers Ted.

"There's going to be a moment when I can see through you and into your darkest corners. I hope that you're ready for that," says Bruiser as he stares into Ted's clouded eyes. He draws back and steps into it, slapping the shit out of Ted. Ted drops to his knees, and a cloud of dark smoke crawls out of him as he hits the floor. The cloud starts to move through the room as if it had purpose, lingering on specific pictures and war memorabilia on Ted's wall. There's a moment where the room stands still, and Bruiser freezes with confusion. Ted falls over, curls up in a ball, and starts crying.

Dick snaps his fingers in front of Bruiser's face, asking, "You okay?"

The smoke penetrates Bruiser, and he starts to laugh in a deep raspy chuckle that feels as if it came from a distant place. He falls back in his chair, saying, "No, not at all. For as long as I've wanted to do that, I thought I'd enjoy it more."

Dick points at Ted on the floor crying and says, "Look, bro, his hair is turning red. Teddy, you soulless bastard."

Ted stands up excited and looks to the mirror. The room is speechless as they watch Ted's transformation. The years seem to shed right off him like a snake molting skin, revealing an old friend from better days. With a gaping smile, Ted says, "I'm a ginger. Do you have a problem with that, Dick?"

Dick laughs and says, "No, it kind of makes sense."

"So, what do you want to call the show, Bruiser?" Bruiser remains silent. "We need a solid pitch for this meeting," says Ted as he unbuckles his belt and shoves his hand in his pants.

"The Hand of God?" asks Dick sarcastically.

Ted entranced by his new reflection in the mirror, drunk off his currently evolving appearance, asks, "What about Delusions of Grandeur?"

"Megalomania with Bruiser?" asks Dick.

Bruiser returns from his energetic retreat, and says in a serious demeanor, "No. I want to change my name, drop the scumbag rep."

"It's going to be hard to shake the image your internet celebrity created. Maybe if you shave that beard and get a high and tight," says Ted as he unbuttons his shirt looking for his tattoos. "We've got to bottle this up and sell it now. We don't need a name or a theme. This is amazing. When they see what you do with Tanner, the show is sold. It's going to be about how much we get for it and who packages it the best."

Dick looks at Bruiser and asks him, "Do you think you can fix Tanner?"

"Dude, he' s a pile of goo. I love the kid, but that's not just tattoos and STDs," says Bruiser as he stares at Ted flexing in the mirror. "But for a mill, I'll damn well try."

"No shit. You're buying drinks tonight," says Dick.

There's a moment where Dick stops and stares at Bruiser as if he were falling in love with him.

"What?" asks Bruiser.

"What did you see inside Ted when you froze up?" asks Dick.

"Some fucked up past lives. I can't really talk about it until I'm done downloading it, but he def had some demons lurking in there," says Bruiser, shaking as Ted's shadows pillage his being.

"Ted's phone makes a weird bird noise, and he stops fawning over his new self, long enough to check the message. He looks up from his phone and smiles, saying, "Let's go. Everybody's here." Bruiser stands up and grabs Ted's glasses off the desk and hands them to him. Ted rubs his eyes and stares off at the far side of his office, saying, "I'm good. Walk with me." Ted slaps Dick on the butt as they walk out the door. "I posted the footage from earlier just to see what kind of a reaction it would get."

"How'd that go?" asks Dick.

"We started getting calls as soon as it hit, but with our 'rep' everyone assumes it's a scam, right? So, I figure, tell them it is. They just want something fresh, but we got some weird feedback."

"Like what?" asks Bruiser.

"No one wants to see you banging handicapped kids just so they can get healed," says Ted laughing.

"That's a human response, maybe after I heal them," says Bruiser playfully.

"You don't think that's weird?" asks Dick.

"Not at all. Just a bit of gratitude from my followers," laughs Bruiser.

Ted, staring at Bruiser with the same weird look in his eye that Dick had, says, "This is going to be a mess."

Dick shakes his head and says, "A real fuck-show. Who are we pitching, Ted?" asks Dick.

"ABC, NBC, TLC, FX, HBO, Vice, Cinemax, Netflix, Amazon, and Hulu. They're all here. The only people I haven't heard from is the government and the religious groups that'll want to confiscate you," says Ted as he stops at the door to the conference room. "How's my hair look?"

"Red, Ted, very red," says Dick.

Ted smiles and says, "You know, you two are the sons Tanner could never have been for me, and I appreciate everything you've done. You guys put me back in the game with Greed, and this next show is going to change the world around us. I'm just humbled to be a part of it."

Uncomfortable with the well of adoration he just unearthed, Bruiser verbally jabs at him, "I've always felt like you were the father I never wanted, and as many times as you've fucked us over, I want you to know; I can't take this." He tries to hand the check back to Ted, but Dick pushes the check back at Bruiser. "I know there's nothing I can do for Tanner."

Ted stares at Bruiser holding the check for a second and says, "I don't have a million anyway. It was a gesture. I just wanted you to know I believe in you. Now that you've slapped me, I don't doubt you for a second," says Ted as he pushes the check into Bruiser's hand. "Maybe it'll clear after we sell this show. So, let's go make a fuck-ton of money!" says Ted as he bursts through the door with Dick and Bruiser in tow.

"I'd like to thank you all for showing up on such short notice," says Ted to no response. The room remains silent as they watch Bruiser drunkenly slither into his seat.

"That's the Second Coming?" moans one of the execs.

"Nice dye-job, Ted. What happened to your face? I need your surgeon's contact info," says another one of the execs.

"Thanks, Shawn. That was Bruiser," he says, pointing at Bruiser, who passed out as soon as he sat down. "Anyway, I assume that you're all here for a good laugh, and to prove that I am the waste of time you think I am, hanging on to the last rung of the ladder."

"That's cute that you even think you're on the ladder, Ted," says Marsha, one of the execs from HBO. "Can we get on with the pitch. I've got a five o'clock with a guy that can levitate."

Ted regroups, points at Bruiser, face down on the conference table, and says, "Look, we all have our pasts. I feel like I was absolved of mine today by the hands of the man we all know as Bruiser, the feckless host of the decadent gameshow Greed."

Bruiser, still face down, waves with a sedated disconcert for the room.

"Ted. Is he drunk?" asks Frank from Hulu. "There's no way this guy is a healer?"

"He was drunk when he came to me and pitched Greed. I was doubtful about a highly intoxicated gameshow host that likes to challenge his guests to test their boundaries in front of the world for money. Bruiser said that since it's the internet, we could do whatever we wanted. Our Greed didn't grant us endless riches by any means, but we can say that we have changed the face of entertainment forever, going where even European networks won't go. Greed is one of the most subscribed shows in the world. Today, we're offering you first dibs on a highly palatable mainstream concept that, if it proves to be genuine, will change the world as we know it forever."

"The only way that guy is going to change the world is by spreading all eighty-seven of his strands of HPV globally," laughs one of the execs.

Bruiser laughs and says, "Thanks, Chuck, but it's eighty-eight now. I have my own boutique strand."

The room groans.

Dick takes a sip of water, stands, up and presents himself, saying, "Today, I watched a girl get the freedom from suffering that we all want. As you saw on the link we sent you, Alex, a beautiful young girl with a lazy eye, was struck by the healing hand of my good friend Bruiser. Now she's devoid of her physical insecurities. I watched Ted's secretary cured from an affliction called aquagenic urticaria, an allergy to water. She hasn't enjoyed a long hot bath — ever. Look at Ted, he looks ten years younger and states his herpes are finally gone. We feel like this show has the power to redirect the current society into an upward spiral, changing the course of humanity indeterminately."

"Hey, Jerry from Netflix. You can't be serious? Bruiser the host of Greed, one of the vilest shows known to man, who is completely wasted right now, is going to heal the world with his 'Jesus powers?'"

As he feels Dick losing them, Ted takes over, saying, "Jerry, I was in disbelief myself until he slapped me. So, moving forward, we're all here to witness a miracle."

Bruiser tries to stand up but is caught off guard by the gravity of the situation — that or the liquor.

One of the execs mumbles, "C'mon, Ted, just sell us the real show and drop the facade."

Bruiser puts his cigarette out on the table and says, "As much as I'd like to slap each and every one of you and free you from your suffering, we're here to sell you a show."

Ted jumps back in, saying, "So, we brought in my son, Tanner. He was born with cerebral palsy and has spent his life confined to a wheelchair or his bed." Ted pulls out his phone and texts someone.

Bruiser leans into Ted's ear and whispers, "I'm not slapping Tanner, not in front of these people. It doesn't feel right."

The room has gone eerily quiet.

"Tanner Needameyer everyone," says Ted, ignoring Bruiser as he opens the door for his son and his caretaker. The silence deepens as the reality of the situation settles. Ted walks over to Tanner and kisses him on the head and looks back at Bruiser, saying, "If anyone deserves a miracle, he does. You can't deny him that."

"Ted, this is dark, even for you," says Marsha as she gets up to walk out. "I can't watch this."

Ted looks down deeply at Tanner and says, "Do this and we'll change the world for the better."

Bruiser covers his face and says, "I don't have to do this to change the world, not here, not now,"

"What are you afraid of?" asks Ted, challenging him.

Bruiser looks at Ted as if he wants to slap him, taking everything back, and then looks around the room to find everyone is recording the moment. "Looking like a complete degenerate by slapping a defenseless handicapped kid in front of the world."

Tanner pounds away grotesquely on his keyboard and we hear a computer voice say, "I've always wanted to be slapped by you, Bruiser."

"I told him he can take over hosting Greed for you if this works, Bruiser," says Ted.

"That's a huge fucking *IF*, Ted! I'm not gonna' break this kid's heart. He's had enough suffering in this life," says Bruiser.

Tanner pecks at the keyboard like a chicken playing piano and it says, "Then what could it hurt?"

Jerry from Netflix chimes in, "Wow. I can't argue with the kid. Let's go. I'm next!"

"You have to start believing in yourself sometime, Bruiser!" demands Dick.

Bruiser starts pacing and says, "This is so wrong."

"We've tried everything. We even tried stem cells, but not even the smallest change!" says Ted.

"You heard the kid, what could it hurt?" says Dick as he watches his friend nervously pace the room on the verge of an emotional collapse.

Tanner gets back on his keyboard, and this time it says, "Come on, hit me, you pussy. I double dare you." The room loses it.

Bruiser walks up to Tanner and kisses him on the head. He looks around the room full of execs with their phones out, and then at Dick and Ted. He shakily winds up his left hand, holding it as far back as physically possible, pauses, looks Tanner in the eyes as he sits in his wheelchair, helpless, twitching away uncontrollably, and as their eyes connect, a thick gob of drool slides out of the corner of

Tanner's mouth. Bruiser sees a flash of light and he hears, *I've served my time. Free me from this cell.*

Bruiser riddled with an apathy birthed by a new feeling of disgust, says, "Fuck it!" He slaps him with an unforgiving left, knocking him out of his wheelchair onto the floor of the conference room. The room moans with disgust, and they all stand up to get a view of Tanner flopping around on the floor helplessly.

"Fuck, Bruiser!" murmurs Dick as he covers his face.

"I found it suiting," says Bruiser.

Tanner looks up at him with a disjointed look in his eyes, and as the two connect, a cloud of shadows escapes Tanner and forces itself on Bruiser.

"Ted, you've done some messed up shit in your day, but—" says one of the execs.

"Give it a second. Bruiser, what's happening?" asks Ted as he watches his son flounder around on the floor.

Bruiser can't respond. His heart drops, and he's overtaken by doubt. "What was I thinking? Me — a healer!" says Bruiser under his breath as he storms out of the room, overwhelmed with embarrassment and self-loathing.

Tanner starts gasping for life and bellowing in misery.

"Someone pick him up. This is a new low, even for you, Ted. What are you trying to prove?" questions John from CBS. "Other than, you have no respect for anything."

"Give it a minute!" yells Ted.

"I guess there are limitations to his newly acquired healing powers," says Dick in a confused tone.

"I saw it with my own eyes. I felt the change inside of me." Ted opens his shirt, revealing a full chest of red hair. "Look, my tattoo is gone. It was terrible, a dragon wrapped around a heart with a sword through it."

"You could have had that lasered off, got some Botox, and died your hair, Ted," says Marsha.

"There would be light scarring. Dick, go get Bruiser," pleads Ted. "I want him to try it again. Maybe it has something to do with the severity of his illness."

The execs all start packing up their things and make their way to the door silently as Dick jumps up and pushes his way out of the room.

Ted walks over to his son, lying on the floor screaming, and he squats down to lift his helpless son, but ends up falling to the floor beneath him. Tanner moans in a puling tone that echoes through the room and forces liquids out of Ted as he clutches Tanner, rocking him back and forth. The conference room clears out, and as soon as the last couple of execs squeeze through the door, Tanner's eyes open, glowing a vibrant azure.

Tanner smiles and moans, "Fuck … you … Dad!"

Ted pushes himself up to gaze upon his child as he speaks his first coherent words and asks, "What did you say, Tanner?"

"This … *sucks*," moans Tanner as he relinquishes to gravity and is pushed forcefully into the floor. He returns to screaming as his limbs straighten, reaching out as if to get away from his person. His body starts to convulse vigorously, and his hair goes from brown to blonde. His arms and legs start to gain mass rapidly and Tanner shouts in a deeply penetrating angelic tone, "Get off me!" He uses his dad for leverage, pushing himself off the ground awkwardly, shaking.

Ted completely confounded, balls up and starts crying maniacally in disbelief. At this point the only other person in the room is Jerry, from Netflix. He's still filming and has barricaded the door. Tanner stands up and dusts off a lifetime of suffering. He offers his hand to his father and pulls him to his feet. Jerry, eyes wide open, asks Tanner, "What are you going to do first?"

"I just want to take a shower — by myself. Nothing personal, dad, but your sponge baths are the worst. You're way too handsy."

Ted, speechless and filled with tears, grabs his son, and pulls him into his chest, shaking with an elated exuberance.

Dick bursts through the door, gasping for air, and says, "I couldn't find him." Face to face with Tanner, Dick looks around the room and asks, "Where'd Tanner go? Who's this guy?"

Tanner waves his hand in Dick's face and then flexes his bicep. "Right here, dick," he says, and ball taps him.

Dick looks deep into Tanner's eyes and examines the new version. He shakes his head and rubs his eyes, saying, "No fucking way!"

Jerry puts his phone down and says, "Well, Teddy, let's talk numbers."

"We'll talk first thing tomorrow, Jerry," says Ted as he pushes Tanner back to soak up his now formidable form.

"I'll get you whatever you want for the show, within reason," says Jerry as he walks away from the conference room, shaking with awe, and shutting the door behind him.

"Dick, find Bruiser and show him the footage. Tell him to enjoy his last moments as a scumbag, internet-gameshow host. I'm going to grab a beer with my son and see if we can't get him laid," says Ted with a face full of tears.

I Found a Reason

Bruiser's eyes open to a scorching sun, endless red rock, and the nape of a beautiful spotted horse. The only thought in his mind that seems relevant is, "Where the hell am I?" he asks aloud.

"It appears to be a land denuded of any life form, sir," says a voice.

Bruiser looks around in search of the origin of the ominous voice and notices a rifle strapped to the left side of his saddle. He grabs the butt stock and caresses it, saying, "Looks like a desert to me, horse."

The horse stops, turns its head, and says, "Exactly, sir."

Bruiser notices a brass plaque on the saddle that has the word 'Desire' clumsily etched into it. He scratches his head and asks, "Well, what are we doing here?"

"You tell me, sir. You brought us here."

"I feel like we're looking for something."

"Sir, I would think water to be in the forefront of our minds. Beyond that, I can't say."

"Water," Bruiser licks his lips, "but this is a dream."

"Is it?" asks the horse, collapsing and pulling Bruiser to the ground with him.

There is a large hollow thud, and he hears, "Bruiser, Bruiser!"

"Bruiser! Get the fuck up, you worthless piece of shit!"

"Dad?" Bruiser screams out and his eyes open, revealing a vignette around the mess he thought he'd left behind. He's lying on the floor, outlined by beer cans and liquor bottles. He looks up through the bottom of a glass coffee table and caresses the belly of a fluffy white pile of chemicals that is trapped on the opposite side of the tabletop.

The banging continues and he hears, "Bruiser!"

"Fuck the fuck off. I'm hibernating," he says.

"Bruiser, it's Dick. Open the door!" he demands.

"Can you text me whatever it is that's so important that you feel the need to disrupt my travels." Bruiser rolls over and starts picking through the flocculant rug like it was a relative primate's back and asks, "You got any weed?"

"Of course!" yells Dick through the door. "Your phones been off for days, Bruiser. I've got Tanner here."

Bruiser looks through a dark tunnel toward the door and says, "Tell him I'm sorry it didn't work, push him back to your Subaru, and fuck the fuck off. It's not my problem."

Tanner yells in a deep, masculine, yet bubbly voice, "Bruiser, quit being an emotional fucktard and open the door."

Bruiser pauses at the sound of his voice, rubs his eyes, and asks, "Who's that?"

"Tanner, and if you don't open the door, I'm going to kick it down!" he says.

"Ha, I'd like to see that." Bruiser finds a roach in the ashtray and lights it.

"I've got a check from Netflix for the new show," shouts Dick through the door.

Bruiser crawls to the door, stands up, opens it, barrels back to the couch, inhales the line he was petting through the glass tabletop moments ago, lights a cigarette, and lays down asking, "Who's the nerd?"

Dick replies, "This is Tanner — new and improved. Look at this stud." Dick grabs his bicep, saying, "He's a Greek god. I almost fucked him the other night — long story. Man, we were trashed."

"Yeah, we were," laughs Tanner, sitting down on the couch next to Bruiser.

"Quit fucking around, Dick. I saw him hit the ground and start screaming. The whole thing was silly. Me, Bruiser, scumbag extraordinaire … a healer. I'm ready to go shoot some porn, do whatever it takes. Let's make some money." He leans over the coffee table and zones out in search of more magic dust.

Dick, hovering over Bruiser, throws a glass of water on him. It doesn't change his demeanor one percent. Dick smears his finger across the table and licks it. He grabs Bruiser and starts shaking him. "B, are you in a fucking K-hole? Get it together, dude! We're fucking rich!" Dick pulls a check out of his pocket and hands it to him saying, "Ted sold the show to Netflix. We leave first thing Monday."

"Thanks, Probst." Bruiser takes the check and wipes the water off his face with it. He swims gracelessly through his K-hole towards Tanner, who's sitting next to him, and asks, "Tanner?" as he grabs Tanner's face and stretches it out like Silly Putty. "This isn't Tanner. This guy's buff, dude. What's really going on?" He looks at the check and tries to make sense of it.

"You're a millionaire, son! And you freed Tanner's soul from his gooey dungeon of a body. This guy's crushing it with the ladies, probably gonna' hit your numbers," says Dick.

Befuddled he says, "You guys sold the show without me."

"You've been plummeting through space for days with your phone off. We had to pull the trigger while we had the shot," says Dick as he takes the check back from Bruiser.

"My phone died," says Bruiser.

"Did you try slapping it?" asks Tanner.

"Or buy a new one. You're a millionaire, dumb ass. Get it together. We're throwing a party for Desiree here tomorrow," says Dick.

"It's Friday?" asks Bruiser.

Dick laughs and says, "Yes sir. We're leaving on Monday to travel cross-country with the show. You're going to change the world forever. You think you'll be ready?"

"One way or another," says Bruiser as the lack of situational levity curls him up in a ball and he drops his head on Tanner's lap.

"Get it together. You need a name for yourself and a name for the show," says Dick.

Bruiser's eyes shut.

Tanner, completely comfortable with Bruiser's head in his lap, strokes Bruiser's hair and says, "Bruiser, you granted my only wish, and I am forever indebted to you. I want to tour with you, walk the earth with you, get bitches with you. I want to be your PA."

"Personal assistant?" mumbles Bruiser as he returns to the desert.

Tanner laughs and says, "Pussy Attendant. I want to bird dog for you. You're the future." To no response, he shakes his deity looking for acceptance, but finds only absence.

"Let's get out of here, Tanner. We've got to go grab some equipment for the bus." says Dick, walking towards the door. "I do believe he's returned to the cosmos. You can hit him up at the party."

Bruiser finds himself on the ground, pinned under his horse. He pets it, looking for a pulse, and asks, "Hey horse, you gonna' make it?"

"My name is Desire. I don't know how you forgot that. And don't worry about me. I'm not afraid of leaving this place," says the horse.

Bruiser digs his way out from underneath Desire, grabs his gun and his saddle bag, and walks over to the horse's head. He kneels and pets its mane, saying, "Horse, I'm going to find you water." He looks off into the distance and sees nothing, nothing but horizon. "Which way do I go?"

He hears a wheezing scream in the sky and looks up to find a vulture circling overhead. He grabs his rifle and lets off some warning shots. This attracts the dirty bird, and as it dives at him, he hears an echoing whisper, *Follow me*.

Bruiser looks around and yells, "Why should I trust you? You're waiting for me to leave so that you can pick apart my Desire!"

"What do you have to lose at this point? You can follow me and possibly die or walk in the complete opposite direction and do the same," says the bird.

"Or I could sit here and just do nothing. It's only a dream," says Bruiser, staring directly into the sun.

"I guess, but how will you feed your Desire?"

Desiree and Less walk into Bruiser's place carrying bags full of party supplies. They step over Bruiser as he has found his way back to the floor, again, and head to the kitchen. "What happened with you guys, Des?" asks Less.

"Nothing really. We've hooked up a handful of times, but I don't think he remembers any of it. He's a drug addict and a whore, not really boyfriend material. I love the guy, but he's too hot and cold. And what's this whole thing about being a healer?"

Less responds, staring at her with his head tilted and asks, "You haven't seen Tanner?"

"Ted's kid, the one with cerebral palsy?" she asks.

"Yeah, Bruiser slapped him and turned him from a vegetable into a prime rib. He'll be here tonight. Try not to fuck him. I'm pretty sure he's already caught something life-threatening hanging out with Dick. I don't know where this healing show is going, but the ride should be a good one. I mean, who would have ever thought, Bruiser of all people, a healer? Shit, a savior? Shit, a millionaire? This cross-country tour is going to be legit. You should ride with us," says Less.

"Have you forgotten? I've got my show in LA. It's my dream and all I have is this one chance. I can't live in his dream, and you know he's going to make a mess of it. He always does," she says, staring at Bruiser while he lays on the floor like an old dog in the sun, barely moving only when it can't take the discomfort of constant comfort anymore.

"Bruiser's a millionaire?" she asks.

"Yeah," says Less, pulling the moist check out of the ashtray fingering one of the many cigarette burns and handing it to Desiree.

"Are you coming?" asks the vulture.

"What else do I have without Desire?" Bruiser stands up and follows the vulture through the desert. *Lost and alone, wandering aimlessly in the desert. I wonder what I did to deserve this. I've been alone my whole life. So, even being alone in my dreams makes sense. I just wish there was someone who loved me. Someone amazing.*

"What makes you think you're amazing and that you deserve someone similar?" asks the vulture. "You've been getting similar, but not amazing. The women you surround yourself with are equals. The hard part is acknowledging how much you suck, and how awesome you're not."

Bruiser looks around for the vulture, pointing his gun in the sky, but finds the bird is off in the distance, too far to hit. He drags his boots through the sand, walking endlessly until he trips over something. He looks down and sees what appears to be a pair of tits poking out of the sand. He drops to his knees and digs frantically, trying to exhume the voluptuous form.

One of the breasts erupts and starts spraying a fountain of liquid. He puts his mouth to the tit, drinking from it without a concern for its content. He uncovers the face connected to the body and stares poignantly at it as it feels like a familiar face. He exhumes the lifeless body and slaps her, hoping for a reaction. "Nothing?" He drags her to a rock where he positions her upright and finds his way into her arms, hoping to hide from the sun and suckle from her well of vibrance. As he lay there in her inanimate embrace, draining her container, her breast erupts in his face, pushing him flat on his back.

"What the fuck?" Bruiser opens his eyes and finds Desiree, standing over him with an empty mop bucket, having just doused him with the contents. There is a life-size crucified ice Jesus hovering over him with a bright light protruding from his chest. Jesus starts dripping blood from his crown of thorns. The blood slowly slides down his body to his pierced feet. "Do you really think that's necessary?"

"How else was I going to get you out of your self-induced coma, loser?" asks Desiree as she walks away from him.

"Take a shot, B," says Less, diverting his attention. "It's a Jesus Jager luge, and I've got a projector coming out of his heart that's connected to my laptop."

"Bruiser, seriously — get up! You've got a houseful coming over," screeches Desiree across the loft.

"That's tomorrow!" he responds.

"It is tomorrow," says Less.

Bruiser crawls back to the couch, looking for something with which to dry himself. "That's just what I need in my loft right now; a visual representation of one of the most loving beings that walked the earth healing people and how he was tortured in prolifically excruciating ways because of it. How long have you guys been here?" he asks as he tries to light a cigarette and can't, because it's too moist.

Less hands Bruiser a cigarette he lit for himself and says, "We've been here all day, setting up and listening to you moan about riding through the desert on a horse with no name."

Dick walks in and does a bump of coke straight out the bag, hands it to Bruiser, and says, "Go take a shower, you schmell, and get your shit together, bro. You've got half of Atlanta headed here, and we want this going away party to be epic."

"Thanks for the wakeup call, Des," says Bruiser.

"It was that or jumper cables and car battery," she says.

"Most people just hit me until I wake up," says Bruiser, walking up the stairs towards the bathroom.

"Second Coming … we're all fucked," snarks Desiree.

Dick walks over to Desiree in the kitchen area and says, "Desiree, leave him alone. He's got a lot on his plate." Tanner walks in with two milk crates full of records. "Shit, look at Tanner. That's a miracle; if I've ever seen one."

"Miracle right here, that's me," says Tanner, setting down the crates. "I'm a free man now, so let's kickstart this moped. I wants to get fucked up." He walks over into Desiree's personal space, putting his hand out. "Tanner, the meat is all mine."

Desiree quivers and tries to say her name. "Des … Desi … ree … ray." She goes to shake his hand and he pulls her in for a hug.

"Oh, the *infamous* Desiree, got it. Somebody cut me a line," says Tanner.

Less and Desiree go silent while they stare at Tanner and then look at each other.

"Did he say lime or line?" asks Less.

"Not even a week as a fully functioning biped, and you guys have already ruined him," barks Desiree.

"I'm not ruined, just making up for lost time," he says as he flexes in the mirror.

The group sits down on Bruiser's wrap-around sectional couch, and they start drinking while they wait for Bruiser to get cleaned up. They watch a compilation of pictures from their past projected out of Jesus's chest. Time passes slowly and people start to show up, filling the loft.

"It's been an hour. Where's Bruiser?" asks Dick.

"Probably passed out in the tub," says Less.

"I'll get him," says Desiree. She climbs the stairs to the loft part of the warehouse and finds three beautiful girls in Bruiser's bed all twisted up in a sexual knot. She stops at the top of the stairs and watches them until one of the girls catches her creeping.

"You're more than welcome to join us," says the girl as she perches herself upon a face, smearing herself all over her friend.

"Sorry to interrupt. I was looking for the host, Bruiser. Have you seen him?" she asks, still staring, wondering how one gets to the point where they're comfortable enough to display themselves in the throes of passion amidst a gathering.

"There's a dead body in the tub," says one of the girls, mid-moan.

"That sounds about right. Carry on." says Desiree. She turns her body, but her gaze stays focused on the girls as she watches one of them fishing around in another as if she were stuffing a turkey.

Bruiser comes to in the middle of the desert flittering like an overturned roach in a puddle of fluids, gasping for air. As he opens his eyes, he finds the lifeless body still sitting on the rock where he left her. The sun is directly behind her, shadowing her front, leaving a halo behind her head. He leans forward, trying to find his bearings in this reoccurring realm of confusion. "Desiree?" he asks gently to no response. "What happened to you?" he asks and slaps her playfully with his right hand in hopes of a revival. Again, there's no response, so he closes his eyes and leans back, returning to the puddle.

"You broke me, stupid. And then left me out here all alone and naked in the sun."

"How so?" he asks blindly, waiting for a response. He sees his friend, the buzzard, circling his micro-oasis. "Is that you, scalawag, whispering thoughts in my ear?"

"Scalawag you say. Why don't you slap her?" asks the voice.

"I tried that," he says, staring up at the sky. "She's dead. I'm going to let her have her peace."

"One would have to be alive in order to die," says the bird.

Desiree pushes the bathroom door open to find Bruiser sitting in the bathtub all shriveled up, covered in bubbles, and passed out with a cigarette's worth of ash hanging from a butt in his mouth. She grabs the hair dryer, plugs it in, and holds it over the claw foot tub, saying to herself, "I'm just going to turn it on and drop it in. If you don't wake up, well, I just killed the reluctant Messiah that was supposed to save us all." She lowers the blow dryer just above the tub, hits the switch and bubbles go everywhere.

Bruiser cracks one eye and looks up at Desiree. The light behind her is creating a halo like the one he saw in his dream. He asks dully, "Is that necessary? You've already douched me with a bucket of water, and now while I meditate in this delightful bubble bath, you're trying to deep fry me."

"Sorry, I didn't have any jumper cables," she says and smiles. Bruiser grabs her wrist and tries to pull her in, at the same time almost electrocuting himself. "Stop, Boozer. You're gonna' fuck up my miniskirt," she says playfully.

"Well, take it off and jump in. There's room for two in here," he says, awaiting his fresh serving of rejection. She turns off the blow dryer and sits down on the crapper across from the tub.

"Is that micro suede?" he asks, trying to catch a glimpse of her panties.

"Vintage, suede," she says, crossing her legs. Bruiser looks around for a cigarette. "What's wrong with you?"

"We don't really have time for that conversation. You know there's a gathering outside this loo," he says playfully?

"If only you knew," she laughs as she lights a cigarette, takes a drag, and passes it to him. "You've been missing for days. I'm leaving on Monday."

"If you could imagine the gravitational pull on my soul right now," he says, relaxing back into his bath, having found his two favorite distractions.

"I can't really. None of it makes any sense," she says.

"Nor should it."

"So, explain it to me. At least where you've been all week. We've been worried."

"*We* have, have *we*? So worried, you almost killed me."

"I was thinking about the greater good," she laughs.

"What's going on with you and this whole blackout bash you've been having, alone?"

"I slapped Tanner, and I thought nothing happened."

"Did you expect to fix him?" she asks.

"No, well kind of, but—"

"And you collapsed into yourself as usual when you thought it failed. Meanwhile, you created a monster, a really, sexy monster."

"You've met him?" he asks with a hint of jealousy.

"Downstairs, and he won't stop talking about you. You should really get out there and meet him. And maybe host this party properly."

"I'm good. I want to tell you about this dream I've been floating in and out of."

"I'm in, but when you're done, you're getting out of that dirty, little puddle you made and joining us," she says.

"Exactly, that's so weird. For daze I've been coming in and out of the same dream where I'm riding through the desert on a horse, dressed up like a gutter punk cowboy, and guess what my horse's name was?"

"Dick?" she laughs.

"No, that's a whole other dream … Desire."

"So, you're being led through the desert by your dick, AKA Desire, and where does it lead you?"

"To a naked girl buried in the sand."

"Exactly. It's about your dick having control over you."

"Like, our friend Dick?" he asks.

"No, silly, your cock. It's led you into every fucked-up situation you've ever been in. It's basically your North Star, but it never leads you home," she says.

"On the contrary, you were the girl buried in the desert," he says and offers her a drag off the cigarette. She refuses it and pauses, confused by the accidental compliment. "And the horse's name was Desire; like Desiree."

"Without the extra 'E,' I get it. So, I was leading you to me?" she asks. "That doesn't register. Tell me more."

"You were dead, or more like an inanimate sex doll," he says and his eyes light up.

"Dead to you! That makes sense," she laughs. "So, you're going to be lost without me is what you're saying."

Bruiser takes a moment to process the overwhelming slice of truth he just got served and says, "Your boobs—"

She laughs and says, "I know, they're great. You gonna' miss 'em?" she asks, takes the cigarette from him, and contemplates hitting it again.

"They fed me as you sheltered me from the sun. That's the place I want to be. That's home," he says.

"Sucking on these?" she asks as she grabs her boobs and squeezes them.

"You're missing the point, Des. I want to make this happen with you. Come on the road with us. I'll pay you." he says.

Desiree stands up and asks, "So you can push me to the side every time some grindy lil' whore comes along. I've got my own future in LA. I'm not going to let you destroy that." She flicks the cigarette into the tub.

Bruiser pauses and says, "I'm sorry."

"For what?" she asks.

"For hurting you, I guess. I'm a self-centered, ego-driven, drug-abusing maniac that's controlled by a scared, scarred child," he says, playing with his bubbles as a child would when completely vulnerable and then attacked. "It's funny, in my dream, I was sitting in a dirty little puddle right before you tried to send me to the next life. I was trying to figure out how to resuscitate you, and there was this buzzard telling me you weren't dead just turned off."

Desiree starts laughing and says, "Now that registers."

"And I couldn't figure out how to turn you on."

"And what did your feathered friend tell you to do?"

"Throw you in the puddle and slap you."

"That sounds like fun, but it'll take a lot more than that to turn me on."

"Look, Des, I want to be happy. I'm tired of hurting everyone around me, and myself. I only know pain and suffering. That's where I've made my home, asking for seconds of the shit this life serves me."

"Well, let me know when that changes. If you could sober up and try not to fuck everyone here tonight, I might think about giving you a chance to hurt me again. But I'd be amazed if you could even walk by the girls clit-wrestling in your bed right now." Desiree opens the door, pokes her head out, and watches enviously as the girls force each other to come.

"There are two girls in my bed, and you want me to walk by them. Can we start tomorrow?" he asks gently.

"Three actually. You're missing out. I'm gonna' make sure they know you have every STD known to man," she says as she sticks one foot out the door.

"You know, you hurt me long before I hurt you," says Bruiser as he looks for a way to detain her. "I'm sure you don't even remember."

Desiree walks out of the bathroom, shutting the door, saying, "Maybe I can make it up to you at the bottom of the pile in your bed."

Bruiser jumps out of the tub, grabs a towel, and follows Desiree out of the bathroom, hoping to join the unsanctioned wrestling match taking place in his bed with the love of his life. He finds Desiree, awaiting his almost definite reaction, standing next to a beautiful, young girl with blonde hair, sitting in the booth, watching the sultry act with a grandiose line of something delightful cut out on the tabletop. The blonde looks back at Bruiser, dripping wet, fresh out the tub and then glances over at Desiree glowing with sass. Bruiser grabs Desiree by the arm before she can react to what she believes is about to happen and leads her to the edge of the loft floor. They look out over his living space to find it has filled up with, yet again, a very eclectic group of people no one really knows.

Bruiser tightens his towel and switches to host mode. "How's everyone doing tonight?" he barks at the top of his lungs. Less, who is currently working the ones-and-twos, sees Bruiser, screaming into the crowd, and cuts the music. "Thank you, Less," says Bruiser and shoots him a sarcastic finger gun. "How's everyone doing tonight?"

The room turns their attention to him, dripping wet and barely able to hold himself up. "We're here tonight to send off my good friend, Desiree. She's leaving us for the left coast because she landed a role on a new television series. So, this will be the last chance you all have to hold her presence in your line of sight before she leaves us for a tour through the idiot box." Bruiser looks around the room and finds, no one seems to be interested. They're all just looking at their phones or filming for no reason other than to let their friends know where said friends are not because they have not been invited. "Alrighty. Have fun and try not to break anything. Fuck it, do what you want. I don't plan on coming back here."

Bruiser turns around to find Desiree has separated herself from his half-naked attempt at honoring her. He reconnects with the girl sitting in the booth. She seems to be the only one entranced by his being currently, so he walks up to the booth, leans over, does a line that was clearly meant for someone else, and then walks by the three headed beast in his bed, analyzing every bit and piece that presents itself. He grabs a pair of torn-up jeans from the floor and throws on a black T-shirt. He walks by the bed again, and his focus is only on the girl in the booth. He sits down next to her and asks, "What do you think?"

"Your girlfriend? She seems like a real bitch!"

He turns to the girl and says, "She's just a friend."

"A good friend to put up with your shit," she says.

"Hey, play nice. I was asking what you thought about the girls in my bed," he says playfully.

"Well, Bruiser, I think the show is worth the MDMA I gave them," she says.

"Is that what that was?" He puts his hand out and asks, "And you are?"

"Angelora, and what is it that you're going to do to repay me for the last of my molly you just disintegrated?"

"Well, dark angel, I'm sure we can work something out," he says, staring her down as if to entrance her with his eyes. "What is it that you do with your days, beautiful? Actress?"

She smiles with his compliment and says, "I'm a massage therapist most of the time, a lover all the time, a model occasionally, and rarely an actress."

"Let me see your hands," he says. She hesitates and then puts them out palms up. "I'm not going to read your lines, silly. Grab my fists and try to crush them as hard as you can," he says. Angelora turns red, trying to crush his fists, and Bruiser starts laughing gregariously. "I don't know if you'd make much of a difference on my back with those soft little digits. Let me ask you this, Angelora?"

"Sure," she says as she stares into the mess her friends are making on his bed.

"I've been seeing a masseuse recently, a large Asian woman with the hands of a Panda Bear. She generally has to smother me with her FUPA to get deep into my spine which doesn't really bother me so much."

"So, what's the problem?" she asks.

"She spends a lot of time on my butt, which I don't mind either. The other day she was massaging my ass and her finger slipped into my outgoing mailbox per se."

"Seriously, what did you do?" she asks.

"What can you do? Her finger was already in there and she gives a great massage, so she can get away with it. I figure she's the one with poop on her finger, but my question is: do you tip extra for that?"

Angelora starts laughing and then says, "That's gross and you're stupid."

Bruiser looks deeply into Angelora while she's laughing. Everything slows down and he sees a faint image of black feathered wings expanding behind her while she's laughing.

"Maybe it's the molly, but I find you delightful. I'm starting a new show on Monday and we're going to be traveling cross-country. I'd like you to join us, but only if you answer this one question correctly."

"I've seen your show and it's über kreepy. I find it demeaning to humanity, and I would never put myself in that energetic space," she says.

"Nice. That was the whole point of Greed: to show humanity in its lowest form, desperation. It worked too well maybe. I found it disheartening as well, to the point that I've been trying to kill myself slowly to cope. This is a new show, something uplifting, that will hopefully remove the desperation from humanity."

"I guess, what's your question?" she asks hesitantly.

"This tour is going to be huge, and I want everything to fall into place. You're stunning, and I'd love to take you on the road with us, but I don't know if you're the right fit. I must know: do you believe in happy endings?" He tries not to laugh as he watches her face while she processes his words.

"Gross! I knew it. My sister said you were a child, and I'm not going to join your traveling harem if that's what you're thinking, loser!" she states and tries to get out of the booth.

Bruiser grabs her and pulls her back in, saying, "Angelora, take it easy. I'm just fucking with you! Who's your sister?"

Angelora starts breathing deeply and says, "Sarah. You broke her heart!"

"Well, that narrows it down."

"Sarah Ramirez, you jerk!"

"Broke her heart. She broke my dick!"

"That's disgusting. Let me out of here, you swine!" Angelora pushes him out of the booth onto the floor and walks over him. He grabs her skirt tail, stopping her, and starts to grovel. "She literally broke my dick. She was riding me and flew right off me. When she came back down, she missed completely and crushed my best friend. I heard it snap and I've been able to hit a ninety-degree angle with a hard-on ever since," he says, grabbing his junk. "Listen, I need a masseuse on the road, and I haven't had any time to find one. I just want to know what you have to offer."

She turns to walk away only enticing him further with her finest quality, saying, "I don't know that I want to! What's to say you're not going to try and Epstein me?"

"I'd probably keep you for myself. You just seem a bit too old to make any money off of trafficking," says Bruiser, trying not to laugh.

Angelora kicks him playfully and says, "You truly are disgusting, and I'm only twenty-three."

"Exactly. Let's just say it pays a hundred grand, the show is up to your standards, and I don't touch you: you just touch me. What do you have to offer?"

Angelora takes a deep breath as she stares at her friends trying to reel her into their moment and says, "Well, for a hundred grand: I'm a lover, a Reiki master, and a channel at times. Not to mention, one of the most beautiful girls you've ever met, aside from my sister. I know about you, and everything seems to be true. Now that I know you, I'm confused because there is something uniquely powerful and attractive about your being. But there's a crackling behind it that worries me. It sounds very unstable, and I believe I can help you with that, but it's going to cost you double — maybe triple." She pulls her card out of her bra and tosses it on the table. "Call me if you're serious."

"I want a massage before the night's over, deal?"

"We'll see where the night takes us," she says, looking back at him as she struts towards his orgy covered cloud and climbs into the bed with her friends.

Dick walks up just as Angelora is disrobed by her friends. He stops dead in his tracks, pulls Bruiser up off the floor, and the two stand shoulder to shoulder, watching the girls.

"Too bad you're grounded," laughs Dick.

"I was just thinking the same thing," he says as Angelora looks him dead in the eye.

Dick pulls at Bruiser's shirt and points at the roof, saying, "It's business. I just need you for a blunt's worth of convo." Dick climbs the ladder to the roof, sticks his head out of the hatch, looks down at Bruiser, "You know, if I was gonna' be a dick, I'd use my pass with Sarah's little sister and her friends, but I'd rather watch you fuck it up with Des, one last time."

"I think I'm gonna' save Angelora for later. I'm trying to get her to cum on the road with us."

Dick lights the blunt and asks Bruiser, "I'm definitely calling dibs then. What do you want with Des anyway? You trying to marry her, or you just gonna' hit it and break her heart one more time before you go?"

"Both would be nice, without the heart-breaking thing. I don't think either one of us could take it."

Dick sits Bruiser down on the couch and says, "So, what the fuck happened to you during the pitch?"

Bruiser hits the blunt a few times and says, "I don't know. Whatever I pulled out of Tanner was a dark entity. As soon as I hit him, I was blinded by doubt and fear. I couldn't wrap my head around being able to heal him or anyone. Then I realized I just cold cocked some handicapped kid in front of the world. The fear consumed me, I got nauseous, and fell directly into a blackout hole."

"We need to work on that," says Dick, "seeing as how you're the Second Coming, and we're about to televise a spiritual renaissance."

"The whole thing is redonkulous, Dick. I'm waiting to wake up from this nightmare," he says and starts coughing.

"A nightmare. It's a dream, Bruiser, we're rich. That's real shit. You can finally take care of your mom, try to find your sister, and tell your dad to fuck off. I mean, beyond the show, you're going to change this rock forever. I've been hanging out with Tanner, and all I can say is *you* turned that kid from a boner killer into a lady killer. Not to mention, he's fucking funny, my dude. You need to spend some time with him. He's been trapped in there for so long. It's like he's been watching and waiting to break out. And Ted would literally suck your dick if you asked. You changed his life and gave him his son. If you can do that for the rest of the world. Bruiser, look me in the eyes, you'll be," Dick tears up artificially, "a rich motherfucker. We both will."

"Fuck off, dude. It's me, Bruiser. Do you think that's how this ends? If it weren't for bad luck … You've seen me at my worst. When was the last time you saw me at my best?"

"Now, brother, right now, and it's better than anyone's best, so try to enjoy it."

"Before they take it away," says Bruiser.

There's a long silence, and Dick returns, asking, "Do you have a name for the show yet?"

"I haven't thought about it because I didn't think it was going to happen. I'll have something for you in the morning."

"Well, let's get this thing going. You've got to do a Jager luge off Jesus," says Dick.

"You know how I feel about Jager, and crucified Jesus doesn't help, you have to know that."

"I know, but it's vintage Euro Jager with deer's blood and opium. I paid out the ass for it. Let's go."

Bruiser hits the blunt, leans back, and rubs his face while the molly invades his gray matter, saying, "Okay, but can you keep this thing low profile. I just want one last night of being a social deviant."

The two climb down into Bruiser's room and find a full-blown orgy in his bed. They stop and watch for a moment, soaking in the performance art that it is, and Dick states, "Too many dudes in there."

Dick pulls Bruiser away from the orgy by his hand like a child. As they hit the downstairs, they find a bad kung-fu zombie flick being projected out of Jesus's chest that's complimented by Less beating up the turntables with nothing but Dub Step.

Bruiser steps into the crowd, looking for something to penetrate, and gets stuck in a gathering he finds to be subpar at best. He makes his way to the middle of the living area where everyone is just standing; not dancing. The MDMA takes over fully, and he decides to get loose, loose in the way of not caring about anything, yet still not being able to dance.

While he's "dancing," he feels a slap on his ass. His eyes light up and all he can think is "fresh meat." He turns around and finds Desiree to be the assailant. He blushes at the sight of her ensemble: blue suede mini skirt paired with a vintage 'Where the Day Takes You' T-shirt that's been mutilated to reveal as much of her as possible. It's accented by the lack of bra and mismatched converse. Her moves are probably worse than his, but it doesn't matter because her existence lights up the room. Bruiser grabs her hand and twirls her, throwing her into the crowd like a yo-yo, and then pulling her back into his arms for a dip. He has her paralyzed in his arms, and this would be when any sensible male went in for the kiss, but Bruiser, being nothing of the sort, pauses and attempts to smile sincerely. He pulls her back to her feet and the two start an old tradition of dancing as awkwardly as possible. Bruiser leans into her ear and says, "I haven't slept with anyone yet, and there was a full-blown orgy on my bed."

"I'd say congratulations, but the night is young," she says and pushes him into the crowd and ducks down, hiding from him. Bruiser returns from his victory dance lap and sneaks up on Desiree. He gets right behind her and pelvic thrusts, pushing her four or five feet into the crowd. She stops, turns around, and Bruiser throws her an imaginary hook and reels her back in. Desiree pulls him in for a slow dance, leans in and whispers in Bruiser's ear, "So, when are you going to heal me?"

Bruiser stutters for a moment at the verbal acceptance she just threw at him, assuming there's a catch. "So, you're a believer now?" he asks.

"I'd hate to have known the man who changed the world and never taken advantage of him," she says, looking into his eyes.

"What makes you think you need it?" he asks softly. "You're perfect."

"If only you knew," she says as she pushes him to arm's length and starts to wiggle around with her eyes closed.

Bruiser bends his knees and drops to the floor, making him about three feet tall so that he can spotlight Desiree while she dances blindly. Her eyes open and she doesn't see him. He pops up from the floor with a smirk on his face and asks her, "What changed?"

"I thought for sure Tanner was a scam when I met him. All I wanted to do was jump his bones and I thought, 'There's no way that you or anyone could turn a helpless soul into that,' but Less showed me the video of his change, and there's no way you could fake that. He's amazing, look at him." She points at Tanner grinding shirtless on two girls in their underwear showering in the blood red fluids dripping from the Jesus ice luge. "I don't know how you acquired this talent, but I assume it comes from a lifetime of suffering and having a heart of gold; even if I've never seen it," she says, smiling at him.

"You're drunk, aren't you?" She makes a goofy, drunk face and nods her head. "Maybe, if you can make it through this party without fornicating anyone, I'll think about slapping your cute little ass and saving you from the perils of the human condition."

Bruiser leans in and tries to kiss her, but she turns her head saying, "You'll just fuck it up, Bruiser."

"Me? You started it," he says.

"Tell me how I hurt you," she says.

"You really have no idea?" he asks.

"No idea at all. Fill me in," she says, while running her fingers through his beard.

"As much as I would like to … fill you in … and out … and in, I don't think it matters. Maybe I'll tell you later when we're lying in bed together."

"I'm surely not sleeping in your bed. That thing has more diseases than the CDC!"

The music cuts off and Dick, who's standing with Less in the DJ nest behind Jager luge Jesus overlooking the crowd, grabs the mic and says, "I'd like to thank everyone for hanging out tonight. I'd like to think we're all as fucked up as Bruiser is or have some plan on how to get there tonight, but that's not what I want to talk about.

This is Des's night. Put your hand up, Des." Bruiser turns to put her hand up for her, but she has ducked down below the crowd. Dick continues, "Desiree, congratulations on the new show and the move to LA. We're going to miss you for sure — especially that guy." Dick tries to point out Bruiser, but he dodges the attention as well. "My longtime friend, more like a brother, Bruiser. You might know him as the host of Greed, the internet sensation, or you might know him from walking by him sleeping in a bush, covered in his own feces."

"Get to the point," yells some guy.

"Anyway, Bruiser and I go back, way back, like before pants had pockets."

"Are you gonna' propose to him or what?" shouts another random guy.

"I don't need to. We're going to be traveling this great nation in a bus together. I'm not going to be able to get away from him. Monday, we leave for a cross-country tour of the US to shoot a new television series that's been picked up by Netflix."

Another random guy yells, "Your show sucks!"

"And that is why we're starting fresh with our new show, sir. I just want to acknowledge this will be the last party here for a while. You should take the time to meet him and maybe trick him into slapping you. He's going to change this world for the better." Dick looks around the room across all the blank stares and points at Bruiser saying, "Fuck it, let's erase the hard drive!" He drops the mic and walks away.

"WHAT A DICK!" yells Bruiser and the music comes back on. He looks for a way out of the crowd, but there isn't one, and he starts to panic. "All I wanted was one last night," he says as he turns around to find Desiree is gone and that he's dancing with a larger Italian male wearing a glittery T-shirt that is way too small for him.

Bruiser fights the crowd and heads towards the kitchen where he finds a group of younger kids surrounding the island. He goes to the fridge and pulls out a bottle of champagne, pops it, fills all the girl's glasses, and sets the bottle down. He then picks up a bottle of tequila from the counter and pours shots until there are no empty glasses left on the counter. He grabs a shot glass, lifts it in the air, saying, "To obtaining all of one's earthly desires in this lifetime or the next." Everyone throws their glasses up in the air melancholically, clink them on the countertop, slam their shot, and return to their phones.

"What is it with the constant adoration of their tracking devices?" mumbles Bruiser.

"It's a sentinel's job," says some kid standing next to him.

"Do what?" asks Bruiser.

"It's a sentinel's job, protecting their virtual egos. No one's worried about being covered in ostentatious tattoos when they're eighty. Laser technology has deemed their permanence irrelevant, but the permanence of their online persona leaves them constantly editing their virtual tombstones."

Everyone lowers their devices and just stares at the two awkwardly, and then return to their phones.

"I never thought about it like that. I guess I'm old school. I'm used to human interaction at parties," says Bruiser. He pulls a blunt out of the junk drawer in the island and lights it, hoping to change the direction of the room. He hits it a couple of times and tries to pass it to the kid next to him. The kid pulls out a pen and waves it in Bruiser's face. Bruiser asks himself aloud, "Does everything have to be digital these days?" He turns to his right and tries to pass it to the girl next to him. She pulls out a pen, hits it, and passes it to him. Next thing you know, everyone has their pens out and they are passing them around the kitchen. Bruiser stares into their eyes and sees no joy, no excitement, not even disdain, just spiritual entropy.

Bruiser licks his lips and turns the blunt around, putting the cherry in his mouth. He puts his hand up and leans into the kid next to him looking to form a tube to be filled with smoke, but he doesn't grasp the concept of receiving a shotgun. Bruiser grabs him by the back of the head and blows an excessive amount of smoke into his mouth and nostrils until the kid starts coughing.

When the kid finally stops coughing, he hands his pen to Bruiser and says, "Hit this, it's Romulan. One hit is like smoking a whole blunt without all the work."

Bruiser scoffs at the kid's technological high, saying, "That's the thing with you kids today, you've taken the living out of life. Everything is so streamlined and efficient that there's no struggle, no work. It's all apps, streaming, and instant downloads. There's no waiting, no process, and I swear if I have to sit through another film about people on their phones texting each other about things that happened on social media and how someone might really find out who they really are by exposing deleted selfies, I swear I'm going off the grid completely — just me and the Luddites."

A girl across the island sets her phone down and asks, "Aren't you that guy from the internet, the kreepster extraordinaire? I heard you had mutant powers."

Distracted from his geriatric rant, Bruiser asks the girl, "What's your name, darling?"

"Most people call me Wiley," she responds.

"First of all, Wiley, thank you for joining the conversation. Secondly, you're stunning. Can I ask you a question?"

"You just did. Would you like another?" she asks him.

Bruiser stares silently at her for a moment and then asks her, "How come nobody dances anymore?"

Wiley replies, "I see people dance at festivals."

"Yeah, that's mindless bouncing: it doesn't count. When I was a kid, we'd go to shows, smoke a joint or what you call an old school of some, well, it was just weed back then, no flavors or brands, and we would dance. No one was ever going to see it again, so it was special to the few that were there." Bruiser picks up another shot and slams it.

The kid next to Bruiser says, "Now, there's forty cameras always staring you down, and if you nerd out, it's over. You shit your pants in public, and your roommates know before you get home."

One of the girls barfs out, "Garrrosss!"

"You've never shat your pants?" asks Bruiser.

"As if!" says the girl, still on her phone.

Wiley jumps back in saying, "I shit my pants all the time. I have IBS."

Bruiser laughs. "So, you live in a constant fear of shitting your pants, embarrassing yourself, and erasing yourself from the VIP list."

Wiley walks around the island to get closer to Bruiser and says, "The sad part is, you get used to shitting your pants and ditching your panties all over the city!"

The garrrosss girl says, "I'd just get it over with and kill myself."

Wiley responds with, "Believe me, I've thought about it."

Bruiser returns to his rant, saying, "But, you're scared of that too. I've tried to kill myself. I wanted to, thought about it at least. My life has been a series of painful letdowns and embarrassments. And then there's the shit I do for money."

"Fucking chicks and fucking with dudes, killer!" says the kid next to him as he tries to high-five Bruiser.

Bruiser pulls the kid's arm down and says, "No, destroying people's consciences so that they can pay their rent, buy some new shoes, or feed their dog. We've all been there, wanting to kill yourself and end it all: start over, hit the reset button, but we're too afraid to do it because we're not sure where you go next. And you'll miss all your shiny stuff. And your 'friends,' what would they post on your tombstone? This life is all we know, so is it nothing, or is it heaven?"

"Probably hell, dude, the way you run the show," says some random kid.

"Fair enough. How could Hell be worse than this life? Maybe we've lived a thousand lives, and that's why we're tired when we wake up. At least I am. I'm tired of making the same mistake over and over and over, throughout every lifetime. Then you realize that you don't remember any of those past lives, so you might as well just have a fucking good time while you're here because you're just going to end up as petrol, like the dinosaurs."

Wiley presses herself against Bruiser, poking him in the nose with the rim of her ranger hat, and starts making out with him. Everyone puts down their pens and point their phones at the moment. Wiley reaches down and grabs his junk, asking, "So, is it real? Can you heal people just by slapping them?"

Bruiser tries to fill her hand and mumbles, "I guess, I mean—"

"It's gotta' be a hoax. I saw the show, and anybody can fake being cross-eyed," says Wiley, crossing her eyes. "That would explain the blatantly obnoxious Jesus Jager luge in the living room."

"Yeah, a miscreant like me with the power to heal people. That doesn't make any sense," he says, deflecting her accusation. Wiley gets on her knees and looks up at Bruiser. He looks down into her eyes: they're beaming light green, and he can feel her silently begging to be slapped. He smirks and says, "You don't have to blow me, at least not in front of all these people."

"I'd let you shit on me if it got rid of my IBS, Bruiser. Right here, right now, on top of the kitchen counter, and in front of all these people. They can film it and put it on the internet. I just want to be able to untether myself from the concept of always being within a jaunt from a restroom." She unzips his pants and sticks her hand in his trousers, saying, "I'll do anything you want for that freedom."

"Anything?" he asks, grabbing her by the wrist as Desiree walks in the kitchen.

"Bruiser, seriously! Leave that poor girl alone! I knew you couldn't do it. One night, Bruiser. ONE fucking NIGHT!" Desiree grabs his wrist and tries to drag him out of the kitchen, but he won't let go of Wiley.

"I knew it, you really do like me," he says to Desiree.

"I don't have time for this high school bullshit. Tanner and Dick have a gun pointed at them," says Desiree, pulling at his arm as he pulls at Wiley's.

"What?" asks Bruiser as he turns his attention to the living area full of panicked strangers.

Desiree pulls his arm and says, "There's some greasy dude with a gun pointed at your friends!"

"Bruiser!" begs Wiley as she is pulled to her feet.

Bruiser looks back at Wiley with her doe eyes leaking with disappointment. He pulls away from Desiree, and with the force from her collapsed restraint, he leans into a solid left-handed slap across Wiley's delicate little cocksucker.

All you hear is a group of groans, "Aweeeee Shitttttt!" and then, "Bruiser!"

Bruiser turns to the living area where everyone is now pressed against the walls with their phones out, filming this random, heavyset dude that's sporting a Canadian tuxedo. He has a gun pointed at Tanner and Dick who have their pants down and are standing next to a blanketed lump on the couch.

"Bruiser, how we doing, buddy?" asks Tanner playfully.

Bruiser glances over at the wraparound couch and points to the furry lump. He walks up to it, ignoring the guy with the gun, and pulls back the blanket, looking for a face to attach to this madness.

Formerly cock-eyed Alex, sticks her head out and says, "Hey, Bruiser."

"Glad you made it, Alex. I assume the guy with the gun is your boyfriend."

"Yup, that's Drew," she says.

Bruiser turns toward Drew and puts his hand out. Drew's revolver starts to shake as he's threatened by Bruiser's lack of concern. Drew denies Bruiser's handshake and asks him with raspy aggression, "You see what you did?"

Alex returns her appearance to publicly acceptable, climbs out from her cocoon, and asks, "Drew, are you off your meds again?"

"I'm not off my meds! I knew your transformation was going to be a problem." Drew turns to Bruiser and puts the gun in his chest, shouting, "I was your biggest fan until you fixed her and ruined our relationship!"

"Yeah, not sorry about that." Bruiser pushes the gun off his chest and asks him, "You wanna' holster that thing, partner? I can't say I've ever seen anyone win their girl back by ruining a party with an active-shooter scenario."

Drew returns the gun to Bruiser's chest saying, "No. I came here to end you before you ruin anyone else's life, but then I walk in and G Easy and Ja Rule…"

"I get Tupac more than Ja Rule, but thanks," imparts Dick.

Drew returns his aim to Tanner and Dick, saying, "… are … are finger-cuffing my girlfriend on your couch!"

"It was under a blanket," murmurs Alex.

"Yeah, I don't see the problem," says Bruiser.

Drew spins around the room, returning the gun to Bruiser's chest, and says, "The problem is you, my man! I used to have a great girlfriend, and I didn't have to worry about her cheating on me because no one else would even look twice at her! AND NOW, BECAUSE OF YOU, SHE'S FUCKING DUDES ON LEATHER COUCHES, TWO AT A TIME, IN THE MIDDLE OF PARTIES!"

"So, you just found out your girlfriend was a closet whore," says Tanner in an overconfident tone. "You already killed the vibe. Why would you want to kill the one person that can help you?"

The whole room sniggers.

"I'm going to kill you and then Bruiser before he ruins anyone else's life. Then all your friends!" Drew says adamantly.

Bruiser grabs the barrel of the revolver and puts it to his heart, saying, "Do the world a favor. Do me a huge, fucking favor, Drew. Pull the trigger and you all can go back to your pointless existence. You can go back to sleep and enjoy the dream with nothing to worry about. Or you can put the gun down. We all know you're not a killer." Drew cocks the gun. Bruiser shakily says, "And you're right, she's too good for you. Alex is a beautiful being and she deserves to be free. She's suffered enough in this life, and she doesn't need your shit anymore. Weren't you tired of worrying about when she's going to leave you and how? It's over. We got that out of the way. Move forward. There's plenty of subpar girls here that can make you just as unhappy as Alex."

The room groans.

"You think I can just put the gun down and enjoy the party!" yells Drew.

"I don't see why not."

"Because I'm tired of getting pushed around and walked all over by you people. I'm in charge now, and I want those two dicks to make out with each other," snaps Drew as he swipes his greasy Hitler youth haircut out of his eyes. "And maybe I'll consider not shooting you, Bruiser."

Bruiser looks at Dick and Tanner.

Tanner steps away from Dick and says, "No way, bro. That's fucked up and down."

"Yeah, man. That's some homo-erotically, weird shit! You got something you want to tell us?" asks Dick.

"He's definitely off his meds," says Alex.

Drew yells, "I TOOK MY PILLS, ALEX!"

Bruiser looks at Dick and Tanner, pleading, "C'mon, Dick, you said you guys almost hooked up the other night. Tanner, you said you owed me one. Get this gun off us and send this nerd home." Tanner looks at Dick. Dick looks at Tanner, and they stare into each other's eyes, debating silently whether they can complete this dare — at least in front of people. "Seriously, you guys have to think about it?"

Drew yells, "And I want to see tongue, now!"

"He's definitely off his meds," says Alex, stepping toward him and attempting to disarm him.

Drew pulls away from her and puts the gun to his head, saying, "I don't need them anymore,"

Alex steps toward Drew as he threatens taking his own life and yelps, "Not one of you accessories with your phones out recording this has called the cops yet?"

"Look, Drew, would you rather watch these two cock-hounds make out, or would you be open to letting me slap you and maybe we can rewire that little hot rod of yours?"

Drew puts the gun to Bruiser's head and says nervously, "You can't fix me. That's a fact!"

"I fixed Alex," says Bruiser, pointing at the perfection she's become. "I can help you."

Drew looks at Alex, understanding she no longer needs him or wants him even, bops Bruiser in the head with his gun, and says, "So, you slapped her hard enough that her eye straightened up. Look at her, you turned her into a slutty, little bitch!"

"Really, Drew." shrieks Alex.

"Really! My Alex would never let those two dipsticks touch her. Let alone, DT her in a room full of people. She used to be soft and sweet, and now she's a pile of broken glass. I'm going to end this now!" Drew pushes Bruiser back a foot with the gun, saying, "You can't fix me!"

Tanner, now at Bruiser's side, pushes Bruiser out of the way, regaining the attention of Drew's rage, and says, "Hey, buddy. Tanner here. The guy who just bookended your girl. If you want to kill anyone, it should be me, the guilty party. I'm fine with it. I've lived more this week than I ever thought possible. You see, I was used to being a vegetable. I had cerebral palsy, and this guy," he puts his arm around Bruiser, "he fixed me. So, the smart thing to do here would be to: let him slap you and see where that goes, or I'll settle with you out of court, and you can watch Dick and I make out. That's only fair, but you can't blame Bruiser for healing Alex. She's stunning and deserves to be free, like me."

"That's not possible. You're stalling!" shouts Drew.

Tanner looks around the room and asks, "How have you not seen the video? Does anybody have the video of Bruiser slapping me on their phone? I feel like that would help right now. Less?" Tanner looks up to Less in the DJ nest and puts his hands up, saying, "If you really think that killing someone or everyone is going to make you a happy person, go ahead and shoot me. I owe that to Bruiser and Dick for the best week a dude could have."

"I'm not making out with you," says Dick.

"C'mon, my guy, not even to save Bruiser," says Tanner, "the Second Coming. You'd basically be making out with a dude to save the world. There isn't a better reason. It's not like he wants us to fuck."

"Put down the gun, Drew," says Alex. "This isn't going to fix anything."

Drew spins the gun around the room in a panic.

Slaphappy

Tanner leans over in Dick's ear and says, "I'd let you fist me while we watch little people, dressed up like stuffed animals, fuck farm animals to save him."

"You've had way too much time on your hands," says Dick.

"Let's just make out," says Tanner. "We owe him that."

"How do we know he's not going to shoot us in the head while we're making out," says Dick. "Let's see how this clip plays out."

Less projects the video from his laptop onto the wall. The sight of Tanner in his prior state stops the room. "So, that was me then," says Tanner. The room moans with disgust when Bruiser slaps Tanner out of his chair. "Wait for it," he says as he watches the helpless heap of flesh that he was transform into his current state.

Drew, mesmerized and disgusted, drops his arms, pointing the gun at the floor. Bruiser sees a hole in Drew's defense and rushes him with a flat hand. Drew catches Bruiser charging him and tries to raise his gun. Bruiser crosses his face with a flat hand and Drew pulls the trigger, sending a bullet through Tanner, dropping him to the floor. Drew falls to the ground and hits his head on the coffee table, letting off another round that ricochets through the loft, hitting one of the ropes that holds Jager Luge Jesus to the railing on the top floor. As Jesus's hand is freed, it drops and swings landing on Bruiser's face, dropping him to the floor next to Drew, and immediately what's left of the party fights their way through the front door.

Tanner, balled up on the ground in a puddle of blood with his friends standing over him, says, "Scratch that off of my bucket list."

Desiree jumps on top of Tanner, saying, "You're going to be okay. Someone, call an ambulance!" she shouts as she tries to pry his hands away from the entry wound in hopes of containing his fluids.

Tanner relinquishes control of the wound to Desiree, saying, "You really are beautiful, I see why he doesn't want you to go."

Only in Dreams

"Jesus," mutters Bruiser under his breath as his eyes open to a pernicious sun leering down at him. He sits up, rubbing his jaw, and looks around in search of an anchor to this realm to which he keeps returning. Memories of unearthing a female form the last time he was here instigate a panic and he crawls back to the boulder where he remembered seeing her last.

Bruiser finds her laid out on the rock, lifeless, cooking in the relentless waves of the unfamiliar star. He climbs up to her and collapses onto her, resting his head on her lap. There's a faint buzzing and a light clicking coming from her chest that pulsates through the silence of this deserted realm. He pulls himself up to her chest and rests his head in the cockles of her heart.

Bruiser remembers having the ability to heal people, so he stands up over her and reaches back with his right hand to slap her, but pauses as he hears a voice whisper, "It doesn't work like that here." He looks around, hoping to find a familiar face, but only finds endless sands as he looks across the horizon. "Try her heart," whispers the voice through the escalating desert winds as it pushes forcefully across his face with no regard for his current suffering. He falls back to her lap and wraps her arm around him, looking for respite from the dust storm that's suddenly taken interest in his person.

"Does she even have one? All I heard was clicking!"

"You'll find all your answers at her core," cries the wind.

"How do I get there?" he asks.

The ominous voice refuses to answer, leaving him to his own devices. He rolls over, staring up at the ball of flames in the sky, and as he looks up his lifeless companion's chest, he notices three circles in a triangle imprinted over her heart. He rests his hand over the three circles and feels a flippant, pulsing sensation. Her chest gives, the flesh starts to dissolve, and he pushes his hand slowly inside of her. As he does, it gets hung up on what feels to be cables and tubing. He forces it deeper into her and feels a rectangular device at the heart of the wires. "I think I've got it," he says to himself.

Bruiser pulls the device out of her cautiously. It's attached to a heavy cable and covered in what appears to be a silicone gel. There's an inscription on the back that says, 'Desire 3355' He flips it over and finds a flickering screen. He detaches it from the cable and the screen goes blank. "What do I do?" he asks the desert, and her body breaks down into a bubbling ooze. What's left of her dissolves and his head hits the rock. There's no response to his query, only the whispers of the desert's breath that aims only to bring more suffering.

Bruiser taps anxiously on Desire 3355 and mumbles, "Just a useless paperweight."

He hears a voice in the back of his head say, "Close your eyes, breathe deep, and think about anything that warms your heart. Connect with Urantia and to the sky from wherever you came. When you truly are free from pain and life flows through you, the battery will charge, and you'll have your companion back."

"Urantia? Sure, that makes sense," he says and looks up to the sun beating down on him, wondering what it wants from him, and immediately it runs past the horizon, setting in the blink of an eye. In its place three moons arise, and position themselves to form a triangle in the sky. "And what would you three want from me?" he asks the moons, only to be answered with an aquatic rumbling far off in the distance. Bruiser looks to the horizon and finds a threatening wall of water moving his way slowly. He climbs onto one of the larger boulders next to him to get a better view and finds he was right, asking himself, "Is that the ocean, in the desert, in a dream?" Overwhelmed by the trembling sensation beneath him, he sits down, crosses his legs, straightens his back, and closes his eyes.

As he tries to catch his breath, the ocean sounds grow louder and more forceful with every breath he takes. The deeper the breath the more resounding the rumble. "What will you do?" asks the voice. Instead of reacting to the ominous voice and opening his eyes to the impending doom, he doesn't respond, and with his eyes loosely shut, takes a deep breath, and exhales. He takes another deep breath and feels the universe, the sea of intricacies that it is, start to flow through him. Moments pass as he solidifies his foundation and then the boulder beneath him starts to vibrate. He hears the voice ask him again, "What will you do?"

Bruiser, agitated by the trickster in his head, opens his eyes to find a tsunami creeping towards him with the volition of a personal vengeance that he acknowledges to be justified. "It doesn't look like there's anything I can do."

"Exactly. You're sitting on the ocean floor, and the moisture you so desire is returning home. Soon your desert will be gone. What will you do?" laughs the voice.

"I don't know the right answer," says Bruiser as his being starts to fill with the realization that he's about to be overwhelmed with the object of his desire.

"What you know as right is wrong," says the voice.

"So, what's left?" he asks, hesitantly.

"Exactly! You can tense up in fear, sit there and do nothing, losing your battle with Urantia, or you can do what's left."

"Who's Urantia and why's she so pissed?" he asks as the water level rises at the foot of the boulder and the towering waves walk him down, "So what's left?"

"All you have left, is what isn't right," says the voice, echoing through his being. Bruiser stands up on the rock with his arms out as the wall of water thunders to him and the incoming desert tide rises, stranding him on the rock. The wave builds as it rushes, leaning over him, blocking the light reflecting off the three moons. As the fear and anger build in him with the realization that he has no control over the world he's been hiding in, he remembers that this world is just a dream, and that the only option left is to submit to something vastly more powerful than the minuscule being he's created. He sits back down in lotus position, closes his eyes, and breathes deeply as the supreme vastness pummels him, forcing him back to another life that resents him equally.

"I don't think he has a pulse," says Desiree, holding Bruiser's head in her lap.

"Have you met Bruiser?" asks Dick. "He never has a pulse, a faint one if any. He'll be fine," says Dick, dragging Drew out of the building with Less.

"He might have a concussion. Jager Luge Jesus got him pretty good," Desiree says as she rubs his head with a delicate resentment.

Dick hollers from the doorway, "Again, have you met Bruiser? He's a walking concussion."

Desiree looks down at Bruiser as he lies there, peacefully, defenseless, and silent. She leans in to kiss him on the forehead, and immediately he barfs out, "All I have left, is what isn't right!" His eyes open to find Desiree hovering over him, staring at him, making a duck face. He stops screaming and tries to regain his composure by asking, "Great party, right?" Desiree realizes who she is really holding as Bruiser puckers his lips begging for some sugar and she drops his head on the floor. "Easy on the melon, love," he says as he fully returns to the room.

Bruiser tries to stand up, but stumbles and lands prematurely on the couch. Desiree is staring deeply into Bruiser, waiting for his standard sarcastic defense mechanism to appear and dumb down the moment, but he's silent as he digs through the coffee table looking for distractions. The silence of the moment pushes Desiree toward him, and she asks, "How's it feel, being slapped by the cold hand of an inanimate Jesus?"

Bruiser rubs his jaw, saying, "Is that what happened? I thought for sure you were trying to tell me you loved me."

"I wish I cared enough to hit you. You'd be a completely different person by now," she says with jest and nudges his arm.

Dick and Less walk back in the room and shout, "Bruiser!"

Bruiser looks up at them and says, "Shouldn't you be at the hospital with your tag-team partner?"

"Tanner? He's fine, B," says Dick. "I think he's upstairs in your bed."

"Well, that's the last place you'd want to be with an open wound," says Bruiser. He tries to get up to check on Tanner and falls back into the couch next to Desiree.

Dick grabs Bruiser by the shoulder and says, "He's fine. The bullet went through him, and the hole closed. Less got the whole thing on tape."

"Sorry about the angle, Bruiser," says Less, handing him his phone. "There was a lot going on."

While Bruiser watches the debacle play out, Tanner walks down the steps from the upstairs bathroom, drinking a beer, and toweling off from a shower.

"Oh shit!" Bruiser barfs out as he watches himself get slapped by Jesus. "Did you post this?" asks Bruiser as he watches his place clear out on the video.

"Yeah. It's got over hundred-thousand hits in the past twenty," says Less as he takes his phone back from Bruiser.

Tanner walks up to Bruiser and pats him on the head like a puppy. Bruiser stands up to inspect Tanner, spinning him around in disbelief saying, "This is too much. You're good?"

"Good as new, Bruiser, better than new, better than the last new," says Tanner with a boisterous smile.

His friends are staring at Bruiser, gazing into his unique being, and he is overwhelmed by a new feeling, unlike the usual sneers of disgust that he gets from most of the world. He sits back down on the couch and consumes the toxic debris that he laid out on the coffee table.

No one says anything.

Tanner, Dick, and Less sit down on the couch, surrounding Bruiser as he tries to return to Urantia, via incoherency, and is once again consumed by the couch. Dick goes to grab the cigarette from Bruiser's mouth, and he flinches. Desiree starts to talk, but nothing comes out. Dick pulls out his phone to check it and sets it down immediately. Tanner is staring hungrily at Desiree, and Less is on his phone, watching his video receive the most hits he's ever obtained in one moment.

Bruiser pops up out of his dark hole, looks around, and asks, "Did you lock the door?"

"You all right, bub?" asks Dick.

Bruiser looks around the room again, saying, "Yeah, I guess." He scans the coffee table and asks, "Does anyone have any weed?"

Desiree replies with, "Don't you think it's time to put it in reverse?"

"Neutral would be nice at the moment," Bruiser says playfully.

Less hands Bruiser a two-foot glass bong and asks him, "You all right, boss?"

Bruiser empties the bowl on the first pull and says, "It's too much, man. If it was up to me, I wouldn't save one of them, present company excluded!"

Desiree snatches the bong from him, asking, "How can you say that? All you've ever done is complain about how 'fuct' everyone and everything is your whole life. You spend most of your time alone or surrounded by rooms full of people, but still alone! You can finally get your way and have the world kneel before you in all your glory, and you want to run away from it because you're too busy wallowing in self-doubt."

"What's that supposed to mean?" he asks.

Desiree clears the tube, stands up, heads towards the door, and says, "It means you finally have the chance to honestly make the world a better place, and you want to run away from the responsibility."

"Apparently you're the one running."

Desiree turns, saying, "Yeah, I'm running, running from you, Bruiser. The only difference between us is that you run so fast there's no warning; you just disappear. I'm leaving because there's no one here. YOU," she shouts, leering into Bruiser's smoke-filled bubble, "created a monster with *your* healing hand. A monster that our friends couldn't resist doubling down on in the middle of a party — in front of her boyfriend. The guy that had a gun pointed at you and everyone else *at MY going away party!*"

"It worked out. It always does if you let it," he says with a freshly humbled smirk.

She looks back at her friends and says, "Well, great. I hope you're happy."

Bruiser stands up and gets in Desiree's face, saying, "You know, with my luck, I'll be the last soul left on the planet without a smile."

"Have you tried slapping yourself?" asks Tanner. "I've never been so happy."

There's another long silence that Bruiser walks away from and makes his way to the kitchen to procure a bottle of tequila and a case of beer. He returns from the kitchen and finds Desiree hugging everyone by the door. "So, you're just going to leave?" asks Bruiser.

"Yeah, what do you care?"

"Fuck, Desiree, you know I care. I'm just no good at showing it," he says, walking over to her with the bottle in his hand.

Desiree turns around, drops her purse, and pauses, choosing her words carefully. "I know you care, but it's only for yourself."

"That's not fair, Des," mumbles Bruiser.

"But it's true. Do you want to talk about how many times you've hurt me accidentally or just the first and the last?"

"Might as well," he says, offering her the bottle.

"Do you guys want to be alone?" asks Tanner.

Leslie bursts through the door, goosing Desiree with the door handle, and the room shouts, "Leslie!"

She goes straight to Desiree and gives her a hug.

"Perfect timing, Leslie. Everyone's here now," says Bruiser, waiting for his hug. "Where've you been?"

Leslie replies, "A date."

Less laughs and asks, "No, really though, sis."

"Yeah, and it was going great until my date checked his phone and pulled up the video of Tanner getting shot," she says as she goes to hug Dick, skipping Bruiser.

"Where's your 'date?' 'She' didn't want to hang with us at the crime scene?" asks Dick.

Leslie shakes Dick while hugging him and says, "I wasn't going to bring 'him' here as much as 'he' wanted to come. You guys are an f-ing mess and we're leaving on Monday, so it just didn't make sense."

"He was lame, and you ditched him so you could come hang with us," says Less.

"Pretty much," Leslie says.

Tanner puts his hand out, saying, "Tanner."

Leslie blows a hot guy fuse and loses her train of thought, along with a few fine motor skills.

"Well, your timing couldn't be more perfect," says Dick, "Desiree was about to enlighten everyone and explain how Bruiser crippled her emotionally, the first and apparently the most recent time."

Leslie smiles. "The first time, he pulled a hit and run freshman year."

"Just disappeared," says Desiree.

"Did everyone know about that except for me?" asks Dick, taking the bottle of booze from Bruiser.

Leslie shrugs and says, "Sorry, Dick."

"Can't wait to hear about the last time." asks Dick. "Were we together then, Des?"

"Can we just drop it?" says Desiree.

"Sounds good to me. Slap-shots, anyone?" asks Bruiser as he starts corralling random vessels on the coffee table and filling them with tequila.

Everyone groans.

Bruiser hands out the shots and starts to make a toast, but all that comes out is, "If I know anything, it's that you all deserve to be healed. You guys have put up with my ego-driven, diva-esque tantrums and my epic rockstar, downward-spiraled blackouts for way too long, especially you, Desiree."

Desiree covers here face and says, "I'm so good, Bruiser."

Bruiser gets on his knees and pleads, "C'mon, Tanner, you're good. Can you spot for me?"

Tanner looks around the room and asks, "Spot?"

"Make sure no one hits the floor," says Dick as he pushes Tanner out of the way. "I got it."

"Na, I wanna' get you again. I don't think anything happened last time," says Bruiser.

"I mean, I feel great, I guess. I don't know that I could eat a bullet like this guy," says Dick, jabbing Tanner in the ribs.

Everyone gathers around Bruiser except for Desiree. Less pulls at her sleeve but she doesn't budge. Bruiser stands up, confronting Desiree, and says, "You're still afraid of me, aren't you? Afraid of my demons? You've always been afraid of me. That's why you went with Dick, that happy-go-lucky fucker." Bruiser pulls at Desiree's hand and says, "You if anyone, deserve it. I want to heal you, so you can go take over Hollywood."

"I thought you said I didn't need it. I'm **perfect** I believe were your words."

"Yeah, but you're not bullet proof. That's new," he says, pulling at her.

"I'd prefer to continue suffering," laughs Desiree.

Bruiser gives up on her, asking, "Who's first?"

Less steps forward and Leslie snickers. "Could you be more up his butt, Less?"

Less responds with, "I just want to get it before it runs out. Besides, look at Tanner. He was a pile of goo the other day. Can you imagine what this will do for me?" Less puts a shot back and puts his chin out. Bruiser lays into his face with his right hand, knocking him into Tanner's arms. Tanner dumps him in the couch. Less inspects his hands, his arms, and then looks down at his feet.

"You feel anything, Less?" asks Tanner.

"No, not really! I mean, my cheek hurts."

Dick inspects Less in a serious manner, saying, "It took about twenty minutes with Tanner, but it was instantaneous with Alex and Tanner's dad. You have any tattoos?"

"No. Come on," says Less.

"What about health issues, any physically noticeable conditions we don't know about?" asks Bruiser.

"Not really, athletes' foot, jock itch, and gingivitis. Otherwise, I'm worried about cancer and mental disorders," says Less as he returns to watching his video trend.

"He's definitely manic," says Leslie.

"It's not mania. I just can't sleep. I'd rather be online."

"Thanks for sharing. Who's next?" asks Bruiser. "Leslie?"

"Sure. I'm game if it means I'll be bulletproof," chuckles Leslie as she slams a shot. "I'm sure that'll come in handy on the road with you guys."

Bruiser slaps Leslie with a stiff right at fifty percent.

"Bruiser! Was that necessary?" yelps Desiree in defense of her friend.

"That wasn't even close to a hundred percent. Do another shot and I'll double slap you."

Leslie rubs her face, saying, "I'll catch up with you on tour if I need it." She does another shot and sits down as everyone stares at her, waiting for a miracle.

Bruiser lights a cigarette. "Anything?"

"Eh, did you hear anything when you slapped me?" asks Leslie.

"No. Nothing," says Bruiser.

"Maybe you lost it when JLJ slapped you," says Dick.

"Who?"

"Jager Luge Jesus," says Less.

"I couldn't tell you how great that would be. Dick, you're up. Let's go," Bruiser says, handing Dick a shot. Dick takes the shot and Bruiser hits him with a solid right. Bruiser stands there, staring at him, waiting for something to happen and asks, "How do none of us have tattoos?"

"We spent all our money on getting fucked up, I guess," says Dick, rubbing his face.

"What's going on?" asks Desiree.

"I don't know," says Bruiser blankly. "Take a shot, Desiree. You in?"

Desiree throws her shoulders up and says, "Eh."

"What are you afraid of?" asks Bruiser.

"Apparently nothing from what I just saw. I knew this was all bullshit!" She looks around the room at her friends and asks, "Leslie, is this a set up for the new show? What kind of hustle are you guys on?"

"I have no idea, Des. If they're up to something, they didn't tell me. Less might know, but it seemed real to me," says Leslie, looking to Less for answers.

"I'm gonna' say I was expecting something completely different," says Less, "but Tanner is all the proof you need."

Tanner winks at Desiree.

"He could be a plant for all I know," Desiree says.

"I was a vegetable, if that's what you mean," says Tanner.

"You know what I mean. You guys fucked up my going away party for a promotional stunt!" she says, staring Tanner down.

Tanner flexes for Desiree and says, "We're not stuntin' on you. I used to be a completely useless pile of goo."

Bruiser steps towards Desiree, there's an exchange of glances and he asks her, "What's the worst that could happen?"

Desiree snickers and says, "I could be infected by your self-loathing, highly toxic, completely destructive misery and fall down into the same blackhole you call home."

There's a silence.

"Should we go?" asks Less.

Bruiser responds calmly, "No, I can hear her yelling at me, but I can't make any sense out of it. I don't know why anyone would turn down salvation," says Bruiser with a little too much bravado.

"Get over yourself. Do I have to say it?" Desiree drops her purse, walks over to the coffee table, and lights a cigarette.

"Yeah, we'd all appreciate that, Des," says Dick.

"Sure. Let's go." Bruiser grabs two shots and walks them over to Desiree. He hands her one and they cheers.

Desiree throws her glass at the wall, and says, "You're a piece of shit. You play the role of the poor abandoned soul that no one can love, but there's no fucking way anyone could get close to you because you're covered in guilt and shame. I'm not going to buy into this whole Second Coming bullshit because it doesn't make any sense that someone so self-righteous would be given the responsibility of healing the world. Why would you have the privilege of doing something Mother Theresa or Gandhi couldn't do?"

He grabs her by the arms and says, "Because I'm a warlock sent from another dimension to change the path of humanity." Less starts laughing. Everyone else goes silent. Bruiser stands there, crosses his arms for a second until he's aware of his own energetic closure, and opens himself up to the attack. "I don't know, Des." The two are face to face, and as much as they love each other, there is a huge invisible wall between them that neither one can figure out how to bring down.

"Why are you so fucking mad at me, Des?"

Desiree looks to her friends silently asking for permission to get awkward and then back at Bruiser, swaying in her silence, and she screams, "APRIL … FUCKING … DUDLEY!"

Dick lets out an, "This should be good!"

Bruiser covers his face.

"Dick and I were on a break, we went out on our first and only real date," she says, searching Bruiser for acknowledgement of the night.

"Seriously!" Dick throws his arms up and walks over to the fridge, grabbing a bottle of champagne.

"Continue," says Bruiser.

"We went to the movies. I let you fuck me in the bathroom," she says, takes his shot from him, and throws it in his face.

"That's what you're mad about?" he asks coyly.

Desiree picks up another shot off the table and hands it to Bruiser. She takes a drag off her cigarette and puts it in Bruiser's mouth. "You didn't pull out, impregnated me, and I killed the fucking baby. I killed it — dead!" Desiree slaps Bruiser and knocks the cigarette out of his mouth.

Once again, the room is silent.

Bruiser stumbles to speak. "Why … why didn't you tell me?"

"Because … April … fucking … Dudley, that dick dock. We went to your friend's party after the movie, and I watched you fuck her in the laundry room. I finally thought we found each other, and you fucking broke me. I was in love with you, Bruiser," she says, and a tear slides down her cheek.

Dick turns up the bottle of champagne and says, "I'm pretty sure you said that was my baby."

Bruiser does the shot Desiree handed him and drops the glass.

"I didn't know what to do, Dick," pleads Desiree. "I'm sorry for putting you through that but thank you for being there."

"It would have been a beautiful baby," says Bruiser, staring back at Desiree with absolute terror in his eyes.

"Until we tore it apart!" she screams.

Bruiser tries to speak, "Look, Des, I—"

"There's no 'look, Des.' I'm not finished. We'll always be friends because I love you, but I feel sorry for you, Bruiser. There's no way you would treat people the way you do if you could see outside of your bubble. The funniest part about this whole Buddha, Nirvana, save the world, bullshit thing is, that on the deepest level possible you're probably just doing it to make the world a better place for yourself, so that you don't have to be around 'subpar' human beings anymore." Desiree turns and goes to pick up her purse.

"No, you're not going to leave me," Bruiser says.

"I am. I'm moving across the country, Monday," she says and starts crying.

Bruiser walks up to Desiree and tries to embrace her, but she pushes him away. "Can I say something before you go?" Bruiser begs.

"Go ahead. Tear me apart."

Bruiser gets in her face, grabs her shoulders, and says, "I hope that we get it right in one of these lives, so that we can fully enjoy each other. Have the same rainy day off, sitting on the porch, laughing about how dumb our kids are, and whose fault that is. Desiree, I love—"

Desiree pushes him with both hands and shouts, "Don't, Bruiser." She opens the door and says, "You don't know what love is. I hope you find someone stubborn enough to teach you what it is; and I'm truly sorry it's not me." She slams the door in his face and collapses on the other side.

Less and Leslie look at Bruiser and say together, "Well, are you just going to stand there, stupid?"

Dick turns around and walks up the stairs to Bruiser's room, towards the roof silently.

"Was that weird for anybody else?" asks Tanner as he watches

Bruiser almost trips over Desiree as he slumps through the doorway. He hears her tears and collapses against the wall next to her, turns up the bottle, and hands it to her.

Desiree regroups, wipes her face, slugs the bottle, and asks Bruiser in a childlike tone, "Where'd you go?"

He pauses, staring down the hallway and asks, "Which time?"

"The last time," she says and takes another swig off the bottle. And as the spirits hit her, she throws it out there, saying, "I wanted to spend my last week here with you. Monday, you let me in for a split second at the Anecdote. I put my guard down and came over here after you ran out of your pitch. You hid on the other side of that door, and you've been hiding from me all week." She looks him in the eyes, waiting for a minuscule piece of truth.

"Desiree, all I know is that in every dream I had while I was bouncing around the cosmos 'hiding' from you, I was chasing you," he says, taking the bottle from her. "I told you: I slapped Tanner, it consumed me, I got stuck in a dark place filled with fear and doubt, and now I think I've lost it."

"Bruiser, you're afraid of being accepted and loved," she says, staring him down and waiting for a reaction. "Being a healer is only going to make more people want to love you and that's what will destroy you."

"I know," he says, sticking the bottle. "Monday night when you came over, all I wanted was to stop everything and get stuck inside of you, forever. You're everything I've ever wanted from this life, but—" He stops, turns, and looks her in the eyes.

"But you're continually shitting all over me and expecting me to wait in line while you figure out where the on switch is for my

120

heart. Bruiser, I'm done. I can't do this anymore. I love you, and I really hope for the sake of humanity you don't fuck this up royally. I'm disregarding my heart and moving forward. If there's anything there, we'll finish this conversation in some other perfect world where we both are ready for one another."

Desiree starts to stand up and he pulls her back to the floor of the hallway, saying, "Des, I … I … love …"

Desiree interrupts him saying, "I love you, Bruiser." She stands back up, grabs his hand, pulls him to his feet, and hugs him shakily, saying, "But it doesn't matter. I know if we're truly meant to be, we will be, but for now, they want us to be further apart. So, come see me when you're in LA on your evangelical, healing excursion, and if you haven't been consumed by groupies or domesticated by that perfect woman that you're in search of, we'll take it from there."

"I guess," he says with a defeated look in his eye.

"What do you mean you guess?" she asks playfully. "There aren't any another options."

"You could come back inside and vibe with us?"

"This party is beat, Bruiser. I'm done here, and I need to finish packing. We can hang out tomorrow if you want?"

"I'd love that, honestly," he says and tries to smile.

Desiree sees the rarity and takes advantage of the moment by leaning in and kissing him slowly and passionately up against the wall and then pushes herself off him, turns around, and walks away. "Tell everybody bye for me and let them know we're doing drinks tomorrow."

Bruiser watches her walk down the hallway, analyzing the moment as he tries to figure out what happened, and as the door shuts behind her, he says aloud, "Love you." He turns and walks into his completely trashed abode to find Less, Leslie, and Tanner staring at him with only looks of discern.

As Bruiser returns to the floor against the other side of the wall he was just holding up, Leslie asks him, "Where's Des?"

"She left. She said she loves you guys and wants you to know we're doing drinks tomorrow." Less and Leslie run out the door after her without thought. "Okay, bye."

Tanner stares at his maker, sitting on the floor in a puddle of despair, overwhelmed with the darker side of reality, and asks him, "You wanna' go make sure Dick hasn't jumped off the roof?"

"I'll meet you up there, T-bone," says Bruiser, staring up at the ceiling. "There's a series of shadows gathering up by the windowsill and they seem to be laughing at me." He rubs his eyes and looks up at Jager Luge Jesus hanging from one hand, melting into a pool of Jägermeister. "This is going to hurt," he says as he slides himself up the wall and pushes off it toward the coffee table, where he grabs all the accoutrement necessary for an urban rooftop camping trip.

Bruiser pops his head out of the portal analyzing the situation and sees Tanner sprawled out on the couch. He climbs out onto the roof carrying a pillowcase full of distractions and asks, "Where's Dick?" Tanner points to Dick, standing on the ledge as far away from Tanner as possible. Bruiser sets down his offerings and runs towards Dick, shouting, "Don't jump! It's not worth it."

Dick turns to him, shushes him, pointing at his phone, and continues his call, saying, "Yeah, I got it, boss. I believe we're ready to start shooting on Monday … What do you mean, you got someone to help me produce? It is going to be a large production. I got it … Look forward to it."

"You okay, Dick?" asks Bruiser.

"Well, I just found out that I paid to have your kid killed and that this whole Desiree thing has been going on behind my back the whole time. So … yeah, whatever."

"Look, I'm sorry, man. It wasn't ever enough to mention, just one heartfelt mishap after another with her. I'm more interested in how you feel after me slapping you."

"I mean, I feel good. I guess. Why? You worried?" asks Dick as he puts his arm around Bruiser and walks him back over to the couch.

"Nothing happened with Less and Leslie," says Bruiser.

"That's what you get when you expect miracles. Do you think you lost it?" asks Dick.

"My head's spinning around so fast right now, I couldn't tell you my last name, but it definitely feels like something's off."

"I'm sure it just hits people differently," says Dick. "I mean, I feel good. I don't know if I could take a bullet in the gullet like the kid, but I don't need it like Tanner and that's all that matters."

"Yeah, Tanner's a fucking anomaly," says Bruiser.

"The things the government would do with you if they found out about him," says Dick as he takes Bruiser's beer out of his hand and drinks it.

"It's not if, it's when. That's what I'm worried about. I could be so lucky as to lose these God forsaken powers."

"I've got to make another call," says Dick. "You should really get to know the kid. It'll change your whole perspective on life. I realized how much I'd thrown away out of boredom," says Dick as he opens his phone and returns to the shadows.

Bruiser sits down across from Tanner and starts rolling up joint after joint.

"What'd you do before Greed?" asks Tanner.

Bruiser pauses, hesitant of all the discomforting affection he knows he's about to receive. He cracks a beer, lights a joint and passes it to Tanner with a beer, and says, "I waited tables and tended bar. Why?"

"I've never had a job, never really done anything other than watch TV. I just wondered how you ended up here," says Tanner.

"Working in a restaurant was just wading through an endless sea of miserable people. I had my guard up the whole time I was taking care of them and their families. I feel like it was a punishment for all the souls I've tortured in past lives, and I thought I was done, but I believe I'm just getting started," he says as he cuts out a series of lines on a silver platter. He hands Tanner the platter and asks him, "Do you remember before?"

"What is this?" Tanner asks as he takes the tray.

"Does it matter? You can take a bullet. I'm pretty sure this won't kill you," says Bruiser.

Tanner sticks his face in the platter and then says, "Before was like watching TV without a remote."

"How so?" asks Bruiser.

"I would dream of places where I was free and in control, and then I'd return to the same place with the same daily routine of drooling on myself while I watched whatever was on the TV."

Bruiser goes down on the silver platter and then says, "I can't imagine."

"Yeah right," says Tanner as he adjusts to his new perspective. "Other than TV, it was listening to my parents argue and my mom crying. I know both were about me."

"I'm sure that's not true," says Bruiser as he forces the illicit particles to gather in his processor.

"No, it was. I was a failure for her, and it shut her down."

"What makes you say that?"

"I felt it all the time. She could barely look at me because I was the reason that he stopped loving her."

"Ted?"

"Yeah, he loves the shit out of me, but he couldn't stand the way she looked at me, and I get it. If I brought something that wretched through my legs into this world, I'd feel at fault."

"It could've been Ted's DNA. He's always come off a little recessive to me."

"It doesn't matter. Either way, I was too much for her and it tore them apart."

Bruiser lights a cigarette. "What happened with your mom? I've never seen her around."

Tanner stops for a second as he clears his throat and motions for a cigarette. Bruiser hands him the one he just lit and then lights another one. Tanner's eyes start to water as he hits the cigarette, saying, "I'm sure Ted never mentioned it, but one day my mom walked into my room, sat down, and started crying. Nothing new there, she always assumed that I wasn't capable of comprehending what was going on."

"There's nothing worse than watching the woman that brought you into this life suffer," says Bruiser.

"That's my mom. I can't remember seeing her smile. She's the one that was supposed to be programming my heart and creating every breath I give, instead she's clawing away at it with every thought that passes," says Tanner.

"Sorry. I had no idea."

Tanner pours a series of whiskey shots.

The two clank glasses and down the lackadaisical poison.

"So, she's sitting there in my room crying, and I see her lean over and start fishing through my pill collection. She starts emptying them all out on the table and then just starts pouring handfuls into her mouth."

"Shit, and there's nothing you can do."

"By the time I had typed the words, 'Stop! I love you,' into my spell and speak, she had already started the process."

"Fuckity fuck fuck."

"Yeah, so she tells me while she's dying, 'You need to forgive yourself here, there, everywhere that you are and have been simultaneously.'"

"I'm sorry you had to watch that."

"She's free. She killed herself in front of me because she didn't think it would matter. The funny part is, that I met her truest self for a moment while she was passing, and she told me she was going to find me in every life until she found my truest self and that she would set that god particle free."

"How so?"

"Of all the dreams I had, there was one recurring theme where I was in a dark place, alone. This me was trapped in a cave that always turned out to be an endless maze. I was being punished by someone that resembled a version of me, not this me, but the mangled, hobbling gremlin I was. The only place I was safe was in the cage at the center of the maze."

"That sounds terrible."

"Well, I could run, so that made it interesting. After she passed, she started appearing in my dreams, no matter what the scenario. I remember the last one before you slapped me." Bruiser watches as Tanner lights up, talking wholeheartedly about something most people would write off as nonsensical. His now blue eyes start to glow as he speaks of it. "I'm lost in the maze, but I'm running, so I'm happy. Lilliana, my mom, shows up and says she knows the way out, but there's something she must take care of before we can go. She takes me to the darkest part of the maze and leaves me there." Tears roll down Tanner's face, but he continues. "She gives me a hug and tells me, 'When the lights come on and the door behind you opens, run fast, and follow that tunnel because it's the only way to get out of the maze.' She kisses me on the cheek and tells me she loves me, that I was being punished for something she did a long time ago, and that she'll find me in every life I live and not to forget this moment. She hugs me with more love than I've ever felt or could fathom she could have. I haven't seen her since, but that was the night before you slapped me."

"So, that's the path to enlightenment?" asks Bruiser.

"If you believe in that sort of thing," laughs Tanner.

There's a long silence while the two stare out into the never-ending sea of molecules. Dick walks up and wades in the silence for a moment and then shouts, "Bruiser," startling the two, "we have to find that hobo that farted in your mouth. Those magical, little, shit particles that were in you are the key. We'll get more, and we'll bring him with us on the road. Maybe if you eat his shit like power bars, you'll eventually become the shit permanently."

"That sounds terrible," says Bruiser. "You're tripping."

"I am, but that doesn't change the fact that we need to find him. Let's just say you lose this power, we're ruined, and we'll lose millions," says Dick.

"Not to mention, the world as we know it will continue to spin aimlessly in the same direction," says Bruiser.

"Let's go find him now," says Tanner.

"I'm way too fucked up for that. Plus, I'm sure there's another wave of people coming through," says Bruiser. He pulls out a pill case and starts crushing little blue pills on the tray.

"Not after that shooting went viral," says Dick.

"Well, let's go find some pussy," says Tanner.

"I'm down," says Dick.

"I'm sure some will turn up here," says Bruiser. "You guys should hang out." He knocks back a line and hands the tray to Dick, saying, "I don't have a pussy, but there are enough drugs here to get us to the point where you won't remember what pussy is."

"Did you say, you don't have a pussy butt? Because I've heard otherwise. Why don't you put down the tooter and come with us? Tanner can get started with his bird-dogging career," says Dick.

"What are you talking about?" asks Bruiser.

"Tanner, you didn't tell him?" says Dick.

"I want to walk the path with you guys. You saved my life and I want to repay you. I want to bird-dog for you on the road."

"You just want to go swimming in an endless sea of Va-jay-jay with us," says Bruiser.

"Well, yeah," Tanner laughs, "obviously."

"How's your dad feel about you leaving?" asks Dick.

"I told him I wanted to go on the road with you, and he threw me the host spot on Greed. I figure I can ride with you and shoot Greed at the same time."

Dick sits down, grabs shots off the table, and hands them out. He's about to toast and Bruiser interrupts, saying, "Hey, Dick, about that whole Desiree thing. I'm sorry that it came out like that. I can't imagine."

"Hey, man, past is the past. I just feel better knowing that I paid to have your seed wiped from the face of this earth."

"That's fucked up, Dick," says Tanner as his shot glass lowers.

"No, Tannerbananner, he did me a favor. Could you imagine having a little me running around right now? It would've ruined me."

Dick laughs and says, "He'd be in high school about now."

"What an asshole, my personality and Desiree's looks."

"Cheers to that," says Dick.

They raise their glasses.

"No." Tanner stops them, saying, "I've never had friends, let alone brothers, and whatever it is you two have been through, it was worth it because you came out of it with—" Tanner pushes his glass to the center and says, "To family."

"He's a trip, right?" asks Dick.

"An acid trip. This kid just schooled me on life. I'm so fucked up, I just hope he reminds me some time," says Bruiser.

"Let's take him for a spin and go pick up some broads. It's disgusting, Bruiser. You have to see it," says Dick.

"There's plenty of time for that on the road. I just want to sit here with my dudes and melt into the couch with the cool breeze on my face."

At that moment, the hatch pops open, and they see a feminine shadow climb out of the portal like a cobra rising out of a wicker basket. "Bruiser?"

"There's your turn up now, you melancholy-go-lucky son of a bitch," says Dick.

Angelora wiggles her way through the hole in the roof, and as she walks up to Dick and Tanner, they jump to their feet.

"Tanner," he says as he puts his hand out and looks her over.

She pauses as she tries to remember how to work her hands and introduces herself. "Angelora."

"Weren't you in that seven-car pileup in Bruiser's bed?" asks Tanner.

"That was me," she says as she pulls away from him.

"You're stunning, nothing but respect. Have a seat. We were just about to fry up some fresh brain cells," says Tanner.

Dick nudges Tanner and says, "Let's get out of here."

"What about dudes on the roof?" asks Tanner.

"We're going to the Pony, remember?" asks Dick.

"You two want to roll?" asks Tanner.

"We've got some stuff to talk about," says Bruiser.

"Why don't you guys talk about it at the Pony?" asks Dick.

"I've got to get up early," says Angelora. "I just wanted to get in a quick interview."

"Swing through after and we'll get weird," says Bruiser.

Angelora tries to sit down in the chair adjacent to Bruiser, but he pulls her by the hand into his lap. "I'm not here to fuck you," she says as she rolls off him. "I'm here for the interview."

"I don't have a table. Will the bed work?" he asks, puts out his cigarette, and slithers over the couch onto the bed face down.

"Sure," she says as she walks over to him.

"Should I strip down?" he asks.

She kicks off her shoes and says, "You can, but it doesn't matter because I'm not going to touch you."

"So far, this interview isn't going well. What are you here to do?" he asks.

She rubs her hands together and places them together in front of her heart, saying, "I'm going to fix the crackling noise you hear when you're alone. Relax, take a deep breath, and think about how you'd like to see yourself in the future. I'm going to align your chakras and allow your true being to shine through." She puts her hands out over his body palms down.

"Is this going to hurt?" he asks.

"Definitely," she whispers.

Bloody Like the Day You Were Born

It's Sunday afternoon in Atlanta and Bruiser has returned to Little Five Points in hopes of finding his homeless creator. There's a river of people moving at a stagnant pace. "One for three. two for five," barks a local artist, trying to reel in an income. "Bruiser!" shouts the artist over the wave of people. "What's up, my dude?"

"Brooklyn, what's going on, brother?" asks Bruiser as he eyes the drawings behind his friend: they're graphite portraits of famous people throughout history, mainly African Americans, other than Kurt Cobain and Elvis.

"Killing it out here. What've you been up to, my dude?" asks Brooklyn.

Bruiser stumbles to explain his current state, "Uh, shit, where do you start? Just trying to get out the A, at the moment. You seen Bootleg?"

Brooklyn laughs and says, "That's funny. That's why I flagged you down. He gave me this to give to you." Brooklyn hands Bruiser a beat-up pack of cigarettes. Bruiser takes the cigarettes from him and opens them to find only one cigarette left in the pack. He pulls out the raggedy bent cigarette and looks at it. "Sorry, I smoked a couple of 'em."

Bruiser puts it behind his ear and as he goes to crush the box, he sees the word "Left" written in Sharpie on the inside of the lid. "No worries," he says, putting the box in his pocket.

"What do you want with that click-clack anyway?"

"He changed my life, honestly," says Bruiser as he hands Brooklyn a twenty. "I can't tell you how much I appreciate you."

A teenage boy walks up to Brooklyn and hands him five dollars, saying, "Let me get that high school combo." Brooklyn hands the kid a Wiz Khalifa and a Snoop Dogg portrait. The kid takes the portraits and turns to Bruiser, asking, "Hey, aren't you?"

"Nope, wasn't me," replies Bruiser.

"Bruiser from Greed. I saw that video from last night. That party looked wild. Tell me this though, when that dude got shot and then the hole disappears, how'd you do that? CG, right? Hey, Skitch, take a picture of Bruiser slapping me," says the kid.

Bruiser scratches his head and mutters, "Yeah. You're right. It was all CG. What's your name, kid?"

"Jordan. Can I get a picture with you, mid-slap? Skitch, get over here!"

Bruiser hesitates for a moment as he notices a crowd starting to build around him. *How do I get out of this?* he thinks to himself.

A voice from outside the crowd yells, "Hey, everybody! Bruiser from Greed is out here healing people! For free!"

"What's wrong with you, kid?" asks Bruiser.

Jordan replies, "Nothing really, I'm fine. I mean, A.D.D., a couple fucked up teeth, and I'm slightly near-sighted." Jordan looks him in the eyes and says, "I just figured a dude like you, always fucked up and banging chicks on camera, had to be frontin'. Something didn't taste right, and I wanted to see for myself."

"It was real, but I think I lost the power," says Bruiser.

"You better do something or you're gonna' get lynched by an unruly mob. You can't go around offering fake miracles without pissing on a lot of people," says Jordan. Bruiser reaches back and slaps the awe off the kid's face with a swift right. He grabs the kid's Snoop Dogg picture and autographs it. "Did you get that Skitch?" asks Jordan as he turns around, hunches over, and grabs his jaw. There is a silence among the crowd. Jordan smiles, the crowd clenches in on them, and he shouts, "He's a fake. I knew he was frontin'!"

"How can I heal you if there's nothing wrong with you?" asks Bruiser. "You've got me fucked up, kid," he says as he looks over the crowd, trying to gauge their level of angst.

"I mean, there's no way you're a healer," says Jordan.

Bruiser catches a glimpse of a sloppy tattoo hanging out of the kid's sleeve and asks him, "That knife tattoo on your arm, is that real?"

"Uh, I drew it with a Sharpie. I'm only fifteen," says Jordan.

"Fuck!" Bruiser looks to the crowd and asks, "Is anyone out there truly suffering?"

"Yeah, aren't we all?" shouts a random voice.

Bruiser wipes the sweat from his brow, a hand goes up in the back, and an elderly woman pushes her way through the front of the crowd, holding a little girl with an extra chromosome.

There's a voice from the inner circle that says, "This should be good."

Bruiser's jaw drops as he finds himself surrounded by a morose mob, five rows deep and growing, all with their phones in the air, filming and says, "Well, this should clear up any doubt." He turns to his friend Brooklyn. "Can you tunnel me out of here?"

"You're on your own, dude," replies Brooklyn. "You're gonna' have to slap your way out of this one, my guy."

129

"I pretty much have to, don't I?" asks Bruiser. "Can you do me a solid?"

"What's that?" Brooklyn asks.

"Can you put the Redd Foxx in a bag for me with Kurt and an ODB." Bruiser hands him another twenty and says, "I have no idea where this is going, but I have a feeling that after I slap this little girl, I'm going to have to make a break for it."

Brooklyn looks at Bruiser like he just dropped a hard R and says, "You slap that girl and one way or another, I'll get you the originals, no charge, real shit."

"Bet," he says, shaking Brooklyn's hand. Bruiser turns to the crowd and starts his speech. "Before we start down this path together, I want you all to know that I have no idea what I'm doing here. I've experienced some very surreal things in the past couple of days, and from what most of you have seen on the inter-web, we are all asking ourselves the same thing right now; is this guy for real and is he really going to slap this little girl? I have to if I'm seriously capable of healing her. I've been highly medicated the past week while most of the 'healing' has taken place, so I hope for all of us this works out, and we all become believers. So, my only disclaimer before I slap this child, is that I ask for patience, it takes a minute to kick in from what I've seen: twenty, thirty minutes, at least — I hope."

Bruiser raises his right hand in the air, dripping with sweat and shaking vigorously. He looks down at the little girl and then up at her grandmother and asks, "What's your name, little one?"

"Peyton," she says.

"And what's your name, love?" asks Bruiser.

"Violet," says her grandmother.

"Could you pick her up for me, Violet?" asks Bruiser and then turns to the crowd, demanding, "Everyone back up three feet. I need room to breathe." He grabs the cigarette pack out of his pocket to light up and finds the empty pack that reads "Left" on the inside. He puts the box back into his pocket, turns to Violet, and asks, "Now, Violet, what's your faith?" stalling for time to gather his own beliefs.

"I'm a God-fearing Christian. Always have been and always will be. Christ my Lord and Savior has gotten me through the worst of times and shown me some of the best. They've been far and few between, but they do exist. I believe in miracles, and I hope for your sake we see one today. What's yours?"

"I guess you could say love. I'd love to see this work out for Peyton. Are you okay with me slapping your baby girl, Violet?" he asks.

"It's not my choice. I don't see anything wrong with her. I love her, and as God's creation she is perfect the way she is. Her father

is over there in the back, and he says that you are the Second
Coming. He saw you on the internet healing people. Is this true?" she
asks.

"Violet, to some extent it is. I've seen a miracle or three with
my own eyes, and I still don't believe it. I slapped my boss's son
out of a wheelchair. He had cerebral palsy, and now he's happier than
anyone I've ever met. There's a possibility I've lost my touch
though. I slapped a handful of my friends last night and nothing
happened."

"Well, I'd hate to think I was standing in front of the only
person that could possibly give my baby a real life and I stood in
the way. Close your eyes and have faith in yourself, knowing that
this moment in time was already designed to bring love and happiness
for everyone here. If you have to slap this child, do it with all the
love in your heart that your belief allows you," says Violet.

"All right, here we go," says Bruiser. He rubs his hands
together and measures the distance to Peyton's face. He closes his
eyes, hoping that the crowd will be gone when he opens his eyes, and
he can go back to being a social deviant. He reaches back with his
right hand shaking wildly and hears a voice in the back of his head
that says, *All you have left … is what isn't right*. He says it again
under his breath, rubbing the tension off his forehead with his right
hand.

"Do it, you pussy. Slap the kid!" says a voice from the crowd.

Bruiser looks around the crowd and finds everyone staring at him
with their basic, hungry, twitchy eyes. He looks at Peyton, and she
smiles at him. "Thank you," he mutters, raises his left hand, and
slaps Peyton at about thirty-three percent. She starts crying
immediately. "FUCKity Fuck Fuck," he says and covers his face.

Brooklyn hands him his bag with the drawings and says, "This
would be the time when you make like a banana and split three ways."

Bruiser drops the bag and puts his arms out, asking for Peyton,
hoping that Violet doesn't tear his arms off at the shoulders. She
hands him Peyton and he pulls the crying child into his chest,
embracing her unlike anyone has in this lifetime. She stops crying
and he starts praying for the first time, "None of this makes sense.
I don't understand what's going on, and I doubt that I, or anyone has
the power to remove an extra chromosome, but I could use some help."

Bruiser looks at Peyton and she whispers without moving her
lips, *What does make sense in this life, really?*

Peyton's dad walks up: he's the type of guy that would take you
off this planet for scuffing his kicks. He's covered in tattoos and
sporting gold from his teeth to his pinkies. He grabs Peyton from
Bruiser and asks, "How's my baby girl?"

"She's an angel," Bruiser says as he tries to sneak a peek at
Peyton's face while handing her to her father.

"I know. She taught me a lot about love. At first, I thought she was my fault, my cross to bear, for all the people I've wronged in this life; but I realized that she was sent here to save me from myself, and I wouldn't change that for the world. At the same time, I couldn't walk past the Second Coming without asking him to save her from this ass-backward place." Peyton buries her face in her dad's chest and starts screaming. The crowd has gone silent with disgust as there is nothing to be said about what just happened. Peyton's dad tightens his embrace as his child screams and says, "Look, I appreciate you trying, but you need to get the fuck out of here, quick, before you get turned into a puddle by these fools."

Bruiser can hear the whispered thoughts of the crowd turning against him as they wait for their miracle. The whispers turn to enraged screams as Peyton's suffering becomes intolerable to watch. Her suffering mixed with his fear of unruly mobs pushes Bruiser forcibly through a hole in the crowd. He turns around and the door of the Porter, a local pub, opens. He sprints for his home away from home, and as the door shuts behind him, he hears Peyton's screams escalate to something like what you would imagine it sounds like when an angel is having its wings ripped off and the moans of a crowd that just watched it happen.

As Bruiser walks into the bar, the first thing he sees is Janeuh. He sits down next to the truth in himself, the fact that he is a disappointment, an emotional miscarriage, and he hears, "What's up, loser?"

He doesn't acknowledge her and lights the cigarette that was behind his ear, staring down the crowd he just escaped as they leer through the window into his haven with their faces pressed against the glass as they search for their beloved confrontation.

"Nice entrance, and not that it surprises me, but why is there an angry mob of people pressed against the window looking this direction?" asks Janeuh.

The barkeep walks up and takes Bruiser's cigarette from him, hits it a couple times, puts it out, and asks, "What can I get for you?"

The windows of the pub start to shake from the furious screams of the enraged mob waiting outside for him. "We're good," Bruiser says, grabs Janeuh's purse, and pulls her out of her chair. "Let's go before this gets weird!" He leads her back through the bar into the kitchen, pulls open the walk-in cooler door, and walks to the back of it. Janeuh is staring blankly at her phone into the abyss of shiny information in her hand unaware of her surroundings. He twists the lightbulb and the back wall slides to the right. He grabs her phone and pulls her into the darkness.

"Bruiser, really? Totes innapropes. When were you going to tell me there's a speakeasy in this shit hole?" she asks.

Bruiser penetrates the bar, slaps a hundo on it, and shouts, "Jesse!"

The barkeep slides Bruiser a Scotch and stares at Janeuh. "Do you have any ciders?" she asks. The bartender walks away. "This is nice, Boozer. It's leathered out and has some fab prints on the wall. But tell me this, as a bartender, how do you make any money working a bar no one knows about? And what-the-fuck was that mob all about?" asks Janeuh.

"Fame. I tell you what, it's truly a curse," he says as he sips his Scotch.

She sighs and asks him, "No, really though? That was unusually entertaining. What's going on?"

He slugs his Scotch and says, "I just slapped this little girl with Down's syndrome, and it didn't go well."

"And what made you think it would? It's asinine to believe *you*, of all people, have the power to heal all who suffer," she says as she looks him in the eyes and rubs his leg.

"Is this how you want to start the conversation, by neg-ing me? As much time as you spend in that damn phone, you haven't seen Tanner, have you?" He gets his phone out and starts looking for the video from the night before. He throws his phone on the bar and plays it for her.

"Who's that? He's hot!" Janeuh says.

"That's fucking Tanner!" squeals Bruiser.

"Your boss's son? With cerebral palsy? Get-the-fuck out of here!" She grabs Bruiser's hand awkwardly and caresses it.

Bruiser pulls away and says, "Yeah, cured! How's that taste? He took a bullet at the house last night. It went right through him and closed like nothing ever happened."

"Yeah, thanks for the invite, dickhead," belts out Janeuh. "So, when are you leaving?"

"The bar?" he asks.

"The state," she says. "Desiree told me you're taking this *new show* on the road."

"Creep much," he says.

"She called *me*. We're friends and that's not going to change. You were just going to ghost me? You didn't think it was important to tell your girlfriend that you were going on a cross-country healing tour," she says, staring at him endearingly.

"I just figured after I woke up to you beating me … It's been a real head-fuck trying to figure out this whole thing. You know, healing people and saving the world from itself," he says.

"And that's why you haven't tried to call or even text me?" she asks as she surveys the bar top for her drink.

"We're leaving tomorrow to shoot a show based around the whole concept of me healing people, and I think I'm losing it, my powers or whatever." Bruiser flags down Jesse and asks, "Two shots of tequila, please, sir, and something for the lady!" Bruiser turns to Janeuh and says, "So don't worry there's still a market for your stem cell project. Assuming the government ever decides to start using them effectively."

"I wasn't worried about it," she laughs. "The job pays shit, but I figure, free stem cells, and I'll live forever," she says as the bartender slides her a glass of white wine.

"If that's what you're into. I'm personally over this life. This place is a fucking mess. We're finally going to kill off the rhino. California is running out of water. The government claims that the rain is theirs, and that collecting it is illegal. We'll never see your stem cells legalized because it would destroy health care, pharmaceuticals, and insurance all together. Two hundred years later, we basically reproduced what we were running from: being overtaxed and enslaved to a level of poverty for the masses. I mean a hundred and twenty years still in debt with bad credit, who wants to live forever?"

"I heard you're a millionaire, so I don't know what you're bitchin' about," she says and takes a sip off her wine. "Who would've figured you slapping people would pay off?"

The bartender grabs a vintage, gold ice pick, hacks away at some imported piece of an iceberg, throws a chunk of it in a glass, pours in three fingers of Glenlivet Fifteen, and slides his best efforts across the bar to Bruiser.

"How's it feel though, all you can eat stem cells?" he asks, deflecting her financial interrogation. "Two more shots, barkeep, if you have the time." Jesse looks around his empty bar and pours three shots.

"Uh, good, I guess," Janeuh says with a tone. "I haven't grown any horns or anything, but I've only had two injections. They felt great, like fairies dancing in my belly," she says and lights a cigarette. "Do you want to slap me?"

"Every time I see you," he says.

"Thanks, but I meant to heal me."

"Of what?" he asks. "You've got stem cells."

"The HPV you gave me!" she yells.

"You can't prove that. And besides, if I cure you, you'll just get it back from the other seventy-five percent of the population that has it. Plus, you'd lose your super cool tattoos," he says as he points to a sad puppy with huge eyes on her forearm.

"Oh, gross. Seriously?" she squeals.

"Yeah, it's the first noticeable change. You'd let me slap you?" he asks.

"I guess. I feel like all the bullshit we've been through, I earned it," she says.

134

"I can't argue with that logic. Let me know when you're ready to part with your precious artwork. So, what did Des say?"

"Basically, she said you fucked her party up and that she can't wait to get the fuck out of Atlanta." They put down another shot with the bartender and he goes back to polishing his glassware. Janeuh processes the toxic molecules and says, "Oh, and that you had a thing for her. It's nauseating. It's the whole reason we didn't work. I'm the complete opposite of what you want: black hair, tattoos, I'm allergic to sunlight, and I'm not bubbly, or anywhere near as whoreish as you like 'em. Plus, I'm way too smart."

"Don't be silly. You're a total whore," he laughs as he digs around, looking for his cigarettes. He pulls out the empty pack again and says, "Actually, you're a perfect mirror of me: dark, sarcastic, addictive personality, and a complete disdain for humanity. Desiree is what I want to be, what I want to have. I'm sorry," he says, putting his hand on her thigh.

"For what? Wasting four years of my life, making me feel like I was never good enough, or for ruining me for any other man on this planet."

He turns to her and says, "All those are valid reasons." He returns to the box Bootleg left for him. He looks into it and reads 'Left' again. He starts pulling apart the box looking for answers. As he unfolds the lid, it reads, 'What's Left.' He hits his cigarette and pulls the rest of the box apart, flattening it out to one of its prior forms, and it reads, 'When right is wrong?' He mumbles, "That's impossible. That's from my dream."

"What's impossible?" she asks.

"The homeless gent, who farted in my mouth and turned me into a healer, *left* me a note that basically quotes a dream I had." His eyes light up with clarity, and he shouts in a gentlemanly manner, "Shots please, sir!"

Janeuh sternly suggests, "Bruiser, slow down. It's early."

The bartender pours three shots of ice-cold Pernod.

Bruiser turns to Janeuh smiling and says, "Or really late. I've got an idea! I never got to shoot our last episode of Greed. Assuming the bartender's willing to hold the camera, I'd like to challenge you Janeuh Rae Golbstein to a game of Greed. Except, if you complete all three dares, I slap you."

"And if I don't?" she asks.

"You have to fuck me, in the bar, in front of the bartender," he says, smiling.

Janeuh takes a sip of her wine and says, "Okay, but not in front of the bartender."

Bruiser grabs her hand, looks her in the eyes, and says, "He really wants to see your tits. I've been telling him how perfect they are for the longest time."

"Okay, but no sex stuff for the dares. I'm not putting these girls on the internet."

Bruiser hands his phone to Jesse and asks him, "You in?"

Jesse looks around the empty bar and says, "Well, I was hoping to finish my book today, but anything for you, B." He puts out his cigarette, grabs Bruiser's phone from him and starts recording.

"Hello and welcome to the final episode … my final episode of Greed. I'm here with my … girl … lover … Janeuh, and filming today, we have my favorite bartender, Jesse. We're going to be delving into the darker side of life, a place we've always wanted to entertain on Greed, but couldn't. That's right folks, masochism. Welcome to Bleed. I'm your host, Bruiser, and I dare you to look away."

"Wait, what?" asks Janeuh as she turns paler than she was, almost transparent.

"That's right, for your first dare Janeuh … Jesse, do you have a knife behind the bar? A sharp one."

Jesse looks at Janeuh and then at Bruiser, saying, "Yo, Brü, I love you, bruh, but—"

"Jesse, do you trust me?" asks Bruiser, throwing a hundred-dollar bill on the bar. Jesse doesn't take the money. "Do you have any serious health issues or anyone in your family?"

Jesse stammers, "My … my mom's got Crohn's disease. I'd assume I do too."

"So, if I told you I could cure you and your mom, you'd go along with whatever's about to happen?" he asks.

"Yeah, but that's impossible. There's no cure for Crohn's," says Jesse, looking at him sideways.

Bruiser jumps behind the bar and grabs Jesse by the arms, saying, "Trust me." He grabs a paring knife and hits the button under the bar that locks the entrance. "Janeuh, you good?"

Janeuh lights a cigarette and stares deeply into Bruiser's eyes, trying to figure out what he has planned, stating, "I'll be better when you tell me what you're doing with that knife."

Bruiser lights up a smoke and pours three shots, saying, "Darling, it's more like what you're going to be doing with this knife. You remember when you were a kid, and you had your first love?"

"Yeah, I guess," she says.

"You wanted to carve you and your lovers initials into everything, circle it with a heart to let the world know you were loved." Bruiser picks her up and seats her on the bar. He caresses her with the knife and then pops the top button off her polka dot blouse with it.

"No, Bruiser! You're fucking around, right? Tell me you want me to carve my initials in the bar or the booth over there," she says.

"Negative. What fun would that be?" Bruiser runs the knife down the inside of her forearm, tracing her veins, and asks, "What's the difference between a tattoo and you expressing your undying love for me by carving our initials in your arm with a heart around it?"

Janeuh looks at the knife, then at her arm, then at the camera, and says, "There was a time when I felt that way about you, and as much as I hate you at the moment, I truly believe if you get your shit together, you will change this stupid world, but I'm not carving our initials into my arm."

"Thanks, but our initials in a heart would help me understand how much you really do love me. I'll give you five hundred dollars. Plus, when I slap you, both the wound and the tattoos will be gone — hopefully." Bruiser smiles and hands her the knife, asking, "Jesse, do you have a first aid kit?" Jesse points to the cabinet under the cash drawer. Bruiser grabs the kit, inspects its contents, pours yet another round of shots, and they imbibe. "You ready?"

"You're fucking serious, aren't you?" she asks.

"Dead. You think you can do it?" He spreads her legs, leans in, kisses her slowly on the lips, leans back, and pushes her skirt up just enough, so that you can see a series of scars on her inner thigh, saying, "This should be a walk in the park for you," as he walks his fingers across the scars.

Janeuh pushes away Bruiser's hand and puts her skirt back, snapping at him, "Bruiser! No sex stuff!"

"Sorry, they always turned me on," he says.

Janeuh pounds her Albariño, lights a cigarette, takes a few drags, and places it in the ashtray. She looks at her forearm and picks up the knife. "Not too deep. I don't know if I can bring you back from the dead." She stares at her arm and slowly traces the outline of the heart. She dips her finger in a shot glass and smears it on her skin. She makes the first cut and her hand clenches up into a fist as the blood starts to slither down her arm.

Bruiser takes a hit off her cigarette and says in a sexual tone, "Nice!" She finishes the heart and leers into him lasciviously. "Is that a nut sack? I thought we decided on a heart."

"As with life, it all depends on how you look at it," she says.

Bruiser turns his head sideways and says, "Oh, I see it. It's facing you, figures."

Janeuh carves the J with one sweeping motion and winces. "The B's gonna' suck!" She pauses and takes her cigarette back from Bruiser, hits it a couple times, slices straight down, and then takes her time with the curves of the B as she's concerned with them being balanced and well formed. She slashes a quick plus sign in the middle for style and says, "There you go. Fuck you!" Bruiser wipes the bloody flesh and pours some booze on it. Janeuh screams as the liquor hits the fresh wound. "What's next, you sadist?"

"Takes one to know one," says Bruiser as he starts to bandage her wound.

"Why do you think I put up with your shit for so long?"

"Let's see number two." Bruiser pours another round of shots. "I feel like I should give you some options." He starts walking around the bar, gathering tools: a wine key, a filet knife, a metal jigger, a bar spoon, an ice pick, and then he grabs a bottle and breaks it. He looks around the bar some more and grabs a large, glass, cigar ashtray and a pool cue.

Janeuh gives him a sneer and says, "Bruiser, what are you going to do with all these objects? I can't take any more pain."

"What else is there?" he asks. "You said no pleasures of the flesh, so all that's left is pain."

"Why don't you ask me a question?" she asks.

"Like a deep, dark secret? This isn't truth or dare, it's Bleed, and I want to see what you'll do for five-grand and a clean bill of health. Besides, I know all your secrets. Like wouldn't it be nice not to have to tell every guy you hook up with that you have herpes?" Bruiser looks at the camera and smiles.

"That's not funny. This is going to be on the internet. You know Becky's clean, and even if I did have herpes, I got it from that rotten piece of meat dangling between your legs," she says, grabbing it.

Bruiser laughs. "You didn't get it from me. It was your first boyfriend, from what I remember. He kissed a bee sting on your eye and transferred it from his lips to your eyes and nose, and if you perform these next two tasks, you'll be free of that burden. So, let's talk about which device you'd like to use."

"That depends on what I have to do with it," she says.

"Each item has a task that I've already chosen, and if I told you, that would take the fun out of the game, especially for Jesse."

"I'm not hurting the bartender!" she squeals.

Jesse steps back, sniveling, and asks, "Wait, what?"

Bruiser lights up a cigarette and pours another round of shots, saying, "It's okay, Jesse. I'm going to heal you, and I'll pay you whatever she makes as well."

"Dude, I don't know. Run me through this whole healer thing again," says Jesse as he wipes Janeuh's blood off the bar top.

"Have you been on the internet lately?" he asks Jesse.

"Yeah, but come on, we've run trains on hookers in here. There's no way you're for real."

"Really, Bruiser!" squawks Janeuh.

"Thanks, Jesse," says Bruiser.

"I just don't really see you as the Second Coming or anything supreme like that. And I thought I heard you say you might be losing your powers," says Jesse.

"You heard that?" he asks.

"Bartender's ears," he says smugly.

Bruiser holds up the disheveled cigarette box and says, "Yeah, but I just figured that out. I was just using the wrong hand. See."

"I don't get it," says Jesse.

"It's a message from Bootleg, the guy that gave me the powers."

"The homeless dude whose butthole you quaffed?" asks Jesse.

"Yeah, basically," says Bruiser.

"Oh, well, that makes total sense."

"So, you're in?" asks Bruiser.

"Five-grand, and you heal me and my mother?" asks Jesse.

Janeuh looks up at Jesse and says, "I promise I'll play nice."

Jesse pours another round of shots and says, "Fuck it. I'm in!"

"Welcome back to Bleed. I'm here with Janeuh and my favorite bartender slash cameraman, Jesse. We're on the second dare. I've laid out a series of devices for Janeuh to pick from, each with its own path toward Jesse's being." Jesse's brow starts to sweat as he realizes what's happening. He waves at the camera as Bruiser introduces each item visually. "Take your time and choose wisely," suggests Bruiser. Janeuh twirls her hair, wondering how each item might be used to inflict pain. She smiles and then points to the ashtray. Bruiser picks up the cigar ashtray and hands it to Janeuh, saying, "Hah, I knew you were going to pick that one. Here's the good news, Jesse, you just made a grand!"

Jesse moans, "Shit," and raises his shot glass in the air, saying, "Ashes to ashes, funk to funky. We all know Bruiser's mom's a junkie."

They do the shots and Janeuh says, "Bruiser, I like him. Can I hit you instead?"

"Nope, it's gotta' be him. Where do you want to film our sex tape?" he asks, pointing to the wrap around booth in the corner. "Over there?"

"What's wrong with you?" she asks.

"It's the last episode of Greed. Our insurance never covered blood, so we avoided it. I want blood! Everything's going to be fine, so grow some nuts and crack this guy's fucking skull. I'll let you do whatever you want to me for the last dare! How's that for fair? Jesse, you in?" he asks.

Jesse puts down the phone and holds out his hand, saying, "Two grand and you've got a deal."

Bruiser picks up the camera and flips it so that it's pointing at Jesse, asking, "So, Jesse, healing you and your mother of a life-threatening ailment isn't enough? You want more?"

"The show's called Greed," says Jesse.

"Bleed technically, tonight, but—" says Bruiser.

"Speaking of butts," interjects Janeuh, "what would you have had me do with the jigger?"

"Exactly that, but ramming it in there with the pool stick," says Bruiser.

"Is it too late to change my decision?" she asks.

"Definitely, are you in?" asks Bruiser.

Janeuh laughs and says, "Throw in another grand for me and we're good?" She throws Bruiser a pouty face and says, "What? I need a new clutch."

Bruiser looks into the camera and says, "And when is too much ever enough?"

Janeuh picks up the ashtray, feeling its weight in her hand, and looks into Jesse's eyes, searching for fear.

"I want to see blood, baby. Hit 'em good," says Bruiser.

She fondles the ashtray for a moment, trying to decide if she wants to break the beautiful piece. It's green glass, and it looks as if it was made during the depression. "So, again, you're not a hundred percent sure you can heal us?" she asks.

The two turn to Bruiser.

Bruiser shrugs and smiles.

Janeuh immediately swings the ashtray across Jesse's head, knocking him to the ground. He twitches for a second and a pool of blood starts to shimmer around his head on the floor. Janeuh turns to Bruiser, who's filming Jesse's convulsions, and then looks over at the array of tools lined across the bar. She goes straight for the filet knife and thrusts it into Bruiser's side repeatedly, twisting it and turning it with every stroke, looking for an organ to pierce.

Bruiser falls to his knees, grabs his side, and drops his phone. His eyes shut and he moans, "What the fuck, bunny?"

Janeuh picks up the phone, turns it on him, and says, "I thought it would be easier if I knocked out the third dare at the same time. You said I could do whatever I wanted to do to you."

"So, you shanked me, repeatedly? Is this some weird prison fantasy? Are you going to rape me next — again?" he asks.

Janeuh puts the phone as close to his face as she can get it while still capturing his expression and says in a sultry tone, "Yeah, do you want to slap me while I do it?"

He pushes away the phone and says, "I don't think I'm going to be able to slap anyone if I bleed to death."

"I thought you were magic and stuff. Why are you still bleeding?" she asks, pushing the phone back in his face.

Bruiser grabs his side, trying to stop the exiting fluids, and says, "I never said magic. I can heal people, apparently, but I've never slapped myself. I think you hit my lung."

Janeuh offers Bruiser her hand and pulls him to his feet, saying, "Calm down, Nancy. You'd be spitting up blood."

The two look down at Jesse to find him still convulsing.

"You definitely clocked him. Keep filming," he says as he inspects the damaged gin-jockey.

"He doesn't look good. Should we get him to a doctor?" she asks, nudging Jesse with her foot. She zooms into a shot of his blood-filled eyeball and asks, "You okay, buddy?"

"Get out of the way. I got it." Bruiser picks Jesse up by the shirt with his right hand, reaches back with his left, slaps him across his face, and releases him back to the bar floor. Jesse's head hits the floor and his eyes open. He rubs his head and looks up at Janeuh filming him. There is a moment of disconnection from the room as Jesse regroups. Bruiser grabs the phone from Janeuh and hands it back to Jesse. He tries to pull him back to his feet, but Jesse resists in his state of confusion.

Bruiser asks Janeuh, "Are you ready?" as he tries to hold onto his upright composure.

Jesse stumbles to his feet and continues to rub his head while still filming the puddle of blood on the floor. "What the what just happened? It's gone!"

"You might have just died. We're not sure. And that isn't the only thing gone," says Bruiser, pointing to where Jesse used to have a fully tattooed sleeve on his right arm. He turns to Janeuh, pushes her arm's length from his chest, cocks back, slaps her with a meek left hander, and then collapses onto the bar top. Janeuh's eyes roll back in her head, and she falls to the ground. There's a cloud of shadows that crawl out of her and envelope Bruiser. He grabs his side and slides into a barstool.

Jesse looks to Bruiser, pointing the phone at him, asking, "Why are you bleeding?"

Bruiser responds, "She filleted me after she hit you."

"A woman scorned. Shouldn't you slap yourself or something?" Jesse asks as he pours a round of shots.

Bruiser looks down at Janeuh and says, "I'm sure it'll work itself out. I'll take a Scotch to go with that shot if you would be so kind?" He looks into the camera and says, "Well, fine people of the outer world, that was our first and last episode of Bleed. I believe we can all see why that wouldn't have worked out in the past. Thanks for tuning in."

Jesse and Bruiser do a shot for the camera and Bruiser's head hits the bar immediately. Jesse grabs the first aid kit and a bottle of tequila. He pulls up Bruiser's shirt, investigating his opening, and says, "Can't have you dying in my bar."

"Yeah, you'd never get your six grand," says Bruiser in a whisper as he tries to regain his composure but can't and returns his head to the bar top again.

"Well, looks like she got your love handle," says Jesse as he grabs some gauze out of the kit and applies pressure to the wound. He digs through the kit, looking for something to tape down the gauze, but there isn't anything left in there. He runs behind the bar, grabs a roll of white tiger stripe duct tape, and starts peeling off a large strip and attaching it to the bar. He doubles up the gauze and starts cutting strips of duct tape. He pushes down on the wound, applying enough pressure to slow the bleeding while he tapes it, covers the wound with more gauze, and then frames it. He grabs two of the larger strips and covers the gauze fully. Finally, he grabs a bandage out of the box, wraps it around Bruiser's waist several times, and pins the end down, saying, "That should do it for now." Jesse sits down next to Bruiser and watches as the last of his tattoos disappear. He lights a cigarette and asks, "When do you want to slap my mom?" There's no response, only the humming of the beer coolers.

"What's a girl have to do to get a drink around here?" asks Janeuh as she picks herself up off the marble floor, startling Jesse.

"What the shit? How'd you get in here?" he asks as if she hadn't been one of the only two people in his bar.

"It's me, Janeuh, Bruiser's girlfriend," she says, staring him down, looking for confirmation.

"But your hair," he says, pointing his limp shaky digit at her, "it's blonde and your eyes — they're blue." Jesse drags her by the hand over to a mirror behind the bar.

Her eyes almost pop out of her new face, and she spits out, "Oh, my greatness. My mom's going to kill me!" She looks down at her arms, now free of tattoos, and rips off the bandage in search of her new wound. She finds it completely healed and returns to her new reflection, spinning around for her own amusement, saying, "I mean, it's not bad. A little too Aryan for the Golbstein tribe, maybe, but I'll take it."

"You look amazing," says Jesse, grabbing her by the waist. He's helpless, drowning in her beauty. Lost in her new image, he pulls her closer, and she's engorged with a new sense of power.

She tries to humble herself and asks, "Oh, yeah?"

"Definitely. I mean, you were beautiful before, but now you're undeniably drop-dead gorgeous!" Jesse leans in to kiss her as he seems to believe it's the only way to move forward.

"Is he okay?" she asks, turning her head and looking back at Bruiser.

Jesse hits her cheek with his face and pulls away, realizing his miss, and trying to evade the embarrassment of rejection. "From what I can tell, he should be all right. I wrapped him up pretty good, but I'd definitely take him to a hospital." With that said, he returns to his hapless pursuit and connects with her face.

Drunk off her new clarity, she gives in and lets him in her mouth, just for a moment, searching him for an undeniable truth that will hold her there. As she realizes there's no connection, she stops him, and pushes back, saying, "I can't. Bruiser could pop up at any moment and catch us."

"I thought you two broke up?" he asks.

"Is that what he told you?" she asks, getting lost in her own reflection just over his shoulder.

"So, it doesn't matter?" he asks, pulling her closer and leaning in for another kiss. She accepts and they rearrange the back bar. As the energetic exchange accelerates between the two, they're distracted by the shaking of one another, and break a series of pilsner glasses. The sound stops their momentum, and they turn to see if they woke the sleeping dragon.

Bruiser pops up squinting, pours a shot from the tequila bottle on the bar in front of him, and downs it. After his libation, he looks up at them, stares through them, and says nothing. He slides off his stool and starts to walk back to the bathroom, stops and stares directly at the two halfway embraced, and says in a childlike manner, "I have to tinkle."

They both frown at his choice of words, and Janeuh says callously, "Bruiser, don't ever say tinkle again."

"Sorry. Bruiser's not in right now. If you'd like to leave your name, number, and a brief message, he'll get back to you as soon as he returns to this realm of confusion … beep," he says and walks off to the restroom, fondling his side, and wincing at his own touch.

"He definitely blacked out. That's his standard outgoing message when he's blotto," says Janeuh. Jesse steps away from her, confused by the surreality of the moment and completely shattered by fears of Bruiser's wrath. His weakness deflates her she-boner and leaves her in need of a drink. "Maybe some other time," she says as she returns to her seat at the bar in search of more volatile liquids.

Jesse turns around to straighten the back bar and says, "Maybe."

Bruiser returns from the washroom stumbling and asks, "Where'd you get the blonde, Jesse? Craigslist?" He laughs as he hovers over Janeuh and puts out his hand, introducing himself to her.

"Dahli," she says and pushes away his hand. "Craigslist? You're going to start this conversation by neg-ing me?"

Bruiser grabs a cigarette off the bar top and says, "Dolly, I do apologize, but I know everyone else here. I assumed—"

"Assumed I was a working girl, thanks," she says and pours a round of shots for the bar. Bruiser does a shot with himself, lights a cigarette, takes a drag, and returns to his former position — unconscious on the bar top. "It's amazing, he really can't tell who I am." Jesse grabs the cigarette out of Bruiser's hand and then grabs Janeuh's hand gently, pulling her over to the booth in the corner, just out of sight. "You know, if he finds us over here, he'll fuck both of us," she says as she slides into the booth submissively next to him, landing with her hand on his thigh.

"As much fun as that would be, I'm rather vanilla when it comes to sex, other than an occasional gaunching here and there."

"Ew, what's that?" she asks, sliding her hand into his crotch for inspection, awaiting a new perspective on pleasure.

Jesse puts his arm around her shakily, still in fear of losing his best customer or becoming his bitch, and says, "Nothing other than a joke."

"No, tell me," she says, leaning into his embrace.

"It's medieval torture. They used to hang people over a large rusty spike and lower them onto it, piercing their rectum and penetrating their whole carnal being until it came out of their upper torso."

"That's D… scusting," she says, as she rubs his member through his pinstriped slacks.

"You wanna' give it a try?" he asks, leaning in for a kiss.

She turns her head, avoiding his failed attempt at arousal, and asks playfully while she latches on to his junk with a fair amount of pressure, "You want to kabob me? With that little spike?" He fights her grasp, confused by the motion. "What are you into though, really?"

"Oppai," he says as she releases his empty threat.

"What's that?" she asks, waiting for his next advance.

"Oppai is Japanese for tits. It's generally Japanese girls with big tits and the things men do to them," he says, staring at hers while he reveals his hand.

"Well, who doesn't love tits?" she asks, giving the girls just enough bounce to unnerve him.

"I heard you had a stellar pair," he says as he pulls the sleeve of her blouse off her shoulder.

She doesn't return it, hoping he's man enough to attempt bathing her neck with his tongue, and asks, "Wouldn't you like to know?"

"I would," he says, caressing her arm nervously.

Bored with his feeble virility, she asks him, "What would you do to see them?"

"Anything you wanted," he says, sliding his hands between her legs, testing her water.

She stops his hand, squeezing it with her thighs, and says, "Seriously though, Bruiser's going to flip out if he catches us."

"But you said he blacked out," he says, squeezing her thigh with a compassionate frustration.

"He just won't remember killing us. That doesn't mean he won't do it if he catches us," she says.

"If he catches us," he says at the same time stumbling over her grand opening with a nervous twitch of the finger. "Cosplay does weird things to me too."

"What's that?" she asks, knowingly aware, stalling as she stretches her neck around the corner, checking on Bruiser.

"Costume play, like dressing up like elves or like anime characters," he says, pulling her back to his attention. He pulls some pills out of his pocket and hands them to her.

"Sounds lame. What are these for?" she asks as she tries to identify the contents in her hand.

He motions to Bruiser passed out on the bar and says, "Knock him out and we'll have some fun."

She laughs so hard she snorts and says, "That's cute. You couldn't knock him out with a Chrysler." She licks her lips gently and asks him, "You want it bad, don't you?"

"What are you into?" he asks.

"Guys that have no understanding of how amazing I am and treat me like total shit," she says, squeezing her tits together, and confusing the shit out of him.

There's a silence, and Jesse slides away from her, saying, "He loves you; you know?"

"That's not fair," is her rebuttal, "and it's fucked up that you know that, and you're still trying to drug him, so you can fuck me comfortably." She lights a cigarette, hoping to appease a stirring hunger that's newly developed inside of her.

"No, really. From what Bruiser's told me, I believe he loves you. He just has no idea how to express that love without putting himself out there, where he can be ripped apart by you, like everyone else that's ever been that close to him."

"As a self-proclaimed Bruiser pundit, what else do you know?" she asks, hoping to find a reason to leave or worse — commit.

"I mean, he tells me everything," he says confidently.

"He does love his bartenders. Okay, blow my mind," she whispers.

His hand returns to her thigh, and he says desperately, "I'd rather blow—"

"Me away with the truth, is what I hope you were going to say." Janeuh takes the Xanax he handed her and says, "No, but seriously, tell me about me through the eyes of the Second Coming, please."

He backs off again and says, "This is going to get weird, isn't it?"

"Weirder than me hitting you in the head with an ashtray, stabbing Bruiser, and then Bruiser possibly bringing you back from the dead, back to perfect health?" she asks, hoping to force some truth into the light.

"Yeah, definitely weirder than that," he says.

"Tell me a story that warms my heart, pushes me closer to him, and I'll show you my tits," she says, pushing the girls up with her forearms.

"Oh, yeah?"

"Tell me a story filled with a truth that makes me cry and rips me apart from him forever, and I'll put that oversized clit of yours in my mouth." Jesse backs off completely with that quip. She can tell he's confused by the last remark, and as he hesitates, contemplating which story will end up with him inside of her. She pulls his hand back to her lap, demanding, "Let's go! Before he wakes up,"

"What do you want to know?" Jesse asks.

"I'm not the one that's going to miss out on the blow job of a lifetime, so I'd say it's up to you." Her thighs quiver as she pushes his index finger inside of her, derailing his train of thought completely. She watches as he stares up at the mirrored ceiling unable to pleasure her and think at the same time.

He pulls away from her and relaxes into the booth, saying, "He said you were one of the most self-serving, arrogant, highly intelligent, spoiled children that he'd ever stuck his dick in, and that you've never had to worry a day in your life. That's why the two of you would never work because you didn't have any gumption."

"I hope that wasn't your attempt at making me cry," she says, undoing the remaining buttons on her silk polka dot blouse and revealing her finest qualities. "And how many children has he stuck his dick in?"

"You know what I mean? He thinks you're a child because you've had an easy life," he says.

She smiles as she realizes she's paralyzed him with her breasts, knowing this is her superpower: the one that contained Bruiser for so many years.

"Can I touch them?" he asks quaintly.

The question provokes the only movement she knows when asked politely to be violated. She returns them to their sling in hopes of giving him the focus to dig in and find a truth, one she couldn't get from the source. "You can't make me cry, can you?" she asks.

"I grew up in a house full of women, and I worked hard to do the opposite. It made me a people pleaser," he says, lighting a cigarette.

"Not a very becoming quality in a man. Do you have a girlfriend?" she asks, trying to stoke an emotional outburst. She watches as his eyes bounce around in his head and he tries to release a group of words he knows he'll regret saying.

"Yeah, and she's great. Why?"

"I wanted to see if you'd lie to me. You seem like a great guy that probably has some safe boring girlfriend, that only sucks your dick on special occasions," she says, waiting for another wimpish retreat.

His hands slither away from her entrance and back into his lap, curled up with one another, and he says, "I wish."

"You must really hate blow jobs," she says, staring off at her former captor.

"I've definitely erased them from my daily agenda."

"Well?" she asks with a cold annoying twinge in her voice.

"Oh, he told me why he'd never love you, and why he kept you in his pocket the way he did," he says, hitting his cigarette.

"That's a start in the right direction," she says, licking her cherry red lips slowly. She grabs a shot glass and raises it in the air, expecting company, and says, "To penetrating me with the truth and changing me for better or worse." They do the shots, and as the tequila travels down her throat and back up her spine, the Xanax pushes down on her as if someone raised the gravity setting for the room.

Jesse catches her energetic deviation and nervously says, "He … he said you had one of the ugliest vaginas he'd ever seen, that it looked like Burgess Meredith's ear from Rocky V specifically, and that he kept you around because he could. He said you didn't have the self-esteem to even admit he treats you like shit, let alone to walk away from him, and that he loved the fact that he owned your heart."

Janeuh picks up her cell phone, looking for the reflection of her new being, staring into the eyes of a person she doesn't know, watching a tear roll down her cheek, and says, "I always wanted blue eyes—"

She slides down to the ground beneath him onto her knees, his eyes expand as he realizes he won, and he says confidently, "I guess, you could say I was suck-cessful in making you cry."

She crawls between his legs saying, "Spare me the pun-ishment and let me try to enjoy this."

He shifts around in his slacks, overwhelmed by what's about to happen. She starts to unzip his pants and her mouth begins to water with an unfamiliar hunger as she realizes she's usually in this position because she wants something, but this time she wants, in a different way, something unexplainable. She looks up at him as he starts breathing heavily in hopes of erecting his coliseum. She grabs it, compares it to her former captors, and laughs at yet another letdown in life. The thirst she feels is new, and all she can think about as she puts his compact, fuel-efficient, two-door hatchback in her mouth, is a steak, a raw one, and how she wants someone to slap her with it and then push her in a cage while she eats the lifeless sliver of bovine. This thought leads to her biting down on him as he attempts to fill her mouth.

"What the ever-loving fuck?" he yells as he tries to jump back and retreat from her consumption junction but can't because she's latched onto his member.

All she wants is to feel it hit the bottom of her stomach, and she asks herself, *Is that weird enough*?

He starts to scream with the pain a man should never know, and then she hears Bruiser's voice say, "I hope you brought enough gum for the whole class?"

Janeuh presses her face firmly into Jesse's lap, to make sure Bruiser's autopilot doesn't recognize her.

"What?" asks Jesse.

"Who orders one prostitute?" asks Bruiser. "Have you seen Janeuh?" She can feel him staring at her ass as it hangs out of her dress, pushing through the tablecloth, threatening him while her face presses into his favorite bartender's lap. Bruiser kicks up her skirt with his foot and says, "Nice."

"She might be in the pisser," says Jesse, "I haven't seen her in a while."

Bruiser walks off pin-balling into the walls of the bar.

"Is he gone?" mumbles Janeuh with his dangling participle in her mouth. She feels what she thinks is the body shaking motion of a yes but is actually him putting his hatchback back in the garage. She returns to sea level, hoping to find a steak on the table. Instead, she finds Bruiser staring at her.

"Didn't see her," says Bruiser as he returns unexpectedly, almost as if he didn't even look for her.

What a turd cutter, this guy. So fucking sexy, but a complete waste of space, is all she can think.

"Thank you," Bruiser says, and sits down next to her, only focused on entering her as that's his only functioning program when he gets this way. "Chellow," he says ever-so-smoothly.

Jesse pops up as Bruiser sits down and leaves Janeuh to fend for herself as she thinks, *The person that sits down next to me is my biggest fear. I'm generally always petrified of this person and his belligerent mood swings, shifting with the wind, but for some odd reason, the fear is what arouses me right now, like I want him to put his hand around my throat and shake me. I don't flinch when he climbs into me as if he knows me, even though he does, but doesn't know he does.*

"What was that?" Bruiser asks her.

"I didn't say anything," says Janeuh as she watches him inspect her. "Can I help you?"

"Have you seen my girlfriend?" he asks. "We were having a moment right before she penetrated me," he says and reaches for his wound.

"Penetrated you? Janeuh?" she asks and laughs as an unwarranted tear slips away from her eye.

"Yeah," he says unaware of her pain.

"What do you want with her?" asks Janeuh as she starts to lose her sea legs. The bars have finally confronted her, and she catches herself thinking, *All I want to do is stick my hand in his chest and strangle his weakest muscle.*

"That sounds like fun. What was your name again?" he asks as he drools over her new presence.

"Penny. Short for Penance."

"Well, that's an interesting name. Is that French?"

"No. What's yours?" she asks, looking his autopilot directly in the eyes and waiting for acknowledgment.

"You don't know me? Everyone knows me. I'm here to save the people of Earth," he says as he infiltrates her thighs and tries to pry them apart.

"Oh, yeah?" she asks as she spreads for him. "Be careful down there."

"Why is that?" he asks in a confused manner.

"Because it's tighter than a dolphin's blowhole. You could lose a finger," she says, smiling.

"I can fix that," he says as he lights a cigarette.

"And tell me how you're going to do that, Scott."

"No one calls me that, Penny."

"Well, what do they call you?" she asks.

"Bruiser," he slurs out.

Bored with pawing at this zombified version of her broken lover, she says, "Boozer."

Jesse comes back with a bottle of wine and opens it for them.

The weird thing is, I have this man I love next to me, flirting with me like he doesn't know the ending, and all I can do is salivate as Jesse pours the wine for us. He's stirring something around in me, she thinks.

"You love me?" asks Bruiser, responding to her thoughts.

"Do you have anything to eat, Jesse? I'm craving steak tartare. Can you make that happen, love?" she asks, watching him avoid eye contact with her purposefully.

"I can bring you some crisps," he says, looking down at the floor.

"Never mind. Sit down and join us," she says, in hopes of being manwhiched.

"Could you bring us another bottle of tequila, my friend?" asks Bruiser, deflecting her request.

Jesse scuffles off, saying, "I'll be right back with that."

"Bruiser, it's me Janeuh!" She grabs his face and pulls it into hers.

"No, I don't see it. It's close, but I'm not buying it. Really, where is she, Penny?" he asks.

Janeuh jumps on top of him, hoping he'll remember her tongue, and he crumples up, protecting his side as she tries to convince him of her identity. Jesse drops off a bottle of Casa Dragones with multiple shot glasses and retreats. Bruiser pushes Janeuh off him and pours some shots.

"You seriously don't recognize me?" she asks.

He laughs and says, "From my dreams, you're stunning." He raises his glass and says, "To firsts, seconds, thirds, and never getting tired of whatever comes after that."

As they clink glasses, he looks deeply through her, trying his best to hypnotize her with his cross-eyed gaze. "Listen, Blueser," says Janeuh, "we've been playing this game tonight, it's called 'If you want to fuck me, all you have to do is make me cry.' Tell me a truth so true that it changes me forever and I'll fuck you, but you only get one shot at it. You in?"

"All the way," he says as he processes the alcohol. The liquid settles, his eyes light up, and he says, "Getting you to cry sounds easy enough. Changing you forever with the truth sounds better than getting laid."

"Game on," she says, looking across the bar into a mirror revealing her reflection. She stares at her new self, wondering if he knows her well enough to point the finger in the right direction. She swirls the wine in her glass, watching the deep velvet crimson juices gracefully dance around, and says, "It's beautiful, vibrant, and well-balanced." She takes a sip of it, and the moment it hits her palette, she forgets everything she wanted to hear, and for the first time feels every particle of her being sing in harmony. The wine reminds her of true beauty and what it means to be appreciated. It leaves her wondering if he's going to hit her with love or bed her with fear.

He starts with, "I can't take the pain of living because I'm too sensitive. I feel everything intensely, but only seem to focus on the painful shit because that's the only feeling with which I'm comfortable. So, all I do is create pain to feel on a regular basis. Now here's where it gets weird, I use drugs and alcohol to remove the discomfort of being comfortable. I create the pain, so that I have an excuse to pleasure myself, and that pleasure brings me more pain. The cycle is killing me, as expected; it's just taking longer than I thought. I'm spinning so fast that I can't find an opening to jump out of the cycle, and I'm trapped in the accelerating momentum of a meteor headed to its inevitable collision. What really hurts me the most, is that no one has ever cared enough to ask me to stop."

"I asked you to stop and that's where you drew the line. You're too stubborn to forgive, and that's why you'll die alone."

Her words don't even hit him. He picks up his wine glass, trying to find the same sensation he saw cross her face moments before. "I wasn't finished. I know my eggs are scrambled, and I can't figure out why I'm trying to put them back into a broken shell," he says, trying to stare through her again and somehow, hits something accidentally.

"How so?" she asks.

He turns away from her as he continues his story, only focused on the wine in his hand, saying, "I had a dream the other night. I was with my mom, dad, and sister. We were walking in to eat lunch together, and if you knew me, you'd know this is something I've never had and the only thing I've ever wanted. Here's the kicker, I see my sister and fall the fuck apart. She disappeared a while ago, and I haven't seen her in years. Dreams are the only time I get that. So, I run to her and hug her so hard that I'm inside of her."

"Your sister?" asks Janeuh playfully, trying to alleviate the mood.

"Yeah, but it's not like that. I just wanted to hold her in my arms and protect her from the universe, but she vanished, along with the rest of my family."

"What happened next?" she asks.

"I'm balled up on the ground with my head between my knees and the world is throwing rocks at me."

"What do you think it means?" she asks.

"I'm afraid of living. I'm tired of doing it alone. I can't do it without the people that love me getting hurt while they try to protect me from myself and—" The bars take over fully as Janeuh watches his heart illuminate in his chest, eventually achieving a blinding brightness, and her head hits the table with the sound of everything on it ringing like wind chimes as she loses her bet with gravity. It echoes through the bar as Bruiser says, "It means, I love you, Janeuh."

That's the Plan Anyway, Now Figure out How to Follow Through

"Make it stop," moans Bruiser as his ears open to his phone's pertinacious vibrance, pulling him through the cosmos back to this three-dimensional challenge. He sits up and is brought to the realization that he's been pierced. He recoils in pain, falling back, and notices a plus-one in his bed: a stunning blonde with firm breasts, voluptuous lips, a tight well-defined body, and not a tattoo in sight — quite the rarity these days. He rubs the girl's inner thigh and notices the sheets covered in blood stains that resemble a half-baked tie-die. His phone rings again. "What do you want?"

"Bruiser, get out of bed," says Dick, "We're downstairs and we need to hit the road — now!"

Bruiser examines the body in his bed and smiles, saying, "Give me ten, maybe twenty." He looks at the girl. "Rise and grind, love." He rolls on top of her and slides his hand between her legs.

"Bruiser, stop it! I told you last night; no penetration," says the girl adamantly.

He starts laughing as he explores his guest further, saying, "It doesn't look like that worked out. Was it your first time?"

"As a blonde. What-the-fuck are you talking about, Scotty?" she says and pushes him off her. "The blood is yours from the hole I made when I penetrated *you* — for the first time." She snickers sadistically and says, "I mean, other than that one night."

Bruiser grabs his side, realizing the mistakes he made last night, and asks her, "Janeuh? What happened?"

She rolls onto him and says, "I only have bits and pieces. You should call Jesse and see if he's all right."

Bruiser grabs his side and asks her, "Why didn't you take me to a hospital?"

"You said it would be bad press," she says. "You don't remember anything?" she asks, revealing a diamond on her left ring finger.

"Where'd you get that?" he asks, ruing his alter ego's slovenly existence.

"Quit playing, Scotty. You asked me to marry you. You said something about true love," she says and pulls the sheets over her new guise. "My parents are going to kill me."

He scratches his head as he looks around the room for his daily accouterment. "Nope, don't remember any of that."

"Shit! I'm going to be late!"

"One more, before you go," he begs.

"I told you, not until you make an honest woman out of me. I love you, and I'm ready for forever," she says as she smothers him with aggressive snuggles. He stares deeply into the reflection of a person who used to be one of his favorite failures. Visually, she is everything he has wanted, but his heart pounds vigorously as he thinks about the internal mess that has brought him to his knees repeatedly. "You can't say it, can you?" she asks with a tinge of frustration. Janeuh pushes herself off Bruiser and throws herself together in a disgruntled manner. She walks down the stairs of his loft, shouting, "You love Dick. I bet you have no problem saying you love Dick," as she storms out of the apartment.

Maybe I fixed her when I slapped her, he thinks. *A millionaire savior with a fiancé. I've got to stop drinking*. He gives her a minute to distance herself, and then rolls out of bed, grabs his standard jeans and a T-shirt, and slips on a pair of gray Chucks. He grabs a jacket, throws it on, and makes his way downstairs, searching the loft for anything that might be of use on his journey. The pool of melted Jesus and his Jager divinity grabs his attention, and he gets lost staring at his mirky reflection. When he returns from the looking glass, he walks over to the bookshelf by the door and fondles his meager collection, thinking that he might catch up on some reading while he's on the road, and then slides the bookcase over to reveal a wall safe. He opens the safe and pulls out a tattered briefcase. He opens it and inspects the contents as if it were gold doubloons and rubies, shuts it, and walks outside to find Dick in front of the building, pacing on his phone.

Dick hangs up as soon as he sees Bruiser and asks him, "Where were you last night? Desiree is pissed!"

"Fuck! That's right. I totally spaced," he says.

Dick goes in to give Bruiser a hug and says, "You missed a good time, but something tells me it wouldn't have been that way if you showed up with whoever that was that just left your place."

Bruiser winces and pushes Dick off him, saying, "That was Janeuh - the new Barbie version. I think we might be engaged?"

"What the actual fuck happened?"

"I have no idea, but it involves me being penetrated and time travel," he says as he lifts his shirt up and removes the homemade bandage. "I have to stop drinking - Scotch."

"Is that white-tiger duct tape and a coffee filter?"

"And the stuffing from one of my couches, I think," says Bruiser, pulling back the makeshift bandage to reveal a meaty, discolored wound that's dripping with puss.

"That's disgusting. Did that happen before or after you slapped that little girl?"

"Listen, Dick, I can explain. I wasn't trying to fuck up the show. I thought I could heal her, but let's be serious, I can't remove chromosomes," he says.

Dick starts laughing. "It looked like you ran off in the video. You haven't been anywhere near the internet since you slapped that poor girl?" Dick hands Bruiser his phone and plays one of the many videos for him.

"How bad is it?" asks Bruiser, staring at the phone.

"It's the most disgusting thing I've ever seen."

Bruiser tries to hand Dick his phone back, saying, "I can't watch it."

The twins come around the corner, carrying a tray of coffee, and Less asks, "Twenty-four-ounce, iced brown bear, right?"

Bruiser drops his briefcase and grabs the beverage, noticing the twins won't make eye contact with him. "Thanks," says Bruiser as he visually interrogates the two.

"You're welcome, sir," they say together.

"What's up with the 'sir' shit?" he asks, embracing the coffee offering. He goes in for a large swallow as Dick forces his phone back to him. You can hear the most horrific grizzle coming out of the phone. It sounds as if the child were being tortured professionally. He spits his coffee onto the ground and pushes the phone back into Dick's hands, saying, "Fuck, Dick, this is terrible! I didn't mean to hurt her. It doesn't matter though, I figured out the problem. It's my left hand. I hit Less and everybody with my right. Wait—" Bruiser looks at his hands, trying to remember which hand he used to hit her.

Dick pushes the phone back at him. "Just watch!"

Bruiser looks back down at the phone as the viewer zooms in for a close up of Peyton. Her face starts to shift and change as the screams get worse. Dick stares at Bruiser, waiting for his reaction. The screams stop and Peyton's face grows anything other than expressionless. Bruiser's eyes water as he hands the phone back to Dick. Less, Leslie, and Dick stare at Bruiser in awe as he emotes.

"How high are you?" asks Leslie.

"Not high enough for this adventure," says Bruiser.

"How'd you figure out it was your left?" asks Dick.

"Bootleg 'left' me a message from a dream that said, 'What's left when right is wrong.'"

"Sure, that makes sense," says Dick, taken aback. "We couldn't have planned a better teaser for the show. I hope it lasts because we're going international. Come check out the bus." Bruiser ignores Dick as he's distracted by a blonde pacing on her cell phone. She's tall, slender, and beaming with confidence. Other than that, the main thing pulling him in is the sundress with converse. Dick grabs him by the neck and reels in his gaze, begging him, "Can you keep this going, Brew? We've got a lot riding on you."

Still ignoring Dick, Bruiser asks him, "Who's that?"

"Her name's trouble." Dick waves the tour bus to pull up. It's all black with tinted windows. Dick grabs him by the arm and pulls him toward the bus, asking, "Do you have everything?"

"Shit, I forgot my hat," he says.

Dick pushes him back towards his place, asking rhetorically, "You have a hat? Hurry up!"

Bruiser hands his phone to Less and Less says, "I thought your phone was dead. What's this?"

"I slapped it and revived it. I've got the last episode of Greed. Bleed. I think. We were shwasted."

"So, that's what happened to you last night," says Less. "Des is done with you."

"Rightly so," says Bruiser. "I'll make it up to her when we see her in LA." Dick, Less, and Leslie huddle around Bruiser's phone and partake in the visual spectacle that is Bleed. Bruiser pops back out of his place, wearing a vintage plaid blazer, a plaid medium brimmed fedora, with a Blue Jay feather in it, a North Face bag stuffed with clothes, and a pillow under his arm, asking, "What do you think, Less?"

"That's definitely too much plaid," says Less.

"No, the show?" asks Bruiser, taking off his hat.

"Sloppy, definitely needs an edit."

Bruiser laughs and says, "I'm amazed we hit record. I barely remember it happening."

"When is that not the case?" asks Less.

"Just watch," says Bruiser as he squats down, reclaiming his breath and grabbing his side.

"Are you okay? You want to get that looked at?" asks Dick as he rubs Bruiser on the head, saying, "I thought you … I mean Tanner can eat bullets like Wolverine and shit."

Bruiser stands up carefully, asking, "Who knows at this point? I think it might be from something evil I slapped out of Janeuh." He looks around and asks, "Where's Tanner?"

"He said he was going to try and meet up with us in LA. I feel like he just wanted to spend some more time with his dad," says Dick.

"I get that," says Bruiser.

Dick pushes Bruiser onto the bus and starts the tour. "So, this is our bus. It's tits across the board. This is Chuck, the driver. Chuck, this is Bruiser. The star of … did we get a name for you and the show?"

Bruiser shrugs. "Haven't had a chance."

"Anyway, Chuck, don't leave unless he's on the bus," says Dick.

"So, this is the living room. Full couch on the right. A dinner table with a wrap-around booth. Behind that is the kitchen. We've got a fridge for beer and shit, microwave, juicer, and an Espresso Machine."

"No fryer?" asks Bruiser.

Dick ignores his snarkasm and continues. "Next, we've got four bunkbeds with doors that slide down for full blackout privacy. On your left is the crapper. The whole room is a shower. We figured that would come in handy. Moving forward, or backward, depending on how you look at it, is the master bedroom slash production office. As you can see, the U-shaped, wrap-around, leather, bench seating is accompanied by a mahogany conference desk. Push that down level with the couch and the seating slides down to form a king-sized bed. Behind you is the tech wall with seventy-inch flat screen that's connected to a Mac Pro editing bay and a PlayStation. The door to the left goes to the master bath that has a two-person hot-tub."

The blonde in the sundress walks up on their tour. "Sorry, lady, we're headed out west, and we don't have room for hitchhikers!" laughs Bruiser. Alone.

"Vanessa," she says, shaking Bruiser's hand firmly. "I'll be the one reprimanding you while we make this leap of faith."

The bus cranks up and takes off into the unknown.

"Less, Leslie, it's a pleasure to be sharing this adventure with you," says Vanessa. "I look forward to working with you. I'm a big fan of the work you two did on Greed." The twins put out their hands to shake with her and Vanessa pulls them both in for a hug, saying, "I love twins. I grew up with a pair. You guys are so weird. It must be nice to have someone so close that you can understand without words." The twins look at each other and laugh awkwardly. "Dick, I'm going to need some chosen one-on-one time. We have a lot to cover before we get to Huntsville." She pushes Dick and the twins out the door, shuts it, and sits Bruiser down, perusing his affections, saying, "I'm going to need you to slap me."

"If that's what you're into? I'd rather start with pulling your hair."

"To heal me," she says, sitting down across from him.

Bruiser grabs her hand from across the table and gives her a slightly off-kilter stare, saying, "I don't think you need it. Honestly, you seem perfect."

"You sure?" she asks.

"Yeah, I'm getting a lot of visuals. Energetically, you have a golden light behind you. I really don't think you need any healing," he says.

"Cut the shit, Bruiser. What you're missing is the genital herpes I picked up in LA," she says.

Bruiser attempts consoling her, saying, "That's LA. Herpes and—"

"Heroin. Getting healed by you is the main reason I took the gig. I was hesitant because I don't generally believe in miracles, but Needameyer owed me a favor. Then I saw what you did to that little girl yesterday. I was like 'There's no way these guys are smart enough to fake that.'"

"Thanks, uh, it's real, for now," he says.

"We just need to get to as many people as we can. You wouldn't believe what people are paying to get slapped by you."

"I don't want their money," he says.

"Well, how do we decide who gets healed first then?"

Bruiser responds to her statement with a sideways look, saying, "Hospitals, schools, churches, homeless shelters. Take the money from the ones that have it and tell them they're getting VIP service. Speaking of VIP, what would you pay to get rid of your herpes?" he asks as he leans back in the couch, staring her down overconfidently.

"I mean, I'm super broke right now."

"I guess we could set up a payment plan, or you could work it off," he says, looking her over as his mouth starts to water.

"I'd rather keep the herpes," she says.

"Oh, come on."

"No way José. You're way too much like my ex."

"He was a great guy?" asks Bruiser.

Vanessa stares him down. "A dirty little whore like his mother," she laughs and continues, "but this meeting isn't about us. It's about the show. We need a name for it. A name for you, a look, an image, and branding. The essence of who you are. What's your religious background, and what's not? That's going to play out big in the end. Once we blaze a trail through the US, there's going to be a battle over who was right."

"Speaking of blazing a trail," he says and opens his briefcase to reveal a Hunter S. Thompson supply of drugs topped with a pair of wooden nun chucks. He pulls out a vape pen with a glass bulb on it, presses the button, fills the bulb with smoke, and points it at Vanessa, saying, "A dab el' do ya'."

She pushes away the pen and asks, "So, that's your religion?"

Bruiser hits the pen again and says, "I do love getting high. I used to read a lot of different stuff, Buddhism mainly. I love to meditate. I've just found drugs gets me to the same place, but faster." He points the pen at Vanessa.

"And where's that?" she asks.

"Far away from this three-dimensional challenge," he says.

"I just need you to be able to form complete sentences when you're on camera, otherwise you're in charge. Are you going to stick with Bruiser?" He shrugs and Vanessa leans back in the couch. "It might work with the whole forcing of enlightenment thing, but it's rather dark."

"I would like to ditch the dirty whore stigma that I've worked so 'hard' to obtain. I have a couple names for the show that I really like. I was thinking 'The Hand of God' maybe or 'In Your Face.'"

Vanessa jumps in, saying, "It's too much. We want to keep God out of this. We need humble. How did you come by your newfound ability?"

Bruiser raises his hand in the air and shakes it, saying, "Some homeless guy on Greed, Bootleg Johnson, farted in my mouth and slapped me. I puked neon green and went into a coma for a few days."

"Well, there's nothing there," she says, scratches her head, and jumps into her tablet.

Bruiser lights a cigarette and says, "I was thinking, 'Children of the Light,' no, 'Future of the Left!' That was it."

"Definitely. You just gave me the chills! But why Future of the Left?" she asks.

"Oh, I figured out last night that it's my left hand that does the healing," he says, digging through his briefcase.

"All right, Future of the Left it is. Starring? We need a face they can relate to."

"Like a persona?" he asks.

"Yes. The face of the man that changed this planet."

"More like a mask you wear in public to hide your true identity, so that you can interact in a 'normal' society."

"I don't want you to wear a mask, Bruiser," she says.

"Good. That's what I like about you: no make-up, no jewelry, and no ego. Just you."

Bruiser picks up the remote to the flat screen and Vanessa takes it from him, saying, "We're going to need some ego here. Are you keeping the beard and the grizzled hair? We can't change mid-season. We'll lose people."

"Gross," says Bruiser. "I don't think you have to worry about branding. Did Jesus Christ have branding? He just was who he was until it killed him."

"We need someone approachable, and we want to leave the host of Greed behind," she says.

"I'm not arguing that, but it's who I am, and that's exactly what brought us here," he says.

"How about your real name? Beauregard A. Derrick." Vanessa stares at him with judgement and then says with her chin out, "The third."

Bruiser puts out his cigarette, saying, "My father's name doesn't matter anymore." Bruiser looks around the master suite and then looks Vanessa in the eyes, asking her, "Do you know how to get this to turn into a bed?"

Slaphappy

She stands up and puts her weight on the desk, revealing some cleavage, and says, "You just push down on the table, I think, but this is no time for a siesta. I'm not done with you."

"That works 'cause I'm just getting started with you. I figure we might as well get comfortable while we work you out, work this out," he says, staring deeply into her sundress.

Vanessa laughs at his toxic masculinity. She sits back down and says, "That's cute. You plan to turn me with complacent penetration?"

"Turn you, like into a vampire?"

"Worse." she laughs. "Turn me straight!"

He marinates on that one for a second and then says, "But your ex, you said he was a …"

Bruiser, filled with nerves, lights a cigarette and Vanessa motions for a drag, saying, "People change, and his disaster of a person turned me off men forever."

"Challenge accepted," he says boldly, almost grotesquely. She returns his confident gaze, breaking his overconfidence and he snivels back at her. "You can't blame me for trying, you're absolutely divine." His phone rings, he looks at the screen, and then looks at Vanessa, begging her for privacy with his eyes. She doesn't retreat from his new lair, so Bruiser put's the call on speaker, sets the phone on the table, and says, "Hey, woman, what's up?"

"Is this really you, Scotty?" asks the voice.

"It's me, ma," he says.

"To what do I owe the privilege?" she asks.

"I figured that since I'm coming to see you, I should probably pick up."

"You're coming to Charlotte?" asks his mother with no luster in her voice.

"Don't blow a fuse, ma," he says while trying to hypnotize Vanessa with his eyes.

Vanessa passes his cigarette back to him and gets on her tablet. The bus hits a rough patch of road, and the back of the bus starts bouncing. Bruiser notices Vanessa's tits fighting to get out of her sundress and loses his train of thought.

Vanessa looks up and notices the liquid cascading out of Bruiser's mouth, saying, "Wrap it up, B."

"Hold on, Ma," he says and mutes the phone. "It's my whore of a mother."

"You can talk to her when you see her. I'd like to set up the show. We're going to be shooting in a few hours, and I want it all to be on paper."

Bruiser sets the phone down, opens his briefcase, pulls some weed out, and starts rolling a joint. He cuts out a line of Oxy, dumps the line into the joint, and puts the phone up to his ear and says, "All right. I'm back." He gestures to Vanessa, asking if she'd like to partake and she swiftly turns down his gracious offer.

Bruiser's mother goes on for moments without a pause while Bruiser smokes his joint in in an attempt to escape his mom's verbal discharge. "Yeah. I'm listening, Dancing with the Stars … silly kitties … Okay … Whatever, the receptions terrible. We're headed to Alabama … What, no, I haven't talked to my sister. Mom, she's not … I haven't talked to her in a while. I've got to go … Yeah, I know. We'll see you tomorrow, Ma … I've got to go … Yeah, I'm sending you money." He ends the call with his mother and stares at the phone for a minute.

Vanessa closes her tablet and says, "Scotty? Do you want to use that name for the show?" He doesn't respond as he is lost, staring through his phone while he smokes his joint. "Hey, you okay?" she asks. "She calls you Scott. We could use that for the show. Where does it come from?"

Bruiser hits the joint real hard. "Yeah, clearly, I have my father's name. He forced that one on her, and she decided I was too cute to call baby Beauregard. So, she just started calling me Scotty. It still confuses me and takes me to a place I'd rather not go."

"Where's that?" she asks.

He shrugs. "Home."

"Noted. Where were we? Greed, you didn't have writers?"

"Nope."

"You can handle free balling a miracle, healing show with no safety net?"

"Sure," he says without hesitation.

Vanessa puts her tablet down and says, "Here's the thing, we can't sell you just slapping people and changing the world. You did a lot of greasy shit on Greed and now you heal children with Down's syndrome. We need a story that explains the transition, something to pry the world away from their perception of the old you that's based on a philosophy or religion. Something that will grab the world and bind them to you."

"How about my drug addiction, and how I found the truth in a deep, drug-induced meditation?" he asks.

"Nope, drugs and sex scare the general public. We need a compelling story that will have people selling their shoes to be healed by you."

"What about, me being from the streets and how I was homeless? You know, like even though I'm a straight, lower-middle-class, Caucasian dude, I too have been thrown away by the world?"

"Nope. What's your thing? Who are you?" she asks.

Bruiser jumps up, battles with gravity for a second, and slides open the door, shouting, "Dick, what's my thing?"

Without hesitation Dick says, "Gettin' fucked up and slaying broads?"

"Thanks, Dick. Leslie, you have anything?"

Leslie responds, "Blowing dudes."

"Only when I'm sober. Less?"

Less laughs. "When you get really fucked up, and there aren't any girls around, you generally won't stop with the whole government conspiracy, alien, illuminati, slavery, Egypt, Atlantis thing."

Vanessa forces herself to stop laughing and says, "That combined with the healing thing will have you on a cross in no time. You want to avoid the government and media."

"What if we make it global? Global suffering, and how we are all enslaved to the point of being too sick to fight, but healthy enough to make it to work and pay taxes. They have us right where they want us; enslaved by our debt. This movement is about freedom from our own personal fleshy cells."

Bruiser sits down next to her, puts his hand on her leg, and she pushes him off her quickly, saying, "A global movement. I don't know."

He stands back up and gets on his soap box, stating, "Democracy in Egypt, Nukes in North Korea, bankruptcy in Greece, global warming, polygamy in the states, Pakistan and India, corporate America, corruption by corporations in every government known to man, human trafficking by world renown pedophiles, the trash pile in the Pacific the size of Texas, rhinos are almost extinct because Asians can't get their dicks hard, and the rich get richer while the rest die funding their movement towards glutinous, financial excess."

"That might work with the whole Buddhist thing. This life is suffering, and the only way around it is accepting that fact and smiling as you take your beating," she says.

"Exactly. What about you?"

"What do you mean?" she asks.

"Where are you from? What's your passion? Why production?"

Without looking up from her tablet, she says, "I'm from Denver originally. I graduated from USC and then I slept my way to the top of this shit covered mountain. I wanted to direct, but I found every set I worked on was a mess and they always needed someone who could get shit done. Someone that could manifest the right solutions and yell at people without having them resent you. My tits did most of the work."

"I get that," he says as he scoots closer to her. "If you could do whatever you wanted and not have to worry about money; what would you do?"

"I'm at the point where I would love a family, a couple of towheads running around, a dumb job, and a boring house in a silly little neighborhood. I wanna' get fat and know that it doesn't matter because I have the love I always knew existed," she says, sliding farther into the booth.

Bruiser stalks her down, sliding closer to her and says, "I couldn't have said it better. So, a hot wife to watch the kids while you're at work?"

"I'd rather stay at home with them," she says as she fights her way out of his grasp.

"Me too."

"Nobody wants to be the one at work while everybody is having a blast spending your hard-earned salary," she says.

"And then you get cancer from the stress of your job, die, and they spend the life insurance on drugs and hookers. If that ain't love," he says and leans in to kiss her.

Vanessa, startled, jumps up out of the booth, saying, "Listen, you need to get your head clear and organize this 'being' that you're becoming. I like Future of the Left. Think about a name for yourself, and a wardrobe to match your new persona. I'm gonna' go check out my bunk while you rest, meditate, or whatever."

Bruiser jumps up with her, saying, "You can have the master suite. I don't need you guys waking me up at six, telling me to get out of your office. Not to mention, no one's going to want to work on my bed."

Vanessa snickers, and says, "You're the master here. Enjoy it. I don't know how you plan on bringing multiple chicks back to your bunk."

"What a thinker." He tries to push down on the table and make the bed, pleading, "You sure you don't want to join me?"

Vanessa opens the door and gets one foot out safely, stating, "I don't know how my girlfriend would feel about that. Seriously though, I need you to focus on connecting to yourself, to others, to the world, and to the universe." As Vanessa is talking about connecting, Bruiser sees a blue flame float out of her chest, and everything shifts in and out of focus. Her face turns gray, and her attributes flatten, leaving the focus on her eyes as they start to glow a bright blue. She smiles and says, "You're about to change the direction of humanity forever."

The vibrance that emanated from her soul forces Bruiser to lose control over his puppet, and he falls back on the table, saying, "No pressure." The table slowly lowers, turning back into a bed, and the light turns to darkness as Bruiser's eyes shut.

The cold transition through utter darkness is lit up by a spectacle of lights similar to traveling at hyper-speed on a solid dose of acid. The light show evolves from a tunneling effect into a pattern of neon paisley designs spinning in unison. The spinning slows down, and Bruiser finds himself hovering over a world new to him. He sees the shadows of beings gathered around a bright, blue light that resembles a bonfire burning, but there's no smoke. There's a collective humming like vibration coming from the group. It's deep and crackling like that of a power line, except magnified.

Bruiser realizes he has no physical form and can't control his positioning. While he's trying to figure out how to move, one of the shadows removes its hood and looks up directly at him. The being has bright, blue, piercing eyes that look through him, yet somehow acknowledge his presence. The creature places its focus back on the blue flame and replaces its hood as the pitch of the humming raises to a higher frequency. The blue light at the center of the being's attention grows almost doubling in size, turning a bright indigo. The humming turns to a buzzing that's somehow more soothing, and it pushes Bruiser into a fetal position. He is haunted with a vision of his mother in one of the few moments in time when she held him.

Bruiser starts to focus on the pain attached to his mother, and he feels as if she is being pulled away from him as images of his life pass by. He witnesses her being abused by different men, men he never knew, some of those being his relatives. He sees her alone, crying, and balled up in a closet as she shrinks into a small girl. The blue flame begins to dim, and as it does, it pulls Bruiser down into it. The hooded gathering looks up, all with glowing blue eyes, and there is a silence. Bruiser's speed has snowballed, pulling him dramatically faster towards the ground and all he can think about is hitting it — hard. Just as he is about to hit the ground, he sees their cloaks blown off by the draft of his movement and finds they are ancient beings, simple in design, and they all appear to look the same in size and stature. He hears a statement that seems to be coming from a collective voice, "You only have two choices in life, one will enslave you, and the other will set you free."

Instead of hitting the ground, Bruiser plummets through it into more darkness, and he hears one final advisory statement from the group, "You will find your freedom in numbers, surround yourself with good people."

"But I'm so alone," he screams into the void.

"By choice," hums the collective mind.

Bruiser is spit out of the ground and grabbed immediately by a hand that slams him to the ground, knocking the wind out of him. His head hits the ground, jarring his sight, just enough to the point where it looks like his vision is losing reception. There's a tug at his leg and he leans forward to find two forms that remind him of Janeuh and Desiree. He feels two more hands grab his wrists. The hands are attached to two beautiful girls that he believes are his sister and Vanessa. They hold him down tightly and start pulling at him. He feels more hands and looks around to find a bunch of dudes. They're all rather white with blonde hair, golf shirts, and khaki shorts.

The conclave of hungry souls starts to claw at him, ripping his skin from the muscle. He struggles for a freedom that he's never desired more, and another being floats down from the sky in the middle of the group and hovers over his core. It has the wings of a damselfly and it's outlined by a glowing, neon-brown light that's distorted like that of a heat wave. The being lands on top of him, starts sniffing him, pets his face endearingly, and then swipes its hand across his eyes, forcing them shut, and sewing them together.

Bruiser fights to open his eyes as he is being ripped apart but cannot. Trapped inside an endless image of himself, he finds a moment in time where he was sitting on his mother's couch, watching TV, and eating wasabi peas. Everything about that moment in time sucked: his mother was being beaten by his stepfather on a regular basis, his girlfriend left him for her ex that also enjoyed beating her, and he was about to be homeless. There was a menagerie of empty beer bottles lined up on the coffee table in front of him. Searching to escape the pain that was relentlessly forcing itself on him, he decided to throw a pea at the bottle in hopes of landing it inside the longneck. It goes in on the first time and one would think that to be enough, but Bruiser continued, landing five in a row – flawless. And that was the first time he heard his name as a distant voice whispered it into his ear from across the void.

Bruiser's eyes burst open to the damselfly whispering in his ear, "I love you." It reaches back, sticks its leg into his stomach through his diaphragm and into his chest cavity, and grabs his heart. Bruiser screams, releasing an energetic light from his hands. His attackers are pushed aside from the shockwave released from his hands, and the being that was holding on to his heart, trying to pull it free, dissolves as Bruiser points both his hands, still emanating light directly into its chest. As he does this, he's lifted off the ground and set into flight.

One would think there was a thrill that comes from the empowerment of flight and the freedom from a ravenous crowd, but all he feels is fear as he looks down to find himself flying over a wasteland. He's pushed uncontrollably toward a building, and realizes he still has no control over his flight. The only thing he can focus on is landing as he finds himself barreling towards a rooftop. As he loses sight from his rotation, he sees the eyes of everyone that's tried to love him but done nothing but tear him apart. He tries to change the direction of his momentum but starts spinning uncontrollably toward the wall of another building.

He takes a deep breath in the middle of his escalating rotations that stops him right as he is about to hit the building. As he stops, he finds himself in lotus position, hovering just over the ground of a dark forest. As his eyes adjust, he focuses on two indigo glowing eyes that are growing closer and closer. The fear returns to his chest, and he remembers to breathe, hoping to stop the threat homing in on him. However, as the eyes grow bigger, he finds they are attached to a ridiculously large wolf. The fear sinks to his gut, paralyzing him, and his heart seizes, his breath stops, and he hears a growl. In the growl, he hears the word Bitté, and his only thought is to say it aloud. "Bitté?"

The beast freezes mid-attack with its teeth upon Bruiser's face and starts licking it. He relaxes into a relieved comfort as the animal sits in front of him smiling, and a blue flame appears in its chest, revealing its true form. "It's a giant, gray wolf, and there is a shadow standing behind it: the shadow of a man in a cloak that has his face shrouded by the hood, revealing only a matching pair of glowing blue eyes and the beak of an Ibis that's poking out of it.

The man steps forward into the light of the blue flame and says, "She is yours. Love her and she will walk with you through hell." Bitté howls and the flame travels from its chest, stopping mid-air, and then connecting the two. The flame grows into a resilient, white light that fills his dream, and he hears, "You must trust her, Zealand. Your life depends on it."

The bus hits a decent sized pothole, and Bruiser awakens, back on the bus, sprawled out over the conference table, hugging his briefcase. He jumps up, saying, "I've got it!" and bursts out of his room, forcing everyone to look away from their devices.

"Got what?" asks Less.

"Herpes, we know," says Leslie.

"Seriously," says Bruiser.

"Yeah, I'd definitely get that hole checked," says Leslie, laughing and pointing at the blood stain seeping through his shirt.

Bruiser caresses his new opening and turns towards Vanessa, asking her, "Are you ready?"

"I've already got it. I was hoping you'd get rid of it, not make it worse, like that festering hole," says Vanessa, pointing at the hole Janeuh made in him. Bruiser lifts his shirt and inspects it. Vanessa steps back as he reveals the infected opening, and she points two fingers at his wound, saying, "Yeah, that's grody."

Leslie laughs, and pointing two fingers at Bruiser, says, "Stick it in him, Vanessa."

"Make sure you wear a glove, though," says Dick.

"All jokes aside, Vanessa. We have a connection. I had a dream when I was out, and I'm pretty sure you're my hellhound. I need you to slap me," he says.

"How high are you, Bruiser?" asks Dick.

"Pretty high, but I was talking to a wolf in my daydream, and I'm pretty sure it was Vanessa."

"This is going to be a long ride," says Vanessa.

"Sorry, that's Bruiser. He generally doesn't make much sense, but given the sitch," says Leslie.

"So, I'm your bitch?" asks Vanessa, "Your 'evil' bitch."

"No, not like that. You're my protector. We sat in front of each other and the blue flames in our hearts connected. It filled the world with a bright, penetrating, white light."

"You'll say anything to get some, won't you?" asks Vanessa.

"Look, I need you to slap me at the exact time I slap you. Our connection was pure light, and it was overwhelming," he says.

"Whatever you're into," says Vanessa.

He stares deeply into Vanessa's light blue eyes and says, "Thank you, are you ready?"

She laughs at his esoteric shenanigans and then looks around the bus, asking, "Sure, should I sit and shake, or would you prefer I play dead?"

"I'd imagine he wants you to roll over," says Leslie.

Vanessa stands up and gets in Bruiser's face. She smiles at him and says, "Anything to get rid of this itch." She raises her right hand, and he grabs it before she can get it up.

He pushes her back to a mutual arm's length, saying, "Lefties. On three. One … Two … Three!"

The two connect at the same time, and as they do, there is a blinding flash of light. The lights on the bus flicker and then go out, and the two collapse to the floor as the bus comes to a halt.

"That's how you do it. I want my money back," says Less.

Leslie laughs and says, "We definitely got duds."

"Chuck. Is everything all right?" asks Dick.

"Sir, the bus just shut off," he says.

"Give it a minute, and then try to start her up," says Dick, standing over Bruiser and Vanessa. He turns to Less and Leslie and asks them, "You think they're all right?"

Leslie gets up, lights her lighter, and leans over Vanessa, saying, "There's no telling." She looks at Bruiser and finds his position to be apropos, saying, "You know, he looks happy. He doesn't really smile, even when he's unconscious." Leslie returns the light to Vanessa, overly inspecting her new boss.

"Get that thing out of my face," says Vanessa, pushing away Leslie's hand.

"I bet you say that to all the girls," says Leslie.

"What happened?" asks Vanessa, pulling herself to her feet. Her body clenches up and pushes her into the corner as a wave of electricity rolls over her being. She can't help but to touch herself through her sundress as her suffering is lifted. "Oh, fuck! That's nice!"

"You okay boss?" asks Less awkwardly as everyone else is trying to ignore their new boss playing with herself in the corner of the dark vessel.

"Sorry. It feels like someone is blowing ice-cold air across my … It feels so fresh and crisp. It's like it'd never been fouled. I'm waiting for it to start snapping." The bus restarts, the lights come back on, and Vanessa finds clarity, realizing how awkward this must look: backed into the corner with her sundress lifted, diddling herself, and her new staff staring at her. She pulls her hand away from her entrance and there is a static shock that jumps from her hand to Dick's. The static charge travels through the bus, shocking everyone, and there's a silence that Vanessa breaks by saying, "Sorry."

"I definitely want a redo," says Leslie.

Redirecting the moment, Vanessa asks, "You think he's okay?"

Dick kneels over Bruiser and slaps him, saying, "Yeah, I'm sure he'll be fine."

"He looks so harmless," says Vanessa.

"What'd you see when you were out?" asks Leslie.

"It's a blur. I mean, I was running through the woods chasing a rabbit and …"

"Seriously though?" asks Less.

"I saw my brother, not the old him, but a version of him that survived," says Vanessa. She returns to the floor of the bus next to Bruiser and can't help but pet him while he lay there, defenseless.

"What did he say?" asks Leslie delicately.

Vanessa mumbles through her tears, "He said trust them. They're good people, and they're going to protect you."

"I wonder who he was talking about," says Less.

There's another silence that Vanessa breaks, saying, "I assume he's slapped you guys."

"Yeah, but with his right hand," says Less.

Vanessa lifts Bruiser's shirt as she's concerned about his hole, hoping it feels as good as hers, only to find it still infected. "Should we leave him here?" she asks, looking around the bus. No one seems to be worried about him. "Bruiser. Bruiser. Bruiser, wake up," she says, slapping him on the face lightly.

His eyes open with an intensity that can't be explained, and the two get stuck in each other's eyes as he says, "Zealand. It's Zealand T. Dahl!"

Touch Me I'm Sick

There's an odd, ambient noise drifting through the southern Gothic church as Bruiser creeps from behind a curtain out onto an empty mezzanine, shrouded by a gray cloak. He looks down at his first gathering and finds there's maybe a hundred people, not quite the turn out they had expected. He watches as the curtains on the main stage open to reveal a motley crew of suffering souls that consists of a child in a wheelchair, a young man laid out on a gurney, an old blind man, and a handful of others varying in need. They all look lost as the spotlights hit them, and the audience stares up at them with their mouths agape.

Bruiser looks up at the ceiling and notices a handful of shadows perched along the edge of the molding. As he tries to focus on his entrance, the ambient whisper lurking through the church begins to growl at him. He puts his hands together and takes a deep breath, hoping to silence the invisible threat. He turns on his microphone and channels these words under the guise of darkness:

"Hark ye, O man, to the wisdom of magic.
Hark the knowledge of powers forgotten.
Long ago in the days of the first man, warfare began between darkness and light.
Men then as now, were filled with both darkness and light; and while in some darkness held sway, in other light filled the soul.
Aye, age old in this warfare, the eternal struggle between darkness and light.
Fiercely is it fought all through the ages, using strange powers hidden to man. Aye, man, know ye this knowing: always beside thee walk the Children of Light.
Masters they of the sun power, ever unseen yet the guardians of men.
Open to all is their pathway, open to he who will walk in the light.
Free are they of dark Amenti, free of the halls, where life reigns supreme.
Given to man have they secrets that shall guard and protect him from all harm.

Slaphappy

He who would travel the path of the master, free must he be from
the bondage of night.
Conquer must he the formless and shapeless, conquer must he the
phantom of fear.
Powers have they, mighty and potent. Knowing the law, the planets
obey.
Work they ever in harmony and order, freeing the man-soul from its
bondage of night.
When darkness is banished and all Veils are rended, out there shall
flash from the darkness, the light."

The spotlights hit Bruiser as he finishes his inaugural speech.
"Welcome to The Future of the Left. My name's Zealand T. Dahl. I
don't know how you found your way here or what you expect to happen,
but that doesn't matter. Tonight, we will unearth the truth from the
lies you call your life and reveal the happy healthy light being
you've always felt deep down inside of the mutation you call home. We
will free you from the current state of inhumanity that's controlled
and confined by a power so dark and shameful that it has chosen not
to reveal itself for millenniums. This group of oppressive, self-
serving, nepotistic, slave masters will no longer control you with
their technology, viruses, and idol worshipping. I will banish the
illnesses that kept you chained to your safe lives on your
comfortable couches in front of your dream boxes."

The room searches for the origin of the ominous voice that just
recited the confusing poem. The audience follows the spotlights to
find Bruiser leaning over the balcony, with his back to the crowd and
his arms stretched out, in what one would call a Jesus Christ pose.
He turns around, looking for praise at the edge of the balcony, and
receives only silence. Bruiser drops his cloak to reveal his standard
attire: gray jeans, white T-shirt, and gray Chucks. He disappears,
making his way towards the stairs that lead to the main stage.

Bruiser walks the main floor, sifting through the blank looks
from a crowd that's clearly underwhelmed by his disheveled
presentation. He scans the crowd, looking for visible defects, and
finds a teenage girl on the back row with terrible acne. He runs up
to her and slaps her first. The girl's parents embrace her, and the
crowd gasps. Before the girl shows any sign of healing, Bruiser takes
off down the aisle slapping anyone he can get his hand on, all the
while running toward the stage.

Vanessa turns to Dick and stares at him quietly as if he had
just run over her girlfriend. Dick grabs her and whispers, "You've
got to trust him. He's never let me down — on camera."

"Of all the wardrobe options," says Vanessa, "he went with jeans
and a T-shirt. He's misjudged this group. Look at their faces, Dick.
I'm surprised they haven't lit their torches and grabbed their

pitchforks. He just slapped a fourteen-year-old girl with a mental disability!" And as she says that; a group in the back stands up and collects their belongings. Vanessa puts her hand up to her ear and whispers, "Bruiser, you're losing them. Do something!"

Bruiser continues down the aisle, slapping as many turned heads as he can. He cuts across the front row, skipping most of the crowd he wanted to slap and climbs the stairs to the stage. He locks onto the boy laying on the gurney, and asks, "What the fuck is this?"

Vanessa jumps back into his ear, saying, "I'm pretty sure they heard that. That's Neil. He's seventeen, and he has Lou Gehrig's disease. It's a disease that causes paralysis due to nerve degradation. I don't know if I'd start there."

Bruiser mutes his mic and says, "I got it. That's exactly where we start. They all signed disclaimers, right?"

Vanessa hesitantly asks, "Yeah. Why?"

Bruiser turns his mic back on, saying, "How's everyone doing tonight? Anyone on the aisle feeling any different?"

A man's voice in the crowd screams, "My daughter's acne is completely gone! The boils healed!"

"Good start," says Bruiser.

Another voice asks, "What does that prove? I want to see miracles, the miracles we were promised."

Bruiser laughs. "Were you all promised miracles?" There's a series of nods from the audience. Bruiser walks up to the edge of the stage and asks, "And what did you pay for these miracles?"

A voice from the front row yells, "Two hundred dollars!"

Bruiser motions to get a microphone to the guest in the front row and then points at the man, saying, "Two hundred dollars for a miracle, you say. That sounds like a steal, and what may I ask did you expect me to heal for two hundred dollars?"

The man with the mic says, "It's not for me." He looks to the woman sitting next to him and says, "My wife has breast cancer, and she has a double mastectomy scheduled next week."

"I understand why you would be upset. She's a beautiful woman. Tell me, sir, how much have you spent so far on insurance, deductibles, and medication?"

The man says, "Hundreds of thousands, and that doesn't include an attempt at homeopathic remedies."

Bruiser paces the stage. "AND I say, you're a damn fool for expecting a miracle for two-hundred, measly dollars." He points to Neil on the gurney, saying, "My friend Neil here with ALS is worth millions. That's what his family has spent on care and miracle cures. I'm sure his parents would spend twice that just to see him be able to wipe his own ass again. I guarantee they've spent at least a hundred grand on stem cells to no resolve."

Another voice from the crowd states, "Only thirty-two thousand, because we couldn't get any more or we would have."

Bruiser motions to get the woman a mic and says, "Like I said, you're a damn fool, but a lucky one. I hope you brought your whole family, because you'll be the first person, that I know of, to demand a miracle and get one."

The man sits back down.

Bruiser points to the lady in the crowd that answered his question and asks, "You, you're Neil's mother?"

The lady stands and says, "His aunt, Lindy. My sister wanted to come, but she had to work, along with his father, and his younger sister. They all have multiple jobs to cover the financing of his every breath."

Bruiser motions for her to come up on the stage and says, "Lindy, come up here, please."

He gives her a hug and asks her, "Are you familiar with my technique?"

"Only what I saw on the internet. I skipped his therapy and brought him here because his family assumes it's all a computer-animated hoax. I figured, what could it hurt?" she says.

Bruiser laughs and says, "It only stings for a second from what I hear, but we're wasting valuable time. May I?" he asks, as he motions to slap her.

Lindy puts her hands up in defense and says, "I don't have any serious illnesses."

"That you know of Lindy, but I feel like you deserve a miracle just for believing they exist."

"Thank you!" she says, lowering her guard and looking deeply into his eyes without judgment.

Bruiser draws back and slaps her. There's a silence in the building. A silence so quiet, you can hear the breeze crossing the room. Lindy just stands there, not even rubbing her jaw, just looking at Neil. Bruiser turns to Neil and pulls him off his respirator, grabs him by his shirt, lifts him up, and slaps him with every ounce of love he can muster. The slap releases a cloud of shadows that overwhelm Bruiser. He lets go of Neil, dropping him like a stray dog that just bit you. The crowd releases whatever breath they had held from the prior slap, and there is a familiar moan of disgust that comes out with it. Bruiser turns to the crowd, saying, "Don't worry, folks. He'll be righter than rain in about twenty or thirty minutes. Give him a week and I'm sure he'll be a complete asshole like the rest of you mildly functioning bipeds." Bruiser makes eye contact with the little boy in a wheelchair next to Neil and asks, "And who do we have here?"

Vanessa whispers in his ear, "That's Franklin. He's eight, and he has stage three lymphatic cancer."

Bruiser looks down at the bald child with the pale skin and dark circles around his eyes. The boy looks up at him and smiles. Bruiser raises his hand, and a man in the front row pops up yelling, "Don't you touch my son, heathen. I've had enough of this freak show. I've seen the things you do on your show." The man rushes the stage and puts himself between the boy and Bruiser.

Bruiser drops his hand and turns to the man, saying, "Healing is about forgiveness. Forgiving him, yourself, and me. For all we know, you gave him this illness. Can you forgive yourself for that?"

The man looks down at his son and says, "No, never."

Bruiser puts his hand on the man's shoulder and says, "None of us do, sir. You're wasting valuable time, every minute being a handful of people's lives changing forever. The funny thing is, you've already signed a waiver, so I'll humor you at the cost of all the people's health in the back row. We can sit here and wait for my friend Neil with ALS to pop up and dance a jig, or you can sample the medicine for him." Bruiser pushes the man gently out of the way, asking, "Frank, what's your dad's name?"

He responds with a nightmarish wheeze, "Jack. My daddy is Jack."

Bruiser puts his hand out to shake Jack's hand and greets him, "Well, Jack, welcome to The Future of the Left." Jack refrains from touching Bruiser. Unfazed by his reluctance, Bruiser says, "So, you know my past, and you doubt our future here together. Healing is about letting go of the past and releasing the pain that we have made a part of us so that we may become whole and new. I've been blessed with a gift that comes relentlessly through my hand and offers a new beginning for anyone bold enough to step forward." Bruiser puts his hand out again, so Jack can shake it, saying, "My name is Zealand, Zealand T. Dahl, Bruiser was a nickname. What ails you, Jack?"

Jack responds, "I'm fine, and I'm not falling for your scam."

Bruiser laughs and says, "What could it hurt? If it doesn't work, I'll let you punch me in the junk." Jack shakes his head and says nothing. Bruiser decides to flip the script, and asks him, "So, Jack, what were you doing watching Greed?"

Jack mumbles, "Nothing, I wasn't—"

"Speak up, Jack!" demands Bruiser.

Jack folds his arms and says, "My friends at work, the other truckers on the road, they watch it. They're the ones that talked me into coming here tonight." Bruiser looks over at Vanessa and Dick. They both point to their wrists. Bruiser looks down at Franklin, the raggedy pile of bones that he is, dwindling away with every breath, and then looks to his father: a blue-collar worker in a pair of Lee's, wearing a flannel, sporting a twenty-dollar watch with a flip phone attached to his hip.

"Jack, if you judge me and hold me to my past, your son could quite possibly die. There are people that won't be healed and could die because of this conversation. We're being selfish. Everyone has pain and suffering in this life. What's yours?"

Jack nervously rubs his arm, revealing a military tattoo. Bruiser's eyes light up, and as he is starting to talk, Jack shouts out, "I have hemorrhoids, Zealand!"

"Are they bad?" asks Bruiser.

Jack shuffles his trucker hat around and says, "Yeah. I drive a rig and sometimes they itch so bad, I have to pull over to get at 'em and give 'em a good scratch."

"Well, Jack, the audience won't be able to see that illness heal, but I'm sure you'll notice right away. Are you going to miss that tattoo?"

"How so?" asks Jack. "It's the first thing to go. You were a Marine?"

Jack barks out, "Fighting Third!"

"Thank you for your service, but it's time to let go of that pain as well. I'm going to slap you, and when that tattoo disappears, I'm going to slap Franklin, along with the rest of the church here today. For your son's sake, and the other suffering souls, I'm begging you, may I slap you?" asks Bruiser.

Jack nods his head and asks, "If it doesn't work, I get to punch you in the junk?" Bruiser nods and then slaps the ever-loving shit out of Jack. He hits him so hard the six-footer almost stumbles to the ground. Jack recoups, lifts his sleeve, and stares at it. He starts to turn red with rage, looks up at Bruiser, and puts his hand out like he's going to punch him. Bruiser turns and slaps Franklin, before he can get his punch off. Mid swing, Jack's lips pucker up and then turn into a gaping smile. At this point, it's too late to stop, and he lands one across Bruiser's dick, knocking him down to the floor. Security rushes the stage along with a few of Jack's friends. Jack looks down at his arm for his tattoo and shouts, "It's gone." He reaches out to give Bruiser a hand up, as security tries to protect Bruiser, but he waves them away. Jack grabs Bruiser's hand and pulls him to his feet. As Bruiser struggles to stand, he sees a shadow behind Franklin hover over him for a moment and then float away toward the ceiling.

Bruiser looks to Jack and finds him smiling at him. He looks past Jack to catch the first glimpse of an angry mob rushing the stage. A moan comes from Neil, who is lying on the floor next to his gurney, screaming and twitching. Security surrounds Neil to protect him from the enraged crowd and Jack turns around to join them. Bruiser looks down the line of chairs filled with suffering souls, and they're all starting to really freak out. He assesses the lineup of people on stage and decides to slap them all before the audience goes ape shit.

He slaps the remaining severely sick people on stage. The first being a paraplegic and the second a blind man. He slaps the shades off the blind man's face and turns to the remaining subjects. They have no visible ailments; at the same time, they don't seem to have the faculties to resist his violent affections, so he slaps them all in one swoop. The audience forces their way onto the stage to crucify Bruiser for his evangelic shenanigans. They're separating him from the last person in line, an older man sitting in a chair, that hasn't reacted to the ongoing chaos on stage. Bruiser looks through the angry mob to the old man and asks, "Sir, what is it that ails you?" there's no response. *Maybe he's deaf*, thinks Bruiser. He tries to push his way through the mob with security, but they hold their wall until the blind man stands up and takes his first look at the world. The blind man smiles and says, "This is what all the hoopla was about."

Bruiser turns to the paraplegic next to him and offers him a hand out of his chair, and the crowd watches as the once physically humbled soul gets out of his chair and takes his first steps. As they witness something like the first steps of a newborn fawn, Bruiser slips through to the incoherent man, slaps the dim look off his face, and then sneaks off the stage, avoiding the mob of people coming for his head, and stops next to Vanessa and Dick.

"What are you doing?" asks Vanessa.

"Half time shots," he says as he places his hand in hers, so that she can feel the shaking that's begging to be healed by the spirits.

"What are you going to do with the last half hour?" asks Dick.

"Clear the stage and line up anyone left, so that I can heal them," he says.

"Where did that speech come from?" asks Dick.

Bruiser lights a cigarette and says, "It was just there after Vanessa slapped me."

Bruiser turns to her and asks, "How are you by the way?" Vanessa stares at him without a response. "Perfect," he says, walking away from them backwards.

Vanessa watches Bruiser scamper off and asks Dick, "So, that's Bruiser?"

"Zealand T. Dahl, apparently," says Dick.

"I just don't get how someone with so much darkness, could bring in so much light to this place," says Vanessa.

"Let me know when you figure him out," Dick says, staring over at Neil and the wall of security that's guarding the boy from the enraged crowd that's fighting to get to Bruiser; whether it's for healing or persecution. A stern chiseled boy, resembling a fitness model, is birthed from the pile of security, and there's a new noise that takes over the church that's made from the sound of people's jaws dropping.

Lindy jumps up and says, "Neil, my baby!"

From deep in the crowd we hear, "That's not him. They made a switch. That feeble boy is in the back somewhere! I want my money back! This is God's house, and we've welcomed Satan!"

Vanessa taps her headset and asks, "Bruiser, where are you? The crowd has turned." Bruiser doesn't respond. "Can you handle this, Dick?"

Dick turns to Vanessa and asks, "The crowd, or do you want me to go get Bruiser?"

"Start with the crowd," she says.

While Dick is looking for a microphone, he gets knocked over by security pushing Neil off stage. Neil puts his hand out, offering Dick a way off the floor. And as Neil pulls him to his feet, Dick gets stuck, staring into his electric blue eyes.

"Neil? Welcome back," says Dick, who won't stop shaking his hand nervously, dumbfounded by Neil's presence.

Vanessa grabs Neil's bicep and says, "He's ripped head to toe, and the blonde hair."

Dick looks at Vanessa and says, "It's amazing, isn't it? He's just like Tanner."

Neil fights Dick's embrace and goes to hug Vanessa asking, "Hey, what's your name?"

"Va … va … Vanessa," she stammers. "Amazing, you're absolutely amazing."

Dick pulls Less over and points at Neil and Vanessa.

Less hands Vanessa a microphone.

"So, what's it like?" she asks. "Waking up to this madness. Going from a useless pile of protein to a, well, let's be honest, stunning, young, exemplary form."

Vanessa points the mic at Neil, and he grabs her hand, saying, "I guess you could say it's like waking up from a really long nightmare. It makes me wonder if that deal I made with the devil was real, and if he's going to hold me to it."

"All right, any plans for the future?" she asks.

"Haven't really had any time to think about it. I mean, I spent most of my days … all my days watching TV. I guess I'd like to see if I can make it inside the box," says Neil staring at her with a lusting glimmer in his eyes.

"Really, no plans to help other children with Lou Gehrig's Disease?" she asks.

"If I'm entertaining them while they lie there, drooling on themselves, that would be helping. But clearly, Zealand is the only one that can truly help any of us."

Dick grabs the microphone from Vanessa and asks him, "So, Neil, what's on your bucket list?"

Neil says, "I just want to get money and fuck bitches."

Bruiser pops up behind them smoking a cigarette and says, "Well said, my friend, well said."

Neil turns around, grabs Bruiser's hands, and drops to his knees. He's trying to talk but can't make it past crying and stuttering.

"You think he's going to end up like Tanner?" asks Dick.

Bruiser shrugs and says, "I hope so. Tanner's a good kid that finally caught a break."

Bruiser pulls Neil to his feet, and as Neil tries to catch his breath, he says to Bruiser, "I owe you one, man."

Bruiser laughs and says, "You want to pay me back, help me clear the stage. Dick, can you get control over the crowd? This is ridiculous." Bruiser pulls Neil out onto the stage with him, and they take the podium as the stage is being cleared. "This is my new friend, Neil. You guys met him earlier. He was melting away on that gurney, couldn't even breathe on his own, and now look at him, he's a specimen of perfection. I don't care if you like me or if you trust me. I can see how you think there was a switch, and that this whole thing is to get your hard-earned dollars. I want to give you your money back and heal you; all of you. I know that you are all here because of one thing — fear. Fear of spending the rest of your life in pain. Fear of your daughter never going to college or your son never having a family of his own. Fear that this whole life was just about pain and suffering. Fear that we all are slaves to something we'll never understand, and that there truly is no freedom for us in this life. You might be right, but I guarantee you my new friend, Neil, here is going to leave this church today and go live his life to the fullest."

Jack walks up to Bruiser and stands next to him with his brand-new son in hand, crying he's so happy. Franklin has a full head of hair and a vibrant smile. His eyes are wide open and shining. He pulls at his father's pant leg, and Jack picks him up and kisses him all over his face as more tears burst from his eyeballs.

What's left of the audience submits, forming a line at the base of the stage, and the first person to walk on stage is a heavy set, balding man in his late thirties. Bruiser offers his right hand for a shake and gets a limp sweaty connection from him.

Bruiser asks him, "What can we do for you today, friend?"

He hears the man's thoughts in a whisper, *I'm a thirty-eight-year-old man and all I do is jerk off in front of the computer. It's miserable, especially since I'm married. It would have been cheaper to stay single and jerk off. Then I'd have two less people that hate me.*

"Excuse me?" asks Bruiser.

"My name's Ted. I have prostate cancer. I don't want to lose my dick! I want to use it to make my wife happy!" he says.

"Well, Ted, are you ready to be happy?" asks Bruiser.

Ted tries to smile and says, "What could it hurt, right?" Still holding Ted's hand, Bruiser ravages his face with his left hand. He hits him so hard that he believes Ted is going to cry, but he doesn't, he just turns to walk away.

As Ted is trying to leave the stage, Bruiser insists, "Ted, stay up here with us and celebrate your new life."

The next person to approach the stage is a woman in her late thirties. She is very attractive, but she has a bad case of resting bitch face; it matches the power suit she's wearing. She walks up to Bruiser with her hands grasping one another behind her back, offers him a stern handshake, and introduces herself, "Smith, Jennifer Smith, and I'm here because—"

Bruiser interjects, "It doesn't matter anymore."

She looks away from him and asks, "But how can you fix me if you don't know what's wrong?"

Bruiser replies, "This doesn't work like your analytical mind wants it to work. All I know at this point is that me slapping you is like rebooting a computer that runs slow and drags. Are you in?"

Jennifer takes her glasses off and asks him, "Can you explain it to me after you hit me?"

Bruiser grabs her hand and states, "I will, Jennifer. I will." He reaches back, and she puts her chin out. He slaps her and she collapses to the ground in tears. Jennifer cries what's left of her broken heart out and then smiles. Bruiser puts out his hand to lift her up and bring her to her feet. He takes her glasses from her and throws them off the stage, asking, "You suffered a heart attack recently?"

"Yes?" she replies as she tries to focus on his face.

"Your father; he was a horrible man. You watched your mother kill him," he says.

"Yes," she says and starts crying again.

"It made you hard and calloused. You've protected your heart from all people, the good and the bad. You're alone and you want a family, but you're a scared child. At the same time, you have the strength and ferocity of a lion. Sadly, that's what you needed to obtain the status you have in life, but it's protected you from love as well. Forget about all that and know now, this new beginning will draw in good people to love and protect you."

She stops crying and gives Bruiser a hug, collapsing in his arms, saying, "Thank you!" She releases him, hands him her card, and walks off the stage.

"NEXT!" yells Bruiser. There's a furry, old man fighting with the stairs to come see him. A middle-aged lady jumps out of her seat to help him. Bruiser walks over to the elderly man and asks him, "Where do we start?"

His nurse, the lady that helped the man on stage, responds, "Well, he has dementia, and he's one of the angry ones."

The old man looks up at Bruiser with a blank look in his eyes, almost with the rage of a demon, that's buried under the innocence of a child. Bruiser hears his thoughts, *I sit every day at the bus stop eating lunch, waiting for her, but she never shows. Where is my Rose?* The man starts crying and then clenches his fist.

Bruiser raises his hand as if to slap the old man's face lightly The old man grabs Bruiser's wrist and draws back like he's going to punch Bruiser. "Sir, I'm going to need you to relax. I can't find your Rose, but I can find you and bring you back to this world." The man hears her name and releases Bruiser's wrist. Bruiser's only reaction is to slap him as hard as he can. He knocks the old dude's dentures out of his mouth and across the stage. The old man collapses to the ground on his back and his eyes roll back in his head. "Shit!" says Bruiser nervously as he nudges the old dude, getting no response.

Vanessa chimes in, "What's going on, Bruiser?"

"I think I killed the old dude," he says.

There's a series of moans from the crowd.

"Your mic's on Bruiser. And is that possible? Just keep the line moving. We'll throw him on the gurney," says Vanessa.

"So, healing comes in many forms. My friend here—"

The old man's nurse jumps in, "Randall."

Bruiser chimes back in, "Randy had been suffering a long time from dementia. The last thing I saw when I slapped him, was an old man sitting at a bus stop every day, eating lunch by himself, and waiting for his deceased wife, Rose, to come home."

Randall's nurse nods her head and says, "The constant confusion, mixed with disappointment, had turned to anger and fear."

"There are better places than this life and I hope that Randall finds his Rose in the next one. So, if we could, I'd like to keep the line moving and continue the healing." Bruiser turns to Randall's nurse and says, "I apologize for the surprise unemployment. Do you mind if I slap you?"

"He didn't have any family, and he left everything to me. So, thank you, I guess. You did us both a favor." She pulls Bruiser down to her level and gives him a kiss on the cheek, saying, "I'm finally returning to Barcelona." She smiles and turns her cheek towards him. Bruiser slaps her and returns to the line of people.

There's a girl standing in front of him barefoot, wearing dirty pink sweats and a wife beater with a Pegasus on it. She has an asymmetrical face that looks as if it were melting. The girl smiles at him with the remnants of a soul that's been devoured by darkness. Bruiser puts his hand out, helping her up the step, and as he holds her hand silently, he is brought to his knees by the pain she's accrued in this lifetime. He asks her, "I assume you're ready to be relieved of your demons?" Bruiser lets go of her hand, turns her head to the right, and slaps her. As he does, a gang of shadows are propelled from their cage and released into the room where they gather by the ceiling, forming a cumulus nimbus with the rest of the lost souls that can only be witnessed by him.

Sometime shortly after he 'killed' Randy, what was left of the crowd submitted or left, moving the line at a faster pace. Bruiser slaps his last guest and as he walks off the stage, he sees Randy's nurse holding Randy's hand. Bruiser walks up to the gurney and the old man pops up gasping for air. It appears as if he's inflating from the gasp of air: his skin thickens, his muscle tone defines, his spine straightens, and then his eyes light up. Bruiser smiles and says, "Randy, great to have you back. To what do we owe the pleasure?"

Randy smiles, revealing a mouthful of his own teeth, and says, "It's a long story. I saw Rose while I was out, and she didn't miss me. It's hard to explain, but I was kind of a jerk to her when she was alive, and I was punishing myself for abusing her. I finally had the chance to be forgiven. Thank you for that. I'm not done with this life, and I'd like to enjoy the rest of it with you, Theresa."

"I really didn't want to go to Spain alone," says Theresa. She leans in and gives Randall a long-awaited kiss. The couple pull away from one another and stare at Bruiser in awe.

While Bruiser soaks up his praise, uncomfortably, only wanting to run away and digest the moment with a bottle, the girl with the Pegasus wife beater walks up to him, saying, "I'd like to thank you."

Bruiser is speechless as the girl is now beautiful, shining light in her purest form. He puts his hands on her face. "Just don't turn into an asshole, Kristen, and we'll call it even."

She smiles and says, "I want to come with you."

Bruiser feels a tap on his shoulder, and he turns to find Vanessa staring up at him with the same look in her eyes as Randy, Theresa, and Kristen. Vanessa grabs him by the arm and drags him through the venue, saying, "Walk with me!"

Bruiser turns back to Kristen as he is being pulled away and motions with his head to follow him. Bruiser responds to Vanessa naively, asking, "What's up?"

Vanessa stops and faces him towards her. "I thought you were just some scumbag that got his kicks driving around Atlanta, ruining young girls, like that one," pointing down the hallway at Kristen. "It started off rough, way too much ego, but when the crowd turned on you, it was a solid kick in the nuts."

"More like a punch," he says.

"Either way, it really humbled you," she says as she drags him through the load-out toward the bus.

He looks back for Kristen, but she's out of sight. "It all came together. It always does," he says and stumbles almost falling.

Vanessa catches him and asks, "Are you okay?"

"Yeah, I think. It's a lot to process at one time: visions, voices, and shadows," he says, lighting a cigarette.

"What's it like," she asks as she takes the opportunity to stare him down while he plays with his slow death, "being able to see through people?"

"It's a lot, processing all that pain, feeling it as if it were my own. I get these flashes of their lives and they whisper to me. I hear them talking in a child's voice. And then there's the shadows."

"What about that mongoloid chick that turned out to be smoking hot?" asks Vanessa, enamored with Bruiser's presence.

"Kristen?" he asks, looking back at the parking lot for her. "That one was hard to watch. She had a lot of shadows. I thought I was just slapping away people's sickness, but I get flashes of their pain and I can feel their suffering."

"Just make sure you're not holding on to it," says Vanessa, smiling with a hint of concern in her eyes.

They stop in front of the bus and Bruiser states, "I'll be fine. You wanna' come in and get high?"

"I've got to shut the show down, Bruiser," she says as she turns from him, almost as if she intended to drop him off at the bus and leave him in solitude with his newly acquired demons.

The door to the bus opens and Bruiser greets the driver, "How we doing, Chuck?"

Chuck responds, "Excellent, sir, another beautiful day,"

Bruiser grabs Vanessa's hand and tries to pull her on the bus, asking her, "You scared?"

Vanessa breaks free from his grasp and says, "Definitely. What did you hear when you slapped me?"

Bruiser walks up the stairs to the bus backwards, waving her in with his hands, summoning her for a meeting with herself based on a truth unbeknownst to her. She follows him onto the bus, still mesmerized by his presence, and he grabs her hand, pulling her back to his office, saying, "There was a dark cloud gathering in the building tonight. Did you see it?"

"Inside the building?" she asks dumbfounded.

"Yeah," he says.

Vanessa stares oddly at Bruiser, as he rushes directly to his suitcase and dives into it. She realizes what she just signed up for and says, "We might need to concentrate on cutting back on your daily regimen of substance exploration."

Bruiser turns on some music and starts rolling a joint, saying, "But, that's where I find the truth, and I don't think I can process all their shadows without it."

"We need to work on that. Tell me about the girl," she begs.

Bruiser's presence recedes and he says, "Kristen, the inbred mongoloid that was raped by her siblings, father, uncles, and how they used to whore her out as a child. I felt all of that and looked into her eye, the good one, not the one that looked like a runny yolk, and felt a depth of pain that made me feel like I'd had an easy life."

Vanessa starts choking on smoke and reality. "Fuck … cough … that's … cough, cough … that's messed up."

Bruiser hands Vanessa a water bottle and says, "Yeah, I really didn't want to believe that anything like that existed in this world."

"What about me? What did you see when you slapped me?" she asks as she puts her hand on his thigh.

He flinches with her embrace, as it pulls him back in the room, and he says, "Honestly, I don't remember. As soon as your hand hit me, I was gone."

"Stop lying," says Vanessa as she takes a swig off her water and looks around the room, saying, "I'm not ready for you to see inside me anyway, but I know you saw something. Where'd you dig that name up from anyway?"

"You like it?" he asks, locked onto her, looking for an honest reaction.

Vanessa looks down at her hands, saying, "Yeah, Beau Derrick would've been a good laugh, as far as the new world's regards towards you."

"Beau regards," he says.

"You're stoopid, but you're cute," she says coyly.

Bruiser, filled with a new confidence, says, "You're the cute one," as he gets lost in her.

Vanessa shifts gears quickly to avoid the road they're headed down and says, "Zealand T. Dahl. I like it. I don't know what I'd call myself if I had your position in life." She gets stuck in his gaze for a moment and regroups, asking, "Where'd it come from though? What's the T stand for?"

"The T stands for Tenderoni."

"Stop! I'm getting out of here before this gets messy," she says as she starts to stand up.

He grabs the bottom of her shirt and retains her presence for another moment. "When you slapped me, I went back to this day where everything was fucked, as always, and I was getting baked on the couch at my mom's place. There were beer bottles all over the coffee table, and I was eating wasabi peas. I had this moment of clarity and tossed five peas in a row in different bottles, effortlessly from the couch. It was like the planets aligned; everything fell into place, and that name just appeared for what I thought was no reason."

"You're truly the most bizarre person I've ever met. Tell me more about Kristen," she says.

"That's her business."

"C'mon!" she begs.

"Do you really want to know?" he asks.

"Probably not. Let me ask you this? Having seen all of that and knowing what she'd been through…" She scoots closer to Bruiser, turns the joint around, and puts it in her mouth. She blows a shotgun into his face in a seductive manner and says, "…and seeing that you've turned her into a beautiful young girl—" Bruiser starts coughing. "Would you sleep with her?"

Bruiser's coughing escalates into an attack at the thought, and he pushes himself away from her. She hands him her water bottle, and he pushes it away, mumbling, "Beeeeer." Vanessa goes to grab him a beer from the fridge and comes back with a six-pack and a bottle of whiskey. As he stops coughing, he blurts out, "That's so fucked up. You're into girls. Would you hit it?"

"She was ridiculously gorgeous after you slapped her." Vanessa pours two shots, raises her glass, and returns to his gaze for a moment. She regroups and says, "To the Future of the Left."

They take the shot and Bruiser says, staring into her eyes, looking for the first sign of jealousy, "She was. She wants to jump on the bus with us."

"Well, I guess we'll find out. But knowing who she was and what she'd been through, there's no way, right." Vanessa stops and looks into his eyes for the truth.

He smirks and asks her, "Isn't this all about forgiveness and forgetting that person, leaving them in the shadows of the past?"

"That's what I figured. You're into some weird shit, huh?"

Bruiser crosses his arms and says, "It's all love. I might have done her before I slapped her." Vanessa starts laughing and Bruiser sticks his finger in her mouth, gagging her playfully. She pushes his hand away and he returns to her gaze, saying, "I'm sure you've done some weird shit before; jerked off your brother, fingered the cat's butt, or watched your mom undress with some weird thoughts in your head." Vanessa pushes him out of the booth, stands up and steps on him on her way to the door. "Vanessa, come back here. I'm just fucking with you," he says, pulling at her.

"My brother's dead. He overdosed, and I miss the shit out of him," she says as her face starts leaking.

"I'm sorry. Come here. Tell me about your brother."

"He was beautiful, a lot like you," she says, hitting the joint and staring at the wall blankly. "Seriously, he was sensitive, powerful, and angry."

"That's a tough life. You couldn't help him?" he asks.

"I was too busy playing with my ex, and he slipped through my fingers," she says, pulling up a picture of her brother on her tablet.

Bruiser leans into her and asks, "Your ex, the last guy you slept with?"

Vanessa laughs and says, "Yeah, the one I said was a lot like you too."

Bruiser lights up another joint, and asks, "Oh, yeah?"

Vanessa stares at Bruiser and says, "Yeah, a real d-bag."

Bruiser laughs and says, "I bet."

Vanessa takes the joint from him and says, "He was amazing, and he knew it, just like my brother. He was bored with this life, and he loved me with his whole heart. It was like having my brother but being able to fuck him. I lost them both at the same time. My brother OD'd, and I pushed Armand away."

"Armand?" laughs Bruiser.

"Yeah, Armand. I used my brother's death to attack him. He'd been cheating on me the whole time we were together. He couldn't say no to a beautiful girl. It was like the minute he did, his ego told him, 'You're old and washed up.' Plus, he would get angry when he was drunk. You could hear his mother in there, screaming at him, and his only defense was violence. I took a couple solid punches from that guy. He sure could make me cum, though. Sometimes, I wasn't sure if it was an orgasm or if I was having a seizure."

Bruiser's ego is thwarted by the challenge. "He was too much like your brother, so you pushed him away because the sight of him was a constant reminder?"

"Exactly. What about you?" she asks.

Bruiser hits the joint a couple times and asks her, "Who was the last guy I slept with?"

Bruiser blows Vanessa a shotgun.

"Yeah, sure," she says, coughing.

"I've never fucked a dude, just haven't met the right guy, I guess," he laughs. "I did spoon a guy once. He broke into my house."

"Go on."

"I was with this chick for a minute. She lived a block or two from me. We had the same last name; it was weird. She was a hairdresser, covered in bad tattoos, loved cocaine, smoking hot, and loved it in the pooper. Anyway, we were at this bar, literally next to my house. I just got off work, and we're getting all sorts of fucked up. We get up to leave and this cat with baby dreadlocks stops me and says, 'You should fuck her. I'm gonna' buy you a shot.' I reply, 'I'm going to fuck her, and I'll buy you a shot.' So, I take her next door, fuck her, and this was my favorite thing about her, she always wanted to leave right after, so that she could sleep in her bed with her dog."

"Perfect," laughs Vanessa.

"So, I'm walking her home, like the gentleman that I am, and we walk past that dude with the dreadlocks in the parking lot of the bar, talking to himself. He's like, 'Hat, get off my head. I'm so tired of you fucking with me. Stay on my head, that's your only job.' We ignore him clearly, continue walking, and then we hear this thud: dude's pin-balling into cars, telephone poles, and knocking over pots on stoops, trying to follow us. I'm not the type of guy to get worked up, especially in my neighborhood. Anyway, I drop her off, kiss her, smack her butt, and decide to take the bike path back. As soon as I get home and shut the door, I hear a knock. At this point it's four-thirty, maybe five. It's my downstairs neighbor and he wants to drink a beer on the porch. My reply is, why not? I have to be up in three hours, might as well. So, we're standing out in front of the building smoking, drinking, and dude walks by us."

Vanessa blurts out, "What!"

"Yeah, bumps into my car and keeps going. I don't think anything of it, you know. Guy's all zombied out on pills — I assume."

"Sure," she says, putting her hand on his.

"It's six, at this point. I walk upstairs, strip down buck naked and climb into bed … and … there's a body in my bed!"

"No!" she squeals.

"And me being me, I think it's another beautiful girl that snuck in to take advantage of me," he says snidely.

Vanessa's eyes light up and she agrees, "Of course!"

Bruiser picks her up and puts Vanessa back on his lap, simulating a good spoon session, saying, "So, I snuggle up, put my hand on her leg." He puts his hand on Vanessa's inner thigh as he says, "Then her stomach." He continues to move his hand with the story. "Then her …" Bruiser grabs Vanessa's boob, and she paws it off immediately. "Wait, none of my girls are A's. I move frantically to her face," he says, smothering Vanessa with his hand. "Then her hair. And that's when it hits me."

Vanessa knocks over her beer, saying, "Baby Dreadlocks!"

Bruiser grabs the spilled beer and says, "None of my girls have dreadlocks. I jump up, grab my junk, and hit the light switch!"

Vanessa turns sideways, so she can see his face, and asks him, "What did you do? Did you call the cops?"

Bruiser laughs and says, "That's funny, most people's first question when I tell that story is, 'Did you kill him?' Being in Georgia, I could have. My favorite is, 'Did you fuck him?' My response being, 'No,' and hearing, 'Oh, that's a terrible story. I would love to have some stranger sneak into my bed. I would teach that little robber a lesson.'"

Vanessa looks at Bruiser and asks, "So, how did he get in your place?"

Bruiser sticks his beer and says, "That's the fucked-up part. I lived on the top floor. It's three flights up and you have to go around back. And the only way in is through the bathroom window, which I generally leave open. He would have had to climb up three flights of porches, through the window, and into my bedroom. And there is no way that guy knew I lived there."

Vanessa laughs and asks, "So, what did you do?"

"I woke him up and told him, 'You have to get the fuck out of my house!' He said, 'Yeah, yeah, yeah,' and then went back to sleep. So, I started clapping, woke him up — again. I got him to the stairs and then pushed him down the landing." Vanessa leans in and gives Bruiser a kiss, a long one.

"What's that for?" he asks.

Vanessa responds, "For not killing him or fucking him."

Bruiser straightens up and says, "I could have, I guess. I'm just not that guy. The funny part is, I ran into him at the pub six months later, and the first thing he said was, 'Thanks for not killing me.' I always remind him that I was the big spoon and tell him not to forget it. Apparently, he was going through a lot at the time. He had lost both his parents in two months' time."

Vanessa pulls her shirt off and attacks him, saying, "That's what makes you a good person, and it's probably how you ended up here." He is overwhelmed at this point, figuring it would have taken months on the road to get her naked. He sits up and starts making out with her frantically. She takes his shirt off and then rips off his bandage, looking for his hole, asking, "Where did it go?"

He shrugs and mutters, "Perfect."

She responds, asking him, "What?"

"Your tits are perfect. They're a handful, but it's how you wear them, confidently with no bra, that does it for me." He lifts her onto the desk and groans as the desk lowers and the parallel couches slide over the tabletop forming a bed at the same time, knocking over the beers, flipping his briefcase, disemboweling it, and sending a vast selection of drugs all over the bus. He pulls at her jeans, trying to find a quick release button, only to be defeated by her button fly.

"I thought you would have mastered the five-o-one by now," she says, laughing at his defeat.

Emasculated, he slides his hand in her pants looking for the entrance to her theme park, and hits the speed bump at the front gate, saying, "That's nice."

She moans deeply as it's the first time in years she's been touched by a man; and as a picture of her girlfriend pops up into her head, she says, "No dicks on the road!" She panics at the reality of the situation and tries to run away with his hand trapped in her pants. She drags him around the bus while he tries to break free.

Still attached to her, he pulls her on top of him and returns to kissing her, and then stops and says, "I'm not a Dick. I'm a Bruiser. Is this because of your girlfriend?"

She dismounts his face and pushes him away, saying, "No. I mean yes, but no." In fear that she has made a huge mistake, she pops her button fly, releasing his hand. "What am I doing? How many girls have you fucked with that story?" Bruiser gets his phone out and starts banging on it like a calculator. Vanessa grabs her shirt and says, "You're just like him. I'm such a glory whore. I can't do this. Do you know how much it costs to get your gold star back?"

Bruiser buckles his belt and asks, "Wait, what?"

Vanessa escapes to her digital assistant and says, "My rejuvagination, revagavirgination, do you have any idea what a procedure like that costs?"

Bruiser lights a cigarette and replies, "Five grand."

She puts her shirt on and screams, "Twenty-thousand dollars, American!"

"So, you're worried your girlfriend will notice?" he asks with his head turned sideways.

"Definitely!" she barks.

He puts his hands on his hips and says, "Huh, I always thought you girls were more accepting."

Vanessa turns to open the door, stops, and says, "It was a present, like a wedding ring."

"Well, you're definitely a hundred times more beautiful than any diamond I've ever had on my finger," he says and laughs quaintly.

She laughs and says, "You would have some smooth shit like that to say. Look, I'm not a disposable hoe. You can't just leave me on the side of the road when you're done fucking me. Could you spend the rest of your life with one woman?"

He laughs and says, "I'm not gonna' lie to you. I have ADD when it comes to girls. I'm good at the beginning of relationships, but I can't move forward into anything serious. I've done it a couple of times and it always ends with me coming really close to catching an assault charge. I was raised by a child that had been abused by an alcoholic. The result was emotional instability with a subconscious aggression towards women that comes from a fear of being hurt by an emotionally unstable woman."

"So, you've thought about it?" she asks.

"When I feel trapped, I can't breathe. I won't ever put myself or anyone in that position again."

Vanessa opens his door and says, "Speaking of which, I'd like to get your mom on the show tomorrow. Can you make that happen?"

"She'd be more receptive to your feminine ways, but I'll try," he says, looking down at his feet.

"I'm gonna' get out of here and go get some work done," she says, retreating from the inevitable. "We need to keep this professional."

"Whatever works for you, boss," he says as she walks away.

Vanessa tries to get off the bus as fast as possible and bumps into Dick. Dick grabs her arm lightly and asks, "Hey, where are you going?"

She responds, "To get this shit show packed up and ready to go!"

"I've got everything in motion with the crew. Hang out and have a beer. I'd like to get in a three-way with you and Bruiser," says Dick.

She laughs and says, "I bet you would."

"So that we can talk about the show," he says laughingly. "What'd you think?"

"I think it's going to be one hell of a ride, Dick."

Bruiser pops out of the bus, saying, "But Seriously, V, I think I could love … Dick, what's up, buddy?"

"He definitely loves him some dick. Great show, bub. How you doin'?" asks Dick.

"Nauseated. Nothing a good buzz can't fix."

"How's your hole?" asks Dick. Bruiser lifts his shirt. "Nice, I was worried about you for a second."

Bruiser lights a joint and hands it to Dick.

Vanessa steps back from the two and says, "I'd love to stay and bro down with you two, but I want to make sure we get all packed up and on the road." She turns to walk away and bumps into Leslie and Less.

"Where you headed, Ness?" asks Leslie.

"I've got a lot to take care of," says Vanessa. She turns to Bruiser and asks him, "When do you want to leave, oh Great One? Tonight, or in the morning?"

Bruiser looks down his crew in question, and Dick explains, "We can leave now, drive through the night, and have all day to mess around in Charlotte, or—"

Bruiser hits the joint and asks, "How long a drive is it?"

"Seven, roughly. How much time do you want with your mom?" asks Dick.

"As little as possible. I need some time to process what just happened. You guys wanna' hang out and drink a couple?"

Dick laughs heartily and says, "A couple. The only time I've seen you drink a couple was in your sleep."

"Why were you watching me sleep?" ask Bruiser dryly.

"Look, I'd love to hang," says Vanessa, "but I've got a full night ahead of me, shutting everything down." She looks at the twins and asks them, "You two good?"

"Yeah, boss, everything looked great," says Less.

"Good. Get some rest. We have a full day tomorrow," says Vanessa, walking off.

"What's her deal?" asks Less. "Did you try to fuck her?"

"Quite the opposite. We were just talking about her crush-proof box, and she ran off," says Bruiser.

Vanessa stops and laughs. She turns around, walking back towards the bus and says, "Actually, we were talking about Bruiser's love of dick."

"I do love me some Dick," says Bruiser, climbing back on the bus, looking for distractions.

"You all right, Vanessa?" asks Dick. "He can be a lot."

"Agreed. Less, can you check into something for me?"

"What's that, boss?" asks Less.

"Can you get a quote on a rescrotification for Bruiser. He said, between pissing and sitting on his balls all the time, he was due for a lift." She walks off and is immediately back on her tablet.

"That's gonna' be a mess!" says Leslie. "You think Bruiser knows she's a lesbian?"

"Vanessa?" asks Less. "It wouldn't matter anyway; I don't think he believes in those mythical creatures."

Kid, You'll Move Mountains

Bruiser pops back out of the bus, armed to the teeth with distractions, asking, "Who wants a beer?"

Leslie bows down in front of Bruiser and says, "I'm in, Oh Great One."

Bruiser sets up some chairs, and everyone sits down except for Dick. He leans over Bruiser with a stern demeanor, asking, "You tried to fuck her, didn't you? I told you to leave it alone."

Bruiser slides back into his folding chair and looks up at Dick with a disgruntled smirk, saying, "She jumped me and then got all weird."

Leslie cracks her beer, smiles, and looks down the drinking line at Bruiser, saying, "Great show tonight."

"You think?" he asks.

"From what I saw," says Leslie. "You could drop the ego, and you'd embrace way more people."

"Bruiser, too much ego — never," laughs Dick.

Bruiser stands up confronting his friends and says, "All that matters is that everyone was healed, right?"

Less looks up from his phone and mutters, "Everyone that stayed."

"Their loss," says Bruiser defensively.

Less says sternly, "We still have to sell it, if we want to reach the masses."

Bruiser starts pacing and asks, "Doesn't it sell itself?"

Dick jumps in, saying, "Let's just say it wasn't real, and you had no superpowers. What kind of show would it be?"

Leslie sets her beer down and stands up, joining Bruiser, saying, "Your 'poem' at the beginning was beautiful, but we're in bumble-fuck Alabama. They don't get it. The show was an absolute mess, and I wouldn't expect anything less from you. I'm sure it'll hit hard in LA, but you're being selfish and expecting them to bow at your feet, when it should be the other way around."

Bruiser gets on his knees and asks, "I should bow at their feet? They're the same people that were poking JC in the gut with a spear when he was hanging from the cross."

Bruiser sprawls out on the concrete and Leslie steps over him, saying, "And that's where you'll be if you don't get your shit together and drop the ego. You need to be blander and more palatable if you want to change this world for the better."

Bruiser lights another joint and looks up to Dick for support, asking, "What do you think, Dick?"

Dick takes the joint from Bruiser. "Honestly, she's right. You can't run around screaming, 'I'm the fucking Messiah. Submit, and I will save you from eternal suffering.'"

Bruiser smashes his fist into his hand, growling, "I'm trying to help them. They think I'm a huckster, just passing through to pocket their hard-earned credits."

Dick picks Bruiser up off the ground and says, "It's hard for me to believe it, and I'm your best friend. Your past is confusing. On top of that, they're not ready to be free. You're forcing a major change on them. We're asking for something more relaxed, like a Christian evangelist or Zen healer, maybe."

Bruiser laughs. "Sounds terrible. I'm neither one of those, Dick. I'm kind of a scumbag and definitely a misogynist, right?"

Less looks at Bruiser and says, "This is true, but you're starting over, and you have the chance to change everything, including your name, which we like. Where did that come from?"

Bruiser leans over Less with his hands on his armrest, stares him in the eyes, and says, "When I hit the floor of the bus after Vanessa slapped me, I saw a wizard that delved in the black arts, and then I found an ancient book floating in another dimension."

"Seriously, Bruiser?" asks Dick.

"I think he is, Dick," says Less.

"I am!" Bruiser has a good laugh and hands out some more beers, saying, "You know me, bro. I'm gonna' do whatever I want, and it'll go wherever it goes. As far as a persona, I'll start working on a mask to cover my deceptive face."

"Good luck with that," laughs Leslie.

"What about this? I keep the hair, shave the beard, throw on a suit, and a pair of contacts that make my eyes look like a reptile?"

Leslie laughs and says, "Keep working on it."

Less stands up and points to the shadows of the parking lot, asking, "What's that?"

"Kristen!" Bruiser shouts out.

"Yeah, how'd you know my name though?" she asks as she walks up to the group.

"I heard people screaming it at you when I slapped you," says Bruiser as he offers her a beer, asking, "You old enough to drink?"

190

She snatches it out of his hand and says, "Not even close."

Bruiser offers her a seat, saying, "Fair enough. What's going on?"

She declines his offer, drops to her knees, and paws at Bruiser's ego, pleading, "I know you've already done more for me than anyone else could but … I need a favor."

Leslie stands up nervously, asking, "All right, Less, let's see if we can polish this turd. You want to help me load the footage?"

Less, ogling over Kristen, says, "I'm good. I'm gonna' drink a beer or six with the new Messiah."

Bruiser pulls Kristen to her feet and asks, "What is it?"

She points off into the shadows of the parking lot at the outline of two girls approaching them and says, "My sisters need you. We don't have any money to pay you, but we'll spread the word and well, shit, whatever else you want honestly." She stares at him with that look; the one that says everything he wants to hear.

Bruiser blindly responds, "Sure. Anything for a fan."

Kristen whistles and her sisters start their trek toward clarity. As they approach, it appears as if they are walking with their arms around each other. They hit the light, startling the boys to the point that their beers fall out of their mouths and hands. Kristen dauntingly introduces them. "They're stuck together. Meet my older sister … s. Kara, Julie, this is Zealand."

"This should be interesting," states Dick.

The girls approach him clumsily as they're attached at the hip, sharing the same two legs, and then split off awkwardly just under the shoulders. They're wearing rags that have been duct-taped and patched together to fit their unique form.

They say together, "Hi, Bruiser!"

He stutters at their sight, not that he's disgusted, but more like bewildered by how he thinks this is going to turn out. "Zealand, whatever, you're familiar with the show?"

"The internet was all we had in the walk-in closet we were locked in most of our days," say Kara and Julie together. They go in for a hug and say, "You're our favorite."

He accepts, awkwardly patting them on their backs and says, "Thanks, but I don't know if I can help you girls."

Kara pleads, "Look at what you did with Kristen. She's amazing."

Julie begs him, "You have to try."

Bruiser hands them beers, and only Kara accepts, saying, "Julie's not much of a drinker."

Julie defends herself, saying, "We share a liver, so I let her do all the work."

"Fair enough," says Bruiser.

"Well, Zealand, what do you think?" asks Dick.

"I think we're going to get really fucked up and figure this one out. Less, can you grab some chairs for the girls."

"We can sit on the cooler," says Julie.

Chairs are complicated," says Kara.

"Less, go grab some more drugs out of my office and your camera," says Bruiser.

"Yes, your Excellency. Your will, my hand," says Less sarcastically.

"I love that he finds humor in my situation," says Bruiser as he returns his gaze to the oddity in front of him, jesting, "So … what seems to be the problem?"

"They're tired of each other," says Kristen.

"I couldn't imagine," says Bruiser.

"We want to be beautiful — like her," they say, pointing at Kristen.

Bruiser scratches his head and says, "I can't promise you beauty. I can't even promise you a separation. I can't—"

"You can. I believe in you, Zealand," says Kristen as Less walks off the bus with his arms full. He has another chair, more beer, a video camera, a longsword, and his twin in tow. Less leaves Leslie standing in the doorway of the bus, contemplating if she wants to witness the upcoming events.

"What are you thinking, Less?" asks Bruiser.

"Come on, it's right there," Less says.

"You want to cut the girls in half and—" says Bruiser as he circles the two, inspecting them as if he had a clue where to start.

"Then you double slap them," says Less.

"Nope," says Leslie and turns around, returning to her editing.

"Do you think you can do it in one swipe?" asks Bruiser.

"You guys are serious, aren't you?" asks Kristen.

"They're not, at all. You're not. Are you?" asks Dick. "You're going to kill them!"

"Stop being such a pussy, Dick. We've got this," says Bruiser as he grabs a bag out of his pocket. "How do you girls feel about cocaine?"

"If it's anything like the fairy dust dad gives us, we love it," say Kara and Julie.

Dick turns to Bruiser, saying, "All right, I can't be here for this. Vanessa will kill me if I let this go down."

"You can't leave. You know Less can't do it in one swipe. We need you to do it," says Bruiser.

"I can do it. Come on, Bruiser," begs Less.

"Zealand, in front of company," says Dick.

"Sorry, Zealand," mumbles Less.

Bruiser goes to hand the sword to Dick, and he refuses, saying, "I'm not doing it."

"I don't care about that." Bruiser points to the white line in the crease of the sword and says, "Pass that around." Everyone goes down on the sword, and when it's done, Dick rubs what's left all over the sword and hands it back to Less. "Any last words…" asks Bruiser playfully, "as conjoined twins?"

Kara and Julie try to look at each other and ask, "You guys are serious?"

"Why don't you try slapping them first and see what happens?" asks Dick.

"What fun would that be?"

"Dick, grab the camera."

"Have Less film it," says Dick.

"He's got the sword," says Bruiser.

Dick tries to hand Less the camera and says, "Give me the sword, Less. I'm not going to let you kill these girls."

Less refuses, saying, "I trust Bruiser, I mean, Zealand, and I believe in him."

"That's crazy, Less," says Dick.

"What isn't these days?" asks Less. "Just hit record!"

"Should we lay down a tarp or something?" asks Dick. "I feel like this is going to get messy."

"Good call. You wanna' grab some Tylenol and some Neosporin while you're at it?" asks Bruiser.

Dick starts to get aggravated with the situation, his voice cracks, and he says, "I'm just saying, you're about to cut these two girls in half with a sword, and you're expecting them to grow new legs and organs. They'll bleed out before you slap 'em. You're not at all worried about killing them?"

Bruiser looks at Less.

Less looks at Dick.

"No, not worried," says Bruiser.

"Makes sense to me," says Less.

"And Kristen, you and your sisters are fine with it?" asks Dick.

Kara points to Kristen, saying, "Look at Kristen."

Julie chimes in, "Do you remember what she looked like? She was a fucking monster."

Kara continues with their fingers interlocked, begging, "We have nothing to lose. You can't even start to understand where we come from and what we've been through. I'd suck a million little dicks to get away from our captors."

Kristen pulls at Bruiser's hand. "There's nowhere to go, looking like they look, without expecting to suffer and be abused."

Julie and Kara simultaneously say, "The circus; that was our plan."

"You see, Dick, we're saving them from the circus, from exploitation," says Less.

"Are you prepared to lose them?" asks Dick.

"There's nothing to lose," says Bruiser.

"Why don't you just try slapping them first, before you go all fucking medieval?" asks Dick.

Bruiser stands in front of Kara and Julie, scratching his chin, and as he comes to some sort of understanding with the universe, he says, "Sounds boring. Less, get behind the girls. I feel like there is something I should say."

"What?" ask the girls.

"A blessing of some sorts, 'cause this is about to be one of the most amazing things anyone will ever see on the internet. Just hit record," says Bruiser.

"Fuck it. Let's go," says Dick.

Less raises the longsword, and Bruiser starts his introduction, saying, "Welcome to Future of the Left. I'm your host, Zealand T. Dahl, and tonight we're in Huntsville, Alabama, where we're going to amaze the world with a new feat of healing. My ole pal, Less, is going to cut these two … this one conjoined twin in half … in one stroke — hopefully. Then, I'm going to slap them and they're going to form two whole people that are finally free from themselves."

"Hurry up! Less's arms are shaking," says Dick.

"Kara, Julie, any last words?" asks Bruiser.

Less sets the sword down, saying, "Give me a sec, Bruiser."

Bruiser stomps his foot adamantly and says, "No more Bruiser, especially when the cameras are rolling. Are you ready?" Less shakes off his reprimanding and raises his sword. Bruiser starts the countdown, "On three. One … Two …"

"No, definitely no!" screams Vanessa from the back of the parking lot. "What the-actual-fucks going on here?"

"Who told Ma?" asks Bruiser.

They all turn to Leslie's shadow, peering through a tinted window on the bus.

"Bruiser! You're not seriously planning on cutting these poor girls in half?" asks Vanessa completely perturbed.

"I would never," says Bruiser.

Less drops the sword and Bruiser lowers his hand.

"I told you this was fucked up," whimpers Dick.

"Dick, when'd you get so soft?" asks Bruiser.

"I think he's afraid of his new boss," says Less.

"I can't lose this job, man," moans Dick.

Bruiser pats him on the back, saying, "You know if you got fired, I'd rehire you as my blunt roller, right?"

"Bruiser!" says Vanessa.

"Zealand in front of our guests!" he shouts.

"Zealand! Did you try slapping them first?" asks Vanessa.

"That's what I said," whimpers Dick.

"What if they get stuck together — forever?" asks Bruiser.

"They deserve to be free," says Less. "I couldn't imagine being attached to Leslie forever."

Vanessa puts her hands out and says, "Less, give me the sword!" She plays with it for a minute feeling the weight and then tests the blade for sharpness, saying, "Slap them first. If that doesn't work, I'll do it."

"Oh man, that's not fair," says Less.

"We all know you can't make it through their hip bone in one swipe, Less," says Vanessa.

Bruiser submits to her, saying, "Fair enough, boss lady. We'll try it your way."

"Zealand, seriously?" asks Less slightly butt-hurt.

"But Less gets to do the separation if the slap doesn't take," demands Bruiser.

"Deal," says Vanessa, surprised by Bruiser's forfeit.

"Girls? Are we ready?" asks Bruiser, and then slaps the girls before they can answer. Their faces curl up, in what one can only imagine is an overload of sensation. They grab each other's faces at the same time, looking deeply into one another while they communicate silently. They struggle to put their faces together and kiss for what they hope is the last time as one. Bruiser is hit by a fog of shadows that are released from the girls. He drops to his knees and collapses to the ground in a fetal position, starts vomiting, and says, "Yeah, I'm done."

Vanessa jumps on top of him, trying to help, but he pushes her away, saying, "You don't want to feel this."

"Thank you for trusting me," she whispers in his ear.

"You don't get the job title of hellhound without getting all of my respect," says Bruiser, and he returns to vomiting.

Kara and Julie, still connected and clawing at one another, jaunt sloppily through the parking lot and waddle off into the darkness of woods. As everyone is focused on our reluctant Messiah, Kristen asks, "Should I go after them?"

Bruiser moans, "Less, follow them and keep your distance. Just make sure they're all right."

With only the light of the full moon and the bantering moans of the two-headed beast, Less walks blindly, holding his blade close, hoping that they were all wrong and that he finally has the chance to cut through human flesh for the best of everyone. He calls out, asking for acceptance of his assistance, "Girls. Kara, Julie, are we all right?" All he hears is their playful moans in the distance.

Less follows their moans as they turn into the bellowing, soul screams of something unexplainable. As he gets closer to the screams, he notices a green light emanating from the girls. The two are caught up in something primal that could be confused with something sexual, or very self-destructive in nature; they seem to be tearing themselves apart. The unholy sight hinders Less's approach as he feels like it's a private moment the two have only dreamt of, and he knows he should keep his distance until he hears them beg for his steel.

"Holy blasphemes fuck! You can take me now if this feeling's going to get worse!" yells Kara, and he decides to investigate. Less cautiously approaches the separation, and the closer he gets, the more horrific the moans get. They've become highly sexual in nature, something far from his comfort zone, but he proceeds. The clawing and pushing have turned to caressing and fondling, and they are knotted up in a ball, something similar to a Celtic knot. There's a light beaming from their core, the place that binds them, and as it starts to flicker, Julie turns to Less and her eyes go pitch black. A deathly fear rolls over his being as she looks deeply into him and growls, "Cut us apart!"

All he wants is to run away. Mainly because they're naked, and he's never seen a physical form like this one. It neutralizes any thoughts about this moment he had bouncing around in his head. Kara looks to Less, and with a siren-like bawl, she says, "Please, just fuck the pain away." He's pulled mindlessly for a closer examination of the moment and finds that they've clawed each other raw in hopes of freedom, and that they are dividing as well as growing the necessary parts to split. It's absurd, yet very intriguing. As he looks for a dotted line to swipe through, he notices that they're connected at the hip and the bone seems to be the only thing hindering their escape from one another.

He raises his sword, and with every molecule in his being, he swings into them. As his blade finishes its quest, hitting the earth, he collapses, and they pull him into their moment. They tear his clothes off and he falls deeply into the girls as he hears, "I remember a time with no sun, trapped in darkness with only the glow of the devil's moon to guide me. Now, I sit here blinded by the light, and I smile to let the gods know I won."

Carol

The tour bus pulls into a cul-de-sac in the middle of Charlotte, North Carolina. What used to be a nice neighborhood has been left behind and is now being consumed by the upper-lower class, no longer the lower-middle class. Bruiser gets out of the bus with his newly transformed band of followers in tow and forges his way through an overgrown yard to the front steps of a modest home that's in need of a serious paint job.

"You grew up here?" asks Vanessa. "On Sheppard Cove?"

Bruiser looks around and replies, "Yep." He knocks on the door to no reply, sits down on the stairs, and couple of cats pop out of the bushes to welcome him. Bruiser's heart is flooded by memories of waiting incessantly for his father's return, sitting on these same steps, and he jumps up, rings the bell a couple times, fidgets with the knob, and then opens the door.

They are greeted by another group of cats in the foyer.

"Dude, your mom's a crazy cat lady!" laughs Dick.

As they walk through the one-story, ranch-style house, they find more cats and a cityscape of empty towering boxes that appear to all be from Amazon. "Ma!" he screams. There is a pungent smell that infects them as they walk through the living room. "It's looking like I might have just inherited a house full of cats."

Dick replies, asking, "How many cats do you think it would take to eat your mom?"

"All of them," Bruiser says, looks out the sliding glass door, and finds his mother's 1976 Grand Prix in the carport. Bruiser opens the sliding glass door, walks out onto a patio surrounded by shrubbery, lights yet another cigarette, and screams, "MOMMMMM!"

"Scotty Potty. Is that you?" shouts his mother.

Dick laughs and says, "I forgot about that."

Bruiser walks his entourage around the shrubs to the back yard. He looks up to his old tree house, built by one of her exes looking for acceptance, to find his mom adorned in her Jazzercise workout gear, feeding the squirrels. "Ma, what are you doing?"

"I'm birdwatching with the kitties!" says his mother.

Bruiser covers his eyes and grumbles, "Seriously?"

"Come help me down. I want to meet your friends!" she says in a childlike voice. Less and Leslie retreat, leaving Dick, Vanessa, Kara, Julie, and Kristen. His mother runs up to Dick and gives him a hug. Bruiser hits his cigarette and looks at Vanessa glumly. His mother turns to Vanessa and asks, "And who is this little number?" She laughs as she plays with Vanessa's hair. "She reminds me of your sister."

"Mom, this is Vanessa. She's the producer of the show."

"I thought my lil' Dickie was the producer," says his mother.

Bruiser laughs. "She's the network producer. She's little Dick's boss."

His mother gives Vanessa a hug and eyes down the other girls. "What about these scamps? Where'd you find them? Working a parking lot?"

Dick laughs and says, "That's funny. Technically we did find them in a parking lot. The twins are Kara and Julie. They were conjoined twins until last night when Bruiser slapped them, and Less cut them into separate entities with a longsword. This is their sister, Kristen, who was technically a mongoloid, no offense."

Kristen looks at Dick, smiles, and says, "Sounds about right."

Bruiser's mother eyes them down and says, "Interesting story, Dickie. They're beautiful, but you need to take them shopping."

"That's all you got from that conversation?" he asks his mother. "We need to take them shopping. Let's go inside. I have something for you."

His mother lights up, excited about her surprise, and starts skipping toward the house. They follow her, trying to avoid making eye contact with the anomaly that is her spandex attire.

"Would you kids like anything to drink?" asks his mother. "I've got Hawaiian Punch!" Bruiser's friends disperse in search of more cats. "So, Scotty, what did you get your mother?"

Bruiser walks her into the living room that's filled with more cats. There's a large rectangular box in the middle of the living room with a bow on it. "It's a seventy-inch flat screen."

His mom looks at it and asks, "Well, where'd you steal that from?"

"Thanks, Ma. You really get me," he says with a morose smirk. He walks his mother to the window in the foyer and points at the bus, saying, "That's mine. There's three more like it, that follow us. I'm a healer with a television show. I'm fixing the world."

His mother retorts, "You're just like your grandfather: delusions of grandeur, built on a foundation of alcoholism and abuse. What's your angle?" Bruiser raises his hand to slap her, but she has already started walking away. "Do you want something to drink?" she asks. "I've got your favorite — grain alcohol and Hawaiian Punch."

Bruiser lights up a cigarette and follows her through the dining room into the kitchen with his head down, saying, "I always liked my Everclear with Kool-Aid, Purplesaurus-Rex, specifically."

She mixes the two a drink and asks, "So, have you heard from your sister?"

Bruiser flicks his ashes in a cat shaped ashtray that he assumes she made and says, "She's been dead for years, Ma."

She sits down with Bruiser and says, "Yeah, but Scotty, you two always were close. I know you talk to her. Especially with your new 'powers.' What does she say? Do you guys talk about me? Does she still hate me?"

Bruiser takes a swig off his delightful concoction and says, "She never hated you. She was just afraid of becoming you."

She looks at Bruiser and says, "Same difference. I guess you're my favorite now." She laughs and rubs Bruiser's hand. A Calico cat jumps up on her lap, and she offers it a drink. "You want some hummingbird juice, little kitty?"

Bruiser tries to grab her drink from her, saying, "Mom, cats don't drink booze!"

"My kitties do. Makes 'em silly," she says.

"You're the silly one. Listen, Ma, I've got a show to film tonight. Do you want to come? I can heal you."

She looks him dead in the eyes and sneers, saying, "I've seen your show. It's disgusting."

"Well, that's not awkward. I guess I should have figured you'd check out Greed," he says, waiting on her response.

She takes his cigarette from him, hits it, and says, "I remember one time, we were leaving church, and we left you and your sister in your dad's gold Camaro while we grabbed some stuff from the convenient store. We came out and found the car in the middle of the intersection, smashed. You almost killed your sister. When we asked you what happened, you said, 'The devil made me do it!' You had pulled the emergency break. I don't know how. You were only five but pure evil."

Bruiser puts his cigarette out. "Because it wasn't me. It was your precious daughter. And what makes it worse, she let a five-year-old take the blame for it!"

"Not my baby!" she shouts.

"And who leaves their kids in the car?"

"You weren't allowed in the store because you got caught shoplifting candy bars," she says.

Bruiser looks up at the ceiling and redirects the conversation, saying, "I talked to the bank. They said you're two months behind on the mortgage. I'm going to take care of it."

She returns to the conversation, asking, "Oh, yeah?"

"And I'm going to put some money in your account for you, but we've got to talk about getting rid of some of these cats. I think you might have toxoplasmosis."

"What's that?" she asks.

"It's a parasitic addiction to cats that you get from their poop," he says, laughing.

"Now who's being silly? I guess I could get rid of one or two of them. If the price is right." She gives him a big hug and asks him, "Do you want me to make you your favorite?"

Bruiser lights up, saying, "Chili mac and cheese?"

She starts digging through the cabinets and says, "I think I've got some of those little gnocchi you liked thrown in there. What did you call them?"

Bruiser sits down at the dinner table, preparing to be fed, and says, "Rat brains."

His mom turns to him and says, "You were such an odd boy."

Bruiser stares out the window for a moment, watching his friends on their cat safari, and returns, saying, "Thanks, one could say that's still true."

She returns from digging through the cupboards and says, "Well, I don't think I have either one of those things anyway. I've got some rice cakes."

Bruiser lights another cigarette, chugs his punch, and mumbles, "It's cool. I wasn't hungry anyway."

"Do you want some goldfish, baby?" she asks.

Bruiser starts to answer her and looks over to find that she is talking to one of her cats. He stands up and says, "I don't think crackers are good for cats, Ma." She pulls a skimming net out of the cupboard and walks over to a fish tank on the counter. Bruiser watches wide eyed as she fishes out one of the goldfish and flicks it at the tuxedo kitty.

He walks over to his mother, grabs her by the shoulders, and reaches back to enlighten her with his open left hand. She drops to the ground, starts crying, and says, "You'll never hit me again, Scotty."

Bruiser goes to pick her up, but she runs off and locks herself in her bedroom. He follows her down the hallway and starts shaking on her bedroom doorknob. "Ma, I wasn't trying to hit you. I'm trying to heal you. Something's not right. I just want to fix you."

She screams, "You're just like your grandpa, a boozer, and a loser! He used to hit me, and no one's going to touch me ever again! The kitties love me, and they don't try to fix me."

Bruiser gets his phone out and pulls up the video of him slapping the girl in Little Five Points. He slides it under the door and says, "Just press play, Ma. This is what I do now. I heal people."

200

She screams through the door, "I saw this on the Facebook! This is what you do now for a living? You slap little children and dupe people out of their money. I don't want to be part of it, and you can keep your money. I'll sell my cats to pay the rent."

Bruiser laughs and says, "Ma, no one pays for cats. They multiply like gremlins. Most people can't give them away."

She responds with a serious tone, saying, "Some people do. I have some very respected breeds here, and there are some really smart ones that I've trained."

Bruiser, frustrated once again with his mother's insanity, collapses on the floor of the hallway, saying, "I'm sure they're amazing, Ma."

"Can you put out the cigarette!" she screams through the door.

Vanessa peers around the corner of the hallway, asking, "What're you doing?"

"I tried to slap her, and she ran off and locked herself in her room," says Bruiser as he takes a hit off his cigarette.

Vanessa sits down next to Bruiser and says, "We've got to get going. I'd rather have you slap her on the show anyway. If you hadn't spent the night messing around with those whores, you would have had more time with your mother."

Bruiser puts is pointer finger over Vanessa's lips and whispers, "She hates whores."

His mother screams through the door, "Scotty! You always have time for your whores, and never any for your mother!"

"Look what you've done!" he begs Vanessa. "Can you help me get my phone back?"

"I can hear you, Scotty! Don't you yell at your sister like that!" she screams.

"Mrs. …" says Vanessa.

"Flamingo." says Bruiser.

"Mrs. Flamingo, we have to take your Scotty. We have a show to shoot. He's going to heal a lot of people. You should come to the show tonight and watch," says Vanessa.

His mother is silent and Bruiser whispers to Vanessa, "We can't go. She has my cell phone. Ma, give me back my phone!" She slides the phone under the door. It's wet. Bruiser wipes it off without even thinking about from where the moisture came.

"Don't you want to give your son a hug good-bye?" Vanessa asks.

"If I come out there, he's going to try to hit me. I know that son of a bitch."

"Mrs. Flamingo, you just called yourself a—"

His mother starts screaming, "I know what I called myself. I'm not coming out!"

"You might not ever see him again," says Vanessa blatantly, hoping for a moment of sanity from his keeper.

"God willing. Take a cat on your way out!" screams his mother.

Vanessa stands up, pulling him to his feet, and the two walk through the house silently.

"Can you pay off the mortgage, get her a live-in nurse, set up an account in her name that will sustain her cat farm, and try to find homes for as many as you can?" Bruiser asks Vanessa.

She pulls out her phone and starts scrolling through an album of his mom's cats, saying, "Thirty-three. At least."

"Cats?" asks Bruiser.

"That we saw. I'll get her an assistant to start a cat-farm foundation. We'll see if we can make some money off it, maybe we can advertise on the show." Vanessa grabs his hand and walks him onto the bus. There's a Calico that follows them onto the bus. She grabs it by the nape and throws it off the bus. "You all right, Scott?"

There's a moment of silence.

"Bruiser or Zealand, please?" He walks back toward his chemical fort, stopping at the fridge.

"Are you going to be all right?" she asks.

"Nothing a bottle can't fix," says Bruiser. "Did that masseuse ever turn up?"

Vanessa pours herself a shot and says, "Angelora, no, she wanted to meet up in New York. You know, I'm certified. I can get in there and work out some of those knots."

Bruiser laughs and lights a cigarette, saying, "I was hoping for a happy ending, not a mediocre representation of a feminist perspective on the downfall of humanity and its relationship to the existence of toxic masculinity."

Vanessa takes a cigarette from him, asking, "What happened in there?"

Bruiser pours a round of shots and says, "I reopened an old wound, and I believe it's infected." Vanessa waves her hands, refusing the shots. Bruiser does both shots and mumbles, "She told me I was finally her favorite."

Vanessa takes a drag off his cigarette and says, "Well, see? That sounds positive."

Bruiser chuckles and says, "Years ago, right after my birthday, I found out my sister died — supposedly."

"Bruiser, I'm so sorry!"

"My sister always called on my birthday. It's the only time I ever heard from her. Anyway, she'd been on the run from the federal government for selling black market stem cells. She was looking at forty-years imprisonment for trying to help people."

"The FDA never did approve them," says Vanessa.

"Why would they? It would cost them billions. Anyway, she gets a call from her secretary one day saying to leave the country immediately. The FBI raided her office because she'd been charging twenty-seven thousand an injection for illegal stem cells. Her boyfriend, the lawyer representing the company performing the injections, BioSpark, was from South Africa, so they headed there to avoid extradition."

Vanessa pours another round of shots. "So, she got out?"

Bruiser takes a shot with her and says, "Yeah. The whole story is ridiculous. I saw so many people cured of lifelong suffering, and knowing they didn't want us to be healthy changed me." Bruiser pauses, takes another shot, and hits his cigarette. "I hadn't seen her in so many years before she went on the run; and now I can't even remember the last conversation I had with her."

"Bruiser, I had no idea," she says, grabbing his hand.

He pulls away from her grasp, saying, "I always felt so alone in that house. Their connection was so strong. They talked and laughed all the time while I sat in the corner. I always felt like she hated me, but it took me a lifetime to figure out that it was just for being a dude."

"Who? Your sister?" asks Vanessa.

"No, my mother. My grandma used to tell me I was just like him, my grandfather, the man that used to beat the both of them. I never met him, but that's all she ever saw when she looked at me."

Bruiser walks back to his room and finds it currently occupied by Less, Leslie, Kara, Dick, Kristen, and Julie. They are smoking a joint around the table. Vanessa follows Bruiser to his room and shuts the door behind them. Bruiser grabs his briefcase and starts foraging through it. He pulls out a bag of coke the size of his fist and reaches into it. There's a rock in the center the size of a ping-pong ball. He puts it on the table, smashes it with his phone, and then proceeds to cut out a line the length of the table with his hand.

Vanessa steps between Bruiser and the line, asking, "What are you doing?" The room empties immediately, leaving the two to their newfound relationship. Vanessa sits down next to him and says, "I get it, your mom's a mess. She's the reason you hurt, and this is to numb the pain. When does it stop though? Your life means so much more to the world now. So much more than this bullshit!"

Vanessa puts her hand on Bruiser's back, and he flinches, asking her, "Does it? Cause it doesn't feel that important at the moment. That's the woman that brought me into the world, and she can't stand me." He goes to stick his face in the pile of drugs and Vanessa immediately swipes the epic trail of powder off the desktop. "What the fuck are you doing?" he yells at her as the air fills with the chalky white powder.

"I was coming back here to fuck you, you stupid shit! Someone needs to tell you how great you are. Apparently, on a regular basis … throughout the day, but I don't think I'm ready to throw away twenty-grand on a self-absorbed, drug addict. I know where that goes!"

Bruiser lights up another cigarette and jests, "I'm hung like a gnat, if that helps. You wouldn't even notice. It'd still have that new car smell and everything." Vanessa looks at him with a stern disdain and Bruiser smirks, saying, "All right, a blowjob it is!" Vanessa laughs excessively, and then there's a silence while she processes her options out of this moment. "A hand-job?" he asks, in a last-ditch effort for any sort of a physical interaction. He takes her hand and places it on his feminist battle-hammer, saying, "Just like three strokes."

Vanessa thinks about it for a moment, leans in as if she were going to kiss him, and stops right at the point where their eyes are locked and staring deep down into the abyss. "I'm not doing this with you!" she says adamantly. "I'm not going to let you hate-fuck your way to the center of my heart just so you can get back at your mom."

Bruiser pushes away from her and grabs a pill bottle out of the couch that he found while fidgeting nervously during their discussion. He takes one pill and crushes another one with a lighter, pushes the line into what's left of the blow and consumes it, reaches into his briefcase, and grabs his wax pen, hits it vigorously and falls over, landing with his head in her lap, looks up at her and says as he powers down, "Fair enough. A friend would be nice and equally refreshing. I'm going to need a moment to… gather my… get her on the show."

She stares at him while his eyes are closed and whispers, "You're such a pleasure — when you're not talking." She plays with his hair, knowing that he's taken solace in there somewhere, hopefully safe from his own repetitive tormenting thought cycle. Her phone starts to vibrate, and she slides away towards the door.

As soon as she opens the door, the girls lock on to the opening, push her out of the way, and cover Bruiser like a blanket. Dick looks up from his laptop and out the window at the torrential downpour that's started, and asks Vanessa, "How's he doing?"

Less and Leslie follow the girls into Bruiser's room and Vanessa looks back at the door, sighs, and says, "We'll be lucky if he's alive when we get to the church."

Dick unfazed by the thought says, "You should have seen him the last time his mom stayed at his place for the weekend. He literally died. She's the chink in his armor and at the same time she is the armor."

"Do you think he'll be all right?" she asks.

"He's been through worse," says Dick.

"How is that possible?" she asks, sitting down across from him as she tries to reconnect to her mobile devices, but can't. She shakes her tablet in the air and shouts, "Titty-fuck-balls."

Dick looks up at her and asks, "Where would you like to start?"

Searching for a user's guide to her talent, Vanessa blurts out, "Relationships."

"Oh, when it comes to women; he's threatened. He uses orgasms to control them as long as he can. And when they fall in love, he uses his personality to push them away, protecting himself from what he believes is the inevitable."

"What's that?" she asks.

"Being trapped emotionally by a psychopath that he loves with his whole heart, but knows will destroy him," says Dick without looking up from his laptop.

"I get that, but girls eat that shit up," says Vanessa.

"Yeah, it drives them crazy when he shuts them out. He's been throwing away Janeuh for years," he says, tripping over his tongue.

Vanessa, looking up as her electronics finally decide to comply, asks, "What's a Janeuh?"

"His fiancé? I guess," he says, looking away.

"Fuck that!" she says, motioning to Dick for a cigarette.

Dick throws her his pack and a lighter, saying, "I mean, no one knows if it's true. They supposedly got engaged in the middle of a blackout the night before we left." Dick interrogates her visually and decides to ask her, "You're into him, aren't you?" Vanessa looks out the window, watching the rain as he reads her face for the truth. Realizing he hit something, Dick says in a snarky tone, "I see the way you look at him, and I don't believe your girlfriend would appreciate it."

Vanessa lights the minty-fresh carcinogen and throws his belongings back at him loosely, asking, "What do you care?"

He fends off the return and says, "As much as I'd like to watch you two fight and fuck your way across America, I'd prefer to keep everything on the bus copacetic."

"Can you get a hold of his mother?" she asks, deflecting his concern.

"Look, he's a good dude through and through. Most people don't get to see it, and I assume he's discombobulated by the thought of showing the world."

"Why?" she asks, only focused on Dick's relativity.

"Because they don't deserve it," he says, defending his emotionally crippled friend.

"Deserve what?" she asks.

"His words," says Dick. "Most people read him as an absolute mess, but his deviousness is penetrating and plants a seed of growth. It sounds bizarre but look at Greed: he was handing people piles of cash, at the same time breaking them down by helping them truly see what they really are. It's unorthodox, but it has its place in this fucked up mess." Dick wipes the sweat off his brow as he looks up from his phone, saying, "She won't leave the cats. She says, 'If I leave, they won't let me back in.'"

"Just get her to the show. It was his last request before he capsized. He wants to slap her, but she's afraid of him."

Dick sits back down and returns to his laptop. In hopes of returning to Vanessa's graces, he divulges Bruiser's Achille's heel. "His mother's convinced that he's the reincarnate of her father."

Vanessa looks up, almost aroused by the truth she unearthed, and asks, "The one that used to beat her?"

Dick takes a second to process the repercussions of his response. "Yeah, every man she's ever been with has hit her. I can't tell if it's bad luck, bad taste in men, or she's just a miserable person that really knows how to push a man to the point where he can't control his hands."

Vanessa scowls at Dick and says, "That's disgusting!"

Dick tries to plead his case, saying, "Sorry, that's the most chauvinistic thing I've ever said, but I've heard her say some shitty things to him: things you know about yourself, but don't need to hear out loud."

"Like what?" she asks.

Dick looks at Vanessa and then stops himself.

Vanessa heckles Dick in an attempt to pry as many secrets out of him as possible. "C'mon, Dickless."

"It's not even the words, Vanessa. She just didn't give a shit about him. It was like she was destroying Bruiser, just to get back at her father."

"How so?" she asks.

Dick shifts around in his seat awkwardly, knowing she's got him by the balls, and says, "Okay, after high school, Bruiser moves back in with his mom and his stepdad."

"Flamingo?"

"Yeah. He was a drunk Belgian dickhead. Bruiser's working two jobs, going to community college, and the guy takes a swing at him while he's sleeping – between shifts."

"He hit her, too?"

"All the time."

"B used to stand up to him, and that's why he threw him out. She never once tried to stop it from happening; more so she stayed with the dickhead and watched as her son (the reincarnate of her father) was being thrown out by a Euro knockoff of her father. If that makes any sense?"

"Wow."

"So, now he's homeless. Me and our good friend come down to kick it with him. We're living out of his truck and bouncing around from motel to hotel to motel. He loses his job waiting tables, because he smells, and then he starts slinging dope. We didn't pay rent for years. Shit, he beat down these two Marines, with a pair of nun chucks, that were looking for me 'cause I wrecked their stripper girlfriend. Most people would've turned to the dark side fighting through the life he was given. He's a good dude, just been through it. And after all that, he still cares what she thinks."

"So, you think he's a good dude at heart?" she asks.

Dick looks down at his phone and says, "Yeah, but his dick's a tornado, and, genitally speaking, destroys everything in its path."

"I guess I'm just going to have to hunker down and pray that he doesn't flip my trailer."

Dick's eyes pop out of his head, and he says, "I got her!"

"Who?" she asks, expecting anything other than what she gets.

Dick snidely says, "Flamingo."

Vanessa looks up and asks, "You had her kidnapped?"

Dick laughs and says, "I catnapped her: I told her one of her cats snuck on the bus, that the driver couldn't catch it, and that she has to come get it. I'm going to send the bus back and if she gets on, I'll have Chuck pull off immediately."

"We'll see," she says, smiling.

"Honestly, I think we're better off if she doesn't show."

"It's what he wants?" she says.

"I'm telling you, it's not worth it. She's bag-lady crazy."

"Ladies, please," says Less, fighting his way out of Bruiser's suite. He shimmies through the door, a hand grabs a hold of his shirt, pulling him back in the room, and the door shuts.

"That didn't look healthy. Dick, you wanna' help him out?" asks Vanessa.

Dick sighs, gets up, and walks back to Bruiser's door. He presses his ear up against it and he hears, "If your sister's open to it—" Dick pushes the door open and shouts, "Less, Leslie, boss wants to talk to you!" He looks at the fleshy blanket that's covering Bruiser and mumbles, "I'm not even gonna' ask. Leslie! Let's go."

"What's going on back there?" asks Vanessa.

"A whole bunch of fuckery," says Dick.

"Less!" yells Vanessa.

The door pops open and Dick grabs Less and drags him back to Vanessa. Less sits down next to Vanessa and notices the screen on her laptop is not responding. "I can fix that," Less says, taking her laptop from her.

"That'd be great," says Vanessa. "My phone's doing the same thing."

Leslie walks into the living area putting herself back together. She stops as she catches Dick and Vanessa staring sideways at her and asks, "What's up?"

Vanessa stares down the twins and says, "Can you guys keep it somewhat professional? I've got enough cats to wrangle with Bruiser's antics."

"Sorry," the twins say together.

"It wasn't us," says Leslie. "It was those three little witches back there."

"What were you two thinking?" asks Vanessa.

"We weren't," says Less.

"Ever since Bruiser slapped us, we've been connected psychically," says Leslie.

"We think they used that connection to get in our heads and take control over us," says Less.

"They've got to go," says Vanessa. "They're beyond creepy."

"You know Bruiser's not gonna' go for that," says Dick as he turns to the twins and leans into them, asking, "I thought the right hand didn't work?"

"We think it's something different," says Less.

"Like a psychic can-opener," says Leslie.

Crack the Skye

Bruiser comes to standing in front of a wagon that's dressed in medicinal bottles and inspirational signs. He has a handlebar mustache and he's wearing a pin striped suit with a bowler hat, shouting, "Come one, come all! Gather round and witness the true healing powers of the Orient. I've traveled the world seven times over, looking for the Fountain of Youth, and I've finally found a miracle spirit for the spirit, per se."

No one steps forward.

As he looks over the crowd, he finds everyone dressed to the nines, standing in the middle of an old western town, fending off a vengeful sun that's eating away at their already chapped faces. "Anyone? I know every one of you fine people in front of me has an illness or an ailment. You can't walk this Earth without acquiring one. How about you, ma'am?" he asks, pointing his finger at an older lady in a faded pink corset that's holding a parasol.

A sickly man, wearing tattered rags, steps to the front of the crowd and says, "Of course, like you said, we all have our sickness, but I don't have any money to throw away to the high hopes of a miracle that don't exist. Not in this world."

"What's in it that makes it so powerful?" asks an older lady in the middle of the crowd.

Bruiser laughs and says, "Well, ma'am, if I told you fine folks what was in it, you wouldn't need my help. I'd be out of a job. The only other job I'm cut out for around here is bartending, and we know the life expectancy of bartenders. So, here's what I'm going to do; the first shot is on me. If you don't feel like dancing a jig upon consumption, I'll pack it up and move on to the next watering hole. What ails you, ma'am?"

The lady walks up to Bruiser and grabs the glass pint out of his hand. She inspects it and asks him, "Where do I start? It'd be nice if I could read this label. Even better if I could hold it without shaking. When I wake up, every bone in my body creaks. And to top it off, I've been coughing up blood."

Bruiser takes the bottle from her and uncorks it, asking, "So, what could it hurt?" He takes a swig from the bottle and hands it to her, saying, "Go ahead." She takes a sip, shaking as much out of the bottle as she can, and collapses. Bruiser watches the dust skulk away from her collapse and shifts gears, saying, "Don't worry, folks. That's a natural reaction with the older crowd. Who's next?"

A girl in the crowd steps forward, and as she makes it to the front of the crowd, her illness is revealed: she's wearing a set of archaic leg braces. The girl asks him in a helpless voice, "Can your potion give me my legs back?"

Bruiser tries to swallow, loosens his collar, and a voice from the back shouts, "I'd pay to see that!"

"As would I. How much for the tonic, sir?" asks the girl.

Bruiser holds the bottle up, looking at it as if it were gold, and says, "Today, and today only, one dollar!"

Another voice from the back laughs and says, "A whole dollar, who's got that? If I had one, I'd buy an acre outside of town, so that they'd have somewhere to bury me when this typhoid fever kills me!"

Bruiser steps up onto a whiskey box, saying, "Typhoid fever, sir, that's the number one curable disease for this specific product. Here's what I'm going to do for you lovely people. Twenty-five cents a bottle, and you can pay me the rest the next time you see me. That deal lasts till sundown. That's a whole bottle to share with your family. If you need to run home and grab your sisters, brother, or your cousins. Hell, your kids have jobs. Ask them for a quarter!"

The girl reaches out her hand with a quarter in it and says, "I'll take one while you still have stock."

Bruiser goes to hand her a bottle and then stops, asking, "Are you sure, Miss?"

"It's Catherine. Catherine Starling."

"Well, Catherine, I can't make you any promises. With your condition, I mean … the results with cripples aren't impressive. You might need two bottles."

The same voice from the crowd shouts, "Don't waste your money on this snake oil. He's probably got magic lanterns on the other side of his cart promising three wishes."

Catherine takes the bottle from Bruiser, looks down at the older lady that's still knocked out on the ground, and says, "Here's to the bottom of the bottle." She puts down the whole bottle as the crowd stares. She looks around, grabs her petite belly, and lets out a riveting belch. Her legs start shaking, she drops the bottle, looks back at the crowd, and says, "I can feel them. It's a miracle!" She spins into a pirouette, jumps through the crowd, and runs in a circle around the gathering.

The crowd goes wild, fighting to get to Bruiser and his miracle tonic. As he's taking the small town's collective savings, he stops and looks into a young boy's eyes that's sitting on his dad's shoulders. He has a cleft palette, yet he's smiling more than anyone in this abysmal setting. His dad hands him a bottle of the tonic, he licks his lip, but with a forked tongue, and then licks the bottle from a distance as his eyes bulge out like a lizard.

Bruiser rubs his eyes in disbelief as Catherine bumps into him, asking, "Are you okay?" Bruiser turns to Catherine and is blinded by a white light. As she emerges from the light, she sprouts a pair of glowing, bright, white wings that span twenty-feet wide. Catherine asks him, "How much have we made?"

He holds up a bag of coins, shakes it, and says, "A few dollars maybe." She kisses him on the cheek and whispers in his ear, "What did you do to the tonic this time? This isn't just opium and whiskey."

Bruiser's words come out very slow and deep as he says, "J u s t s o m e o f t h e f l o w e r s I f o u n d g r o w i n g o n a c a c t u s." He scans the crowd, and his hallucination has turned the crowd to death, a reptilian, slithering death. Their skin starts to molt, and they begin feasting on one another. "W e h a v e t o g o n o w, l o v e. G r a b y o u r b r a c e s," demands Bruiser.

Catherine pulls at his sleeve, saying, "W e c a n ' t l e a v e t h e m. T h e y n e e d u s." The crowd turns their attention to Bruiser and Catherine, and they fight for the first taste of the two drifters.

Bruiser grabs Catherine by the arms, saying, "I've turned them into monsters that want to consume us."

Catherine's eyes light up into pure white light, and they beam directly into his as she says, "You can't help them until you face yourself, forgive yourself, and let go." He releases her arms, falls flat on his ass, and he is pulled through the ground as he stares up at the unforgiving sun. Instantly he's pulled, almost as if by a string attached to his back and shuttled off into darkness.

"I'm the monster, I guess. I've no idea why you gaze at me like I'm the answer to your problems," he says into the darkness as it becomes a bright white light. Bruiser finds himself on stage, propped up on a mic-stand. He's wearing the same clothes from his dream, yet in a more familiar reality, mumbling into the microphone at a fully packed church.

Dick scratches his head as he stands next to Vanessa, watching Bruiser confusedly fight to reenter this bastardized realm of inequities. "What exactly was your plan with Bruiser, huh? Prop him up with the mic stand and just wait for the Christians to start throwing stones?"

Vanessa quivers and says, "Coffee had him in the room long enough to dress him and put him on stage!"

Dick laughs. "You should've known he was beyond gone when he asked you for that bowler hat."

Vanessa stares into her tablet refusing to acknowledge his professional impudence and barks, "You're the one that said he always comes through, Dick!"

Dick covers his face and says, "Not when his mom's involved. That's a situation none of us can triangulate."

Vanessa shakes her tablet, as it refuses to work, and demands, "Well, Dick, you're the fun police now, and you're in charge of monitoring his consumption from here on out."

Dick watches as Bruiser flounders on stage and says, "You know that's not going to work, Ness. I generally do the complete opposite."

Vanessa drops her tablet gracelessly and says, "It's that or you're fired!"

The two stare at each other silently.

Dick grabs Vanessa's arm and shakes it, saying, "Poppers, Ness!" Dick gets on his walkie and asks Less, "Do you have Bruiser's d-fib kit?"

"Yeah, but I couldn't find the adrenaline," replies Less.

"You're going to jump start him?" asks Vanessa confusedly.

"Basically, poppers and Verbooty!" insists Dick.

"What's Verbooty?" asks Vanessa.

"He got it from some guru in India, Sai Babbah. The guy materializes it in his hand from the cosmos, and it has a vibrant healing energy. Bruiser likes to snort it."

Bruiser falls over onto the floor of the stage. Less runs up to him and sets his camera down. He digs around in his hip-pack, pulls out some smelling salts, and breaks it under Bruiser's nose. He pulls out another bag of lavender powder and dumps it in Bruiser's hand. Bruiser's eyes burst open as he re-enters the room. Less hands Bruiser the bag of ethereal dust and grabs his camera as Bruiser looks down at his hand, dumps the rest into it, and snorts a face full the lavender rocket fuel. Less runs off to the side of the stage as the curtains open to a despondent applause. Bruiser tries his best to compose his earthly form and says, "Sorry about that, folks. I was having some technical difficulties. That's the thing about time travel. It really does take it out of you, or you out of it." There's nothing but a menacing silence filling the room. "Where was I?"

A voice from the crowd shouts, "That's what we're trying to figure out! You're thirty-minutes late, and we all paid for a miracle!"

Bruiser starts pacing the stage. "That sounds about right. How's everyone doing tonight?"

Another voice from the crowd shouts, "Not good. That's why we're here!"

Bruiser laughs and says, "Exactly. It's great to be back in Charlotte. Is everyone familiar with what's about to happen?"

Many voices from the crowd shout, "A miracle!"

Bruiser walks to the front of the stage and presents himself to the crowd. He takes off his bowler hat and throws it, then takes off his suit coat and button-down, leaving him in a T-shirt, pin-striped slacks, and a pair of black Converse. "That's absolutely right, my friends. What you're about to witness is nothing other than that, a miracle. Before we get started, I'd like to introduce the woman that brought me into this world. Mom, are you out there?"

There's another long silence among the crowd. Bruiser looks over at Vanessa, off stage, and she motions for him to keep moving. He continues to pace the stage, digging around in his pockets nervously, and says, "I've been given a gift, but she's afraid of my hand. My mother has been a constant, reoccurring pain in this life. She is in the early stages of dementia from what I can tell, and I'd love nothing more than to balance the scales by slapping her and healing her. I wrote this for her, and I hope reading it to you helps you to understand what it means for me to be here with you, as I try to put my own personal pain aside and focus on healing strangers. So, if you could all focus on getting her here as a group while I read this, maybe we all can move forward together."

"The hardest part of this life has been watching the one person who's supposed to love and support you, struggle with life as she's beaten down by it. The constant barrage of pain from your loved ones formed a house with no doors, allowing no one in or out. I watched everyone else in our family slowly tunnel their way out. Being the youngest, it took me a while to figure out where they went and why. As time passed, I watched the world around me develop, and I realized you weren't even close to sane. You carried a hatred for a man that no longer existed. You never released that anger, even though you shared it with everyone around you. The hard part is, I know that you're not aware of it and that you have no control over it. That's what hurts; you're a kitten with needle sharp claws, tearing away at the flesh of everyone that tries to hold you, purring as you do it. I know you have no concept of pain, because you've felt it so long that it has become you. I hate that I couldn't protect you from this world, and I wish you nothing but happiness, if not in this life, then the next."

The crowd stares at him awkwardly, confused, and agitated.

"Where's this going?" asks a man from the crowd.

"We all have pain, deep emotional pain that resides within us and spreads until it becomes normalcy. If we don't address it, it will ultimately present itself in physical illness. I've been given a gift, the power to remove whatever it is that ails you physically, along with the emotional pain that traces back beyond this life and even further back through past lives. All I ask, is that you release the beliefs that you've been programmed with and open your heart to the possibility of wholeness, so that you can share that love and heal others around you." Bruiser stops, holsters his microphone, kicks off his shoes, and with only his pin stripe trousers to guard him, he says, "We're in a Baptist church. I assume we're all God-fearing?"

A stern voice from the crowd asks, "Does it matter? We all know you're a fraud and that this is all acting and CG. So, why don't you get on with it."

Bruiser motions for the crew to spotlight the man in the crowd talking to him and says, "And let's just say I was the Second Coming, or just a relentless Messiah in my own right. What makes you think that I'd want to heal a man heckling me in a crowd of God's children? Stand up, sir."

The man stands and says, "Well, if you are the Second Coming of Christ, the return of our Lord and Savior, I would assume you would have to heal all of us whether you wanted to or not."

The crowd laughs exuberantly, and another voice says, "We've all seen your show and we know that the Second Coming would never have been a drug addicted pervert!"

Bruiser laughs at himself and asks the crowd, "But why would he come back after being crucified for trying to heal us the first time? Two-thousand years later and you're still not ready." The crowd hisses at Bruiser and he fights to tame them. "So, let me ask you, sir, do you have a serious ailment, or did you just come here to prove me wrong?"

The man stammers, saying, "I… I… brought my daughter. She has Spina Bifida."

Bruiser scans the front row of wheelchairs and asks, "What's her name?"

"Alice, my sweet Alice," says the man.

A twisted little beauty of a teenage girl waves her hand. Bruiser walks to the edge of the stage and says, "Are you ready to explain to your daughter months from now, that you came to see the greatest healer on this planet, and because of your own insecurities, she will die in that wheelchair never having known true freedom?"

The man scratches his head, trying to decipher what Bruiser is getting at, and responds, "No, no, I'm not."

Bruiser turns to the girl and asks the man, "So, you do believe in miracles?"

The man hesitantly walks to his daughter's chair and starts to push her up a ramp to the main stage. Bruiser's security grabs her chair and finishes the procession. He reaches Bruiser and tries to debunk him, saying, "Listen, Leland, Bruiser, whatever your name is, I don't know what makes you think that I'm going to let you slap my daughter on live TV when your own mother won't let you slap her."

Bruiser looks down at Alice and says, "You're not his burden. He's yours, isn't he?" She smiles innocently, and it pierces Bruiser's heart. He looks up at her father and says, "First of all, this isn't live. Secondly, what's your name, friend?"

The man gets behind his daughter's wheelchair and says, "Fred."

Bruiser puts his hand out and says, "Fred, I don't know what ails you, but I can cure it. What I can't cure is your personality."

The crowd gasps and he continues, saying, "And from what I've seen, that only gets worse when suffering is lifted. So, tell me what I can fix; then I'm going to slap you into believing in miracles, and I hope the crowd joins you."

Fred's jaw hangs loosely and a whisper slips out of his mind, *Ever since her mother left us, I have been overwhelmed and know that I can't give her what she needs. I loved her mother and I understand why she left. My heart is broken, and death seems like the only cure.*

Bruiser's only reaction to this voice is to slap the 'living shit' out of Fred. Fred is thrown back by the surprise assault, and Bruiser puts his hand on Fred's shoulder, saying, "I'm sorry, and we forgive you. I heard your true being speak, and I realized you don't deserve to suffer. We'd like to meet the beautiful person that hides underneath the crass persona you've created."

Fred takes off his glasses and rubs his eyes while he decides how to react. He points his finger and grumbles, "You know, I've taken a lot of shit from a lot of people, but never from such a piece of—" He stops and leans into Bruiser's space, analyzing his content, and smiles, saying exigently, "Holy shit!" The crowd gasps, and he hands his glasses to Bruiser, saying, "I've never been able to see without these."

Bruiser throws Fred's glasses over his shoulder, leans in and whispers in Alice's ear, "And as far as your mother goes, I'm sorry. I've watched all the women in my life suffer, and the thing I like about you, Alice, is that you're smiling despite it all."

Fred rubs Alice's shoulder, saying, "We've tried everything they offer, even stem cells directly to her spine, and nothing."

Bruiser squats down to Alice's eye level and asks her, "Where'd you get the stem cells?"

Answering for her, Fred says, "Bio … Biospark, I think. We had to go to Tijuana to get them."

Bruiser looks up at him and says, "That was my sister's company."

Fred puts his hand on Bruiser and asks him, "Didn't she get chased out of the country by the government for injecting fetal pig cells into children's brains that were suffering from birth defects?"

Bruiser returns to Alice, saying, "I mean that's how your government spun it. Alice, do you mind if I slap you?"

She struggles to shift her weight in her chair and says, "I just want to be free. If you told me you had to hit me in the head with a sledgehammer to feel whole, I'd let you. So, if you want to slap me; do it now, and we can move on to the rest of the crowd."

Bruiser turns to Fred and asks, "May I?"

Fred looks at Alice and says, "Please and thank you."

Bruiser reaches back with both hands and slaps her on both sides of her face at the same time. She collapses in her wheelchair and Bruiser looks to Fred, saying, "With the serious cases, it takes some time. Why don't you stand next to her and enjoy the show?" Bruiser returns to the speechless audience and asks, "Who's next?"

No one comes forward.

"You *are* a monster!" screams a lady in the audience.

Bruiser scans the crowd, saying, "I'm here to help. Who's next?"

Another voice from the crowd barks, "Why don't you go slap Satan, false prophet."

The man stands up, grabbing his wife, and they start to walk up the aisle. Bruiser jumps off the stage and runs into the crowd, chasing after the couple. He catches up with them and pulls at the man's sleeve, asking, "Where are you going?"

The man turns around and says, "There are no miracles in this life. We're meant to suffer. It's our punishment for abandoning God's word. There's no way I'm letting the damn devil lay his hands on me or my wife. You may enjoy slapping crippled children, but I refuse to sit here and watch." Bruiser hears the man whisper, *This life is a lie. You're worse than the priest that used to touch me.* He grabs the man by the wrist and notices a bandage on his arm. The old man fights Bruiser's touch, saying, "Let go, heathen!"

Bruiser looks him in the eyes and says, "They used to hide pedophiles in your churches, because they thought God could fix them. It's not your fault. I want to help you let go of that pain." The man stops, frozen by his words. Bruiser rips the bandage off to reveal a milky, white, gaping hole in the man's arm.

The man attests, "It's skin cancer, or it was. I had it removed, but it's not healing." Bruiser tightens his grip and slaps the man across his weathered face. Less is on top of the hole, zooming in with his camera. The close-up of the man's wound is on the giant flatscreen above the stage, and the crowd watches as the hole begins to close. The old man shouts, "Great Scott! I guess that's twice I've been wrong today! My wife told me to believe in miracles. I said there was no such thing. Would you slap my wife? She's been suffering from diabetes for twenty years. It's gotten so bad they want to cut her legs off."

Bruiser turns to the man's wife and slaps her across the face. She regroups and kisses Bruiser on the cheek. The couple starts crying in each other's arms as they revert visually a good twenty years in front of the camera. At this point, Bruiser is surrounded by a crowd of the sickly, fighting to get slapped by him. He's overtaken by a heartfelt panic and shouts, "Less, stick to me!"

Less pulls at his arm, saying, "I'm on you, not that I have a choice!"

Bruiser looks at his security as they fight to surround him and says, "Don't worry about me. Stay on the cameraman and make sure he gets the shot." Bruiser starts slapping his way out of the crowd in a frenzy. People are dropping to the ground, while others climb over them to make sure they get slapped. One of the security guards sees Less struggling and picks him up and puts him on his shoulders. Bruiser pleads into his microphone, "Vanessa, help me out?"

He slaps his way down the aisle and forces his way to the front of the crowd where he slaps the whole first row of wheelchairs. And as he does, he notices two men with ridiculous mustaches, dressed in white linen suits, Hawaiian shirts, and wicker fedoras. They stare through Bruiser, slowing down the moment, and distracting him from his cause. Bruiser trips and falls into the lap of a handicapped boy in a wheelchair. He continues to stare at the two guys, adorning the white linen, until he hears, "Get off me, you pussy," come from the mouth of the boy he just landed on.

Bruiser feels a mob forming around him, so he slaps the boy and kisses him on the cheek, saying, "I'm sorry. Please, forgive me." He stands up and motions security to cut off the line at the stairs. He walks onto the stage and sees his mother standing next to Chuck, shaking her head at him, having just watched his reckless antics. He runs over to her to give her a hug and smothers her with his embrace, saying, "You made it. I can't wait to slap you."

She tries to push him off her and asks, "What's going on here, Scotty?"

He waves his hand over the mob of people, fighting to get in line, and says, "Miracles, Ma. Miracles." He points to Alice, who has started convulsing so hard that she falls out of her chair. "Alice had spina bifida."

His mom laughs and says, "She doesn't look too good."

Bruiser whimpers, "It takes time with the more serious cases. Can I heal you?"

She steps back hesitantly, saying, "I don't know. Maybe I could watch a little bit longer."

Bruiser winds up, disregarding her ambivalence, and says, "I don't even know why I'd want to help you. You're probably happier in your little bubble, removed from all the thoughts that torment you."

She laughs and asks, "What are you talking about?"

Bruiser is pushed back by a compassion that's risen from his deepest confusion and says, "There's a darkness hiding inside you that you have locked in a closet, but you've locked yourself in there with it."

She starts crying frantically and screams, "What do you know about my pain?"

Fred leaves Alice's side and runs over to Bruiser's mother. He puts his arms around her and tries to comfort her by saying, "He fixed my eyes. You need to trust your son."

She pushes Fred off her, screaming, "I don't have to do anything! I brought him into this world, and I know he's pure evil."

There's a gasp that moves through the crowd like the wave at a baseball game, and Bruiser hears, "And that's his mother. If she says he's evil, he's got to be."

Vanessa whispers in Bruiser's ear, "It's gone tits up, Bruiser. We have to shut it down."

Bruiser looks back to the crowd and says, "I'm not going to let her take this from me." He raises his hand and goes to slap her.

Chuck pushes her back and puts himself between the two, saying, "You can't force it, sir. She'll come around. Let her watch."

Bruiser stops mid-swing and moans, "All I want is to see her happy. To see her smile sincerely. Get out of my way, Chuck."

There's a new noise from the crowd, almost as if you ran heavenly awe through a wah-wah peddle. Everyone seems to be pointing at the part of the stage behind Bruiser that Alice collapsed on. Alice's eyes have opened, and they are glowing a vigilant light blue. Her hair is blonde, thick, and flowing, and her body has become vibrant and developed. She stands up as if she were breaking out of cement, every movement signifying new life. She glides over to Bruiser and hugs him with a force that almost knocks him down. She turns to her father and hugs him as he breaks down with tears. She turns to Bruiser's mother, puts her hand under her chin, and stares deeply into her. She slowly moves into the point where their lips touch, and her eyes shift to a garish Cerulean blue, paralyzing his mother. Frozen, almost hypnotized by Alice's presence, his mother hisses, "Well, aren't you just a feisty little trollop. I'm guessing you're on his side."

Alice grabs her by the throat. "You know he loves you." She lifts Bruiser's mother up, and with her free hand, penetrates her abdomen, pushing through her diaphragm and up into her chest cavity, saying, "And you're done tormenting him. He's not your father!" Alice forces Bruiser's mother off her hand and across the stage. There is a burst of fluids, and the only thing left in Alice's hand is his mother's decrepit heart. Alice takes a bite out of it and smiles as his mother's blood drips down her chin.

Slaphappy

Bruiser just stands there, overtaken by a ghastly tint, void of words or actions while his mother's body hits the floor. He watches Alice as she voraciously devours his mother's flesh with nothing but the childish delight of innocence in her eyes. He turns to the crowd in a panic, concerned with the uproar, and sees the two guys in white linen, sitting there with their phones out, filming the event without one iota of discernment for the madness. Bruiser drops the moment and crumples to his knees, swaying over his mother, and he's immediately hit with a bright white light that overtakes his composure and punctures his heart. He double slaps her, in hopes of resuscitation, and drops to the floor next to her. Tears run down his face as he whimpers with an unforeseen pain, and he's overwhelmed by dark shadows that follow the light into his chest.

As what's left of the crowd stares at his benevolence, he rolls over and embraces his mother's lifeless carriage. He looks up at Alice, slovenly covered in his mother's blood, she smiles at him, and as she does, security jumps on top of her. The three oversized security guards fight to subdue Alice. One is holding her legs down while the other two fight to keep the arms, of a once helpless girl, pinned. The guard with her left arm looks at Bruiser and yells, "We need back up!"

Alice hurls the two guards holding her arms down into one another and kicks the last one off the stage. She stands up, saying, "You're free now, Dad; make the most of it," and hops off through what's left of the crowd as it separates to avoid her.

Alice's father stands, wide eyed, covered in blood, and says, "We were never meant to be happy."

Bruiser, holding his disheartened mother, looks up at Fred and says, "Well, if that isn't a miracle."

Fred drops his head and walks away. "Your mother was right."

Vanessa and Dick approach Bruiser cautiously as he battles for a reprisal of his emotions, saying, "Give it a minute. She's going to be fine."

Dick pulls at him. "We need to get you out of here, buddy."

With a despondent look, Bruiser says, "I can't leave her. I slapped her, and she's going to be fine! I still have to heal the rest of the crowd!"

Vanessa kneels beside Bruiser, saying, "Bruiser, everyone left — screaming. The show's over. She doesn't have a heart. She's not coming back."

Bruiser clenches his mother's hand, saying, "You don't know that. I have to be with her when she comes back."

Dick pries Bruiser off his mother and pulls him to his feet, saying, "We'll bring her to you." He walks Bruiser off the stage, towards the bus as the paramedics take over.

One of the paramedics turns to Vanessa and asks her, "You ever seen anything like this before?"

Vanessa shakes her head and hands him her card, saying, "Can you let us know if anything changes?"

The paramedic covers Bruiser's mother's face with a sheet and asks her, "Like what? You want me to call you if she gets less dead, lady?"

"What the fuck just happened, dude?" Dick asks Bruiser, as he drags him down the hallway toward the bus. Bruiser doesn't respond. Dick lights a cigarette and hands it to him, saying, "It's funny. I thought you'd be smiling."

Bruiser's eyes light up with a fury and darkness that Dick has never seen before and he solemnly utters, "My mom just had her heart excavated and eaten by a teenager that was completely harmless until I slapped her!"

Dick, trying to console him says, "I'm just saying, I thought you'd be happier. You're free of her burden now."

Bruiser, devouring the cigarette in hand, fights to contain the emotional catastrophe that he is, but can't, and releases it all. "She suffered her whole life. She deserves a better ending. I felt the light leave her body, and I felt her pain as if it were my own. I felt it settle in my soul, and I realized that I never understood the suffering she had endured on the way to giving me life. I've got to go back there, Dick! She's not dead! She can't be!" He tries to pull away from Dick, but he won't let go. Bruiser drops to the pavement and leans back against one of the wheels of the tour bus. Trembling with befuddlement, he pulls a vile out of his pocket, empties the contents onto his flagina, consumes every particle, and then looks up at Dick, asking, "Do you think it was my fault?"

Dick looks away from Bruiser while he tries to quantify what good a lie would do for this situation. "If we weren't here, it never would've happened. You were pretty fucked up, so maybe you need to be in the right space to heal people." Bruiser's eyes tear up and he tries to force down the pain, returning it back to its home. Dick can see his friend suffering at the hand of his words, and he tries to recover by saying, "I mean, you've healed a couple hundred souls. So, what if one rips your mom's heart out and eats it? I wouldn't call that a complete failure."

Dick pulls Bruiser to his feet and the two walk onto the bus silently. They walk back to the master suite and find Kara, Julie, and Kristen playfully rolling around in his bed. The girls pause upon the sight of Bruiser's new fashion statement, and Kristen asks, "Rough night?"

Bruiser removes his blood splattered T-shirt and walks silently back to the bathroom.

Dick slides into the pile of girls, saying, "Look at all these beautiful creatures. Yesterday they were useless discards of society, genetic degenerates, and now they're absolute divinity."

Julie chimes in, "That worship you."

Bruiser pops out of the bathroom, scrubbing the blood off his face, and Kara gets on her hands and knees and crawls to the edge of the bed moaning, "And would never abandon you."

Bruiser fights to ignore their siren like taunts and returns to the bathroom as Dick pulls Kara back to her sisters, saying, "And they haven't eaten anyone. Have you girls?"

Kristen jumps on top of Dick, saying, "No one that didn't want to be eaten." Kara and Julie follow her lead and try to undress Dick.

Bruiser sticks his head back out of the bathroom and finds Dick down to his boxers, covered in the sister. "Dick, don't you think this is fucked up?"

Dick lies there, powerless as the girls scour him. "Which *this* are you talking about?"

Bruiser walks back out of the bathroom. "Dude, my mom's dead, and we're fucking knee deep in a pile of handicapped kids!" He's greeted by Kara, sitting on the edge of the bed with a mirror in one hand and a straw in the other. There's a variety of chemicals that she's placed with a razor blade that form the word *LOVE*. Julie and Kristen naturally gravitate to Bruiser, and they take turns between worshiping him and consuming their love. Bruiser picks up the razor from the mirror and shuffles around the granules of despair so that they spell *LIVE* now and walks back to the bathroom with it.

"You going to be okay, bub?" shouts Dick as he watches his friend plummeting home toward the darkness.

Bruiser cackles and says, "I really can't take this shit life anymore, Dick. I feel like I'm kicking a dead whore."

Dick tries to refrain from laughing and says, "Horse … kicking a dead horse, Bruiser."

Bruiser sticks his head out the bathroom and says, "That's whores' hockey, Dick. Why would I be kicking a dead horse?"

Dick quaintly asks, "Why would you be kicking a dead whore, Bruiser?"

Bruiser straps on a serious face and says, "Clearly because you can't get caught with another dead hooker and you really hope she's going to wake up. My point being: everything I touch turns to shit. I can't have anything good in this life. I even turned this blessing into a full-the-fuck-on disaster."

Dick lights up a blunt and says, "I'm just saying, get your head straight. You need clarity with this much responsibility."

Bruiser guffaws at Dick's impeding new belief system and says, "Fucked up or sober, it feels like the universe is using my luck as a cage, like nothing can work out. My dad, shit, my mom was there to torture me emotionally like she was getting paid to do it."

"Technically she was," says Dick.

"With my luck, she'll come back to life just to finish the job. My sister turned into a distant voice and then nothing. And don't get me started about every time I've ever tried love."

Dick lays back down in the pile of girls and says, "That almost killed you — twicet, from what I remember. What about Greed? That was a good time."

"Dude, that show made me the same thing as my mother, just tormenting people to fund my drug habit and sex addiction. I thought I'd finally caught a break with this healing thing, and I could start to feel good about myself, like I won or at least, I was able to contribute and help free some of the others trapped in the same karmic cages as me."

"Karma, Bruiser?" asks Dick.

"Fate, the divine plan, the universe, or whatever this is that we're swimming around in."

There's a knock at the door.

"Who is it?" asks Dick.

"It's Vanessa. You guys okay?" she asks and pokes her head in the room. "Seriously, Dick!" she screeches, bursts into the room, and stops, lingering over Dick and the girls as she processes the seriousness of the debacle at play. Dick points towards the bathroom in hopes of redirecting her attention toward a reflection of Bruiser leering at himself in the bathroom mirror silently.

His mother's reflection is glaring back at him through the mirror while he stares down at the word *LIVE* scraped out of toxic molecules. He points the straw at the L, and as he analyzes his next move, debating where it will take him, he feels his mother's ghostly reflection staring through him. He looks up and directly into her reflection and notices her features and his are so similar; the only difference being the weathered sadness in her eyes that he has not yet achieved. While he's lost in her eyes, he sees the reflection of his chemical diversion now spells *EVIL* in the mirror. "Maybe you're right," he mumbles, shakes his head, and decimates the four-letter word.

Vanessa returns to the debauchery in Bruiser's bed, asking, "Can you give us some space?" Dick scrounges for his clothing and finds his way off the bed. Vanessa puts her hand on his chest, stopping him, and says, "I was talking to them. Girls, can you fuck off?" The girls, without hesitation, pop up out of the bed and disperse in a vaporous manner.

Vanessa looks Dick deep in the eyes, and says, "There are two dudes, dressed in white linen, outside the bus that want to talk to him."

"The two mustache dudes from the show?" asks Dick as he falls back to the bed, "What do they want?"

Vanessa lays down next to Dick, puts her pointer finger over her lips, and whispers, "They're feds. They said they can clean up this mess."

Dick sighs. "I knew there was something off with them. Bruiser's not going to like this."

The two are startled by Bruiser standing over them holding the mirror covered in a new substance: not white, and not brown, more red than anything. The two instantaneously pop up off the bed as Bruiser asks them in a childlike tone, "Like what?"

Vanessa pauses, returning with, "We've got to get rid of those girls, Bruiser. "They're creepy—"

Dick finishes her thought. "As fuck."

"Dick, you were just trying to fornicate them," says Bruiser.

Dick crosses his arms and says, "That's what's creepy. I didn't feel like I had a choice. They had a power over me that I can't explain." Bruiser pulls a clown-sized straw out of his pocket and does a line. He tries to pass it to Dick. Dick looks at Vanessa and pushes it away, saying, "What is that? The colors are off."

Bruiser does another line and says, "What one would call a suicide, I guess, like when we were kids at Burger King, and we'd mix all the flavors of soda. It's cocaine, molly, Oxy, Happy, Smiley, Verbooty, PCP, supposedly a little Meow Meow, and maybe some Flakka."

Dick's brow starts glistening with the thought and he asks, "No Krokodil?"

Bruiser smiles with a devious glimmer and says, "No, but I do believe there was some DMT in that Blunt you just smoked. So, you might as well just do it to take the edge off."

"Dude, I've got a show to produce," says Dick.

"Really, Dick? Do you?" asks Bruiser.

"If we do — I need to have my head on straight, and I need the same from you."

Bruiser flicks the giant straw at Dick, yelling, "You really do think this is my fault!"

Dick gets in Bruiser's face, grabs him by his shoulders, and says, "Whose fault is it, Bruiser? This whole thing is pretty fucking surreal. You don't know what you're working with. I'm just saying, what could it hurt to slow it down a little."

Bruiser shrugs Dick's hands off his shoulders and returns to the pile of dust saying, "All alone, naked in the sun. Dick, what's she paying you to try and sponsor me? I'll double it."

"It's not about the money. I can't watch you do this to yourself anymore!" shouts Dick. "You have the opportunity to change this world for the better. When are you going to let go of the past and move forward?"

Bruiser scoffs at Dick and hands the mirror to Vanessa. She takes it from him and resends the invitation to his gala of martyrdom by setting it down on the shelf across from the bed, saying, "Bruiser, we really, really need you to get your shit together."

Dick jumps back in, saying, "You've made a complete fucking mess out of this show. If you keep this up there's not going to be a show, no one will get healed."

"Fuck you. Fuck her! Fuck everybody! I'm done with churches full of Neanderthals that are heckling me while I try to help them!"

Vanessa tries to console him, saying, "That's fine, church is definitely not the place for your veracious turpitude. We'll write that off to growing pains." She looks into his eyes, begging for a connection, and gets nothing but a snarl from deep inside his being. He picks the mirror up off the shelf and returns to the bathroom, slamming the door behind him. "Well, see? That wasn't so bad," says Vanessa glumly.

"Did you see his eyes?" asks Dick.

"Yeah, he's *fucked* up," says Vanessa.

"That wasn't the drugs," says Dick, looking into her eyes for validation, "He's always been able to handle his shit. There's a darkness in his eyes I've never seen before."

Vanessa grabs Dick by the arm and walks him out of the room, saying, "I got this, Dick." She shuts the door behind them, staring back at the master suite.

Dick pulls at her, asking, "You sure, Ness? He can be a complete shit-bag when he gets this fucked up."

She pushes Dick toward the front of the bus. "Yeah, I've been through worse. We need to buy him some time to get his head straight before he talks to the feds. Talk to the girls and see if you can get them to distract the two linen dicks. We need to get them as far from the bus as possible. Tell Chuck to lock the door and drive off as soon as possible."

Dick leans in. "What are you going to do with him?"

With a smile on her face, Vanessa leans into Dick's ear and whispers, "Give him what he wants." She pushes Dick off the bus and makes her descent toward Bruiser's den of iniquity. She tiptoes to the bathroom door and wiggles the handle gently, saying coyly through the door, "Bruiser, we need to talk."

Bruiser stares back at the mirror silently. His mother's reflection has returned, staring at him with her analytical motherly discernment. He does another clown-sized line and shouts through the door, "Talk about what, Vanessa? How you're trying to save your job by fucking me into complacency."

"It's not like that, Bruiser."

Bruiser splashes water on his face, and his mother's reflection dissipates slowly. He turns to the door and says, "It's business and you want something from me; compliance." Bruiser returns to his hodgepodge of delights, and there's a silence that follows. It leaves him contemplating why he loves his precious distractions as he gracelessly pushes them back and forth with a razor blade. "Vanessa, I'm so tired of being a piece of shit. I've been holding on to a darkness that isn't mine, and it's tearing me apart. I can't." A single tear rolls down Bruiser's cheek. He puts his left hand out and puts the point of the razor blade to his wrist. "I feel like there's this world of ancient beings that's watching me suffer as I plummet through darkness alone while my love fills their souls."

"Bruiser, open the door so that I can look you in the eyes when I say this."

"Anything you can say to me you can say to the door."

"That's a-door-able, but I need you to stop being such a mope and open the fucking door!"

"I'm good. I'm fucking done with this hapless pursuit," he says as he runs the blade back and forth across his wrist ever-so-lightly. "I've been fighting this life so long that I forgot what I'm fighting for, and I'm tired, really tired."

Vanessa starts banging her head against the door, begging him, "Just open the fucking door!"

"I'm taking a shit. Leave me alone."

"I'll give you five minutes and then I'm coming in."

"Can you just say whatever it is that you need to say, so that you'll feel better about yourself, and then leave me alone!"

"Bruiser, cut the shit. Take off your mask, open the door, and let me in! I'm not doing this with you."

Bruiser doesn't respond to her. Instead, he leans over the counter, does a line, and turns to the hot tub, razor blade in hand. He climbs atop the edge of the tub, staring down into his distorted bubbly reflection, watching his tears as they're enveloped by the chemically enhanced water. He puts his right arm out on his leg and puts the blade back on his wrist.

Vanessa kicks the door startling him and says, "You have the ability to change this planet forever, like no other, but as long as your mother controls your emotions, she'll tear you apart. You have an unsurmountable mountain of pressure on you, and you can't just expect to do it fucked up like this. I need you sober and present if we're going to do this. Can you do sober?"

"Gross," he mumbles.

"Bruiser, tonight was a fucking disaster; your mom's dead!"

"You don't know that. I slapped her, and she's going to be fine," he says.

"You truly believe that?" she asks.

"Wholeheartedly," he says.

"Well, you're going to have to explain that to the feds. They're outside the bus waiting on you. They said that they can erase the situation if we help them out," she says and holds her breath waiting on the meltdown.

"Well, that didn't take long," he says and then bears down on his wrist with the blade. "You expect me to work with them, trust them — the darkness. The same people that ripped off our wings, used our feathers to rest their weary heads, and then told us we were just stupid fucking humans!"

"What was I supposed to do, Bruiser? Tell them you're not interested in covering up your mom's death, so that you can continue healing people and creating more heart-eating teenagers?"

"That was a fluke, Vanessa. There's something else at play here," he says snidely. "Look, it doesn't matter anyway. I'm done with this life. I'm tired of fighting to obtain a level of happiness that can't exist. We're meant to suffer, and I'm done entertaining them. There has to be a better place than here."

"Bruiser, open the door."

"I'm kind of busy," he says with a broken tone.

Vanessa lets out a disgruntled howl and kicks the door with a fervent release, breaking the seal. She opens the door and finds Bruiser squatting on the edge of the tub with the razor blade pressed into his wrist. "It's up the river not across the street," is all she can say. Bruiser puts his hand on his head, mimes like he's taking off his mask, and sets it down. Bruiser slides into the tub, turns the blade ninety-degrees, and traces a vein up to his elbow. Vanessa steps forward, leaning on the edge of the tub, asking, "Aren't you afraid of dying?"

"I'm afraid of living, Vanessa." Bruiser presses the blade into his forearm just enough to puncture the skin.

"Bruiser!" she yelps, "what-the-fuck is wrong with you?"

"I have the heart of a twelve-year old girl."

"It is rather gauche — your heart," she says shakily, reaching for the razor. "Let me take your darkness."

Bruiser puts his arms under the bubbly guise and says, "You wouldn't last eight seconds with my demons."

Vanessa watches as the water slowly changes hues and demands, "If I'm your 'hellhound' it's exactly what I'm here for! Own *your* path and all you can do is grow from it!"

"Well, here we grow," says Bruiser as he bears down on the blade, dragging it up his forearm in a pernicious manner. "I'm going inside now, and I'm going to reverse the gravitational pull of everything." He furrows deeper into his flesh with the blade, ripping through his person in search of a freedom that can only come from the truth.

The water turns into a broth of shadows swimming in his essence and Vanessa jumps in the tub and takes the razor from him, shouting, "Bruiser! There are other ways to get to the same place. This is the fear winning."

Bruiser laughs and says, "Fear deserves to win. They played a better game."

Vanessa climbs on top of Bruiser, straddling him and kisses him all over his face, trying to penetrate him with as much love as she can. "I'm not going to let it win, Bruiser!"

Bruiser murmurs from a distance as his eyes roll back in his head. "I don't think you have much say in it."

Bruiser's eyes open to a bright light clouded by dancing shadows. He takes his first breath of a stale metallic air as his hands stretch out, caressing the cold metal slab that he's lying on. Confused by his whereabouts, he looks around and finds himself in an empty room made completely of metal. He tastes the air again, finding it to be unfamiliar and unfulfilling.

"Am I dead?" he asks himself as he sits up slowly, toying with his equilibrium. He finds himself in some sort of cell with an opening that's filled with an overbearing light that spans from wall to wall. "This doesn't look like hell, maybe I've been abducted," he says as he cautiously slides off the table onto the cold metal floor. The floor gives a little as he steps onto it, and the movement spooks him. He tries to return to the table but can't as it is melting into the floor. He watches the table dissolve and says, "Definitely an abduction, but by who?" Bruiser walks toward the opening, finding it so bright outside of his room that there are no shadows to give the outside world definition.

"Hello!" he shouts to no response, as if he were yelling underwater. He turns to his new surroundings and squints his eyes aggressively, trying to sharpen his focus and force himself awake, but nothing changes. He looks down and finds himself garbed in a tight skin-tone onesie that's so tight it barely leaves room for breath. He tries stretching it out in hopes of loosening the hold it has on him, but it doesn't give. "That's cute, I wonder what this would look like in black?" His suit turns black with the thought, and he returns to the blinding opening, asking himself, "Could it be heaven?" He laughs gregariously and runs towards the bright opening, but his attempt to leave the room is thwarted by an invisible barrier that forces him to the floor.

He stands up and reaches out to touch whatever it was that humbled him. His hand sends out a wave of neon vibrations and he tries to push his way through the wall, but it pushes back, and there's a heat that courses through his hand as his suit turns pure white. He squats, looking at where the wall meets the floor. There are no seams where they meet and no break in the continuity. He puts his hand back on the wall and finds it to be fluid as if he put his hand on the meniscus of a flowing creek. His suit forces a breath out of him, and he decides to sit down in hopes of embracing the moment.

As he squats to sit down on the floor, it raises, forming a cube for him to rest on. One would think the metal floor to be cold and firm, not leaving room for comfort, but it gives and embraces his form. *Solitude*, he thinks and shuts his eyes, returning for a lungful of the unfamiliar air. His eyes open as the shadow of a feminine form appears on the other side of the blown-out opening. He rubs his eyes and says, "Definitely a dream."

The shadow responds, saying, "That would be so much easier to explain. We don't have much time. I need you to open your heart, knowing that it's safe here." She puts her hand on the invisible wall and says, "Let go of the darkness and absorb the light. It's the only thing that can protect you now."

Vanessa can feel Bruiser's form collapse into the tub as he releases the magic that was contained. "We'll see about that, Bruiser," she says, reaches back, and slaps him with a left. His being sinks deeper into the shallow hole. Vanessa grabs his belt, pulls him back to sea level, and slaps him with a right to the same resolve. She double slaps him, but his light refuses to return. Her anger retreats, and she breaks down in tears. "You're not going to do this to me, Bruiser!" She draws back again and says, "I'm not done with you." She slaps him repeatedly with both hands until she feels a spark of life that announces his return.

Vanessa leans back in the tub and releases an expired breath she'd been holding onto. She grabs his wrist and pulls his arm out of the burgundy water in search of what she assumes is a fatal wound but finds nothing that denotes his attempt. Bruiser's eyes open, he smiles for a split second, and then his face returns to bothered. Vanessa pushes herself off him and climbs out of the tub, stripping down as she does. She grabs a blood-stained towel, removes the excess fluids from her form, and wraps herself in it. She walks over to the bed and falls into it.

"Why would you do that to me?" she asks with a despairing tone.

"This isn't about you. I saw her," he says as he finds himself stewing in a pot of his own juices.

"Who?"

"My sister. I have to go back," he says.

"Sure, Bruiser, we can get into some weird kinked out version of *'Flatliners,'* or you can come over here and fuck me until the rest of the world disappears," she says and rolls out of her towel.

Bruiser looks over to the mirror on the counter and then at Vanessa, the exquisitely beautiful woman offering herself to him. He stands up and watches the blood-red water run down his body as he disrobes and starts to towel off, saying, "I'm sorry."

He walks over to the bed and stares down at Vanessa in her unprotected form. She squirms around playfully as she's analyzed and asks him, "For what, exactly?"

He lays down on his side across from her and says, "For sharing. I generally prefer to keep my madness to myself."

Vanessa grabs his hand and says, "Bruiser, I've known you for two days now. You're a full-on fucking mess, and I can't imagine what loving you feels like."

With a face full of sarcasm that covers a hint of the truth, he asks her, "Are you saying you don't love me?"

She releases his hand, puts hers on his face, and pushes him on his back, saying, "I was disgusted by you from what I saw on the internet, but as soon as I met you, I felt something," She rolls on top of him, and straddles him, "in my soul. There's something we have to do together. I feel like I have to help you."

Bruiser tries to push her off him, saying, "Look, you don't—"

She fights to remain atop her paramount. "I'm going to fuck you," she says, pulling at him.

Bruiser interrupts her disposition saying, "Listen, I'm not worth it. You have a girlfriend that loves you." He looks away from her and says, "I'll just fuck you up, like everything else I touch."

"I was saying, I'm going to fuck you, just not tonight. When's the last time you let someone just hold you?" she asks him with a seductive smile.

"I don't know. Maybe never," he says solemnly.

"Let me be the big spoon," she says and falls back into the bed wedging herself underneath him. She rolls him on his side and wraps herself around him like a backpack. Bruiser fidgets nervously to find comfort in her arms. "Just let it happen. Put down your agenda, and maybe we could just lie here appreciating 'this' while we have it."

"Thank you," he whispers. "You've definitely got your work cut out for you. I feel like I've been forcing myself to suppress that person, because no one's ever valued my heart. All I've done is submit to the agenda and let it compress me into a lifeless sediment with no sentiment for this life. I just want to walk freely with my heart wide-the-fuck open, connected to the world." Bruiser rolls out of her embrace and confronts her, asking, "Do you think you could love me — forever?" He stares deeply into her with his third eye to the ground, waiting to hear the truth.

Vanessa smiles with a sympathetic glimmer and says, "It's the only reason I'm here, stupid. And once again, my heart has me stuck in the same karmic pattern of saving someone great from themselves."

Bruiser slides on top of her, staring into her eyes, and leans in for a kiss. Vanessa doesn't fight his touch. The connection blinds the two, and they get lost in their spiritual locus. Bruiser feels his agenda filling with blood and pulls away, asking, "How about a virgin massage?"

"What's that?" she asks as she returns slowly to the room.

Bruiser dismounts her and rolls her over on her stomach, saying, "I'll show you." He rubs his hands together to warm them up and begins slowly introducing his touch to her with a light amount of pressure. As he touches her, she begins to let go of her protective energy. Bruiser slides his hands across her back, caressing it as a wave does the sand. He pulls the tension down her arms from her shoulders and out of her fingertips. He starts kneading her ass and gets distracted as her pussy peeks out at him. He pulls away and moves towards her legs, saying, "You truly are beautiful."

Vanessa turns her head, looking back over her shoulder, and says, "There's some coconut oil in the bathroom?"

Bruiser crawls off the bed and walks into the bathroom where he's confronted by his warm bubbly jus and is reminded of the metal room. He looks down at the floor covered in a bloody rosé and then at the mirror on the counter. He picks up the straw, assuming that to be the fastest way back to his metal cell and leans over making eye contact with himself in the mirror. As he contemplates shedding his mortal coil, he's once again confronted by his mother's reflection. There's a ringing in his ears and he hears his mother say, "I've found a place filled with light where I'm strong and no longer afraid. Please forgive me and know that you deserve all the love your heart can hold … Pick up the phone."

Bruiser drops the straw and hears Vanessa say, "Bruiser, your phone's ringing — it's your mom."

He smiles as the darkness disperses, and revels with the joy of his mother's words. He returns to the mirror covered in misleading substances, saying to himself, "No harm, no foul," and leans over and removes the flirtatious tricksters from atop the mirror. The bus gears up, shifting beneath his feet, he slips, falling and hitting his head on the corner of the hot tub, and the only word imaginable slips out of his mouth, "Perfect."

In My Time of Dying

A vast ball of radiated plasma dances daintily in the sky, gently caressing the epidermis of our reluctant messiah. His eyes open to a vivid cobalt sky, and the thought of something so far away affecting his being, thwarts his processor. In a waking panic, he releases a pent-up breath, and he's immediately startled by the boisterous laughter of three little towheads running off into an ocean view. The saline breeze pushes gracelessly over his form, and he hears, "Do you think you could be happy here with us, doing nothing - forever?"

Bruiser turns to his left to find a woman with a blank face in a white bikini sprawled out on a beach blanket lying next to him. He smiles as he fondles the granules of sand beneath him while he processes the concept of contentment, returning with this question, "Don't you think it's strange that you can feel the touch of something so far away?"

"Yeah, reminds me of your heart; either way it's only an eight-minute drive if you're a beam of light, but way to avoid the question," snarks his female companion.

"Forever is just so much longer now, compared to when they invented it," he says and rolls over to look her in the eyes, but finds only an empty blanket. "Barf," he mutters and returns to his back, saying, "All alone, naked in the sun, right here where you left me." As he says that, the sky glitches and leaves an opening that gives way to the metal ceiling for which he so yearned.

"Welcome back," he hears dance through his cell.

Bruiser sits up in search of the ominous voice and stretches out, consuming the unfamiliar air again, saying, "Thanks for having me." He slides off his catafalque and turns around to watch it dissolve back into its surroundings.

He starts to pace, inspecting this relatively new, but somewhat familiar surroundings, and he's instantly reminded that he's overflowing with fluids. "Well, I'm not asleep. At least, I can't remember having to piss in a dream."

Bruiser is naturally drawn to the blown-out opening again, like a fly to a flatscreen, looking for escape, but finding only a wall. He remembers the gateway offering no clarity or freedom, yet he tries again to stare through it, searching for a relative being with a rational explanation. Coming up unfulfilled, he turns to the wall behind him and walks toward it, asking himself, "I wonder what's out there." With that thought, the wall turns into an endless sea of stars. He walks up to the wall and puts his hand on it. As he thinks about sitting down to enjoy the view, the floor forms a pulpit underneath him. He relaxes into his seat, shuts his eyes, and takes a deep breath. As he breathes in, the window returns to a blank metallic wall, and he thinks to himself, *You were the one that wanted to come back here.*

A concerned voice from beyond whispers in his ear, *But where are you, and what does it matter?* The whisper challenges him again, saying, *This is all you've ever wanted; a life free of chaos - yours or anyone else's.*

Bruiser's eyes open as he states, "I'd rather be at the beach surrounded by chaos." The wall returns to the view of the beach, and the crashing waves return him to a meditative state. The first thought he hears as he shuts his eyes is, *The government put you in here. They drugged you and kidnapped you so that they could experiment on you. They don't want you healing people. It's the same thing that happened to your sister and you walked right into it.*

His eyes burst open as he thinks of his sister and an image of her, emaciated and curled up in a ball, gasping for the will to live appears on the wall, and he's reminded of his last moments on Earth. The image of him lying on the floor of the bus supersedes his sister's image and he says, "I'm pretty sure I drugged myself."

"You're never getting out of here!" shouts a voice.

He yells back at it, "I'd be fine without your worries!" Bruiser takes a deep breath, shuts his eyes, and tries to force the last moments of his chaotic life far from his presence, but the visions of his mother's anguish leave no room for serenity. His eyes open, and as they do, the last show in Charlotte replays on the wall in front of him — not from his perspective, but as if he were watching it on TV. He watches as Alice breaks free from her crippled form. The process of her reforming and coming into the room is frightening. There's an absent look in her eyes as she grabs his mother by the throat, smiles, reaches into her chest, and pulls her heart out of it. As he watches his mother relieved of her burden, he's reminded of his loss and the probability that he'll never truly be happy. He closes his eyes forcefully as she takes her last breath, and when his eyes reopen, he sees the two mustache dudes, filming the morose acts, smiling with a twinkle in their eyes.

The wall glitches, returning to space, and looking to fill an empty space in his mind, he asks, "What happened after that?" There's another glitch, and the wall returns to just being a wall. He closes his eyes and breathes in, thinking, "Maybe if I fall asleep here, I'll wake up there."

What if here is there, and you just end up somewhere else — somewhere worse? questions a distant voice. Bruiser tries to get comfortable and return to his meditation, but he's interrupted by a voice as it asks him, *What are you running from? I thought you wanted to be here.*

He takes another deep breath, and as he releases it, he feels something land on his neck and crawl around. Without hesitation, his eyes open and he slaps the back of his neck. Coming up empty handed and frustrated, he decides to return to his meditation in hopes of finding some basic understanding of bliss, and immediately he is taunted by another voice that says, *You're losing it, nerd. It's hot in here, and your skin's crawling. Ignore the need to respond and leave the line of communication open between the subconscious and the conscious.*

Bruiser deepens his breath, removing himself from the cell, and sending him spelunking inward as he thinks, *Breathe deep or this will surely lead us straight to space madness.* The micro-tickling sensation returns tenfold, and he tries to resist, but can't and opens his eyes in search of the irritant.

He takes another deep breath that begs for a silence from all the restless voices that are running through his psyche, and he hears, *What makes you think you're in space?*

The sensation arises again, and fully aware of his need to brush away the agitator, he resists and lets the feeling subside. But the feelings of discomfort snowball into the belief that he truly has an insect doing a trek around his person. As he resists the agitation, a neon, purple light erupts from his third eye that sherpas him through the transcendental valleys at the base of a spiritual mountain.

The first thought to arise on his internal journey is, *You're tired of being alone, at the same time you're defeated in a room full of people.* With the next breath he gets, *You've been given a gift you perceive as a burden, yet the only burden is the ancient one that weighs on your soul, leaving you void of content and happiness wherever you are.* The thought leaves him with a vision of struggle in a post-apocalyptic world where he sees nothing but pain and fear that's represented in every action.

Refusing to open his eyes, he immediately feels that little something tickle his arm, but this time it penetrates him. His eyes open immediately to reveal a metallic mosquito on his arm, imbibing his life force, and he says, "Even you want something from me space parasite."

Bruiser tightens the skin on his arm, detaining the insect while he contemplates killing it. It offers him a choice as it fills itself mindlessly with his life-force: Offer it a way out of this dream by letting it drink itself to death or relieve the physical constraint that's keeping them bound to the moment and make a new friend.

He releases the tension, and before it can escape Bruiser's person, his left-hand swoops in on the little bugger, and he captures the parasite between his thumb and pointer finger. He laughs at the minuscule being as it wiggles frantically trying to free itself from the eminent doom. Bruiser can feel its life-force pulse through his hand as he holds its existence in question. *"Do it. Just smash me with your mighty fingers, ending my struggle."*

Bruiser laughs and unleashes the small being, saying, "Lucky for you, skeeter, I'm short on friends, and the internal dialogue is nothing other than frustrating." He releases the bug, and watches as it falls to the floor, exploding upon impact, and turns to a puddle of bubbling, metallic ooze that changes colors like an oil spill. Filled with guilt for the life he just smote, he dryly says, "Back to the internal dialogue it is." He kneels and pokes at the puddle with his finger. It begins to grow and starts to take somewhat of a flesh-tone. A hand forms from the puddle, and it reaches desperately, trying to pull itself out of the puddle.

Bruiser contemplates giving it a hand and helping it, but as it's starting to take form, he's overwhelmed by the fear of an intruder. He looks around the room for an object to defend himself, and immediately remembers there's absolutely nothing in the cell. He watches as the hand turns green and takes on a scaly texture. It's followed by a head-sized ball with snake eyes. The semi-formed being emerges, along with another hand, dripping in metallic ooze. Slowly, the fully formed being emerges from the puddle, and there's a familiarity that Bruiser is stunted by as he looks into the eyes of the transmuted being. The two stare each other down for a moment as the being gathers its composure, and Bruiser throws out his best guess, jesting, "Dad?"

"Kind of," laughs his new cellmate. "You know where I can get a drink?"

Bruiser looks around the cell and says, "Good luck with that. I'm still trying to find the pisser."

The being pulls at Bruiser's onesie, saying, "Go in your nano-suit: it filters the urine and returns the distilled water back to your body."

Bruiser jumps back from his touch, asking, "Why should I trust you?"

The being chuckles and then asks him sternly, "Don't you think it's time to start trusting people?"

Bruiser walks around the being, studying his composure, saying, "I guess, I just assume you want something like the rest of the world. Didn't you sneak in here to get slapped?"

The being stops Bruiser's aimless pacing by putting his hand on Bruiser's heart, saying, "Quite the opposite, I'm here to heal you."

Bruiser is left speechless while making an odd, judgmental face. His new friend asks, "Are you okay?"

Bruiser's facial expression changes from confusion and discern to relief and content as his suit turns a tie-dyed pattern and he says, "Give me a minute. I'm distilling in my pants suit. Who are you?" he asks his cellmate.

The being responds, "I am Ü. Who are you?"

Bruiser laughs and says, "I was just sitting here trying to figure that out."

The being repeats himself, saying, "My friends call me Ü."

"You have friends, Ewe?" asks Bruiser.

"All over this universe and throughout most dimensions," he says, "and you're one of my favorites."

"What's your whole name Ewe?"

"Ü it's short for Manüre," he says.

"Like the fertilizer?" asks Bruiser.

"Exactly, but we don't have time for civilities, Zealand."

Bruiser smiles as he hears his chosen name and says, "You can call me Bruiser. Welcome. This is my cell." He points out the empty metal room, saying, "Take a seat, friend."

Ü continues to stand, staring down Bruiser, and asks, "You really don't remember me, sir?"

Bruiser looks at Ü closely and says, "Sorry, this is my first … second time here, wherever here is."

Ü scoffs at his clouded naivety, saying, "That's odd. Someone's clearly erased a major piece of your storage. We're inside you, Zealand. You're always here."

Bruiser tries to deflect the obscure thought, saying, "As long as I'm not inside Ü, we're doing good." He stares at Ü, waiting for him to laugh at his joke, but it doesn't happen. Instead, Ü returns Bruiser's gaze with his weathered, distant, and somewhat familiar reptilian eyes. "Why am I here?"

"You come here to remind yourself of the connectedness of everything. Everything is a small piece of a sea of energy that's connected by subatomic particles. Here, everything is controlled by thought: your suit, the walls, the floor, and the lights — everything. It all moves and changes with your thought. It's the same in all your other lives as well, but you seem to forget that."

Bruiser squints and makes a constipated, poop face, asking, "Well, then why can't I leave?"

Ü shakes him and asks, "Why would you want to? This is the only place you're safe." Bruiser, completely confused, turns his head sideways as his face starts to drool with ignorance. Ü responds to his absence, pointing to the wall, saying, "You're caged by a single thought at the moment. It's left you stuck in a repetitive thought process that won't allow you to be free."

The wall returns to visions of his life, and shuffles through all his damaged relationships with everyone he believes he has ever loved. Bruiser watches the series of traumatic interactions with a deep pensive stare and asks, "And what would that debate be about?"

Ü walks Bruiser's closer to the wall, saying, "Love or the lack of it that stems from the inability to forgive yourself and the world around you. The last time we talked was in this same place under the same circumstances. You kept going on about how you were the zero point, and that's where the changes had to be made. I made a number of modifications to your being, but something went wrong."

Bruiser stares back at Ü, begging for more answers, asking, "Modifications?"

"I'm kind of your spiritual mechanic, but more like a programmer," says Ü, rubbing his scaly hands together.

"That makes sense," he says sarcastically.

"You're not going to remember most of this when you get back to your vacation home, Urantia. It's on the verge of collapse, and it's threatened by a force of darkness that's been looking for you since the beginning of time itself. You only show up here when you're … deceased in one of your many lives." Ü pulls up a piece of Bruiser's life on the wall, and it shows Bruiser, smashed on the bathroom floor of his last moments, cursing the gods as he battles with gravity.

Bruiser scratches his brow, asking, "I'm dead?"

Ü swipes his hand and moves to one of his lives in Atlantis, and then branches off into parallel universes where Bruiser is known for battling darkness fearlessly under different levels of situational gravity.

Bruiser rubs his leg anxiously and asks, "I've lived all these lives, Ü? On Urantia?" Bruiser walks up to the wall close enough to analyze all its intricacies.

Ü puts his hand on Bruiser's shoulder, saying, "This might hurt, but technically sir, you're living them all at the same time."

Bruiser, fully enthralled as he watches his lives play out, says, "That explains why I feel tired all the time. How is that possible though?"

Ü has a good belly laugh and says, "Bruiser, last time I explained it to you, you killed me, and then you killed yourself. Here we are, back in the same spot, and you don't remember any of it."

Bruiser puts his hands together and apologizes, saying, "My bad, Ü."

Ü pushes Bruiser's hands down and says, "This is a safe place where your truest form, the original, before you started the simulacra process, resides. From here, you can jump in and out of any of those lives you're living that need your undivided attention. It's

a hub you can visit whenever you want respite from the never-ending
cycles you've chosen to reenact."

"Why would I want to come back here?"

"To listen to the universe. It's about to change infinitely.
You've been suffering at your own hand, playing the martyr, and we
need you embrace who you really are, so that you can prepare Urantia
for the return of the Winged Planet."

Bruiser looks at Ü sideways, asking him, "Urantia?" He turns
back to the wall as it returns to a portrait of endless space,
saying, "And in all reality I'm trapped in this cell alone."

"Your truest self, or what the humans refer to as the soul, is
here, protected, and more so hidden," says Ü.

Bruiser turns from the wall and asks, "So, what do we do, Ü?"

Ü puts his hand on Bruiser's shoulder and says, "There's no time
to explain, there is a line forming outside your cell right now of
beings that need you, but I need to heal you first. Something we did
to you has you consuming darkness and holding on to it, instead of
transmigrating it to the light. I need to fix it before it destroys
us both. Lay down on the bench." Ü puts his hands on Bruiser's
shoulders and pushes him down on his back as a metal bench forms
underneath him. He puts his hand over Bruiser's heart and says,
"Close your eyes." He puts both of his scaly hands over Bruiser,
palms down, and scans his being, saying, "Take a deep breath and
visualize your future. See yourself surrounded by light and love."
Bruiser releases two child-size breaths from his lungs. "Deeper,"
requests Ü as he waits for a true release of breath. "There's someone
here," says Ü. Bruiser's eyes open and he sits up. Ü pushes Bruiser
back to horizontal, saying, "Not here here. You have a dark entity
that I've never noticed before. Close your eyes and breathe. I'll do
the rest."

Bruiser is pushed through darkness as Ü manipulates the inner
workings of his transcendental being. There's a silence that's sealed
with a frost that pushes through his being, and as he drifts through
the solitary nothingness, he's reminded of his friends and the
holding pattern that they must be stuck in. His eyes open to a
broadening blue sky and he smiles as the silhouette of a flocculant
man's head leans into his scenic view, blocking the sun.

"Manüre?" asks Bruiser, reaching for familiarity.

"Tell me how you really feel," says the man as a sour, onion
smell hits Bruiser's olfactory canal, and he pops up as he realizes
he has his head in the lap of a random vagrant.

The man asks him, "Could you spare some change?"

Bruiser digs around in his pockets as he analyzes his new surroundings. The man puts his hand on Bruiser's, stopping him from his search, and says, "No, are you ready for change? You're tired of suffering at your own hands. You're tired of the blatant oppression, and you want to fall back in love with this world that surrounds you."

Bruiser looks at the man with a tilted head and says, "Sounds about right, but who are you, and what do you know?"

The man puts his hand out for a shake, saying, "John, John Johnson. You don't remember anything from last night?"

Bruiser continues rifling through his pockets in search of an anchor to this reality, asking, "Do I owe you money?" A tinnitus like ringing penetrates Bruiser's being, his vision blurs, and he's pushed back into John's lap, rubbing his temples. The sky glitches, leaving an opening, that returns Bruiser back to his metallic cell.

"I don't even see how you're still alive. Did you do all this? It's all bubble gum and duct tape," says a shadowed form that's standing over Bruiser with its palms directed at him. The man circles blindly over Bruiser, stopping at his head, then to his feet, and then over his chest. He opens a vortex of light with his hands over Bruiser's chest, puts one palm over his heart, consuming his darkness while the other one pushes the energetic tornado of darkness off into the nothingness: far away from Bruiser's chest. As the darkness dissipates, he starts to pull a coil of light up and out of Bruiser's chest, saying, "To dance with the devil and not fall in love. It's the hardest test a soul can endure. You've hallowed out an endless cavern in your soul with the darkness you've consumed, and it's time to fill it with light. The shadowed form pushes both hands into Bruiser's chest, saying, "Here he is, the one that's been attached to you for lifetimes. I don't know how I've never seen this before. He crushes you at every apex and controls you with a fear that can never be relinquished; especially when you're intoxicated. Do I have your permission to remove him, Bruiser?"

Bruiser's eyes open as the darkness starts to throb inside of him and he barfs out, "Where am I?"

John points to the Lincoln Memorial, saying, "Washington, DC."

Bruiser sits up, discombobulated from his travels, and pulls out his phone. He turns it on and rifles through it, searching frantically for any clues that will lead him back to some feeling of normalcy. The texts and voicemail messages are endless and seem to go on for days. Bruiser drops a pin, sending it to Vanessa, and throws the phone over his shoulder. His panic subsides, and he asks his new friend, "You got a smoke, dude?"

John rummages through his pockets, finds a short, and offers it to Bruiser, saying, "I thought you quit."

Bruiser laughs and snidely refuses the half-smoked cigarette, asking, "How'd I get here?"

"You were here when I got off of work last night."

"Work?" asks Bruiser, challenging his words.

"Yeah, I beg for money in a couple different locations. I make people feel better about their hapless pursuit of the reward they'll never obtain. Does that count as work?" he asks and pulls out a brand-new pack of Dunhills. Bruiser reaches for them, but John pulls them back, saying, "I want you to be completely aware of the decision you're making, knowing that there's no wrong decision. You've quit, and that's one of the hardest things to do in this life. If you smoke a cigarette now, and don't appreciate the one full breath you have, you'll regret it and spend the rest of your life chasing it; stuck between the two thoughts. If you're going to smoke, love it, or it will kill you."

Bruiser puts his hands in his pockets and says, "I'm not even sure I quit." He takes a cigarette from John and asks him, "You live here, on this bench?"

John lights a cigarette and says, "Yeah, Lincoln was a great man, a savior of the people. People that needed a fearless leader to speak on their inequality, and free them from oppression. Bruiser, this planet was built on slavery, and it still exists to this day. Our slave quarters are nicer now, but they've hidden it so well that most people don't even know they're enslaved. We've been programmed by the media to consume at a rate that no one can keep up with. They've got us chasing a twenty-four-carat dream, pulling a cart full of fear-mongers, and the one percent holds the whip."

"No truer words," says Bruiser as he stares at the cigarette John handed him, contemplating the only question that matters. John takes a drag off his cigarette and blows the smoke subsequently in Bruiser's face. "How'd you end up homeless?"

"You mean free. I used to be a producer in Hollywood. I was attending a benefit at the White House. I'd been partying all night, and I woke up here, on this bench, to a call from my wife. She told me she'd been cheating on me with my associate and that she was leaving me. So, I just walked away from that person — the one with the whip."

"Don't you miss it: the fame and the money?"

"I had everything I'd ever wanted, yet something was missing. All the drugs, the cars, fucking models, led me to an empty existence. Now, I've got all day for my thoughts, and occasionally I get the chance to make someone feel better about their life. What about you?"

"I'm in entertainment. I'm the host of a new show called Future of the Left."

John looks over at Bruiser and lights up, saying, "Zealand T. Dahl, I thought you looked familiar!"

"Bruiser works," he says.

"The Second Coming spent the night on my bench," he says and laughs. John stands up, leans over Bruiser, and starts talking, but in a different voice; deeper and more penetrating. "Your worst enemy is your ego."

Bruiser stares up at John blankly while he tries to ingest the strange man's words and says, "My whole existence is ego. It fuels my everything."

John smiles and says, "It's our only defense, and it was created by a child that was afraid no one would love the real you: the sober you, the poor you, or the inadequate lover—"

Bruiser stands up and gets in John's face, saying, "Slow down there, bub, I'm a great lover!"

John grabs him by the shoulders and says excitedly, "There it is. Remember that voice and where it comes from, and then silence it." The tour bus rolls up to the curb, fifty feet from the bench and honks its whaling horn. "Do you need to go?"

"They can wait," says Bruiser.

"Can you?" he asks.

"Can I heal you?" asks Bruiser.

John looks Bruiser in the eyes and asks, "Does it look like I need to be healed? I have no dis-ease."

Bruiser digs through his pockets, asking, "What about money? Can I give you some money for taking care of me?" Bruiser pulls out his wallet and opens it looking for cash to give to John. He pulls out his driver's license, stares at it for a moment, and scratches his head, asking himself, "Zealand T. Dahl? Sure, that makes sense."

John stands there, laughing, and says, "I don't need anything. That's my freedom. May I finish healing you?" John lays Bruiser back down on the bench and puts his hand over Bruiser's sacrum. John's eyes close and he says, "You turned your heart off when you accepted that entity into your being. It's served its purpose, and now you must forgive it for tormenting you. Love it. Ask it for forgiveness and let go of it, knowing you don't need it to protect you anymore. Give it the love we all desire and fill the empty space it left in you with light, so that it can't return to its home."

Bruiser mumbles, "I'd like to see that."

John puts his hand over Bruiser's temples and says, "When you believe it, you'll see it." His hands light up and fill Bruiser with a fragmenting vibration that blurs his perspective.

When the vibration passes, Bruiser opens his eyes and finds himself
back in the metal room that's now filled with dark shadows, swimming
in circles around his being. *If you want to save these people,*
whispers Ü, *you have to change your whole perspective. In that life,
you played the victim, suffering at your own hand, because you
believed it brought growth. And it did, but you're done with that
thought process now. You're about to hold the whip, and it's your
decision what to do with it.*
    Ü steps back from Bruiser and starts to do movements similar to
Tai Chi, but more aggressive. His hands activate a sphere of energy
that surrounds Bruiser and fills it with a blinding light. Ü spins
the sphere around Bruiser, and as he does, Bruiser starts to convulse
and expels a burgundy fluid that resembles a fountain of red wine. Ü
steps back, puts his palms together, and closes his eyes, saying, "I
love you. Please, forgive me. Thank you. I'm sorry."
    The white light is devoured by dark threads of smoke, and as
they fill the sphere, they form a face. The face of the shadow that
Bruiser has been holding onto since the beginning of time. It forces
its way out of the sphere and grabs a hold of Ü, shaking him at his
core, asking, "Are you coming with me? I've always wondered what a
reptilian soul tastes like, assuming that you have one." The shadow's
mouth opens, revealing a blackhole, filled with lost souls that are
spinning in the absence of light.
    "Release him!" shouts Ü as his eyes light up a with a neon,
lime-green fire. He grabs a hold of the shadow's mouth, pushes it
back inside the sphere, just over Bruiser's heart, and his hands
light up a with the same light that was emanating from his eyes. "You
have an alien implant in your head that helps you see, but the wiring
is fucked. I can fix it, but I have to—" And before he can finish his
words, he's swallowed by the shadow. It retreats back inside Bruiser,
and he starts convulsing, his back arches as an endless tapeworm of
darkness bursts out of his chest and integrates itself with the
metallic cell as it slowly slithers down the walls of Bruiser's
catafalque, across the floor and up the walls to the ceiling,
embedding itself in the metal as it goes.

Bruiser's phone rings and his eyes open to John, standing over him
with his hands shaking. Bruiser stares up at him, silently, asking
for permission to answer his phone, interrupting the esoteric
surgery. John turns from him, and Bruiser grabs his phone from behind
the bench. "What up?"
    "Dude, you gonna' fuck this guy or what?" asks Dick, standing on
the steps of the bus, waving at Bruiser. "Just get his number and
let's get out of here."

Bruiser laughs and turns back to John but finds no one. He heads to the bus, looking over his shoulder in hopes of one last glimpse of his transient healer. As he walks up the stairs of the bus, he's greeted by Chuck, saying, "Good evening, sir. How are we today?"

"I've seen better. I woke up with my head in a homeless man's lap."

"These things happen, sir," says Chuck.

Bruiser pats Chuck on the back and says, "They do, more often than I'd like to admit. Where is everyone?"

"In your quarters I believe, sir," says Chuck as he releases the air brake.

Bruiser walks down the aisle expecting a surprise welcome that's followed by a blunt, but slides the door open to find Dick, Vanessa, Less, and Leslie all on their laptops, silently click-clacking away. "Welcome back?" he mumbles to himself.

Vanessa looks up from her screen, looks at Bruiser, and says, "Have a seat."

Bruiser, unamused by the vibe he just penetrated, passes by the table, and walks into the bathroom. He turns on the water, to muffle the relentless piss he's about to release, and gets stuck in a gooey moment as he watches the water freeze into droplets mid-air. He hears Ü whisper across dimensions, *Enjoy every breath you take. The world you think you're returning to is nothing like you remember.*

Bruiser shakes his head erratically, hoping to reset this reality, and walks back into the room solemnly. He sits down next to Vanessa, and she slides over. He looks at her screen, and it's blank. He looks at his friends, and they all avoid eye contact with him. "What's going on?" he asks in a precocious manner and then looks down at his palms.

Everyone shuts their laptops simultaneously. Vanessa watches Bruiser, staring deeply at the palms of his hands, and says in a stern voice, "Listen, Bruiser, do you know where you've been for the past few days?"

He looks up from his hands, saying, "No, but the homeless man, whose lap I woke up in, said I quit smoking and I feel amazing. So, if this is an intervention, I believe we're on the same page."

Dick joins Vanessa, saying, "We just can't have another episode like Charlotte!"

The vision of Bruiser's mother being held in the air while Alice rips out her heart flashes in the forefront of his mind's eye. "Listen, you know me. I … I can handle my shit, and I know the drugs have nothing to do with what happened. I feel like there's something larger at play." Bruiser searches for approval in his friend's eyes but finds only disdain for his presence.

Vanessa grabs his hand and says, "Your life means too much to this world to just throw it away over some trite, mommy issues.

Bruiser, when you crassly dug through your arm with that blade in hopes of escaping the suffering of this life—"

Less, trying to rearrange the tension in the room, asks, "Didn't you flatline last time your mom was in town?"

"That was just some dirty, dirty heroine." Bruiser turns to Dick and stares him down, demanding support with his eyes.

Avoiding Bruiser's eyes, Dick says, "I guess it was just a coincidence your mom was in town."

Bruiser stands up and silently looks over his flippant band of followers, soaking up their unfamiliarity, and then walks out of the room.

"Do you think it's him?" asks Less.

"Who else would it be, Less?" asks Dick.

"A really bad knock-off, that they just dumped in front of the Lincoln memorial." says Leslie.

"Anything's possible with those guys," states Less.

Bruiser returns with an armful of bottled waters, and everyone stares him down, looking for flaws. "You guys seriously think I was abducted … and cloned?"

"Do you think you were abducted?" asks Less.

"I have no idea where I've been, but I was hoping you guys could help me figure that out." Bruiser holds firm to his stance, hovering over his friends. "I woke up with my head in that homeless dude's lap, and I keep getting these flashes of a cold metallic cell where I was being healed by this reptilian being that spawned from a metallic mosquito." Dick pulls Bruiser into the booth by his hand, lights up a cigarette and offers it to him. "I'm good. Apparently, I quit."

"Definitely a clone," says Dick, without a doubt.

"He looks great, though, considering. Can we keep him?" asks Leslie as she fidgets nervously with herself under the table.

Frustrated and tired of defending his existence, Bruiser reaches in his back pocket and says, "Thanks, Leslie." He pulls his ID out of his pocket, hands it to Less, and adamantly says, "Explain how I woke up with this in my wallet!"

Less passes the ID around the table, saying, "Easy, you blacked out and went to the DMV."

"I can barely make it there sober," says Bruiser.

"Great picture, though," says Leslie as she over analyzes the ID. "Zealand T. Dahl."

"And how-the-fuck did I end up in Washington D fucking C? The last thing I remember was Charlotte!"

"That's what we were trying to figure out," says Dick.

"I want the truth. Tell me what happened after the show?"

Vanessa takes her time organizing her next words. She pulls Bruiser back into the booth, puts her arm around him, and says, "You were Dirt Deviling some fucked up concoction you made. You said you were tired of this life, locked yourself in the bathroom, and slit your wrist in the hot tub." Bruiser's eyes bulge out of their sockets as he looks for a scar, finding nothing. Vanessa takes a sip of water and says, "I brought you back — from the dead. And in a moment of weakness, I decided to let you violate me."

"Bruiser's eyes bulge further from his face with a disgraced fervor as he says, "There's no way I would forget that."

Vanessa smiles and says, "We were going to, but you went back to the bathroom to get some coconut oil. You never came back, and I found you on the floor, in a puddle, bleeding out of your nose."

"We tried to find your adrenaline pen, but—" says Less.

"It's in my briefcase," says Bruiser interrupting Less.

"It wasn't there; we looked," says Leslie.

Dick gets up and walks out of the room, closing the door behind him. Vanessa, looking down at the tabletop, says, "We knew the bus wouldn't get you to a hospital in time and they were waiting outside for you."

"Who?" asks Bruiser.

"The two mustache rides that were dressed in white linen," says Vanessa.

"Yeah, they had some naloxone, and they said they would help you, but we had to help them," says Less.

Bruiser slams his fist on the tabletop and says, "So you handed me over to the feds."

"It's not like that," says Vanessa.

"Less, you know how I feel about the feds!" shouts Bruiser.

Dick opens the door, after hearing Bruiser pop off, and shouts, "You were dead, Bruiser! They said they'd clean up the mess YOU made!"

Bruiser looks at Dick, smoking a cigarette, and his lungs tighten. Flustered, he fights his way out of the booth and storms out of his room past Dick, shouting, "Fuck dude!"

Dick follows him into the living area, saying, "Dude, you were all-the-way dead. Game over. No one gets healed!"

"There was adrenaline in my briefcase!" shouts Bruiser.

"There wasn't. We checked," says Dick.

Vanessa follows the two into the living room, shouting, "You're alive, Bruiser. That's all that matters."

Bruiser, now cornered by his producers, says, "So, you just handed me over to the fucking Romans. Those two Tommy Bahama wearing, fear and loathing in Portland dickheads. Are you even sure they are feds?"

Dick sits down in the dining booth and says boldly, "No, but there weren't any other options!"

Bruiser sits down across from him, takes a deep breath, and looks into his eyes. Vanessa sits down next to Dick, and Bruiser can feel that there's something off with the two but can't grasp it. "Vanessa, I get it! I don't expect you to fully understand how I feel about the government, but Dick, you know—"

Vanessa defends Dick, saying, "Look, Bruiser, we couldn't afford to take a risk with your life. It's too important."

"Important to who?" Bruiser asks defiantly.

"Humanity," mumbles Vanessa.

"If it's so fucking important, why would you put it in the hands of the evil empire?" Unable to look them in the eyes, granting them the power, Bruiser says, "I've been homeless three times, lived in a crack house, shot at, beat down in a Mexican gang fight, and died—three times now. I've always thought the world was out to get me, but I'm starting to think that I'm the one trying to kill myself, and that the universe keeps saving me, just to let me know I'm better than that."

"We have so much more than a show to lose. From what I saw the other night in Charlotte, whether I created this or not, there is something larger at play than what my hands are accomplishing. The more light I bring into this world, the more darkness follows to consume it. Healing that many people was clearly a beacon for darkness. I saw my sister struggle when she tried to heal people. The government went out of their way to make sure she didn't. I'm worried about you, my friends, and I need to know that you are ready to walk through every layer of hell with me. I … we have more than a show to lose, I need you guys to protect me, and I need to know right now where you guys are at."

Dick pulls at his wrist, saying, "Bruiser, we need you to protect us."

Vanessa joins Dick, saying, "Some kid ripped out your mom's heart and ate it. What's next?" Bruiser, undaunted by their pleas, gets up and tries to walk away. Vanessa jumps up and pushes Bruiser into a corner, saying, "You're really going to just walk away from this?"

"Yeah," Bruiser says, his head drops, and he continues to walk away. Vanessa retreats to the booth, sliding into Dick's embrace. Bruiser looks back and catches Vanessa looking into Dick's eyes endearingly. She gives him a kiss on the cheek, and Bruiser, completely butthurt by the sight of their connection, returns to the table and shouts, "Alice could have killed all of us, but she went straight for my mom! Don't you think that's odd?"

"I guess," the two say together.

Vanessa breaks down in tears, drops her head on the table, and Dick rubs her back gently as Bruiser stands over the table, completely dumbfounded by their connection. He stares her down, almost as if he were trying to look through her and startle the dreamer inside, hoping to hear the one truth he needs to hear most;

but he can't hear either of their thoughts. Bruiser concedes to their emotional wall and sits down across from the two. He goes to grab Vanessa's hand, but she pulls away.

Dick removes his arm from her, leans into Bruiser, and grabs his hands, saying, "When you died, it broke us, Bruiser. We all want a better future: a future with happy, healthy people, far from suffering. You're the only one that can truly give us that." Dick rubs Vanessa's leg with his free hand, trying to comfort her as he stares into Bruiser's eyes, saying, "Vanessa lost her brother to an overdose. You're my best friend, and I was sure I'd lost you this time."

Bruiser in a childlike tone, says, "I'm not going anywhere."

Vanessa looks up, wiping the tears off her face, and says, "We need you to take this seriously."

Bruiser stops in his emotional tracks as he starts to understand how much these two honestly love him, and how he broke them. He tries to rationalize his existence, saying, "That was an anomaly, and you can't blame me for it. I need some time to figure this out." He slouches back in the booth. "Guys, I'm sorry. I've been selfish with this life, because I felt entitled to the mediocre existence that I deemed comical, if anything, to validate the series of attacks I've felt from it relentlessly over the years."

Dick looks at Bruiser with a twitch in his eye and says, "Nobody truly cares. Get over it. We need you to figure this out with your head on straight, or more people are going to die."

Vanessa shrugs Dick's arm off her and says, "Look, if you can make the effort to keep heart eating zombies out of our life…"

Less walks in, sits down next to Bruiser, and interjects, saying, "Zombies would imply that they died and came back to life. Alice is something more complex and perfect."

Vanessa continues, saying, "Whatever they are. If we see more, you'll definitely have the government up your ass."

Bruiser looks at Dick, then Vanessa, and then back at Dick. "They're already up my ass, with a tracking device."

There's a moment that passes where everyone sits in silence, and they exchange glances; nothing more. Less straightens his back, puffs his chest out, and hoping to end the silence, jumps back in with, "I met the beast with three backs, and it gave me something. Something I have to tell you."

Vanessa and Dick turn to one another and smile as if they'd known each other for lifetimes. Bruiser unable to take the turn, pushes Less out of the booth, and says, "Can we do this some other time, Less? I'm beat. I slept on a bench last night, and the rest is a blur." Bruiser leans down into Vanessa's ear, kisses her on the cheek, and says, "I couldn't say it before, but the only thing I thought about while I was out; was you." Vanessa starts laughing and stands up, pushing Bruiser towards his room. Bruiser turns around as she's pushing him into a corner and he asks her, "Why is that funny?"

She leans into him and says, "Because you had me. I was all in, and it meant nothing to you. You still walked into that bathroom and cleaned your plate with no regards for me or my heart; it was standard boyfriend behavior."

"But I'm not your boyfriend," he says.

"No, you're not. You're someone's fiancé. More so, you're just a geriatric fuck-boy, and that's all you're capable of, Bruiser."

His heart skips a beat as he remembers all of that to be true, he looks at Dick over her shoulder, asking, "Where'd you hear that?"

She pushes on his chest, saying, "Does it matter?"

He pauses as he regroups, returning with, "No, but there's no validity to it. Janeuh said I asked her in the middle of a black out before we left."

"Bullshit!" mumbles Vanessa. She pushes him into the wall, shouting, "I know you, and you'll say whatever it takes to get inside me."

Bruiser grabs her by the hips, saying "It's not like that, Vanessa." He pushes her to the other side of the hallway, out of Dick's view, and whispers to her, "You're stunning, smart, kind of funny sometimes, and I know you can handle my shit."

She looks back for Dick's gaze, and as she finds the moment clear, she says, "I'm not denying we had something, but you're truly a disaster of a person, and I don't want to handle your shit!"

Dick picks up on bits and pieces of their conversation and makes his way toward them. Vanessa finagles her way out of Bruiser's embrace as Dick approaches them and barks, "Bruiser!"

Bruiser responds with an agitated rumble, saying, "What?"

Dick pulls Vanessa from Bruiser, puts his arm back around her, and asks her, "Can you give us a minute, love?"

She gives Dick a kiss on the cheek, and as soon as she walks away, Bruiser bucks up on Dick, pushing him into the wall, saying, "What-the-fuck, dude. You know I've got feelers on this one!"

Dick puts his hands on Bruiser's shoulders and then pulls him in for a hug, saying, "I know, buddy, but you had your chance, and I'm calling dibs. Do you think you can just let her be happy?"

"With you?" asks Bruiser, laughingly.

"Yeah, with me," he says without any inflection of doubt.

Bruiser shrugs Dick's hands off and says shakily, "I'm not going to let her go, Dick. This is Desiree all over again."

Dick turns around to walk away, and looking back over his shoulder, says, "You already did, Bruiser. You dropped her right into my arms. Besides, you owe me dibs, so the conversations over."

Bruiser, defeated, drops his head, and says, "Seriously, Dick, that's how you're going to play this?"

Dick stops and turns around, saying, "We're shooting tomorrow, or do you want to take a couple days off while you adjust to sobriety?"

"I'll be all right, but what about the Charlotte show?"

Dick sits back down in the booth with Vanessa and Less, saying, "Nobody believes it was real. I guess your scumbag rep finally paid off. We can pretty much book as many shows as you want, whenever you're ready."

Bruiser watches the three whispering across the table at each other, and blinded by jealousy, he says, "I'm ready."

Dick leans in and goes to give Vanessa a kiss, but she pulls away from him, saying, "Cool, tomorrow we're in Boston, and then New York! David Blaine wants you to slap him on camera, and then Springer wants you to do a show."

Less turns to Dick and Vanessa, and asks in a whisper, "Do you really think it's him?"

"Who else would it be?" asks Dick.

"I'm telling you it's a clone," says Less.

"Don't be ridicu-Less," says Dick.

Bruiser walks down the hall toward his room, looking back over his shoulder, and sees Vanessa touch Dick's face. She leans in and starts to make out with him. The distraction leads Bruiser directly into his door, face first, and he hears, "Come in."

He opens the door and finds Leslie burrowed beneath his sheets. With a newfound fervor in his pants, he asks her, "What the actual fuck is going on?"

She squirms around restlessly under his sheets as she thinks about the possibility of Bruiser inside of her, saying, "I just figured you could use a good snug after everything you've been through."

Bruiser kicks off his shoes and takes his shirt off. "No, Leslie, you're good." He climbs into his bed with her and sneaks a peek at what she decided to be too much or too little. She went with her favorite Hello Kitty panties and a wife beater. It screams hit me, but don't hurt me.

"You're talking about Vanessa and Dick?" she asks.

"Yeah, it's like I'm in some parallel universe, but it's so familiar. It reminds me of—"

She finishes his thought, saying, "The whole thing with Desiree?"

Bruiser pauses and then returns, asking, "How'd you know I was coming back here?"

He hears a whisper from her heart, *I've never seen him smile before, and I realized at that moment, he's never seen me this way before. I guess he couldn't see me lurking around in the peripherals of his obsession.*

248

Bruiser responds to her thought, thinking to himself, *I was too busy putting up numbers, sport fucking to fuel my addiction while distracting anyone worthwhile from getting caught in the bear trap that is my heart.*

She nuzzles her head into the pit of his arm, saying aloud, "You have to protect something so powerful, yet so fragile."

"What?" he asks confused by her penetration.

"Ever since you slapped me, I can hear people's thoughts the same way you hear mine," she says and wraps herself around him.

His being gives in to her advance, and he rolls her over, keeping her under his arm, asking her, "Is there anything else I should know?"

Aroused by his line of questioning, she blurts out, "I had a dream about you! We had a child together," and her whole body tenses up while she waits for him to run away.

"What was its name?" he asks, without hesitation.

"I don't remember, but she was beautiful," says Leslie, as she forces herself further into his embrace, and then relaxes. She plays with his scent, thinking, *His arm around me feels familiar, like a blanket protecting me from everything evil. It offers, not the warmth you would expect, but more the chill of a cool breeze.*

In response to her thoughts, he says, "You feel familiar in my arms as well."

Looking for clarity, she asks him, "You're attracted to me?" Bruiser stares out the window of their mobile home, caressing her arm with his thumb, rolls over on top of her, and kisses her. She responds to his soft, nonthreatening, nor obligatory connection, saying, "I feel like you've always avoided me."

"Leslie, you're amazing, and I **was** avoiding you." With that, he rolls back over and returns to the ceiling. Leslie gives him some breathing room. "I've always had a thing for you, but there was Des, Janeuh, everyone else, and definitely Less; it would destroy him."

There's a knock at the door.

"Less, go away!" screams Leslie.

The door slides open, and Less forces his way into the room. He dives into bed with them, and physically imparts his person on the two; almost as if they were his parents and offered the only refuge one desires in this life.

Bruiser asks Less, "What's up, buddy?"

Less climbs into Leslie's arms and says, "I know you're tired, but I really must talk to you about the Kara and Julie thing. There are things that, I believe, will only make sense to you."

"Well, I'm at half-mast if you're trying to reenact that moment," he says.

"Less, do you mind?" asks Leslie.

Less burrows deeper into Leslie's embrace and says, "I don't mind at all. Bruiser, do you mind?"

"I do, Less. I was hoping to rest my head in an effort to leave this strange place," says Bruiser.

Leslie pushes at Less. "Less, I was trying to fornicate the Second Coming in hopes of bearing his first born, but we can talk about how you cut those poor girls in half some other time." Leslie steamrolls over Less, pushing him away with her feet while sliding back into Bruiser.

Less pushes himself, uncomfortably closer to them, and says, "Here's the thing, Bruiser. Ever since you slapped us, we can hear each other's thoughts, but not like an echo, more like we're sharing the same brain."

Leslie presses against Bruiser, wrapping her legs around his, so that he can feel her throbbing angst for the rapidly dilapidating moment, and says, "We can feel each other, like we're sharing the same heart; it's so weird."

Less sits up and tries to remove Leslie from her illicit pursuit, blurting out, "And there's no way I'm going to feel this moment."

Bruiser pops up, frustrated, and asks, "Are you two trying to double team me?"

"Not at all," says Less. "Quite the opposite. I can't … I won't, feel the two of you going at it."

"You sure, Less?" asks Leslie. "I figured after the twins; you'd be more open to the diversity of emotions this world has to offer."

Bruiser, filled with new varieties of confusion, says, "I can't. What happened with the twins?"

I was so fucking close, Less, thinks Leslie as she tries to pull Bruiser back into the bed.

You weren't, retorts Less.

Get out of my head! silently screams Leslie, trying to force him out of her mind.

I'm doing you a favor, Leslie! Less barks silently.

She volleys with, *You're not. I finally had him all to myself and you…*

"Can you two keep it down?" asks Bruiser as he retreats from this life, collapsing into Leslie's arms. "I'd really love some sleep, more so, just some good clean silence."

Leslie takes a moment to embrace Bruiser as his defenses shut down. Her eyes shut, as she follows Bruiser into the depths, and she's left with this thought, *I can feel his presence leaving the room as he falls out of his body and into the cosmos. He grabs me by the heart and drags me down into the nothingness with him.*

When Leslie's eyes open, she's finds herself in the same bed, next to Bruiser, but the windows of the bus are blacked out. They appear as if they've been sealed, and there are only a few slivers of light fighting to get through. She looks to her left and finds Less as his eyes open and he enters the room. The bus hits a bump in the road and swerves. They hear a shotgun blast ring through the cabin and Leslie shakes Bruiser, hoping to awake his protection, but he refuses to entertain this realm. She feels a light breeze on her shoulder, and she hears Less say, "Hurry up and wake him. We have to get out of this twisted dream!"

"I tried; he's not responding!" she states in a panic. "Where the fuck are we?" There's a thud on the door, that leaves the twins short of breath, and Leslie has to ask, "What was that?" Her hands begin to tremble, and she asks him again, "Less! What was that? What's going on?"

Less shakes her, saying, "We're in his head, and we have to get the duck out of here!" She tries to free herself from the thought but is interrupted by another thud at the door. "Hold your horses, we're coming." He feels Leslie stumbling back toward her waking life, grabs her by the chin, and shakes her, trying to break her free of her panic, saying, "We came here to get him. You have to wake him, so we can get out of here!"

She screeches, "How!"

The door bursts open and standing in its place is a guy that resembles every bad guy from every eighties college movie, but buffer, like his workout regimen was from the future. Less jumps up off the bed and grabs his longsword from the corner of the room. He tries to unsheathe it, but there's not enough room to pull it out; let alone to swing it freely. He decides to use it as a flex, and wedges himself into the doorway, protecting two of his favorite people with only the glare in his eye, asking the intruder politely, "Can you give us a minute, Chad?"

"I've got this, Less, shut the door and don't open it!" shouts Dick from the front of the bus. He slams the brakes, throwing the intruder toward the front of the bus, and there's a series of shotgun blasts that are followed by another knock on the door.

Less opens it, hoping its Dick, but it's not. It's the khaki-clad Chad. He's been hallowed out by two of the shotgun blasts, and the flesh is growing back, filling the holes. His eyes are glowing a garish indigo blue, and they're accompanied by a perfect smile that's dripping with hunger. Less pushes him back with his sword and shuts the door in his face. He turns around to check on Leslie; who's curled up in a ball rocking away in a panic. "Leslie, I need you to get it together, or we're not going to make it back," begs Less, clapping his hands in her face.

She returns to the room in a panic. "What do you want me to do?"

Less turns to the door, waiting for Chad to force his way back through it, and says, "Lay down next to him, get in his head, find him, and bring him back. Lez, you're a goddess with supreme psychic abilities. It's the only reason any of us are still here." He hopes the words penetrate the wall of fear she's built, and that they will retrieve the spiritual sprite that she is.

Leslie covers her face, falls back into the bed, and releases her dainty version of rage, squealing, "I don't know where I am, what's going on, and you just want me to climb inside him."

The door finally bursts open, pushes Less to the ground, releasing his longsword from his grasp. Khaki-clad Chad asks playfully, "I was curious how you felt about the future, and if you had any plans for salvation?"

Less struggles with what he assumes is going to be his last thought on this bus; and knowing he doesn't want this perfect man inside of him, he scans the room in search of shade-tree weaponry, but only finds his longsword lying on the floor across the room. "Fuck, dewd. Now's not the best time. These two are kind of in the middle of a serious power nap. You wanna' try back in fifteen, maybe twenty?" he asks as he rolls over to his sword and grabs the hilt with both hands.

The Chad takes two steps closer to Less, saying, "I just need your friend's heart, and I'll be out, bruh."

"Whose heart?" asks Less as he struggles to return to his feet, sword in hand.

"The maker," is his response.

"Who?" asks Less.

"Zealand!" he barks, losing his cool. He kicks Less in the chest, knocking him back to the edge of the bed.

Less quivers with the hit he just took, looks down at his sword, and then forces it inside Chad, saying playfully, "Oh, Bruiser. I mean, now's just not a good time. Is there any way you could take a seat in the waiting area?" Less directs him with his hand toward the living area, saying, "Mr. Zealand will be right … with …" Khaki-clad Chad pushes his fist into his stomach, penetrating his last meal.

Less screams out, "Leslie!"

She pops up out of her psychic state, and with the sight of her brother's suffering, releases a harmonious scream from a dimension unbeknownst to them.

Chains

"I got it," says a voice that echoes through the metal cell, and a bolt of white lightning shoots out of Bruiser's chest, disintegrating the dark parasites that had contained him. His back arches, and Ü appears over him with his hands shaking fervently as he pulls what seems to be an endless tapeworm out of his chest. Ü gets to the tail end, holds it up in the stale air, licks his lips, puts it in his mouth, and slurps it up playfully like a ramen noodle, saying, "There's no room for love in a heart that's filled with fear."

Bruiser's eyes open and he pops up off his couch-bed, gasping for air as he's birthed from a state of dismay, and a guttural bellowing that's coming from deep within Leslie. She has a withdrawn look in her eye, as if she's staring through the wall of the bus, and when she's finally exhausted her spiritual self, she screams, "Less is dying! Bruiser, slap him! Please!"

Bruiser looks to his left and finds Less shaking uncontrollably. He rolls onto Less and pins his arms in hopes of containing his flailing. "What the fucks?" He raises both of his hands, cocking them for a life redeeming slap, and they light up and start crackling like a high-tension power line. He double slaps Less, and he is instantly propelled back into the room, gasping for air. The force of his return pushes Bruiser off the bed, onto the floor.

Less scans the room as he returns to it, asking, "Leslie?"

"What?" she asks.

"Did we get him?" asks Less.

"Who?" she asks.

"Bruiser. Where is he?" asks Less.

"Fuck dewd!" says Bruiser, pulling himself up off the floor.

Less rolls over onto Leslie and gives her a vigorous embrace, saying, "I told you it would work!"

Bruiser lingers over the twins, hands still shaking, and asks, "What-the-absolute-fuck just happened?"

"You were in a coma," states Less.

"When?" asks Bruiser.

"Just now, when we were on the bus," says Less.

Bruiser digs around in his boxers. "We're on the bus now, Less."

Less sits up, looks at Leslie, and smiles at her with a new respect. "We '*Dreamscaped*' you, Bruiser. It was a different version of the bus in a darker reality. There was this super-buff, blonde, kid that wanted your heart."

Leslie sits up, pushing Less off of her, and says, "I don't think it was a different reality; I think it was the future, Less."

Bruiser scratches his butt as he makes his way to the pisser, saying, "Either way, I'd fuck a dude for a cigarette right now. How long have I been out for?" he asks.

"Daze, we honestly didn't think you were coming back," says Less.

"Speaking of fucking dudes, one of them fisted Less," shouts Leslie.

Bruiser pops his head out of the door while continuing to piss, laughs, and says, "Oh man … I always thought I'd be there for his first time."

"You were there," says Less, "just very unconscious. I'll say this though, for my fist time…" Less clears his throat, reiterating, "for my first time, I really thought there would have been more blood." Less motions the frat boy reaching inside of him and acts out how he was worked like a puppet.

"Less, you were **literally** covered in it, and you almost died," says Leslie.

"But I didn't, and it worked," says Less.

"You were a full on badass, BTW," says Leslie.

"Thanks," says Less.

"Bruiser really was trapped in there, and we saved him. You saved him." Leslie stares emphatically at Bruiser, begging for his antiquated affections as he returns from his epic piss. "Do you remember dying?" she asks Less as she watches Bruiser walk out of his room.

There's a moment that passes where Less looks for words that don't exist to explain a place few souls have traveled with gimcrack to remind them of the inter-dimensional byways. Less returns with, "They asked me if I wanted to continue with this life, or I could choose from a thousand lives, all being grander than this, free of suffering, and full of abundance in forms unimaginable to this world."

"There's my two favorite bosses," says Bruiser as he walks into the living area to find Dick and Vanessa on their laptops. "Where are we?"

Vanessa shuts her laptop, jumps up, and hugs Bruiser, smiling against her will, saying, "More like when are we."

Bruiser sits down in the booth as he rifles through his abstruse journey. Dick lights a cigarette, sits down across from him, and stares down his friend as he tries to figure out what-the-fuck happened, asking him, "You okay, buddy?" He hits his cigarette a couple times, blowing the smoke in Bruiser's face incidentally.

Bruiser starts coughing, waves the smoke out of his face, and says, "I don't know, help me out," Dick offers Bruiser a cigarette and he stares at it, baffled by the fact that there is a decision at play, and then pushes it away from his person. Dick puts the cigarette back in the box as he glares at Bruiser through one eye.

Vanessa sits down next to Dick and slides Bruiser a large mug of coffee, saying, "We're in Boston. You've been hibernating for three days."

Bruiser looks at Dick dimly and then turns to Vanessa looking for clarity. He takes a slurp off his coffee and asks her, "I've been in a coma since DC?"

"We didn't stop in DC, other than to drop off the girls," says Dick.

Bruiser's face drops and he whines, "For why?"

Vanessa puts her hand on Bruiser's and says, "They were too much of a cringe show, Bruiser. You've been out since the show in Charlotte." The connection startles him and he flinches. They stare at Bruiser with discernment as they analyze his being. He twitches as he drinks his coffee, and Vanessa says, "Look, Bruiser, we have to get this conversation out of the way…"

Bruiser returns the look of concern and responds, asking, "Is this an intervention?"

"Definitely," says Vanessa.

"Look, I'm fine with it, honestly. I feel like we've already had this talk, but I want you to know that I'm done getting fucked up and letting that demon take over. I just don't know how to do sobriety, so I'm going to need some help."

The two stare at Bruiser in disbelief, having expected more of a fight. Dick guffaws and asks him, "Who are you and what have you done with Bruiser?"

Bruiser waves at them and says, "It's me. I just can't take it anymore. I've been consuming pain and darkness like it was going to get me into heaven with a flash pass. The only thing I know, is that getting fucked up has been part of my punishment, and I need to figure out how to forgive myself. I'm done suffering for the entertainment of others."

"Yeah?" they ask together.

"Yeah," he says, and breaks down in tears, covering his face, ashamed of his vulnerability. Vanessa rubs his arms as she tries to comfort him. He shrugs her off, and shudders, overwhelmed by an emotion he'd heard of, but didn't believe existed — regret.

Dick, uncomfortable with Bruiser's emote, pulls out his phone, taps the screen a couple times, and slides it toward Bruiser's emotional collapse, saying, "Dude your mom, though." Bruiser freezes up at the thought of his mother's demise as it floods his mind for the first time in this reality. Dick taps on the tabletop, trying to grab Bruiser's focus, and says, "This is gonna' blow your mind. She told me to call her when you resurfaced."

Bruiser's eyes light up as his processor overheats with the thought. He looks up at his friends and asks, "She's alive?" Dick pushes the phone into Bruiser's hands. He wipes the tears from his face, and as his mother's image presents itself via video chat, he barfs out, "Maaa!"

Dick and Vanessa get up and stand behind Bruiser, so that they can watch the conversation. "There's my special boy," says his mother. "I don't even know where to start with you." There's a long pause and then she says, "Thank you."

Bruiser's heart stops beating for a split second, and then he erupts with joyous emotion, unguarded, saying, "You look great; great like thirty. How do you feel?"

His mother pulls the phone away from her, so that they can see the whole package while she spins around, saying, "I was thinking twenty-four. I've never, ever felt this good." She playfully waltzes through her house, reveling in her new form, and then stops to say, "I can't even put into words the amount of respect I have for you. You're a complete mystery, Beauregard."

"I'm glad you made it to the show, Ma. I was worried about you."

"I've been through worse," she says lightheartedly.

"How is that possible?" asks Vanessa from the corner of her mouth, and as she asks herself that question, Bruiser's mother walks past a pile of dead cats stacked up in the corner.

There's a gasp from the three, and Bruiser asks his mother, "Ma, what's that in the corner?"

His mother immediately walks away from the pile of bodies, toward the kitchen, saying, "Oh, bless their sweet little hearts. I don't know what happened. It's like the kitty plague around here. Must be that toxoplasmosis you were talking about."

"Yeah, I don't think that's healthy," says Bruiser.

"Okay well, I've got to go. I've got a hot date with a young man, and I want to look my best. I'll call the vet tomorrow," she says and ends the call.

"You do that, Mom. I love…" he mumbles as her image freezes in the middle of his words. "She's fine?" he questions, handing Dick his phone back.

Dick sits back down in the booth and says with a smirk, "She's cute. I don't know if I'd say fine, but definitely cute."

Vanessa rubs Bruiser on the back and asks him, "Bruiser, you can say no, but do you think you'd be up to shooting a show tonight?" Bruiser doesn't respond. He just stares deeply out of the window. "Bruiser?" she asks, pulling at his attention.

"There's nothing I'd rather do more." he says, and then shouts, "Chuck! Can you pull over at the next bar you see?"

"Yes, sir," says Chuck.

"Bruiser, do you really think a bar is the first stop on the road to recovery?" snips Vanessa.

"I'm so hungry I could eat a prolapsed rectum. Do you think I could borrow Dick, Vanessa?"

"I kind of need Dick," she says, stopping herself as she realizes what she said.

"Well, that's new," says Bruiser laughingly.

"Seriously though, he's my hands. Every time I touch anything electronic it shits the bed. It's gotta' be flipping Mercury retrorape or something."

"Use the twins," says Bruiser as Less walks in the room with Leslie in tow.

"Use me, please," says Less.

"That works for me," states Vanessa. "You two can run inside and eat, girl talk, or whatever. We'll wait out here in the bus." Vanessa turns to the twins, and asks, "You two all right?"

Leslie stares awkwardly at Bruiser, saying, "Yeah."

Less sits down with Vanessa's computer and says, "It wuzz nutz! We were on the bus, Dick's driving, and there was this preppie dickhead with blonde hair and blue eyes, that was trying to get at Bruiser's heart, but I had my sword and I shoved it into him, he shoved his fist into me, and then Leslie lets out this sonic squeal that paralyzes him and wakes Bruiser."

Vanessa stares begrudgingly at Bruiser and says, "I can't imagine what being in his head was like."

Leslie sits down across from Bruiser, staring at him with a doughy set of eyeballs, and asks, "Aren't we already in his head?"

The thought slows Less down as he pushes around the concept of a waking life in someone else's dream. Everything gets really gooey, and then as he returns, looking up from the laptop at Bruiser, he asks him, "Are your dreams always like that, Bruiser?"

"It wasn't a dream," says Leslie. "I think it was the future."

"What do you think it was, Bruiser?" asks Less.

Bruiser takes a sip of his coffee, shrugs, and says, "Honestly, I feel like I've been bouncing around for lifetimes trying to find my way back to this place." He's reminded of a vision of Vanessa and her new relationship with Dick. He pushes at her, making his way through

Vanessa's presence, and fighting his way out of the booth. He stands up and looks around the room, analyzing it, questioning the validity of it all.

"Either way, it was awesome," says Less sitting down in Bruiser's spot, next to Vanessa. "I can't believe we actually brought him back."

"Awesome, Less, you almost died," says Leslie, still visually attached to Bruiser's presence.

"All that matters is that we saved him," says Less.

"You planned that?" asks Bruiser, trying to grasp the concept.

"Yeah, we used to jump into each other's dreams when we were kids. When you wouldn't wake up, we figured, why not try," states Leslie, still ogling Bruiser.

"That's truly bizarre," states Bruiser.

"Bizarre," laughs Vanessa. "You're telling me the twins jumped into another reality that you were trapped in where there was a dude like Alice that was trying to kill you; and all you have is truly bizarre. It's absurd. Aren't you worried that that dream is the future and that you've created an epidemic?"

Bruiser tries to laugh off the concept. "An epidemic of beautiful blonde people that eat human hearts — that's absurd."

"The future actually makes sense, Bruiser," says Leslie.

"It's a reality that will never exist," says Bruiser with a gruff twinge in his voice. "That whole thing with Alice and my mom happened because I was fucked up and had been holding onto all the darkness I'd been taking from people when I healed them. It was tearing me apart at the seams. I had so much darkness attached to the relationship with my mom; it broke them. She's fine. I'm fine. I just need to figure out how to process the shadows and we're good."

There's a long group silence that Dick breaks, saying, "I'm pretty sure she's one of them."

"Who?" asks Bruiser. "My Mom?"

"Blonde hair, blue eyes, and a pile of dead cats in the corner," says Dick.

"My mom has always had blonde hair and blue eyes," says Bruiser. "And you think she's eating her cat's hearts?"

"Anything's possible at this point, Bruiser," says Vanessa.

"What about Tanner?" asks Bruiser as he starts to pace around the bus's foyer. "He changed, and he never attacked one of us."

Dick scratches his chin, saying, "That's valid."

"Shit, Janeuh's one of them too, then," says Bruiser.

"Your fiancé?" asks Vanessa.

Bruiser, stunted by Vanessa's awareness of his situation, turns to her, and says, "Yeah … my fiancé. Vanessa your hair's blonde. Your eyes are blue. Have you had any cravings?"

Vanessa twirls her golden locks with her finger, saying, "No, but—"

The bus comes to a stop in front of an old Bostonian pub, and Bruiser walks toward the front of the bus, trying to fend his way out of the conversation, saying, "Let's write it down as absurd, and we'll say it was my fault, because I was fucked up. I'm … 'sober' now, and until it repeats itself, we keep healing people." His friends stare at him sideways as they all try to compute the complexity of the reality at hand. "You coming?"

Dick gets up and walks off the bus as Less and Leslie look to Vanessa, asking her silently if they can go with them. Vanessa watches as Less gets her laptop to work, saying, "Would that we could. I've got to confirm our booking with the venue, and we need to get all our fucks in a row." Less slides the laptop back at her, and as soon as she touches it, it turns into a bastardized version of the matrix. She shakes her laptop vigorously, and then endearingly looks for a moment of eye contact from Bruiser, asking him, "Can you slap my computer?"

"I don't think it works like that," he says and walks toward the door.

"Bruiser!" shouts Vanessa.

"What?"

"No drugs, no booze, no whores, and definitely don't eat any prolapsed rectums."

"No whores! Seriously?" says Bruiser as he makes a playful moue, turns around, and walks off the bus to find Dick, sulking with his head down. He fishes for a truth, asking, "What's going on, buddy?"

Dick doesn't look up, he just continues to deadeye the river of oncoming traffic, thinking, *How the fuck is he just gonna' give up getting high while he's knocked out after killing himself — twicet?*

"Dick!" shouts Bruiser, "I can hear you."

Bruiser dismounts the curb pushing himself blindly into traffic, expecting to part the sea of automobiles, assuming that they know who he is, and more so, will stop submissively.

Dick pulls him back by his shirt and asks him adamantly, "What's wrong with you?"

"They'll stop," he says with a little cock in his voice.

"Of course," says Dick, pushing him playfully back into traffic. Bruiser, still with no regards for oncoming traffic, jaunts across the street as Dick slowly steps into traffic with his arms out, hoping to stop anyone that might have missed Bruiser's abuse of his pedestrian empowerment. Dick almost trips over the curb as he jumps out of the way of a PT Cruiser that's clearly being controlled by an avid texter. Bruiser receives him, holding the door open as he's mildly amused by Dick's near mishap. Dick punches Bruiser in the arm and flashes his cigarette. Bruiser shuts the door and the two linger in front of the pub while Dick embraces his slow death and Bruiser flicks away at his phone like the answer might be inside. Baffled by his friend's adoration for his tracking device, Dick pulls at him, saying, "I miss you, buddy."

Bruiser looks up from his phone and says, "I miss me, too, Dick. Apparently, I'm making up for lost time with the universe."

"I get that but," says Dick.

Bruiser stops him in the middle of his thought, asking him, "What's really going on with you?"

"Where was I in that dreamscape scenario with Less and Leslie?"

Bruiser drops his hands and says, "Driving the bus."

Dick wipes his face with frustration, saying, "Exactly! Less is chopping up zombies. Leslie's … well Leslie's a mermaid/siren, I guess. You, of all people, are healing souls on an infinite level and creating a new race of humans. Vanessa destroys anything with a microchip. And I'm driving the *fucking* bus!"

"Somebodies got to drive the bus. Do you want to trade?" asks Bruiser with a hint of seriousness.

"I'm just saying, where's my superpower?" asks Dick.

Bruiser shrugs at him, saying, "That's probably what you get for having my seed wiped from this world. You want me to slap you again? I can double slap you this time."

Dick looks at him in a serious manner and says, "I'm good. I don't think I could pull off the blond hair." He opens the door for Bruiser, bows, and points inside with a flat hand. Bruiser grabs him by the back of his shirt and pushes him through the door, but before entering, he turns his phone off and throws it in the trashcan by the front door.

Dick looks over the bar as they walk into your standard Irish pub in the middle of Boston: lots of shamrocks, Guinness signs, and a bunch of drab, curmudgeonly looking dudes that smell of misery. Bruiser blindly walks up to the bar, guided by his oversized organ (his liver of course.) Dick pulls at Bruiser, trying to avoid the gathering of kindred spirits, and Bruiser turns to Dick, asking, "Shots?"

Dick almost slaps him and says, "Dude, Bruiser, Zealand … we're not fucking around with you."

"It's a shot … or two. It's not crack, bub," he says, looking over at the bartender: a large, tattooed, bald, bearded Irishman.

The bartender overhears their conversation and asks, "IDs?"

A cute young redheaded dread, with big tits that are fighting their way out of a crop top, adorning an apron, walks by just fast enough to put a crick in Bruiser's neck.

Bruiser tells the bartender, "Thanks, but we're gonna' grab a table, somewhere in her section," guessing with his finger pointed toward the tables.

The two find a booth in the back of the pub, and before they can sit down, Bruiser blurts out, "So you're fucking her?"

"No matter who you're talking about, sadly, the answer's no," says Dick, staring into his menu, ignoring Bruiser. He looks up and asks him, "But just for fun, who are we talking about?"

Bruiser stares Dick down with a vengeful eye and says, "Vanessa! When you guys picked me up in DC, you were up Vanessa's asshole. You told me you were using your dibs, and then you told me to deal with it."

"Bruiser, you overdosed in Charlotte, on that suicide bullshit you concocted, and hit your head on the hot tub when you collapsed. We shot you up with some naloxone we found in your briefcase. You barely came back, just enough to where you were breathing, and hopefully didn't suffer any brain damage. We've been driving around in circles, with you in the back, playing out your sleeping beauty fantasy while we waited for you to come back!" Bruiser is immediately pushed into his menu by a ringing in his ear. He makes an uncomfortable face as he tries to stay in the room, but can't, and finds himself back in his metal cell. Dick watches his friends suffering and asks, "You okay?"

The ringing subsides and Bruiser returns energetically, stumbling back into the pub. "I'm pretty sure you guys handed me over to those linen clad, government dicks!"

"Slow down, B. What?"

"I get this ringing in my ear, my vision blurs, and I see this metal cell I was trapped in. I was on a spaceship, or maybe it was an underground bunker. I don't know, but I'm pretty sure those two linen dicks were there," says Bruiser, staring Dick down with a vengeful eye.

Dick starts laughing and says, "Maybe you did catch the brain damage. Bruiser, you've been in the back of the bus the whole time. We've done nothing but risk our freedom to protect you!" Dick returns the vengeful eye to Bruiser.

Bruiser won't stop interrogating Dick with his eyes, and barfs out, "So, you're not banging Vanessa?"

"This is why you brought me here: to interrogate me?" asks Dick, dropping his menu. "You really think we'd hand you over to the feds?"

The waitress approaches the table, nullifying Bruiser's rant, and says, "Hey guys, how we doing today?"

"Can we get two waters?" asks Bruiser as the waitress sets down two waters. She gets lost in Bruiser's presence and fights to pull away from his tractor beam, asking him, "Do I know you? You look familiah."

"I doubt it," says Dick.

The waitress walks off, scratching her head.

Bruiser takes a swig off his water and asks Dick, "So, you and Vanessa definitely aren't fucking?"

"Bruiser, she's my boss. You're my best friend. We're not all vagina-blind like you. And what does it matter? You're engaged, tragically in love with Des, and you owe me dibs!" Dick stops as he comes to the realization that his friend has come down with a bad case of feelings, laughs again, gregariously this time, and says, "You like her, don't you?"

Bruiser rubs his eyes and says, "You don't have to be a Dick about it. My head's fucked up, dude, but yeah, maybe just a little."

Dick tries to regroup, asking, "You ever thought about celibacy? I feel like you'd get a lot more done."

Bruiser pulls out his ID and hands it to Dick, asking, "What about this?"

Dick looks at the front of the ID and says, "Beauregard A. Derrick the turd." He flips it to the back where the magnetic strip is, bends it, and then holds it up to the light, asking, "Help me out here, what am I looking for?"

Dick tries handing it back to him, but Bruiser pushes it back at him, saying, "The name!"

"That's your name, Beauregard A. Derrick the third." Dick stares at him awkwardly and asks, "You sure you don't want to take a couple days off and regroup?"

Bruiser looks at the ID baffled, and puts it back in his wallet as the waitress saunters up to the table, asking, "You guys ready to ordah?"

"How are the fish and chips?" asks Bruiser.

"Fried," says the waitress.

"We'll take two, extra tartar sauce," says Dick.

"You want anything else, B? I don't see any prolapsed rectum on the menu; you want some wings or something?"

The waitress lights up and starts tapping on her book with her pen. "Hey… Yah that healah, Bruiser … Zealand, right?"

Bruiser's chest puffs up and slyly he says, "Depends on what you've heard. What's your name, darling?"

"Chelsea. It is you! I was trying to catch the show tonight, but I can't find anyone to covah my shift."

Bruiser grabs her hand and starts stroking it, saying, "We'll see how the chips are, and maybe I can save your soul from this peril we call life."

She bounces around with a newfound joy, saying, "I'd love that!"

Mesmerized by her elation, Bruiser asks her, "How'd you hear about the show?" He pulls the waitress into his lap with a finely tuned stare.

She settles into his lap saying, "It's all anyone is talking about. No one thinks it's real. Is it?" They stare at one another with a silent intensity that can't be explained.

"Do you have any sweet tea?" asks Dick, breaking the moment.

Chelsea stands up at Dick's request, and Bruiser pulls at her, asking, "Where you going?"

She glides out of his grasp, saying, "To grab you two a Pepsi."

"Hurry back," he says with a tinge of cringe.

Dick, who's stuck in his phone trying to avoid Bruiser's vulgar display of power, throws his phone on the table, saying, "You were just grilling me about Vanessa, and now you're trying bang the waitress."

Bruiser ignores Dick's provocation and ogles the waitress's departure. He returns to the table pushing his water to the side, and points at Dick's phone, asking, "What's she want?"

Dick grabs his phone as another text pipes through. "Vanessa's up my ass about your consumption. She said that if I can't control you, she'll replace me with someone who can. Are you really gonna' do this?"

Bruiser scans the bar, asking, "Sobriety? Just saying it makes me nauseated, but I'll try; like our lives depend on it. I can't promise you anything in New York, though."

"Vanessa told you about that?" asks Dick. "David Blaine wants to shoot on the streets with you, and then he's throwing a healing party at his place. He's raised some major cash for you."

Chelsea returns with three shots.

"Fuck!" belts out Dick.

"So, Chelsea, what is it that ails you?" asks Bruiser.

She drops the shots on the table and says, "We can talk about that aftah you eat." She picks up her shot and says, "To living your life free of fear, no matter how great the evil."

Bruiser goes to pick up his shot glass, but Dick swipes it from him, saying, "Dude!"

"C'mon, it's just one shot," he begs Dick.

"There's no such thing," says Dick.

"Zealand, your boyfriend is totally lame," states Chelsea.

"He's not my boyfriend. He's my long-lost father, and he's doing all my shots for me until he gives up on this fool's errand," says Bruiser.

"Oh, I see it now," says Chelsea, staring at Dick sideways.

"Cheers," says Dick as he bangs both of his shot glasses on the table and then does them. Chelsea slams her shot and walks off. Dick adjusts to his new unhindered perspective and asks, "You really thought we turned you over to the government?"

Bruiser watches as the spirits take over his friend, and he says, "Dude, one minute I'm in the bed with Vanessa, and the next thing I know, I'm trapped in this chromed out cell. Then I get spit out onto a park bench with my head in some hobo's lap. You guys pick me up and then I'm in a three-way dreamscape with the twins. It's too fucking much, and you're telling me I was just in another one of my drug-induced cocoons?"

"Yeah, basically," says Dick.

"What happened with the feds then? They were waiting for me outside after the show, right?"

Dick looks away from Bruiser, toward his phone, and says, "No body, no crime. We took off when you hit your head. They couldn't find your mom, Alice is a missing person for now, and I assume what they think they saw was good old fashion Bruiser shenanigans."

"I never thought being a shit-brick would come in handy, but I'll take it."

Dick sighs and says, "You seriously thought we'd turn you in? We've been through too much. We wouldn't even take you to a hospital." Bruiser stares deeply into Dick, looking for a whisper of truth, waiting for him to break, and all Dick has is, "They're definitely curious about what's going on with you, and I guarantee they won't leave us alone. That's why we need you at one hundred percent — flawless."

"Look, I'm sorry I doubted you guys: you specifically. My heads twisted something fierce, and I can't tell what's real anymore."

Dick leans back in his seat and soaks up Bruiser's admission, saying, "I don't think I've ever heard you apologize to anyone for anything — ever." He stumbles over his next question, asking, "What did you see when you slapped me?"

Bruiser hesitates and then says, "Nothing that I remember."

"So, nothing dark from my past?" asks Dick.

Overrun by hunger, Bruiser searches emphatically for the waitress, asking, "Do you have anything dark in your past; other than me? Things always seem to work out for you."

"I guess," says Dick, settling into his new perspective.

"Dick, you're nothing but light and love. That's why Desiree chose you: you're safe and easy. It was so hard watching you with her. There's no way I could watch you do it again with Vanessa," he says as he fidgets with his hands nervously.

Chelsea drops off the fish baskets and asks, "You really serious about healing me?"

Bruiser starts scarfing fries, before they hit the table, and responds with a mouthful, saying, "Yeah, you sure you don't wanna' save it for the show tonight?"

Chelsea looks down to the floor and says, "I can't get out of work. I tried." She returns from the floor, grabbing Bruiser with a desperate glance, and asking, "Is it real? Can you heal me?"

Bruiser answers her with a lowly grin, saying, "There's only one way I can answer that, love."

She puts her hand on his shoulder and begs him, "Can you do it now?"

Bruiser shifts in his seat, laughs, and says, "Let me put down this basket of cod and … You sure the bartender isn't going to mind if he sees me slap you?"

Chelsea looks to the bar and scoffs, asking, "Who? My brothah?" She points to an old suspect looking dude at the bar and says, "The ownah is the one you should worry about, my pops. He's twelve beeahs short of a six pack, so there's no telling with him."

Dick watches Bruiser as he blindly walks towards another mishap and interjects, saying, "We definitely need you to sign a waiver." He starts digging through his pockets, expecting one to be crumpled up in there, and says, "I can print one. Is your printer Bluetooth?"

With a smirk on her face, Chelsea says, "Can you have someone fax it here? It wouldn't mattah anyway, I'm only seventeen."

"Shouldn't you be in school?" asks Dick.

"Oh, I graduated a yeah early, so that I could wait tables full-time." she says and waits for them to get her joke, gives up, and says, "I'm kidding. I'm going to Hahvahd next yeah, assuming I make it."

Bruiser looks up at Chelsea and says, "I don't care about waivahs; you deserve to be happy."

"Chels!" yells the bartender, pulling her from the table.

Dick leans into Bruiser and pleads, "We don't need any more bad publicity, Bruiser, and we definitely don't need a lawsuit."

Bruiser throws Dick a sad puppy face and says, "Dick, she's smart and beautiful. If I don't slap her, I could be doing the world an injustice. She might be the first female president."

Dick pushes his basket to the center of the table and says, "You just want to fuck her."

Bruiser takes the fries out of Dick's basket and aptly states, "That would be against the law!"

Dick groans and says, "When are you even going to consider listening to my opinion, man?"

With a mouthful of Dick's fries, Bruiser says, "Sorry, I forgot I had a new life coach."

Dick slams his hand on the table, demanding Bruiser's attention, and says, "I'm your producer, Bruiser, whether you like it or not."

Bruiser backs off with his hands in the air, saying, "Welp, boss, I'd rather it happens here, than in front of a crowd."

Dick lowers his tone and says, "How about this, we'll leave it up to how severe her illness is. It could just be menstrual cramps, and she's over exaggerating."

Dick pauses and then analyzes the room, asking, "Aren't you worried about her three-hundred pound, tattooed, southie bartendah bruh squashing you?" Dick searches for concern of any type from Bruiser.

Bruiser looks at the brick shithouse of a bartender and asks, "For healing her?"

Dick's phone lights up again and he slides it to Bruiser, saying, "It's Janeuh."

Bruiser pushes it away like a dirty diaper and throws his hands back in the air.

Dick laughs and asks, "What, are you allergic to phones now or just fiancés? Put your hands down. You need to call her at some point."

He shows Bruiser the menagerie of texts from her, and Bruiser pushes it away again, saying, "I would, but I threw out my phone on the way in here."

"Why'd you do that?" asks Dick.

"I can't have them following me around," he says inspecting the darker corners of the bar.

"Who?" asks Dick as he tries to figure out who Bruiser is looking for. "Dude, your head really is fucked, isn't it?" Dick's phone lights up again and he says, "Vanessa's ten-times hotter anyway." He forces his phone into Bruiser's hand, saying, "Just break it off properly with Janeuh."

Bruiser takes his phone, submitting gracelessly, and says, "She's got my grandma's ring. Not to mention, there's part of me that thinks I fixed her when I slapped her, and I feel like it couldn't hurt to keep one up my sleeve."

Chelsea chimes in, "And that's exactly how I came down with the virus."

Dick's face emotes nothing but confusion and he asks hesitantly, "You've got AIDS?"

She drops three more shots on the table and says, "No, but I'm bipolah, and I'd love to get off this rollahcoastah." She smiles sideways at Dick and says, "I took care of your bill, gents. Ah we going to do this?"

Bruiser looks at Dick, waiting for the okay. Dick begrudgingly takes the shot from Bruiser and raises both his glasses in the air. Chelsea looks at Bruiser. Bruiser looks at Dick and asks, "So, **boss**, are we gonna' do this?"

Chelsea catches the moment and snuggles up to Dick, throwing her tits on his shoulder. Dick looks at Bruiser and says, "We don't really have a choice, do we? How about this, Chelsea, throw four or five burgers and a couple sampler platters on the tab, box it up, and we've got a deal."

Chelsea jumps up and down ecstatically and starts clapping. When she's exhausted herself, she runs over to the POS and puts in their order, and when she's done, she runs back to them, grabs them both by the hand, and drags them down a hallway past the kitchen and bathrooms to an emergency exit that leads to an area behind the building.

Dick pulls out his phone and points it at them, saying, "For the internet."

Bruiser laughs and says, "She's bipolar, Dick. It's not gonna' come across on film."

"Just in case," says Dick.

"In case of what?" asks Chelsea.

Bruiser grabs her by the shoulders and straightens her out, saying, "In case you turn into a zombie." Bruiser turns to Dick with that 'what-the-fuck' face. Chelsea drops her check presenter on the ground and kneels on it. Bruiser tries to pull her back to her feet and says, "Oh, no. It's not like that."

The back door burst open and her brother yells, "Chelsea, yah whore. You out heah gettin double dicked by the dumpstahs again. You're mothah would be proud, God rest huh soul."

Bruiser slaps Chelsea. Chelsea's brother takes a swing at Bruiser. Bruiser ducks and pops back up, responding with a slap across her brother's face.

"Shamus, you faht sniffah!" shouts Chelsea. "It's Zealand T. Dahl, the saviah, and he's healing me."

As she finishes her sentence, she falls over and starts vomiting. Shamus rubs his jaw and says, "Looks like that's going well. This guys a scumbag. He's gonna' try to stick it in your poopah."

Dick, while trying to hold the camera still, laughingly says, "There's no telling at this point."

Bruiser kneels, rubs Chelsea's back, and looks up at Shamus, saying, "I'm pretty sure I got rid of your herpes, Shamus. I'm sorry there's nothing I can do about that accent."

Chelsea wipes her mouth and starts laughing.

"What aah you laughing at?" asks Shamus, "You have the same accent."

Chelsea points to Shamus's arms and says, "Your sleeves, Shamus, they're fading!"

Shamus presents his arms and says, "I know. I've had them for years."

Chelsea screams, "No, Shamus, look!"

He looks down and screams like a small child, "Ah! I thought you were a fraud, a trixstah. It was all supposed to be CG. That was ten grand in aht you just erased. Whose gonnah pay for that, you bastahd?"

Shamus flexes his chest at Bruiser and Dick jumps between them, saying, "If you want, we can mention your bah at the show tonight."

"Everybody knows my bah, Jack," says Shamus.

Dick pulls his card out of his phone case and says, "Here, give me a call. I've got a dude in New York that'll set you up. Better yet," Dick takes the card back from Shamus and writes 'free entrance plus infinity sign' on the back. "Bring anybody you want, and Bruiser el' slap the shit out of all of 'em."

Shamus takes Dick's card and asks, "You sure?"

Dick's phone lights up and he answers it, saying, "Vanessa … Yeah, we'll be out front." He hands another card to Chelsea and says, "You too, if you end up getting your shift covered."

Chelsea gives them an overzealous hug, kisses Dick on the cheek, and then Bruiser on the lips passionately, saying, "You guys should come hang out aftah the show. I'll buy youse a drink."

"Thanks for the meal," says Bruiser.

"I wish I could do more," says Chelsea, pulling Bruiser by the hand.

Shamus nudges Chelsea, saying, "Keep it in yuh pants, yuh dirty little slag."

"Any othah day, that would be true, Shamus. Today, I got a clean bill, you faht sniffa."

Change

Bruiser and Dick are sitting on an old, beat-up, plaid couch in the belly of a moldy locker room, at the heart of a high school auditorium that clearly hasn't seen any action in decades. Bruiser is watching Dick smoke a cigarette like a dog waiting for scraps to hit the floor. He offers Bruiser a cigarette, saying, "All I'm saying is that you need to call your fiancé, just to let her know you're all right. She sounded worried."

"All I'm saying is, fuck off," says Bruiser, refusing the carcinogenic delight. "I'll talk to her after the show, Dad."

Vanessa sneaks up on the two and snarks, "Quite the fashion statement, Bruiser. Jeans and a T-shirt; didn't see that coming."

Bruiser takes Dick's cigarette from him and puts it out, asking, "Am I overdressed? This place looks like it should be condemned."

Dick leans into Bruiser's ear and says, "You're the one that said you were done with churches?"

Bruiser laughs and says, "Dick, I don't want any cocaine! Get it together. I really can't tolerate this behavior anymore."

Vanessa shouts, "Dick! Seriously? Are you drunk?"

Bruiser intercepts her wrath by saying, "I tried to stop him, but I think he might have a problem."

Vanessa looks Bruiser up and down, looking for a tell.

"He made me pinch hit for him," slurs Dick.

Vanessa grabs Bruiser by the shoulder and shakes him, saying, "Can we seriously talk about your wardrobe choices, and your plans for morphing into something more iconic than jeans and a T-shirt?"

Bruiser laughs and says, "I was really surprised when they told me we didn't have any tuxedos in wardrobe." He penetrates her with a cunning smile. "You're going to love my suit jacket. It's vintage Ralph Lauren. Can you grab it for me, Dick?"

She gets lost for a moment and returns, saying, "You're about to change the world indefinitely for better or worse, and you have no problem looking like a complete schlub."

Dick fights his way off the couch and stands up, saying, "Schlub would be an improvement," and walks away.

Bruiser grabs Vanessa by the hand, pulls her into his lap, and lightly says, "Hey."

She rolls off his lap, asking, "You alright, Bruiser?"

He looks away from her gaze and says, "It's a lot. I can't honestly say I'm super stoked about consuming a room full of shadows, and I'd fucking love a cigarette!"

"So, smoke one."

"I don't want to smoke, I'm just nervous. I'm about to be overflowing with toxic energies, and I'm not sure that I know how to process the shadows — especially sober."

She looks around the room, checking to see if they're alone, jumps on him, and attacks him with an overzealous hug, saying, "We'll figure it out. Just focus on keeping your heart open and everything else will fall into place."

Dick breaks the moment as he walks up and hands Bruiser his plaid jacket, saying, "Serious five, Bruiser."

Bruiser slaps Dick on the butt as he walks off towards the entrance to the auditorium and says, "I'll be there when I get there."

Vanessa takes the jacket from Bruiser, saying, "Very hobo sheik. I can't say I like it, but it's a step in the right direction." She throws the jacket over her shoulder and leans back into him, saying, "It's not yours — the darkness. You choose to hold on to it; like you get off on the feeling, just like any other addiction. When I slapped you, after you double suicided yourself, I felt that energy pass through me when it left you. You just have to let it flow through you."

He grabs the side of her face, caresses her adoringly, and says, "I wish it was that simple, love."

Less and Leslie walk into the locker room, and she pulls away from his deviant strokes, saying, "It is, it's a choice to be happy and feel good. You choose the pain and the darkness because you don't have to worry about losing it."

Dick walks back in the locker room and shouts, "Seriously, Zealand! They're flipping chairs. Let's go!"

Bruiser looks down at Vanessa with a forced smile on his face. She returns the gaze, and her reflection pushes down on his fleshy motor. He leans in to kiss her, but the twins pop a bottle of bubbles that startles the two, and she evades his PDA, saying, "Can we return to this after the show?"

Vanessa jumps up, pulls Bruiser to his feet, and walks him over to Dick and the twins. "Finally, a drink. I really didn't want to do this sober." Bruiser pulls the bottle in for a closer inspection and says, "Oh, that's so cute — sparkling cider."

Leslie, pulling at his shoulder, says, "Welcome to sobriety. It's pear; if that helps."

"It doesn't a… pear to," says Bruiser glumly.

Less points at the plaid sports coat draped over Vanessa's shoulder and blurts out, "Are you wearing that tonight, B?"

Bruiser laughs at the tribal concern for his presentation and says, "I was, why do you ask?"

"The only thing it goes with is that couch," says Less, pointing at the defeated support device. "It's just not you, bud."

Vanessa throws the jacket on the couch, saying, "He's not wrong."

Leslie fills the champagne flutes and hands them out, saying, "Cheers."

Vanessa puts her glass in the air, and says, "To the Future of the Left, where the recessive will become the dominant."

"And may we be blessed by the lack of presence of any Aryan cannibals tonight," adds Less.

Everyone groans with Less's blatant disregard for the moment.

"We're done with that program, Less," says Bruiser.

"What program?" asks Less.

Bruiser walks away from the group, saying, "Fear, Less. We're inventing the future as we go now, and there's no room for fear in the blueprints." He walks out onto the stage of the high school gym, sporting his standard: jeans and a T-shirt with his glass of faux bubbles in hand. He stares blankly out into the speechless auditorium, pondering the concept of how he's about to ingest all their pain and suffering, and his thoughts are interrupted by a faceless voice that shouts, "Who's this bum? You here to save us, tough guy?"

Bruiser finishes his bubbly juice and throws the glass off the stage, saying, "Yeah, I guess. You guys up to it?"

Another random person from the crowd shouts, "Seriously, bro, they promised us miracles. Are you the warm-up act?"

Bruiser laughs and says, "I'm Zealand T. Dahl, your savior for the evening, and if you keep heckling me, I'll let your soul continue to plummet into darkness at an accelerating speed."

Yet another random voice heckles him, saying, "Zealand. You sure it's not Bruisah, that scumbag from the intahnet? That's why I'm heah. I need to make some cash. Dare me, I'll do anything."

Bruiser starts to pace the stage as he teeters on running away from their suffering and protecting his clarity, or diving headfirst off the stage, right into the center of their cauldron of shadows, and getting lost in it forever. He stops pacing, takes a deep breath, making room for all their suffering, and says, "Sure, I dare you to come up here and let me slap you?" He motions for the heckler to come up on stage. The guy stands up. He's a classic blue-collar dude: blue jeans, straight-fit, Hanes T-shirt, a ten-dollar haircut, and a lost look in his eyes. The heckler looks at his friends, smiles, and then high fives them as he makes his way across the row. Bruiser waves him up onto the stage, saying, "C'mon up here, buddy." The guy climbs on stage, shakes Bruiser's hand, and then turns to the crowd and waves. Bruiser pulls at him, asking, "What's your name?"

"Derrick Brumfield," says the heckler.

"And Derrick, what brought you here tonight?"

Derrick points at the audience and says, "My friends, we all watch Greed religiously. We heard last minute, you wah doing a show here in Boston. They said it was something new, where you heal people, but, c'mon we know you. We figured it was a scam, all paht of yuh new show. You know like Kauffman, but you get a whole room full of people to let you slap 'em."

Bruiser puts his hand on Derricks shoulder, saying, "Not at all my friend. I'm tired of that person, and I'm here at the mercy of the universe to heal you. What ails you?"

Derrick bunny ears his pockets, saying, "Sure, I'm broke, that's what 'ails' me." The auditorium breaks out in a blind exacerbation of laughs and Derrick, somewhat confused, asks, "Aren't yah gonna' dare me to do stuff for money? I'll do anything."

"You sure? Anything?" asks Bruiser.

"Anything!" he says.

"You know the rules, right?" asks Bruiser, looking over the crowd.

Derrick responds exuberantly, saying, "I get three dares, and you can double the money if it's something twisted that I don't want to do. I get the cash aftah I complete each dare, and if I do all three, I get to slap you, but if I can't complete all three dares, you get to slap me, right?" Derrick starts jumping up and down nervously, fist pumping, and Bruiser hears a childish whisper from Derrick, *I'm in love with my friend, Todd, but he's so straight it's boring, and I know he'd murdah me if I tried anything.*

Bruiser paces the stage for a moment and then says, "You've got a heart condition that needs to be resolved, or it will destroy you slowly and painfully."

Derrick looks out to the crowd and says, "That's news to me, tough guy. How do you know that?"

Bruiser stops in front of Derrick and stares him in the eyes, saying with a penetrating concern, "I can feel your pain, and I don't want you to suffer anymore. I want you to be free. So, here's the game, one dare for five grand. Are you in?"

Derrick looks down at his shoes and asks, "One dare for five grand? This should be good. Yah, I'm in."

Bruiser looks down at his belt buckle and says, "You know what, Derrick? I'm going to double it; and you only get one chance to say yes, or I get to slap you."

"Bet!" Derrick says excitedly.

Bruiser laughs and puts his hand back on Derrick's shoulder. Derrick looks around the room as Bruiser pushes him to his knees, saying, "Ten grand, Derrick. You have friends and family here?"

Derrick's processor starts to smoke with anticipation as he stares off into the crowd, saying, "Yeah, I know everybody on the South End."

Bruiser looks out at the crowd with him, saying, "Derrick, for a quick ten grand, I want you … in front of all your friends … to swallow my love." Bruiser undoes his belt buckle and says, "You only get one chance to answer." Derrick's face turns white, he stands up, and steps back. Bruiser buckles his belt, saying, "Is that's a no, Derrick?"

There's a holler from the crowd, "I'll eat his dick fah ten grand."

Bruiser looks for the voice, finding a larger woman in the back row, that's wearing a moo-moo, that's seen butter days, trying to make her way up front. He yells back at her, "Sorry, this dare's just for Derrick." He steps closer to Derrick and puts his hand on his shoulder. Derrick falls over, desperately trying to get away from him. Bruiser leans over to pick Derrick up, saying, "That's definitely a no. Tell me you couldn't use ten grand, Derrick?"

Derrick barks at him, "I wouldn't do it fah a hundred grand."

Bruiser raises his left hand and asks, "So, that's a no?"

Derrick starts to walk off stage and says, "Yeah, that's a hahd no, like no way in hell — NO."

Bruiser walks Derrick down as he tries to escape his reckoning, saying, "Where you going, buddy?"

Derrick stops, turns around, and puts his chin out, saying, "That was the least cool thing I've seen in a long time, Bruisah."

Bruiser slaps him with all the love in his heart he can muster and says, "Sorry, it's a different show now, but I think you're going to like it." As Derrick's presence starts to melt from the slap, Bruiser grabs him, gives him a hug, and whispers in his ear, "There's nothing wrong with loving whoever you want. You're going to have to deal with it eventually. If you don't, it will eat away at you until you're a hollow cracked shell of a person."

Derrick walks off the stage, rubbing his face.

"Who's next?" asks Bruiser. *There's that silence again,* he thinks and starts to panic. He searches the crowd for visible ailments; ones that would instill confidence in his gift. He catches one of Derrick's friends trying to push a girl out of her seat. The guy fights to stand her up and he says, "I'm not gonna suck yah pissah, but my sis will. Get up there, Geri."

"That's why you all are here? No one wants to be healed, freed from eternal suffering?" Bruiser points to an old lady in the front row, asking, "What about you, love? We could add twenty years to your life."

The old lady stands up slowly, creaking with every movement, and says, "Sounds terrible. Will I still be in debt, with bad credit, and stuck in this shithole?"

Bruiser laughs with the room and says, "I can't fix that, but just to clarify, I'm not here to trick anyone. I was given a gift, the power to heal all wounds, and since we have the time, I'll just explain how I see it."

Bruiser paces the stage, channeling these next words. "The emotional pain comes from the mind and presents itself as physical suffering. The mental suffering comes from a lack of control over your daily existence. There is a googolplex of things going on in your body right now, so much that, if you had to consciously control them all, you would blow a fuse and have a nervous breakdown.

"The mind communicates with the body by way of electrical frequency. Cells communicate with the same vibration. Cancer is just another way of the mind saying it's unhappy with this life. As it fails to communicate with the cells, they're lost. With no true purpose, they self-destruct, as do humans.

"Your father wasn't there, your mother didn't hold you, your sister was jealous of the light in your eyes and the attention it obtained. Or maybe your friends didn't understand why you smiled and laughed, so they fed off your love and happiness, taking it permanently, against your will. This is when we began to build walls to protect our light from the parasitic relationships. This light is love, the frequency of healing. Some of us come into this life with illness and struggles from past lives, but we all start out this life as pure light.

"The more we hate, the less it flows. We hate our bosses, our friends, and even our family. Hatred harbors the powerful beams of light, and the flow becomes limited and inconsistent. Light cannot be contained and must flow continuously. When it stops, we're defeated.

"Let's say *you* chose this life, planned every moment of it, all to help you grow, love more, and expand so that you could share more light. A light so bright that the flesh dissolves. When we find that there's no one to hold our hands, or to catch us when we slip off the major cliffs in life, or to support us with unconditional love, our light starts to flicker with resentment.

"Could you imagine watching your children suffer and not doing whatever imaginable to make sure they continue to smile, but we can't be there all the time to protect them from this life. Eventually, they stop smiling and turn into assholes. Now, the only one we can hate is ourselves, and that's what is happening. We must be that person for ourselves. We make choices without concern for anyone's happiness, other than our own. When the consequences kick in, we realize who we are and punish ourselves. No longer wanting to live with the choices we made, we chip away at the vessel, trying to get off this rock as fast as we can, while we entertain our struggle by judging everyone around us, hoping to make it to the top of the biggest pile of trash with the best view.

"I've come here today to free you from this repetitive cycle. Do yourself a favor and allow yourself to be loved for the first time, truly. Find comfort in your flesh and use that to bring comfort to others. Who's next?" he asks, expecting blind submission, but receives only crickets.

A voice from the crowd asks, "Where'd yah get your infahmation?"

Bruiser searches the crowd for a face and says, "I've been through a lot in a short period of time."

"That's great and all, but I'd just like to be able to walk up there and tell yah that yah wrong, face to face," says the voice.

Bruiser, still searching for the man's face, asks, "What's stopping you?"

A man in a wheelchair rolls out of the crowd and says, "Just my legs, or the lack thereof."

Bruiser finds himself stumped as he connects the voice with the face of the man in the wheelchair. The man is missing both of his legs, just above the knees. He points to his security and asks, "Can someone get him up here?" One of the crowd members pushes him up on stage and Bruiser shakes his hand, asking, "What's your name?"

The man replies, "Andrew, Andy."

Bruiser looks down at his nubs and asks, "How'd you lose your legs, Andy?"

Andy shifts his body in the chair and says, "I left them in Iraq. Stepped on an IED. Spun me around in the aih."

Bruiser scratches his head and says, "Andy, I'm going to be honest with you, I've seen some amazing things recently, but I don't know what I can do for you. Worse case, we get rid of those tattoos. Have you thought about prosthetics?"

Andy, shifting back and forth in his wheelchair, says, "I have, but I can't affahd the ones I want, even with government assistance. Besides, I'm waiting on the cyboahg models that hovah. I just want to be whole."

"Don't we all?" asks Bruiser as he gets lost, staring off into the crowd. His eyes get caught by three bright lights in a triangle as the ringing in his head comes back, pushing him to the floor, taking him back to the metallic cage.

Bruiser sits up on the metal bench, trying to focus on the bright blinding wall, and as he does, it starts to dim. His eyes adjust, and he finds the shadow of a boy that seems to be peering in through the opening as if it's a storefront window. Bruiser shuts his eyes and deepens his breath as a line gathers behind the child. The silence Bruiser has found in his current meditation is unsettling, and just as he thinks he is free from the voices that linger and haunt him, he can feel his skin suit absorbing his sweat and he hears, *Let them in.* His eyes open to an endless pile of people, staring at him through the invisible wall, and he hears the voice say, *Heal these people and try to focus on turning the darkness to light.*

"But how?" asks Bruiser.

Fear controls you and the tension contains the darkness. Know there is nothing that they can take from you, because you are always here and safe. Rather than holding on to the darkness and protecting the world from it, laugh at it, give it the love we all deserve, and release it back into the world.

"Who are these people, and what do they want?" he asks.

They're figments, says the voice, *just parts of yourself that need love.*

Bruiser's eyes open and there's a man that resembles Ronald Reagan, a younger version with blonde hair. He is staring blankly into Bruiser's eyes as a gob of drool seeps out of the corner of his mouth, and he does nothing to rectify the situation. Bruiser watches as the spittle traverses his leisure suit with no guidance. *Why are you so afraid of them?*

"I don't know. They look harmless, but they never are. And it's always the ones you let in that hurt you the most."

Who taught you that? Bruiser looks for the voice in his head that instilled that thought but can't locate where the subtle whisper comes from. *Who did you see when you looked in the mirror?*

Bruiser is taken back to the moment before he died and he lets one word free from his heart, "Mother?"

His eyes stare down the crowd as they fight to get through his door, stepping over one another, fighting to find their own serenity. He shuts his eyes and hears, *She was beaten by this life, and had every right to fear it. She passed that on to you, to protect you, but it holds no meaning at this time. Let go of that voice. What can they truly take from you? Other than what you let them. This device, that you built and programmed to protect you, has convinced you that you are the most amazing person on the planet and that there's no one else worth meeting. The sad thing is that there are others, and you'll never meet them, because you're too busy convincing people how amazing you are. The really sad thing is that they already know. The child you're protecting is even more amazing, but they'll never know that person either, because you've negated that being's existence. You've deemed their emotions invalid and nonfunctioning. When do you start accepting them and their broken selves, along with your own? Stop dancing around, screaming how fucking beautiful you're not, and just cool the fuck out.*

Bruiser's eyes open and he analyzes the mob of seemingly mindless beings waiting for his touch. They show no emotion and the only thing that seems to drive their meat carriages is forward momentum. As the crowd grows, the ones in front are being pushed into the invisible gateway, and yet still show no emotion. Bruiser scratches his head as he watches them being compressed against the invisible wall. He realizes that the fear and disgust in his heart is what is keeping them out, and he hears, **Let them in.**

Bruiser is immediately returned to the stage in Boston, and as his vision clears and the ringing subsides, he looks Andy dead in the eyes and says, "Andy, I read somewhere that healing comes from accepting your situation, because there is truly nothing you can change, other than your own outlook. You can't run from the past or to the future."

Andy rolls in, saying, "Well, yah right there!"

"All you can do is enjoy the moment and know that everything changes constantly. Accept who you are and try to be better. Andy, I accept you for who you are and know you're a beautiful person. Can you let go of who you are and open yourself up to the possibility of being whole?"

Andy rubs the armrests of his wheelchair, saying, "Anything to get my legs back. I'd suck your pissah religiously for that freedom."

Bruiser laughs awkwardly. "I wasn't really going to let him … I couldn't even get it up—"

Andy puts his chin out, the best he can, and says, "Me neithah. It's been so long I forgot what it looks like."

Bruiser reaches back with both hands while looking deep into the crowd, the spotlights blind him again, and all he can hear is, *I got tired of running from myself.*

Bruiser releases, knocking Andy out of his chair and onto the hardwood floor. The room goes silent, and then there's a voice from the crowd, saying, "I think I'm gonnah puke. Will you help that guy off the flarh? He's a vet and a cripple. He dahserves bettah. Yah fucked up, man, seriously."

Bruiser looks down at Andy on the floor, out cold, yet smiling like a baby to the point where he should have his thumb in his mouth with a blanket wrapped around him. Bruiser returns to the crowd and says, "Give it a minute. The more serious cases take time."

"You think we're gonnah fall for this, you shyster?"

Bruiser looks down at Andy and then back at the crowd. The sound of metal chairs screeching against the hardwood floor as people start to get up, pushes Bruiser into a dead stare while he processes his miscalculation. At that moment, the doors in the back of the auditorium burst open, and a crowd walks in led by Shamus, yelling, "Everybody, sit down! This man changed my life today. He got rid of my herpes in the middle of an outbreak."

There's a shout from across the room, "Shamus, what'd he pay you to pull this shit?"

Shamus looks around the gym as he's walking up the aisle with a grip of people behind him. "Who's that? Uncle Bunky? Get up here old man. He'll fix yah Parkinson's!" Shamus takes the stage, steps over Andy, and walks up to Bruiser, shaking his hand, asking, "What's Andy doing on the floor?"

Bruiser looks down at Andy, saying, "Growing legs — I hope."

Shamus kicks Andy playfully, saying, "He's a vagabond anyway. Don't listen to these hooligans, I got you." Shamus takes the mic, looks back at Andy on the floor, and says, "You know, I could care less about half you southie fuckahs, especially this guy." He points to Andy curled up on the floor and says, "Guy owes me a grand easy, just in bah tabs. Sadly, I'm related to the other half of youse. This guy over here, Bruisah, Zealand, healed me today." Shamus rolls up his sleeves and says, "Every last one of youse has sat at my bah, and I know you remember the tattoos from my knuckles to my neck. Some of the best aht in Boston. Tico, you here? He had better be. We all know he got the hep from a needle. Somebody find Tico and drag his ninety-pound ass down here." Shamus looks back at Bruiser, then over to his family that he dragged on stage with him, and continues, "It's always been hard to explain, but I used to have tha ADD, tha OCD, and probably dyslexia. We all know ma was ah drinkah; and she passed me down some unwanted gifts. But aftah Brewsah slapped me today, it was like everything made sense. I don't know, like I said, I could care less about half of youse, but I was sitting there with this flood of cleah thoughts, and it came to me: Bruisah's crossing the country and he's going to change the world forevah. If we don't take advantage of this guy today, we're going to get left behind like the apes when the other ones stood up and started talking." Everyone returns to their seats and there's a silence that crawls through the auditorium, thanks to Shamus's words.

Bruiser takes the mic from Shamus and says, "Look, I've been a piece of fecal matter for the longest time." He looks down at Andy on the floor, silent and lifeless, while Shamus checks his pulse and continues, saying, "And I'm tired of it. Aren't you? How many people here have you shit on — figuratively: friends, family, lovers, your children, or mainly strangers. We used to be majestic beings, and I know that more than anything. They turned us against each other, a long time ago, with one word — survival. How many times have you used that word to get what you want?" Bruiser returns to pacing as he reads the crowd, saying, "I can't do it anymore. What are we holding on to? What's so great about this life?"

Slaphappy

A voice in the crowd asks, "Yo, Shamahz, you serious about this guy?"

Shamus grabs the mic, holding on to it with Bruiser, and says, "You know, no mattah how much he paid me, I'd never lie to my family. Get Gigi up here!" Shamus motions for someone to push his grandmother on stage. "Yah think I'd let anybody touch my Gigi?" Shamus helps her on stage and says, "You're all afraid of happiness. Everybody that comes up here and lets my new friend, Bruiser, slap 'em, gets a beer and a shot at the pub latah — if that's what it takes."

A line starts to form at the bottom of the stage and Bruiser reaches back to slap Shamus's grandmother, visually asking him for permission. Shamus nods, and Bruiser slaps the geriatric woman with a vivacious amount of zeal. There's a startling scream from the stage, and Shamus drops to the floor, grabbing Andy's hand as his screams bellow through the auditorium. "How can I help, buddy?"

Bruiser squats down next to Shamus, inspecting Andy. "Thank you, Shamus, but I have it from here. Get Gigi out of here. I don't think you want to be anywhere near this."

Andy points to his legs, or lack thereof, and screams. Shamus pushes down on Andy, saying, "I'm not going anywhere, Bruisah."

Bruiser looks at Andy's nubs; they're cut off above the knee and his jeans are folded back and pinned down. Andy gives out another wailing scream and says, "Can you take off my pants? I can feel my legs, and it sucks!" As he says that, a golden light beams from his eyes. Shamus tries unpinning his jeans, but the pressure is too much. He grabs a knife off Andy's waist and removes the first pant leg. A fleshy little flipper emerges, spewing a bright light as well. Shamus cuts off Andy's second pant leg as he screams religiously for help from any God that will assist him. He clenches Shamus's hand as the auditorium full of people stare wide eyed with their mouths agape. Slowly the flippers become the shape of feet and start extending. Andy's eyes open, and they're a vibrant Royal blue. He looks up at the crowd, staring back at him, and then down at what is happening to him.

Bruiser shutters with fear that he has created another, asking, "Didn't you used to have brown eyes?"

Andy looks down at his newly formed legs and says, "Yeah, I didn't have legs either. What color are they now?"

Bruiser looks over his shoulder at Less, who's filmed the whole epimorphic regeneration, and then looks back at Andy. "Blue. They're blue, my friend." Bruiser and Shamus pick up Andy and put him back in his chair, and while his new legs take form, he watches Gigi battle with her rebirth as she sheds a good thirty years. Bruiser tugs at Shamus's arm, and they watch together as she stands up out of her chair. Andy sees her feat, tries to get himself erect, and almost falls, but Bruiser catches him and returns him to his wheelchair, asking, "Shamus, can you?"

Shamus wheels Andy off the stage and parades him around the building. Bruiser finds that the disposition of the crowd seems to have turned ever since Andy was brought back from defeat. He slaps his way through a never-ending river of suffering people and notices a celebration of life that he'd always yearned for, but never expected: the room has stopped, everyone is smiling, and they are open and connecting to one another. It's the closest thing to humanity he's ever seen up close.

Realizing that he's done here, he fights his way through a sea of adoration until he bumps into Shamus on his phone. "No more calls. I can't feel my hand. I'm going to have to use my feet if you call anyone else," begs Bruiser.

Shamus puts his phone down and hugs Bruiser as Andy jumps through the crowd, landing on his shoulders, saying, "You're a good man, Bruisah. I never would have thought it was possible. I was defeated in life: my spine was broken, my legs were missing, and I was ruined from fighting a war for a corporation that doesn't even remembah my name. I had tried everything; even stem cells, but nothing could return the feeling of being whole."

Bruiser stops, looks up at the cloud of shadows he just realized are lingering over him, and asks Andy, "Stem cells?"

"Yeah, for spinal development," says Andy.

"Do you know where they came from?" asks Bruiser.

"No clue, it was all secret government reseahch. Why?"

Bruiser looks out at the crowd of fresh souls enjoying their new lives, and ignores the voice in his head, saying, "No reason."

Shamus drops Andy and puts his arms around the two, asking, "You're comin' back to the bah, right?"

Andy responds for Bruiser, saying, "Of course, after I go pick up some new pants."

Shamus pushes Andy off him, saying, "Obviously, you Goldilocks, you'd neva pass on a free beer. I was talking to Bruiser … sorry Zealand."

"Bruiser's fine, but I can't."

Shamus looks Bruiser dead in the eyes. "You have tah. We're going to celebrate you and tha new life you gave us to fuck up, Bruisah. You've changed these people, more so, this city, the city we love. This place was known for people being able to handle suffering and diversity. I'm interested to see how they handle a life without pain and sickness. You havtah join us for a drink."

Bruiser surveys the crowd for an instant out, and finding none, he says shakily, "Honestly, I'm trying to quit. It's a long boring story but—"

Shamus shakes him, begging, "C'mon, just one drink."

Bruiser laughs nervously as he's confused by his own path toward a continued sobriety and says, "There's no such thing where I'm from, but Chelsea's gonna' be there, right?"

Shamus stops shaking Bruiser and grips his arms tightly, saying, "Easy, B, I can get you any dime in the city, and I appreciate what you've done, but … Fuck it. If you promise to take her with you, you can havah."

Bruiser has a good hearty laugh and says, "I'm good, I've got more than enough problems at the moment." Shamus shoots him some sad puppy dog eyes and Bruiser gives in to him, saying, "Okay, one drink."

Shamus envelopes Bruiser with a bear hug, shakes him like a martini, and sets him down, saying, "If I don't see you tonight … I expect you to stop by the bah next time you're in town." Shamus pulls his phone out of his pocket and hands it to Andy, saying, "Take a picture of me and Bruisah for the bah."

Bruiser walks through the crowd, floating on all the love in the room, all the way backstage where he's addressed with the same affection from his crew. Vanessa, the first to grab him, pulls him in and kisses him on the cheek, whispering in his ear, "Thank you."

He stops, as he feels something unfamiliar in his pants move, and asks her, "What was that for?"

She stares up at him endearingly, locked into his eyes, and says, "A great show … that we can use … where no one died."

And all fluffed up from her compliment, he says, "Technically, no one died last show."

Vanessa slaps him playfully and says, "Technically you did — twice. But you know what I'm saying."

She turns from his cockiness and starts to walk away, but he stops her, raising his voice and lowering his ego, saying, "It was a good crowd. And as much as I thought that I could do without Boston, it turned out."

Less walks in, sets down his Steadicam rig and asks, "What about Andy?"

Bruiser stops, returning from a moment he'd prefer never to leave, and says, "It's definitely the stem cells." He fidgets with his hands nervously as they continue to shake with all the anxious shadows, he's just acquired from an auditorium full of people.

"What's the stem cells?" asks Leslie.

"The blonde hair and blue eyes, like—" says Less.

"Alice, Tanner, Janeuh, and my mom. They all had stem cell treatments. Andy was telling me the government tested them on him to see if it helped with spinal injuries," says Bruiser as he sits down, receding into the couch.

Dick sits down next to him, asking, "You got stem cells from your sister? Have you had any … cravings?"

Bruiser elbows Dick in the ribs and says, "For human hearts, Dick? Fuck off. I feel like … I hope that was an isolated incident." The spirits start to take over and he leans back, looking to the ceiling for comfort. His face starts to turn a eucalyptus green, and his leg starts twitching.

Vanessa catches his retreat and asks him, "Bruiser, are you okay?"

He doesn't respond but stands up loosely and is immediately pushed to his knees by the recurring ringing in his head. Vanessa puts her hand on his head and catches a static shock that leaves her shaking her hand. Bruiser starts to puke, but pushes it back down, and as his eyes open, he asks, "Who do I have to feltch to get a drink?"

"Bruiser!" yelps Dick.

Bruiser stands up, steadies himself, and walks off, saying, "I need something; I don't know how to do this sober,"

"You think he's all right?" asks Dick.

"These large sessions seem to take their toll. We should have started out with smaller crowds," says Vanessa, staring at him as he walks out the door. She follows Bruiser out the door, shouting, "Bruiser!" across the parking lot, trying to retain his presence, but he doesn't respond. She drops a canter in his direction, trying to catch him.

The doors of the bus open, inviting Vanessa inside, and she asks the driver, "What's up, Chuck?"

"Speaking of upchuck, is Mr. Dahl all right?" he asks.

"Who?" she asks.

"Zealand," says Chuck.

"I'm sure he'll be fine. He's a resilient SOB," she says and walks back towards Bruiser's room, but is stopped by the sound of upheaval as she passes the community crapper.

"Bruiser, are you all right?" she asks and opens the bathroom door to find him kneeling in front of the toilet, expelling a dark red stream of fluids. "What's up, Chuck?"

Bruiser looks up with a face-full of tears and asks her, "What?"

Vanessa whimpers at his suffering, saying, "Sorry, I was attempting humor. That doesn't look good. Are you okay?" She walks into the small, tiled shitter and goes in to rub his back. He flinches as she touches him and begs her, "Can you grab me a beer?"

Vanessa backs away timidly, debating the outcome of this conversation. She returns with a bottled water and catches him looking in the mirror, staring so deeply that you would think he was staring through it into another dimension. She approaches him with the bottled water, asking, "See anything in there you like?"

He turns to her, and she smiles. It stuns him for a moment and then he says, "No, I think it's broken."

She hands him the bottle, stating, "It's a process. Do you want to talk about it?"

He takes a swig, rinses, and spits, saying, "I've never felt that much love directed toward me. You would think it was the best feeling, like the highest high, but it hurts." Bruiser pushes past her towards his room.

Vanessa follows him and finds him frantically digging through the couch. She grabs him by the arm and sits him down at the table, saying, "We got rid of it."

"What? C'mon!" he moans.

"There were a couple life sentences in there," she says, looking into his eyes, reading them, and gauging his suffering. She pulls his nun chucks out of the couch cushion and starts swinging them over her head in a rather respectable manner.

She stops swinging them and goes to hand them back to Bruiser, but he refuses her, saying, "Hold on to those. They look happier in your hands."

She drops the nun chucks and in an endearing tone, says, "I'm proud of you."

"For sharing my toys?"

Vanessa sits down next to him, saying, "Bruiser, we expected a mess worse than Charlotte, and it was the complete opposite."

She grabs his hand and Bruiser pulls away, saying, "You expected the same debacle, and still followed me in there?"

She puts her head on his shoulder and says, "Yeah, and it was worth trusting you. The show was amazing; the energy in the room was so much more vibrant than the other two shows. What happened in there?"

Bruiser dimly responds, "In the gym. I'm just tired of running from this life."

She puts her hand on his thigh and says, "No, after you hit your head, when you were in … inside yourself. You're so different. Something changed."

He's silent as he tries to conceive explaining his transcendental journey to her. He grabs her hand, stopping her unceasing strokes. "It's hard to objectify something so surreal." Vanessa, feeling the rejection of her touch, gets up to give him space, but he pulls her back to the seat and tries to smile at her.

"Try me," she says playfully.

He takes a swig of water, rubs his face as he organizes his thoughts, and turns to her, saying, "I was trapped in this metal cell that changed with my every thought. Like, if I thought about sitting down, the floor raised to seat me. If I thought about a moment in time, it appeared on the wall. I was alone, and it felt like I'd been trapped there since the conception of time itself."

Vanessa reaches for his hand, grabs it, and pulls it to her heart, asking, "Where do you think you were?" She answers her own question, saying, "Trapped in your subconscious, maybe."

He fights to pull away from her heart, not wanting to infect her with his energetic trembling, saying, "It was too lucid to be a dream, and I keep returning there. My ears start ringing, my vision blurs, and I'm there, like a window opens to that place."

"Why do you think that happens?" she asks.

"I feel like I'm still there watching myself in that moment, but I believe it's to remind me."

"Of what?" she asks, rubbing his thigh.

"This reptilian looking dude showed up that reminded me of my dad. He worked on me and found something attached to me that thrived off the darkness. I think the attachment was my grandfather. He said that he was the reason why I was naturally drawn to pain and suffering. He was kind of an evil dick that I never met but programmed me with enough fear to keep me docile and in disbelief for an eternity. Anyway, the reptilian guy removed him and told me that I have to learn how to process the shadows. That I must send them to the light, or it will destroy me. But the main thing that sticks out, was the endless line of people, outside my cell, that needed to be healed. And with the whole connectivity of the cell, I couldn't figure out how to open it."

"Or why," she says.

"What do you mean?" asks Bruiser.

"Metaphorically speaking, the cell is your heart. You're trapped in this impenetrable sanctuary, and you don't know how to let people in. Your father, who you could look at as the father, God, was healing you and encouraging you to open up, so that you can heal them, or love people, that is. The real question is: who built that sanctuary to protect you? Or was it to protect them from you?"

An intense pain rolls through Bruiser and crumples him up into a ball. He curls up with his head in her lap and submits to the darkness, saying, "That's fair, I feel like everyone takes a piece as they pass through us, and I'm definitely tired of being a part of that parasitic exchange."

Vanessa lets Bruiser find a temporary sanctuary in her lap, asking him as she strokes him, "You can't be happy living like that — alone, trapped in an impenetrable cell."

He recedes into her as he embraces the familiar thought, moaning, "Happiness has never been on the list."

She shakes him as he digresses emotionally, saying, "Happiness is all we have, and it comes from letting go of the pain and the fear of the pain that we use to protect us long after the threat exists.

Your grandfather, the one that created the people that hurt you, is a strong image; and I'd love to think that removing that program would be freeing but—"

Bruiser kicks at the couch as the darkness rumbles around in his being, saying, "I feel like the darkness is so much more intense and threatening without him."

She tightens her hold on him, saying, "It's not yours. Let it pass through you."

Bruiser sits up, looks into her as his eyes flood with mirky shadows, and he growls, "I wish it were that simple."

Vanessa jumps on top of him, straddling him, and says, "It is, Bruiser. All you have to do is believe it, and you'll see it. Just relax, let me take it, and I'll fill your heart with more love than you've ever known possible." She grabs his face with both hands and the darkness starts to retreat from his eyes.

He tries to pull away from her, saying, "Sounds great, but I don't know how."

Vanessa fights to stay on top of him. "Just let me into that rock full of darkness you call a heart, and I'll show you how."

He flinches at her words, trying desperately to break the hold she has on him. "That's what I get for opening up to you?"

She can feel the darkness returning as he looks her in the eyes, and she tremors with regret as she realizes her mistake. "I'm sure there's a diamond in the middle of that lump of coal," she says and leans in to kiss him. He tries to pull away, still offended by her words. Vanessa grabs his hands and relentlessly opens her heart, saying, "Fill your heart with my love, use that diamond that you forged to project a light so bright that the rock dissolves."

Vanessa forces herself on him and he retreats, asking, "What about your girlfriend?"

"I think you'll like her," she says and connects with his face. He doesn't pull away this time, she does, asking, "What about your girl-fiancee?"

He tries to return to her face, disregarding Janeuh's existence, but stops and says, "I don't think you'd like her." He pulls Vanessa back into him, asking, "So, you want to fuck?" Resenting himself as he lets the phrase slide past his teeth, he laughs nervously.

"I thought for sure the 'infamous' Bruiser could come up with something more penetrating than 'you wanna' fuck.'"

Bruiser grabs her and pulls her back into him, saying, "Sorry, you retard me emotionally. I've never had to ask, it just happens, but you're different."

She flinches and tries to pull away but finds she can't run from him. As she returns to him, he sees an indigo flame light up in her chest, her third-eye illuminates, and a pair of giant white wings sprout out behind her. He withdraws from his pursuit, saying, "I'm just trying to fuck this up. Aren't you worried about soaking up all this darkness?"

Vanessa leans forward, hovering above him, eye to eye, and says, "It sounds like you're more worried about my love invading your haunted sanctuary of souls. Tell that voice in your head to shut-the-fuck-up. Let go of all the chatter in your dumb brain and allow yourself to be loved. Consume all of my love in this fleeting moment where we've found each other and know that this too will pass. Just let go … you're safe here."

"Fuck, you're beautiful — it's blinding." He pushes himself up and leans into her, kissing her deeply, and there's an energy that builds between the two that feels like they're headed towards an even longer conversation.

He takes off her shirt and slides his hand up her mini skirt, waiting for her to pull away, but she stops and shakes him, saying, "I'm serious, let me take the darkness from you."

She rips his shirt off and scrapes his chest lightly with her nails. He grabs her hands, stopping her, and says, "It would tear you apart." He smiles and rubs on her gates lightly, testing the waters.

She starts to purr like a brand-new beamer and reaches into his pants, grabbing his dick as if it were the first and last time, she was ever going to touch one, saying, "Well then, let it. Let it tear us both apart." She moans into his ear as she chews on it, saying, "There's no room for love in a heart filled with fear."

"That's the second time I've heard that." Bruiser's stomach clenches up with her familiar words and from the arousing suspicion that he's about to win, at least actually get what he wants: That being a somewhat sane, completely beautiful, and equally amazing woman; something he never deemed himself worthy.

"What do you think it means?" Vanessa asks him.

"Ever since Bootleg slapped me, I've been hearing these murmurs from people. They're like echoes floating through time, that are trying help me." he says, rubbing her stomach ever so lightly.

Vanessa pulls down his jeans and starts sliding back and forth on his pummeled horse. The two stare each other down without flinching. Vanessa continues to slide across his dick, and without the use of her hands, she forces him inside of her. She stops moving and lets Bruiser just be inside of her. They get lost in each other as they drown in the connection and the overwhelming comfort that resides in it.

"So, that's what it feels like to stick your dick in twenty-thousand-dollars," he says with a nervous laugh, subversively hoping to break their bond.

Gyrating around him slowly, she puts her hand over his face, and as he lolls into her, she whispers, "Shut up." Moment's pass, and she pulls her hand away from his face to find his eyes closed. She

286

battles with her ego, trying not to let the situation offend her, but breaks it and demanding his presence, shouts, "Bruiser!"

Dick kicks open the door with the screen of his phone pointed at the two, shouting, "Bruiser, I've got Janeuh on FaceTime!"

Vanessa covers up and turns to Dick with an unchallengeable look in her eye, growling, "What a Dick!"

He covers the phone with his hand, and all you hear is Janeuh screaming through the phone, "Fucking, really, Bruiser? Nothing's changed. You're out there saving the world and you still can't keep your dick where it should be!"

Dick realizes what a dick he truly is being and ends the call, saying, "Nice rack, boss."

Vanessa's eyes fill with darkness as she finds herself caught in a situational mouse trap, and she points at the door, demanding Dick's absence.

Dick stares at his friend, void of movement, and then at his boss, asking, "Are you okay?"

Vanessa jumps off Bruiser and pushes Dick out of the door, saying, "What the fuck are you doing, just barging in here like that?"

"I really didn't think that you two would—" Dick tries to get another glimpse of his friend through the doorway, but Vanessa blocks his view, and he apologizes, saying, "Sorry, I tried to call you."

"My phones dead. Everything I touches seems to break," she says, looking back at Bruiser frozen in a coital moment.

"Appears that way," says Dick as she backs him out of the room and slams the door in his face.

Bruh...

"So, I'm inside this chick, trapped inside her disease infested uterus," says Bruiser as he hits a blunt, stretches, and takes a swig of coffee.

Dick takes the blunt from him, asking, "Was she hot?"

Bruiser shakes his head as the dream ventures back into his forefront, and he says, "I'm telling you, I'm literally inside of her uterus, Dick. It was hot and steamy in there, and I'm playing whack a mole with her nodes or whatever. And every time I whack one, two more pop up. All I want to do is leave, but I can't find my way out of her."

Dick hits the blunt a couple more times and passes it back to Bruiser, saying, "I would say, in this scenario, slap the nodes, heal her, and then go toward the light."

"What time are we supposed to meet Blaine?"

Dick snatches the blunt from Bruiser, as he walks off toward the bathroom, and says, "Vanessa said he'd be performing on the streets of Brooklyn all day, and to just find him."

Bruiser returns from the bathroom, more disheveled than he went in, saying, "So, I go toward this speck of light and crawl into a tunnel that starts out fleshy and moist, but leads me into something similar to a sewage drain, from what I can tell."

Dick lifts Bruiser's bed, turning it back into a table, and asks, "You sure you were in the right hole?"

Bruiser laughs and asks, "Is there a wrong one? So, I'm crawling through this tunnel: It's slimy, it stinks, it's moist, and it smells like shit. I hear something behind me that startles me, so I start crawling, but the faster I crawl toward the light, the smaller the tunnel gets, and the closer the predatory noise gets behind me. I finally push my way to an opening and I'm immediately, without choice, spit out into an alley. The alley's so dark, I can't really see anything other than vague forms at this point. I hear footsteps followed by these braindead moans, and now my heads spinning with paranoia and I'm shaking with fear. You know it's not my style, but I'm freaking out. I take off running down the alley and I start to see images of faces, beautiful faces, smiling at me in the piles of trash as I run by them. I start kicking over the trash piles, trying to jump over them, but the more trash I kick, the more bodies fall out. There's no emotion on their faces and I don't see any blood, so I'm thinking they're robots or something similar. I trip over this one pile and fall, landing face to face with my fathers, and all I can think is, 'When was the last time I saw you and why are you here?'"

"Weird," comments Dick, jumping into his phone.

"I go to touch his face, his head rolls over, and it starts spitting out this Kelly-green fluid with the texture of a synthetic oil. And the next thing I know, I'm covered in homeless dudes. Homeless robots maybe. I feel one of them grab my arm and bite it, and instantly something pushes them all off me."

"Who do you think it was?" asks Dick.

"It felt familiar, but it's more like a what than a who. I jumped up so fast that I left my shoes in the alley. Now I'm running barefoot through an abandoned downtown area that kind of looks like LA, but there's no streets: only sidewalks. I look up and there's no skyline, just endless towers. I run into a dead end that resembles the favelas in Brazil: they're smaller shacks, that go up and back, like they were built on a hill. I start climbing them: not like hardcore parkour, more like a soft-core parkour; it's clumsy. Mainly because I'm so afraid of these homeless guys from the alley that are trying to rape, murder, rape, and consume me. As I get higher up the hill of shanties, it starts to look more like lower-middle class. There are three-bedroom, ranch houses stacked on top of each other, and it feels like I'm running through the neighborhood I grew up in, except it goes up instead of across. I run up the walkway of a house that looks like the one I grew up in…"

"Creepy. Cats everywhere?" asks Dick.

"Yeah, robot cats that are watching my every move. Then a light in a window catches my eye, so I run over and look in the window. It's all fifties-style, nuclear family: clean cut, two-point-five kids, dad's smoking a pipe, all that, but they move like robots," says Bruiser as he sips his coffee and tries to figure out how to turn on the television.

Dick takes the remote from him, saying, "Are the homeless guys still trying to rape-murder-rape you?"

Bruiser smiles and says, "Yeah, I can't shake 'em. I look up and see McMansions everywhere, and I decide that I'll ditch them in one of the giant houses and hide out for the night. As I make my way up to the closest abode I can find, I notice that the lights are out and nobody's home, but there are alarms on the windows. Instead of running up, I go over, or down the aisle of these luxurious homes that all seem to be abandoned, and I hear something in a bush. I haul ass, and the next thing I know, I'm standing on top of fifty feet of well-balanced patio furniture that's about to topple and lead me right back into the mouths of these cannibal, robohobo rapists. And for some odd reason, I'm holding two pint-glasses of rosé that I can't spill, or the universe will collapse on itself — surely."

"I'm really starting to think you have the brain damage,"

Bruiser continues, saying, "Definitely. So, I start kicking the furniture out from underneath me at the robohobos, knocking them out one by one, until I hit the ground, and then I chug the rosé. What do you think it means?"

Dick shakes his head and holds his hands up as Vanessa bursts in, yelling, "It means you're late and we need to find David Blaine. Let's go!"

"Ten more minutes, ma!" says Bruiser.

"BZ, you're smoking weed for breakfast?" asks Vanessa.

"I'm just holding it for Dick," he says and tries to hand her the blunt. She turns around and tries to slam the door, but it just makes a light ding.

"You think the dream was about her?" asks Dick.

"I was inside of her while I was having it, but how so?"

"You were safe inside her, playing a silly game, and when you left, darkness was all there was," says Dick.

"What about the thing with my dad?" asks Bruiser.

Dick pulls Bruiser to his feet and pushes him towards the door, saying, "Queerly — I mean clearly, your dad's the dirty, homeless, soulless, robot chasing you. You're tired of running from dirty old men that are trying to consume you, and all you want is to go home to a nice house and drink rosé on a pile of lower-upper-class, patio furniture."

Bruiser tries to exit the bus, but the light of day pushes him back onto it. He takes the end of the blunt from Dick and says, "Well, when you say it like that, it sounds a little fem, but I think dreaming about being pounded to death by some soot covered, hobo, whiskey-dick bot, while it bites chunks out of me and thrusts away blankly into my second to last meal, is totally normal."

"Wait, what?" asks Dick as they stumble out of the bus to find Less and Leslie geared up and ready for the day.

Less smiles at them and says, "I can't say I miss New York."

Leslie turns and says, "How could you? The only time you've been here was when we shot Greed, and that was a disaster."

Dick laughs and asks, "Are you talking about the part where we got held up on camera by some tweaker, train kids, or when Bruiser blacked out at Scores and got us thrown out for starting an orgy with a handful of cocktail girls in the back?"

"Nice, Bruiser," says Vanessa.

Bruiser looks Vanessa in the eyes, while Leslie tries to put a mic on him, and says, "You've got to give me credit for the cocktail waitress, dancers would've been too easy."

"Most of that," says Less, "mainly the homeless 'girl' I hooked up with, that turned out to be a guy. Roberto, that lascivious little devil."

Leslie deadeyes Less, saying, "I thought you would have figured it out when she told you her name was Bob."

"'She' told me it was short for Roberta," says Less.

"The worst part about hooking up with the destitute is that they always try to move in — immediately," says Vanessa, stunning the group. She walks off on her phone, saying, "Sorry."

"Who's she talking to?" asks Bruiser.

"Her girl, from what I can tell," says Leslie.

"You think she's gonna' tell her?" asks Dick.

"She seems like that type of person," says Bruiser. And effectively changing the topic, he says, "You guys geared to the teeth? I don't want you to miss a moment of what happens in New York."

"You're serious about this whole film everything documentary, B?" asks Less as he digs through Leslie's backpack.

"Yeah, and not to compare myself, but can you imagine if JC had a film crew?"

Less responds, saying, "Yeah, I'm definitely going to need more tape, batteries, chargers, and an assistant."

"Use Chuck, and give him a camera," says Dick.

"I want a real PA," says Less querulously.

"Well then, find someone here that wants to work for free, loves to travel, and maybe moonlights as a bodyguard," says Dick, lighting up a cigarette, and walking away from Less and Bruiser.

"Or a Shaolin monk," says Leslie.

"Do you still have Bob's number? I'd imagine she's free," says Bruiser as he jaunts off to catch Dick and Vanessa.

He sneaks up on them as Vanessa's ending her call and jabs her in the ribs playfully, startling her, and she turns around, asking him, "And when were you guys going to let me in on the documentary?"

Bruiser leans in to give her a kiss and says, "Hey?"

Vanessa pulls away, yet smiling, and says, "Let's try to keep it professional."

Assuming her girlfriend to be the source of this rejection, he says, "A little bit late for that. How's your girlfriend?"

"She's definitely pissed."

"About what?" he asks, toying with her.

"You, stupid. I had to tell her," she says and tries to distance herself from him.

Less walks up on the end of the conversation, asking, "Told her what?"

Leslie joins them, saying, "Told her about his dumb, dirty dick."

Bruiser scampers after Vanessa, catching her right as she catches Dick. He places himself between the two, asking, "Are you pissed because I didn't mention the documentary? It's going to produce itself."

She shrugs him off, saying, "I don't have to produce. I love all facets of the process."

Bruiser pulls at her, saying, "Less wanted more people with cameras in their hands."

"I'd like that," she says in a childlike tone.

Bruiser tries to smile at her and says, "Cool, I'll run it by him." She doesn't return the smile but stops and waits for Less and Leslie to catch up as Bruiser continues to walk away.

"You ready for New York, Dick?" Dick doesn't respond, so Bruiser pokes at him, asking, "You all right, bud?"

Dick stops and looks up at the sky, saying, "You know I'm not. I'm just a useless sidekick that's here for comedic relief and exposition."

Bruiser grabs Dick by the shoulders and shakes him, saying, "Well, could you at least be funny." He smiles and double slaps the shit out of Dick. Dick rubs his face indiscriminately and pulls Bruiser into a surprisingly empty coffee shop. Bruiser looks at Dick, waiting for a reaction. Dick looks at his hands and spins in a circle, searching for any sort of change. Bruiser scoffs at him, saying, "Dude, spend less time worrying about your superpowers, and more time thinking about how we're going to spend all this money."

Dick, mildly ruffled, says, "It's not even about that. I love the money thing. It's easy thinking about that, but—"

Bruiser slaps him unsettlingly hard on the back, saying, "But … this 'is' about the whole superpowers thing."

"Yeah," says Dick with an ornery tone.

"What do you think your power would be?" asks Bruiser.

Dick stares off at the blackboard, looking for his second cup of the day, and as he figures it out, he looks back at Bruiser. "I'd be happy if I could fly. You always talk about it happening in your dreams, and it sounds like a good time. Other than that, laser eyes, invisibility, or whatever Tanner got, maybe, I don't know. What do you think it is?"

"I saw it when I slapped you just now."

"Two large Kenyans, black," says Dick.

"Do you want cream in that?" asks the barista.

"What?" asks Dick as he looks into the barista's eyes, repeating himself, "Two Kenyans, black, black."

Bruiser puts a twenty on the bar and the barista pushes it back, saying, "I couldn't … Zealand." Bruiser looks around the coffee shop and finds himself surrounded by fans with their phones out, filming. "Help me out here, Zealand?" asks the barista as he points to eczema splotches on his skin.

Dick goes to grab the coffees and stops himself, pulls out his phone, and starts filming. Bruiser looks at the barista and says, "Lean forward." The barista puts his hands on the bar and leans in close enough to kiss Bruiser. Bruiser backs off and slaps the dude.

"Owwie!" says the barista as he leans back into his new self, rubbing his jaw.

"Did you think it would feel good?" asks Bruiser.

"Kind of," is his response.

Bruiser puts a blue bill in the tip bucket, turns around, and smiles into every camera pointed at him, asking, "Who's next?" He realizes that it's everyone and starts slapping people randomly. All you can hear is the pleasurable moans of people as they ease into their new perspective. "With the more serious cases, it takes time. Hopefully none of you have had any stem cell treatments, as we are finding complications with those that have. Spread the word, find the voice of love in your heart, and listen to it," says Bruiser as he grabs the coffees and tries to evade the scene. He tows Dick out of the shop, who's still filming, and tries to hand him his coffee, saying, "Put that thing down."

Dick disregards his request and asks him, "Isn't that a little careless; even for you?"

Bruiser takes a long, deep sip off his coffee and asks, "Tipping a hundo on coffee? I guess."

"Healing strangers and just walking away with no concern for their path, or even a thought about your responsibility for it?" asks Dick as he tries to film and drink coffee.

Bruiser looks back to find the crowd from the coffee shop, tracking them with their phones out, and says, "I feel like me and the universe are cool. It kicked me in the dick and told me it'll work itself out. You got a cigarette?"

"You quit," says Dick.

Bruiser looks over his shoulder and points out the crowd following them, saying, "The thought of being trampled by the shadows of a New York, city-block-sized crowd is making me nauseous."

Dick pulls at Bruiser's sleeve, saying, "Get used to it; it's only going to get worse. You'll be lucky to survive your newfound responsibility for humanity."

Bruiser pats Dick on the back. "My responsibility for the human race is nothing, compared to the garbage you're going to have to dredge Lil' Dickie through to fulfill your purpose."

They turn another corner, finding a relatively intimate group of people in a circle, and as they approach the edge of the gathering, Dick asks him, "Wait, what?"

Bruiser peers into the group, only to find David Blaine with a handful of cards. David takes a sip of water and asks the person of interest to put the card back into the deck. Bruiser looks over to the right of the crowd and finds Less, standing on a dumpster, filming the event. He looks back and finds his following has grown, and that they've surrounded him. Bruiser turns to Dick and says, "Intercalarius is the word I heard when I slapped you."

"What?" asks Dick.

Bruiser acts like he's looking for his phone, saying, "I don't know. I had a vision of you in a pyramid with green skin and you were procreating with everyone you came across, because you were a supreme being. The pyramid was a vortex of light, and you were at the center of it. Humanity left you gifts of gold, food, and small children. It was bizarre."

Dick hands Bruiser his coffee, jumps in his phone, and then looks up from it, saying, "It means 'of insertion,' or 'to be inserted.'"

"That makes sense."

"But that's not possible, B. I'm sterile," mumbles Dick.

"Not anymore," says Bruiser and he pushes his way through the crowd, towards David. David takes the deck, throws it up into the air, pulls out a lighter, and spits a fireball that devours the deck midair.

"Where's my card, man?" asks the participant.

"Good question, my friend," says Blaine as he pulls Bruiser into the circle and slaps him. "Do you have this man's card?" Bruiser rubs his face and empties his pockets, and as he does, a three of hearts appears in the handprint David left behind. David points at Bruiser's face and asks the man, "Is this your card?"

The crowd starts awing and laughing. Bruiser looks around, clueless to what's going on, and the participant leans into Bruiser's face, asking, "How'd you do that?"

The crowd applauds as Bruiser continues to rub his face and David grabs Bruiser's hand, stopping him from rubbing it, and shows it off to the crowd, yelling, "Zealand T. Dahl everyone. He's here to save our souls!"

The crowd goes silent as David shakes Bruiser's hand. Bruiser pulls him in for an embrace and he leans into Blaine's ear, asking, "How do you want to do this?"

David laughs and takes a step back, saying, "Let's start with the question on all our minds, Zealand. Is your magic real or is it just an illusion? Are you truly a healer or just an actor? Anyone can pull off illusions, but magic—"

Bruiser looks at the cigarette, loses himself in the burning cherry for a moment, and throws it on the ground. He looks up to the crowd and asks confidently, "How many people still believe in magic?" He spins around, looking for raised hands, but no one responds.

David jumps in, saying, "We're all just looking to catch a fraud, because we stopped believing in magic a long time ago. It's the same thing with miracles."

"And that's why we suffer," says Bruiser, "because we stopped believing."

David pulls a razor blade out of the air and lets out a deviant chuckle, saying, "There's only one way to make them believe again, and that would be to let them witness it." He forces an opening directly into his wrist, running the blade up his arm, and stopping at his elbow. An ejaculation of blood covers Bruiser's face and splatter paints his white T-shirt. He drops the blade and begs, "Save me, Zealand, if you can!"

Bruiser pulls back with both arms and stretches out like the wings of a seagull, stopping midair to catch the offerings of a tourist, and then fervently attacks David's face with both hands at the same time. David steps back and runs his hand down his arm, wiping away the blood, along with the opening, leaving his arm unscathed. He stretches his arms out in a Jesus Christ pose, palms up, leans his head back, staring up directly into the sun, and says, "Have fun with that, Zealand." David is immediately covered in a brilliant white light that leaves the crowd blinded. His body is propelled into the sky, and he disappears, leaving Bruiser in the middle of a crowd of anguished souls.

The inner circle pushes in, clenching around him like a sphincter threatened by a cold finger, and he hears, "Heal us, Zealand!"

Bruiser spins around, slapping the first row in one desperate swoop, and says, "Fuck, dude!"

Dick turns to Vanessa and says, "I knew we should've brought security!" He yells over the crowd, "If you've been slapped by Zealand, please step back, and allow others through!"

The second row starts fighting their way through to him and Bruiser looks up to Less, standing on a dumpster, asking him, "You good, Z?"

"Never been better," he says as the crowd consumes him.

Vanessa pushes her way into the shrinking circle, holding a camera, and blocks for Bruiser, saying, "I got you."

Dick follows her lead and jumps into the crowd with them, asking, "What can we do for you, Zealand?"

Vanessa pushes back on the crowd, shouting, "Everyone will have a chance! I need everyone to take two steps back!"

Dick spreads his arms as he tries to block for Bruiser, saying, "We're going to have to fight our way out of here, Vanessa. You watch zombie flicks?"

She grabs Dick and says, "Yeah, stack up!"

They turn their backs to Bruiser, covering his, and the crowd goes mental. The looks in their eyes is that of a hunger that comes from lifetimes of starvation. Bruiser looks around the crowd, saying, "I'm definitely getting Blaine to teach me how he flew off like that." He raises his hand high above the crowd, shaking it as if he were about to start speaking tongues, and says, "Come and get it! I'm done fucking with all of you." He raises his other hand and starts spinning, as if he were fighting his way out of an Emo mosh pit. Bruiser forces his way through the crowd to the outer rim, stops, and turns around. He stares down the path he made on his way out as he realizes he left his friends in there to fend for themselves. He charges the lane, grabbing Vanessa and Dick, and pushes his way out the other side, slapping as many as he can on the way out.

"You all right, Zealand?" asks Vanessa.

"I feel a little violated, but I'm sure it's something I need to get used to. You guys get out of here. I've got to grab Less and Leslie and finish off the crowd."

Dick lights up a cigarette and offers it to Bruiser, saying, "We're not going anywhere, B."

Bruiser looks at the cigarette, takes a deep breath, turns it down, and fights his way back to Less, asking, "Lift me up?" Less pulls him up, and as they hover over the crowd that now has no visual end, Bruiser turns to Less, asking him, "What do you think, buddy?"

Less pats him on the back and says, "You're in control of the future, and you're changing it exponentially right now, make it beautiful."

Bruiser puts his hands together, palm to palm, in front of his heart as if to pray, and says, "Thanks, I needed to hear that." He puts his hands over his head and motions as if he were diving in the crowd, but stops and yells, "So, how about this? Erybody back the fuck up. This is madness and we're better than this." The crowd goes silent. "I plan to heal everyone here, but it's not going to happen if you continue to behave like animals. Can ev-er-y-body stop, take a breath, and chill the fuck out, or is that me asking for a miracle?" The silence sustains. "Cool, everybody take three steps back, and at the first tinge of discomfort, I bail." Bruiser takes a deep breath and says to himself, *thank you.* He jumps down off the dumpster and slaps away at the crowd until there's no one fighting for his attention.

He stops and stands in the middle of the crowd as an unfamiliar wave of energy rolls through him. He shuts his eyes and feels his being flutter. And in his moment of clarity, he has a vision of the crowd tearing him apart to nothing. He opens his eyes in a panic and looks over the overwhelming crowd for a familiar face. "I guess this would be a perfect time to have a phone." He spots Less, still on the dumpster, and makes his way back to him, slapping stragglers on the way. He reaches out and offers Less a hand down, asking, "How'd it look?"

Less takes his hand, saying, "Redonkulous. Why didn't you leave when you had the chance?"

Bruiser laughs and says, "Because that wouldn't have changed anything. Did you see how everything stopped and everyone chilled out exponentially after I slapped them. Imagine a world like that, where everyone got it, and we all loved freely and appreciated one another."

Less looks at Bruiser sideways, confused by the lighter side of his friend, and says, "Sounds boring. Did you see the linen, mustache dicks?"

Bruiser looks around nervously, asking, "The feds from the Charlotte show? They're here?"

Less stops him, saying, "I don't think they're feds."

Bruiser scratches his head and says, "Yeah, they're definitely something different."

Less asks him, "What do you think they are, B?"

Bruiser and Less get to the edge of the crowd and they hear, "Mr. Dahl! Zealand T. Dahl!" yells the voice.

Bruiser stops, looks around for the origin of the voice, and with a serious tone says, "Honestly, Less, I have no idea, but I'm pretty sure we're going to find out."

As he says that, they are interrupted by a man in a suit, that's standing next to a limousine, saying, "Mr. Dahl, Mr. Blaine would appreciate some chosen one-on-one time with you before the party starts."

Bruiser starts to get in the car, notices Less hesitating, and asks him, "You coming?"

Less pushes him in the limo, saying, "I'm gonna' walk back to the bus. I'll see you there."

"Less, don't spend the whole day looking for Roberto," laughs Bruiser.

"Ha, I could be so lucky as to run into that scamp."

To Hell with Good Intentions

Bruiser climbs the stairs of David's penthouse, out onto the rooftop, and is immediately confronted by the vastness of the New York City skyline and an even more overwhelming sight: a blonde-haired, blue-eyed version of the freshly slapped David Blaine sitting on the ledge of the high-rise. Bruiser, still covered in David's blood, cautiously skulks his way over to the ledge and sits down next to him, asking, "How'd you know I could save you? Weren't you afraid of dying?"

David turns to him and says, "I was more afraid of you not being real, Bruiser, and with your rep, we assumed you were just an illusion, so we had a team of people ready to pull me out."

"I've been getting that a lot lately," says Bruiser.

"Don't get me wrong, I loved Greed. I might be one of the few people that actually respects you for that show. You're such an eloquent scumbag. When I saw the Future of the Left stuff on the internet, I couldn't figure out what you were up to. I mean, the cockeyed girl, that's easy. The little one with Down's: I figured CG, maybe you green screen it, fix it in post, and then degrade the video for the web, but it looked pretty clean, and there were too many other angles from random phones. And fuck, the last episode of Bleed, that's what really sparked my interest. But the one thing that pushed me over the edge," says David, patting Bruiser on the back, "was the kid with ALS, from the pitch meeting. That was by far, the sickest thing I've ever seen on the internet. It was horrifying, at the same time very satisfying. And then there's the Charlotte show—" David blows another fireball, lighting a cigarette. He tries to hand it to Bruiser, but he refuses.

"You saw that? How?"

David wipes his mouth and smirks, saying, "The dark web."

Bruiser asks naively, "Really?"

David looks at him and says, "No. I know people, Bruiser. There's a lot more to this life than we can process. When I saw the Charlotte show, I was blown away. You're doing auditoriums full of people. That's a serious hustle."

Bruiser turns away from his hungry gaze full of adoration and says, "That's what I wanted to ask you about."

David, still staring at Bruiser with a glint in his eye, says, "Yeah, the crowd seemed to turn on you. You've got way too much ego in your presentation."

Bruiser has a good laugh at himself and says, "I've definitely heard that before. You're amazing the way you control the crowd. My crowds are always heckling me and trying to burn me at the stake."

"Magic's fun to watch," says David as he pulls a flask out of thin air and takes a swig. "You've put yourself on the highest pedestal. I mean, healing the world — the Second Coming. I don't believe they're ready for that. This life is all about suffering for them, and technically what you're doing is helping the class cheat on the final exam. There's no freedom from suffering in this life; only freedom from this life."

David tries to hand Bruiser the flask, and Bruiser takes it from him hesitantly, saying, "I never thought about it like that." He leans over the ledge and looks down into the abyss of industrialized humanity, asking, "You ever think about jumping?"

David looks over the edge and says, "No, not really. I think I love myself too much to do it."

Bruiser leans back and returns to the vast skyline, saying, "I've always felt like if I jumped, I'd split into two versions of myself. One version of me would hit the ground, and the other part of me that wasn't afraid would just fly off into a new reality."

David turns to him and asks, "Like heaven?"

Bruiser laughs and says, "Or whatever, just a break from this repetitive life where I seem to be making the same mistake over and over … and over." He hands the flask back to him without drinking from it.

David, mildly offended, asks him, "You're not going to have a drink with me?" He gets lost in his reflection in the flask for a moment and then sets it down on the ledge, pulls out his phone for a better view of his new image, and stands up, saying, "I'm going to try and get used to this. I can't believe I'm one of them."

"One of who?" ask Bruiser naively.

"Blonde hair, blue eyes."

"Oh, that. I think it's a sign of ultimate health that comes from the stem cells." Bruiser stares at David as he takes in his new look, and asks him, "Where'd you get yours?"

David sits back down and says, "I'm not supposed to talk about it, but one of my old friends started a company called—"

"BioSpark?" asks Bruiser.

David's eyes light up and he says, "Yeah. How'd you—"

"That was my sister," says Bruiser as he's stunted by David's new penetrating blue eyes.

David smiles and says, "Now you have to have a drink with me, Scott. Fuck me, I used to party with your sister in nineties-New York when she was modeling. She really loves … loved you." David puts his arm around Bruiser, pulls him in for a shaky embrace that leaves them teetering on the ledge, and says, "Damn, I miss that girl."

"More than anything," says Bruiser solemnly.

David looks over the ledge, down to the buzzing city street, and says, "She said you were an amazing kid, but I … she never … So, when you slapped me, did you fix everything?"

"And then some. How do you feel?"

David stretches his hands out as if he were trying to pop every joint in his arms at one time and says, "Supremely crisp and crackling. I can feel the power crawling through my being. I just wasn't sure if—"

Bruiser pats him on the leg and says, "You don't have to worry about any STDs or your liver. I'd be a little bit more selective when it comes to sexual interactions, and I think you'll be—"

David laughs, interrupting Bruiser, and says, "This life. How'd you know about that?"

Bruiser leans back over the ledge, looking down at the street, and says, "I get glimpses of people's thoughts when I slap them. I saw piles of girls when I slapped you, and an image of you yelling at your dick."

"Your sister was the same way — super intuitive. Do you know what happened to her?" he asks, handing Bruiser his flask - again.

Bruiser accepts it and takes a healthy swallow. He looks at David as he releases a repressed fury, saying, "She was on the run from the government for selling black market stem cells and ended up in South Africa with her boyfriend, fiancé or whatever. She was having a hard time out there; being tracked by the US government, but not contained. I think she faked her own death and disappeared to India, or Iran, maybe, she was doing a lot of stem cell work with their government, mainly burn victims, but there's really no way to know. I'd give anything for one last moment with her."

"I'll see if I can make that happen."

"What are you talking about? She's alive?" he asks coyly.

"You activated the nanotechnology in the stem cells with the frequency they've spent years trying to find, and you're telling me that you're not working with her?"

"Not at all."

"That's absurd! You're telling me that you just happened to figure out how to activate the sleeper cell and you triggered the next step on accident."

"The next step?"

"In evolution. We're the future."

"Are 'we'? As much as I'd like that to be a good thing, healing the planet, and as awkward as that would feel," Bruiser pats his heart and says, "there is this underlying tone of life that I don't trust. Like you said, this life is suffering, and if that statement is true, what I'm doing is pointless. The only thing that is inevitable is what's in the darkest part of my heart where all fear comes from."

"What's that?" asks David.

"The end," says Bruiser as he looks down, down, down to the trail of humans, fighting their way through the day.

David laughs and asks, "Of what?"

Bruiser continues to stare down into the human traffic of metropolitan Manhattan and says, "Everything."

David looks down with Bruiser and says, "Humans are all sharks and cockroaches, this dream is lit by chaos, and there is no bad or good, only change, a constant change that will continue for eternity. There's darkness attached to everything in this life. That's the balance: the blistering sun that makes you appreciate the shadow of night. You can have all the love in your heart, with the best intentions, and create more pain than the darkest soul that torments those same loving souls and squeezes nothing but more love out of it, turning it into an even bigger ball of light."

Bruiser claps his hands together. "That's just it. I have the best intentions for this gift, but there is this underlying fear."

David puts his hand over Bruiser's heart and demands, "Fuck fear! The only thing you should really be afraid of is yourself and the power you hold. Your place in this narrative will affect humanity infinitely and indefinitely, more so than anyone that's ever lived. Your decision could take us all straight to heaven, or you could just blindly trample through hell, shutting the gates, leaving us all void of love, trapped in this dark, loveless place forever."

"No pressure. And that's the thing, I realized that I don't know love. I don't love other people, generally, they disgust me with their minutiae, self-absorbed struggles as they push everyone down in front of them to obtain a moment of freedom from their own self-disgust. I don't even love myself. I've been beating the shit out of myself for lifetimes. What I'm really worried about, is that I'm transferring this hatred into the world subconsciously and it's going to return to cage me."

"Maybe, you'll change that. Do you know what we are?"

"Supreme beings," says Bruiser in a mocking tone.

"That 'are' going to plow the earth and make it fertile for a new seed." David puts his hand on Bruiser's shoulder and says, "When I saw that girl lift your mother up by the throat, stick her fist into her, pull out her heart, and eat it, I only dreamed that I would become one of the survivors."

Bruiser turns Wite-Out white and looks at David, asking, "Survivors?" David sits in silence, looking up at the setting sun, contemplating his next words while Bruiser looks over the ledge, contemplating flying away from the conversation, and then spastically kicks the Converse off his feet into the river of people below.

"What are you doing?" yelps David.

"Testing your chaos theory. My shoes just made a leap of faith for us." The two sit and wait patiently for something to erupt beneath them on the sidewalk but find no repercussion from Bruiser's Converse plummeting to their destiny. "You know she's still alive?"

"Who? You're mom? How is that possible?" asks David.

"Same as you, she got stem cells from my sister. I slapped her after Alice ripped her heart out." Bruiser looks back down at the street, still in disbelief of his own actions, and asks David, "Aren't you just a little bit afraid of what you are?"

David follows Bruiser's gaze back down to the street. "As much as you're afraid of what you've become. Maybe this is what we need to end the suffering: a new being strong enough to endure this life. Bruiser, there's a shift coming, an energetic shift, and I know you can feel it; the purging."

One of David's assistants, a squeaky little guy in a piano tie, bursts out of the access door to the roof, shouting, "DAVID! DAVID!! I need you downstairs for a conference call, and your house is starting to fill up with people."

David steps off the ledge, looks back at Bruiser, and his eyes flicker like a neon sign as he says, "Embrace your demons and then come down, when you're ready. They're waiting for you."

Bruiser rubs his eyes, David disappears, and he gets trapped in his head for a moment as the voices, take over, demanding, *What the actual fuck? Why should you even care? No one ever loved you, and now you're in charge of healing them and creating a new supreme race. You expect it to turn out for the better. Just jump, and there's nothing left to worry about.*

He shakes his head and says aloud, "Do the world a favor."

Bruiser walks into David's penthouse, and there is that moment when the room stops, you forget to breathe, and everyone turns to you, analyzing your whole being. Bruiser: everyone he'd ever wanted to meet in one room. The room: homeless dude – clearly, no shoes, dirty gray jeans, and a plain white T-shirt covered in magician's blood. The room returns to its conversations prior, yet at a more selective volume, while still observing their savior.

Bruiser scans the room, looking for a safe place to start as he crosses the magician's minimalist penthouse, continuing to be scrutinized and misjudged. His palms begin to sweat and he beelines towards his sanctuary.

"What can I get for you?" the bartender asks.

"A bottle of tequila — something nice," states Bruiser.

The bartender presents a bottle, saying, "We have Casa Dragones, Mr. Blaine's favorite. Would you like it in a snifter?"

Bruiser reaches for it, saying, "I don't need a glass."

The bartender pulls the bottle back and says, "Sorry, we don't do bottle service." Bruiser digs around in his pocket, pulls out a crumpled hundred, and slides it across the bar. The bartender takes it from him, saying, "I do appreciate the tip, but—"

Bruiser looks over his shoulder and sees Vanessa and Dick smoking on the patio. He asks the bartender, "Do you have a pint glass?" The bartender pulls one from underneath the bar top and Bruiser says, as politely as possible, "Fill it."

He sneaks off toward the patio, assessing the crowd, and as he walks out onto it, Vanessa opens her arms to hug him, asking, "Bruiser, where'd your shoes go?"

He leans into her and says, "They fell off when I was sitting on the ledge with David."

Vanessa slaps Bruiser on the arm and says, "Bruiser! You could have killed someone!"

Bruiser rubs his arm, saying, "I was just testing a new theory. Where are Less and Leslie?" He takes a sip off his solution as he stares endearingly at his boss.

Vanessa looks away from his hunger, saying, "They're around here somewhere, but David said that we can't shoot the party tonight. He said something about celebrity privacy." She reaches for his glass, takes a sip, and spits it out, squalling into the breeze, "Tequila, Bruiser. A pint glass of tequila?"

Bruiser says dryly, "It's really good tequila; if that helps."

Dick pulls out his pen, hits it, and offers it to Bruiser. Bruiser hits the pen, and Vanessa snatches it from him, screeching, "Seriously, Bruiser! Are we doing this?" She hits the pen and says, "You're willing to risk it, with a golden magician walking around?"

There's a silence and it's filled with an unsurmountable frustration that's been festering between the two all day. "What? It's just weed," he says as he starts to shake with the setting sun.

Bruiser tries to curl up in Vanessa, but she steps back from him and stares at him with disappointment, saying, "And tequila. What's next?"

Dick takes his pen from Vanessa and moonwalks away from the awkward silence, saying, "Crack would be my best guess. I'm gonna' go peruse the crowd and leave you two to it."

"You saw David?" asks Bruiser.

"How could you miss him? My heart dropped when I saw him," says Vanessa as she stares into his eyes, begging for some sort of truth to validate his degradation.

Bruiser returns her gaze, asking her to concede with his eyes, and says, "I was just on the roof with him, and he didn't try to eat me. You've got to let go of the Alice incident." He leans in with every ounce of love he can muster and tries to kiss her.

She pushes him away, saying, "I've got a bad feeling about this, Bruiser." She distances herself further from him and crosses her arms, asking him emphatically, "Aren't you just the slightest bit worried about Blaine?"

Bruiser inches back towards her, saying, "No, oddly enough, he knows what he is, and more so, wanted to become one, and extremely more so, believes 'his kind' are the future." He leans back into her and uncrosses her arms.

She stares back at him blankly and asks, "You can't hear my thoughts, can you?"

He steps back with the thought and says, "No, why?"

She laughs and says, "Because you'd know how stupid I think you are for buying his shit. He's trying to turn you into a monster."

Bruiser stands there, speechless, as he tries to process her line of thinking. He stumbles to protect his new life, saying, "He's a good dude. Goes way back with my sister and admitted to having been an avid consumer of her stem cells."

"So, it's definitely the stem cells?" she asks.

"Seems that way. He mentioned something about the stem cells being infused with nanotechnology, and how they couldn't find the right frequency to activate them."

Vanessa grabs him by the arms and looks up at him, saying, "Until you came along. Bruiser, that room's full of money. What if they've all had stem cells?"

Bruiser laughs at her concern and says, "What if? What if they all turn and decide at the same time, they want to try human flesh? What are the odds?"

He leans into hug her, but she evades his affections, saying, "You think I'm crazy, Bruiser? We have to get out of here!"

"Calm down. We can't leave, Dick said they were paying us."

"This is true."

"How much?"

"Enough to buy you a castle," she says moistly.

"Just what I need – more walls. How much though?"

"Fifty thousand a head, a hundred people maybe, five-mill, I guess."

"Fissuck. That's a lot. Any cash?"

"A mill."

"Is it on the bus?" he asks.

"It's here," she says.

"Get it on the bus now, just in case you're right," he says as Dick walks back out onto the patio, interrupting them with a tall and leggy model-esque girl in tow, saying, "Look who I found."

304

The girl walks directly up to Bruiser, puts her arms around him, and kisses him on the cheek, gently, but in a sensual manner. Bruiser gives the girl a warm embrace and says, "Put Dick in charge of it."

Dick melts as he watches the girl latch onto Bruiser and then asks, "In charge of what?" Vanessa leans into Dick's ear and whispers. With a disgruntled tone Dick asks, "Right now?"

"Yes, right now," snarks Vanessa.

Dick looks at the girl and then leans into Bruiser's ear, saying, "Dibs."

Bruiser stares awkwardly at the girl, trying to compose a conversation that will reveal her name. His processor begins to smoke with confusion.

"Angelora," she says, burrowing into his presence, "your masseuse … I helped you release something … on your roof."

"Nice!" says Vanessa.

"Angelora. Hey, sorry, I've been through a lot in a short period of time. How'd you end up here?" he asks.

"I'm in town visiting a friend, a model, her roommate knows David. She totally freaked out when you walked in. There's a whole group of girls that want to meet you!" she says as she awakens lasers from beneath Vanessa's eyes.

Bruiser looks down, past his blood-spattered shirt, to his bare feet, and says, "I was hoping to change before I jumped into the crowd."

Angelora pulls at his hand, saying, "I love it. Its totes fashion forward. Let's be honest though, you could wear a bikini made from human flesh and no one would look at you incongruently." She pulls Bruiser into the den as he looks back to his friends for protest, finding nothing but envy in the form of distant sneers.

Dick sighs and says, "He puts in no effort, he's a total scumbag, and he slays." He looks at Vanessa trying to figure out how she fell for it, while she watches Bruiser walk away with Angelora. She doesn't respond and Dick asks her, "You mad?"

Vanessa puts her hands on her hips, saying, "How could I be? She's fucking stunning, I'd let her fart in my mouth. Has he ever had to work to get a girl?"

Dick snickers, saying, "They tend to just fall in his lap, literally," and points to the den where Bruiser is being consumed by a flock of elevens.

Vanessa takes Dick's cigarette from him and says, "Being a millionaire messiah isn't going to make it harder for him, that's for sure."

"This is my good friend, Zealand T. Dahl," Angelora announces to her friends.

The girls stand up and surround him, fighting for his attention.

Adrianna, a voluptuous Brazilian model, makes eye contact with him and says with a thick accent, "BRUISER! I love 'Greed.' I always wanted to be violated on that show. You're my favorite. Can we shoot an episode tonight? I dare you!"

Bruiser blushes for the first time ever, or at least in the new millennium, and a tall blond lingerie model interjects, asking, "Zealand, can we talk about the shift taking place in the universe right now? Things are moving into a new dimension, the fifth, I believe, all light. Do you think we're ready? Can you heal me and help me prepare?"

Angelora pushes her back into the pile, fighting to regain his attention. She drags Bruiser back to the circular, sub-level couch where the girls are entertaining two dudes that are trying too hard to impress them with their lack of concern for fashion. They're wearing a collection of threads that look as if they were motivated by three decisions: mescaline, unlimited funds, and quantum camouflage.

"Nice shoes," says the plaid gentleman on the left, "I didn't know widespread was in town!"

Bruiser sinks into his instant harem, staring down the two quasi-familiar faces, and says, "Nice dick broom, fuck-o."

The plaid guy on the right giggles in an annoyingly high-pitched cackle and then whispers in his friend's ear. He turns to Bruiser, and with a thick German accent, says, "Nice dick broom yah, ha-ha. I'll pay ten grand for that shirt though — it's grotesque. Twenty if it's David's blood."

A stunning Asian girl in skintight, paper-thin jeans, and a silk blouse that accentuates every molecule of her upper half, pulls Bruiser away from their aggressive conversation, asking, "Are you going to heal us tonight?" She magnetizes his gaze to hers and says, "David was saying that he believes you're the future."

Bruiser laughs and says, "Of the left." He looks the girl down and up, contemplating where to start, and says, "I love your necklace."

He caresses the light, airy chain that holds the weight of a resilient stone as she replies, "Thank you, I made it. I'm a jewelry designer. Sung, Sung Song."

He pulls his hand off the necklace and slides it down her silk blouse, stopping on her waist, waiting for rejection. "Beautiful, Sung. I'd like to see more … of your collection."

Sung doesn't stop him, saying, "I've got a few pieces around here somewhere if you'd like to help me find them." She pulls at him, trying to remove him from the pack, but he's somehow distracted by the hyena-like cackling coming from the goons across from him.

Without breaking his concern for the two, he asks, "Do you know those guys, Sung?"

Slaphappy

She grabs his flocculant beard and tugs at it, saying, "I know that they're friends of David."

Bruiser pushes her hands off his critter, saying, "They rub me the wrong way, Sung. Maybe it's how they layer plaid in an only mildly offensive way."

Sung leans into his ear and whispers, "They're hard to talk to, like they're high off of something vaporous." As Sung finishes her words, the guy on the left pulls out a handkerchief, sticks his face in it, and returns with a distorted grimace.

Angelora grabs Bruiser's face and pulls him back to the pile of girls, saying, "Zealand!" She climbs over him, blocking Sung, and placing him next to her friend, Morgan, a stunning redhead that's spilling out of her dress.

"So, are you going to heal us?" asks Morgan.

"I'd love to try," he says, getting lost in her affections momentarily, and then returns his gaze to the two plaid suits. Angelora leans over him and starts making out with Morgan. She takes Bruiser's hand and slides it up her dress. The two dudes in plaid get up while he's distracted and bookend the pile of girls. They paw at Angelora's friends, and the cackling returns. It unnerves Bruiser, pulling him out of his passionate distraction. He leans back as the girls slither over him like snakes in a pit, fighting for his affections, closes his eyes, and as he returns to the room, he says, "They're … the linen mustaches from—" As the words cross his lips, his face is covered by silk with a masculine hand behind it, and a collection of fumes enter his mind's eye, pulling him out of the moment as the girls bury him in flesh and his eyes shut.

The first thing said by Bruiser as he comes out of the cloud, fighting his way out of the pile, and jumping to his feet, is, "Hey, Grant! Could you guys fuck off with the drab conversation and maybe go do some more of that coke my overdraft fees paid for!" The two plaid gentlemen stand up, ready for whatever's next, sandwiching Bruiser as he returns to this realm, and Bruiser clenches his fist, asking, "Kruder, Dorfmeister, what is it with you two lizard dicks? What do you want with me?"

"Are you saying we have green scaly dicks?" they ask together.

"I'm saying you're some weird reptilian detectives!"

They lean into his ear, breathing heavily as if the oxygen in the air were a foreign concept, and they say together, "We just want you to love us." They kiss him on the cheek simultaneously and Bruiser pushes them shoulder to shoulder, slaps them both out of instinct, and is overtaken by a cloud of green smoke.

"Ewwww! My turn, my turn!" screams Morgan.

Blaine pops up from the green cloud behind Bruiser and blows a fireball, saying, "Looks like the guest of honor started without us." He puts his arm around Bruiser and says, "Turns out, me and this guy,

307

Zealand T. Dahl," Bruiser puts his hand up waving like a prom queen, "go way back. I know we all put down an exceptional amount of money in hopes of a miracle, and all I can say is, he delivers."

A voice from the back, snarks, "Nice hair, did he do that too, Dave?"

"Yes, and thank you," he says as his eyes glimmer unnaturally. David leans into Bruiser's ear and asks him, "How do you want to do this? Form a line?"

Bruiser feels an awkward tension in his shoulder as David leans on him and he says, "No lines. I want this to be a personal experience. Tell them they can get as fucked up as they want, just don't crowd me." Bruiser looks down at his feet and asks David, "Can you find me some shoes and a clean shirt? I have the worst looking feet."

David steps back and looks down at Bruiser's feet, saying, "Don't sweat it. It works." He looks up at the crowd and says, "If everyone could give Zealand some space. He's asked for an intimate healing experience on a more personal level. Zealand, everyone." He gestures to Bruiser and sits down on the couch in the pile of girls Bruiser was just entertaining.

The room applauds Bruiser for an overzealous amount of time, and while they are applauding, Vanessa runs up and gets in his ear, preempting his speech, asking, "What do we do if every one of these people turn?"

Bruiser pulls her off to a corner and says, "That's ridiculous."

"Ridiculous? You're drunk and we talked about this. You're okay with creating a room full of monsters?"

"They're not monsters, they're the future, apparently."

"I need you to trust me on this one," she says, looking him deeply in the eyes. "Let's just go."

Bruiser scans the room as he feels all the eyes on him and the judgement forming in the moment, and says, "You know I can't do that."

David breaks the lover's quarrel, asking, "Is everything all right, Zealand? The 'future' is waiting."

Bruiser gives him a double thumbs up, smiles, and waves at all the hungry souls. Vanessa grabs his face, asking, "You're not really buying into this whole thing about them being the future, are you?" Bruiser stares back at her blankly, wanting to be honest with his voice, but holds back. She releases him, saying, "Get your head out of your ass! This is about the money and the fame. Do you really think you're the creator of a new perfect human race?"

"When you say it like that, it sounds a little farfetched, but it's going to be fine. What's this all about?"

"Alice," she says.

"Forget Alice, my mom has that effect on people! It was a fluke. Let it go, Vanessa!"

"You think it was a fluke, that Alice ate her heart? I heard them talking about stem cells, and I'm pretty sure everyone here has had them."

"That's impossible."

"Look around at these people. Do they look sickly? Every one of them has an STD for sure, but do you think they all gave you fifty-grand to get rid of HPV?"

"Fifty-grand is nothing to these people. This is something to talk about with their friends over dinner," says Bruiser, looking around the room for passing judgments. "I'm in control, and I don't need any negative thoughts attached to this moment. You don't need to be here for this, neither do they," he says pointing to Less and Leslie.

"Seriously?"

"Seriously! You're freaking out. I think it's the darkness you pulled off me last night when I was inside of you, and I don't want it to tear us apart. Just get out of here and walk it off. Everything will work itself out," he says and hugs her.

She shrugs him off and walks off to the twins.

The room goes silent.

David stands up, grabbing Angelora's hand, and says, "Come on, girls." He turns to Bruiser and says, "Zealand, find us when you're done," and pulls his harem, hand in hand, out of the room.

The room stares at Bruiser intimately as he sweats out another pause, filling it with, "First things first," and walks straight to the bar, saying to the bartender, "I'll take another pint." The bartender slides him the bottle of tequila he asked for prior, and he asks him, "Can I slap you?"

"I didn't pay," says the bartender.

"We'll call it a tip," he says and raises his hand.

The bartender leans forward and asks him, "Who could turn down a clean bill of health?" Bruiser slaps the bartender, he rubs his jaw, and presents a grandiose smile as all his gray hairs turn brown.

"Excellent," says an over-sized man in a tuxedo, standing next to Bruiser. "What else will that southpaw of yours fix?"

Bruiser, stunned by the man's presence, says, "You … you're my favorite director,"

"And you're by far my favorite healer," says the man.

"It can cure anything, from what I've seen, not to mention retard the aging process and even regenerate lost limbs."

The man pushes his chin out and says, "Well, Zealand, what are you waiting for?"

There's a silence that fills the penthouse as they wait for the miracle at hand. Bruiser raises his hand and stops to ask, "Have you had any stem cell treatments?"

The man pats his face and says, "Does it matter? You have my money." Bruiser stops as he digests the line of thinking just offered, raises his hand, and slaps him. The man hands him his business card as his face begins to change and says, "I can make you a pile of money. Are you headed to LA?"

"We are," says Bruiser.

"I'll throw one of these at my place in the hills, but I can fit ten-times as many people," he says as his appearance reverts to a version of himself from better days. The man drops to his knees and the room freezes. Bruiser offers him a hand up, and the man looks up at him as his eyes start to glow a bright blue and his hair fills out with golden locks. "Have you ever thought about acting?" Bruiser has no response. "Call me when you get close to Los Angeles," he says, walking away in full health, twenty pounds lighter, floating in his tuxedo.

The room turns to Bruiser with that hunger again: the hunger for a miracle. His only thought being, *Is it worth five-million dollars to create a room full of these creatures*? His eyes fade in and out as he envisions the room progressing through to a full towhead movement and his heartbeat pulsates through his ears. He closes his eyes, takes a deep breath, and feels a cool breeze pass through his being as he hears an inner voice say, *She's infected you with fear and doubt. There's no wrong or right here, only what's left. Open your heart, embrace your demons, and let this shoe land where it must.*

Bruiser proceeds to clear the room slowly, working with small talk, poignant jabs, and surprise slaps. As the night dwindles, he finds the room to be filled with perfection — and a fresh cloud of shadows. *She wasn't wrong, but she wasn't right,* he thinks to himself as he wades through the crowd, looking for the truth at the heart of the matter. Finding no threat of heart-eating celebrity, he finishes his patrol and sneaks off, dragging his shadows along with him in search of David — more so his harem. He finds a hallway with no doors and walks down it until it dead ends. "Perfect time to have a cell phone," he says to himself as he stands there, blankly, scratching his head as an unmarked panel opens.

He is greeted by Angelora and a chorus of, "BRUISER!"

"Come up here now, silly!" sings Sung, standing on the edge of the bed, fully naked, staring down the stairs at him.

Angelora kisses him on the cheek and takes him by the hand, walking him up the stairs to a bed that's perched on a ledge that overlooks David's grandiose bedroom. As Bruiser climbs the stairs to his newfound haven, he finds by far the most beautiful thing he's seen in this life: a pile of models, naked and undulating in his direction. Staring down into an anomaly of flesh, he says, "I was wondering where you beautiful creatures had gone." The girls stare up at him with a diverse selection of hunger in their eyes. He starts to climb into bed but stops as he spots an ancient samurai sword mounted on the wall. He walks over to it and says, "Kamakura Katana, I wondered where you went. This blade auctioned for a half mill."

He goes to pull it off the wall and hears Sung moan, "Bruiser, put that silly toy down and come slap the evil out of us."

Bruiser turns back to the bed and watches Sung as she rolls around, gyrating her naked figure in the pile of perfection. He caresses the ancient blade and says, "Sung, I doubt there's an evil bone in your body, but if there is, I'll find it."

"Bruiser, put down the katana and come downstairs!" echoes David's voice through the bedroom.

Bruiser looks around the room and then back down at the girls, asking, "Where are you?"

David yells, "I'm in the bathroom! Underneath you!"

Bruiser hangs the sword back in its place and tickles the girls' feet as he dismounts the bed. He walks down the stairs and into the bathroom where he finds David surrounded by a mirky fog of shadows. Bruiser looks around the bathroom: It's all gold and marble, with a sauna, hot tub, stripper pole, a seventy-inch flatscreen, and a marble booth with a mirrored tabletop. Bruiser catches David staring into the tabletop, running his fingers through his fresh golden fluff, asking, "How'd it go out there?"

Bruiser, still overwhelmed by David's dump palace, says, "Well, you've got some new friends."

David breaks from his own gaze, turns to him, and sternly says, "I already know everyone out there." He takes a swig of water, flips out a Zippo, lights it, and blows a fire ball that warms the room.

Bruiser steps back from the flame, saying, "I was going to ask about that: kerosene? 151? lighter fluid?"

David does another one, wipes his mouth, and says, "Water. It was water, Bruiser. I used to use kerosene, but you slapped me after my fireball and the kerosene must have fused to my DNA or something. I don't know how, but it's beautiful."

David motions for Bruiser to sit down and Bruiser joins him, sitting down across from him with an energetic hesitance, as he looks at the mirrored tabletop, mumbling, "I know how this ends."

"You'll be fine, Bruiser. What I'm having a hard time understanding, is the new hunger inside of me."

Bruiser leans back, and hoping these aren't his last words, he asks him, "For human flesh?"

"Don't be daft. For power. I'm ready to shed this three-dimensional life and wake up to a world where I can live to the new potential you've given me." He pulls out a mirrored box from under the table, opens it, takes out a cigarette, lights it with a fireball, shuts the box, waves his hand over it, reopens the box, and it's now full of white powder.

Bruiser shifts in his seat. "How'd you do that, magic?"

David laughs and says, "No, just an illusion, but the shit inside, that's magic … and maybe a little PCP." He pulls a platinum tooter out of the air and goes to hand it to him.

Bruiser's voice cracks as he says, "Well, I appreciate the heads up. We were just talking about the protocol for introducing people to PCP, and how not mentioning it is a bit rapey."

David laughs and says, "Yeah, common courtesy, but it's not the PCP you have to worry about."

Bruiser pushes the tooter back, saying, "I love that bitch, but like every other woman in my life, she's been trying to kill me for years."

David scoops a handful of the white powder out of the box, dumps it on the table, and laughs as he pushes the magic dust around with a playing card, saying, "I didn't think that these third dimensional novelties would be a problem for you anymore, Bruiser."

Bruiser watches as David cuts out a line the length of his arm and then looks to the door, begging for a divine intervention. "Quite the opposite, it turns everything inside out," he says as his brow begins to sweat.

David stops in his powdery, white tracks and asks him, "How so?"

Bruiser looks deeply into David, looking for a truth that he might be able to use to buy his freedom, and hears no whispers to define the fear inside of him. He looks up to the mirrored ceiling and says, "I can't really explain it, but it's like someone with a dark sense of humor takes over my vessel."

David looks up from his illicit toils and snarls, saying, "Someone that's been hiding in you for lifetimes?"

"What do you mean?" asks Bruiser.

David finishes the fat, dragon tail he'd been working on and asks him, "Could you imagine if your life just went on forever with no interruptions? You'd have to sit there with all the fucked-up shit you've done, and no matter what good you did, you'd still be haunted by the darkness you've embraced to survive. And we're rather civilized at this point — the dark ages were unimaginable."

Bruiser stares at the pile of confusion as the darkness inside of him bangs away on his subconscious, begging for freedom, and he says, "I feel like I've lived a hundred lives on this planet and I'm tired of coming back to this irreparable mess!"

David presents the substance with his hand, saying, "I believe that those people that you've been, the ones that helped you survive the darker ages, are still in there, and they're going to help you change this world for the better."

Bruiser starts to shake with internal frustrations, saying, "The ones that want me to plummet into darkness with you. Listen, Dave, there's nothing I'd love to do more then throw back some lines with you, dude, but I can't. I know what it feels like to say yes, never looking back at sobriety, walking away from this moment defeated while I continue to destroy everything in my path. I believe there's a part of me that has the strength to say no, and I walk away with a new confidence in myself. Like, I level up into a new person, and that's where the light comes in and fills me up. I'd love to know what it feels like to become that person."

David sticks his face in the dragon's tail, exhuming as many magic particles as he can, and says, "Sadly, you never will, Scott. You're still looking at this life with a binary, black-and-white mindset, I'm telling you, we live in the gray. Right now, is about deciding what will bring the most growth. Jump off the ledge with me and I'll teach you how to fly. Do a couple lines, entertain me, and I'll give you Janine."

"Who?"

"The katana over my bed."

"Seriously? She's worth a half mill."

"A whole, but listen, I think you're astounding. I loved your sister, and I wish she were here to see this. I know she would be proud of the person you've become." He sticks his face back in the pile and returns from the delights handing Bruiser the platinum tooter.

Bruiser pushes his hand away, saying, "I have a deal with Vanessa, I can't."

David pushes the line closer to Bruiser with his hand, saying, "I won't tell her."

Bruiser clears his airways incidentally, saying, "She'll know. Once you open the cage, you can't put that beast back in, and it goes on for days." He gets up and steps away from the table.

David lights another cigarette and puts it on the table where Bruiser was sitting, saying, "You're the talent, and you're irreplaceable. She's your producer, and she'll just have to deal with it. I have this feeling you've done more for less."

Bruiser looks down at the granules of white enlightenment and watches as they glimmer with the light reflecting off the mirrored table, saying, "You know, if this shit was black, nobody would do it, but it looks so pure and good." He picks up the cigarette and hits it hard, hoping that it hits the spot that's itching for other things.

David watches as he hits the cigarette and says, "Humor me and I'll fill your head full of truths that will change the whole direction of your movement."

Bruiser submits gracelessly, grabbing the platinum tooter. He stares at the life-altering dust as he lingers over the table in debate. "What could it hurt?" he asks himself as he leans over and tears into a headful of pure confusion.

David watches Bruiser as the mystery substance takes over and he assimilates to his new perspective. Bruiser looks at David as his face slowly turns green, his eyes go black, his skin begins to form scales, and he sprouts dark, leathery wings. Bruiser hears a whisper from David say, *Come with me, and walk the earth. I've been here since the beginning of time forging the grids for this moment.* David blows a fireball and starts laughing in a deep maniacal tone.

Bruiser shakes his head, everything goes back to normal, and he finds himself, limp and lifeless, saying, "That's definitely not coke. What is it?"

David pulls a razor blade out of thin air and dredges it through his forearm, saying, "Like I said, magic. I got it in Kenya from a witch doctor." The gash heals in front of Bruiser's eyes and David says, "He's the one that taught me to breath fire."

Bruiser does another line and says, "Oh, you were serious. What's the hangover like?"

David releases a guttural laugh that shakes Bruiser's core and says, "It's a real motherfucker. When I did the first line, you just turned into a giant ball of white light." He wipes the sweat that's been accruing on his face and asks, "What did you see?"

Bruiser laughs and says, "You turned into my mother."

There's a pause and the two stare at each other. David breaks the silence, saying, "That's not the first time I've heard that; your sister said the same thing."

Stumbling to find the right words that fit the moment, Bruiser says, "Seriously though, you turned into a fire breathing dragon." He continues staring at David, looking for a glimmer of fear from that statement, but finds none.

"I know what I am. Do you know what you are?"

There's a silence while Bruiser digs around, looking for an answer that he doesn't have, and David states, "You're the missing link. It happened with humanity a long time ago when we transitioned from apes to functioning bipeds. Scientists have proven that it would have taken tens of thousands of years to make that jump, and I know that man evolved because of alien interference, whether it be technological or physical, they were the only influence on our rapid, genetic expansion. You're not one of these simple, three-dimensional breeders, Bruiser. You're a Starseed that's bridging the gap to the next step in evolution.

Bruiser blindly asks, "I always related more to being a wizard than an alien, but I'm game. Tell me more."

"They're the same thing. Where do you think the stories came from about the great ones that changed the world?" David lights another cigarette for Bruiser with his dragon breath.

Bruiser takes the cigarette from David and devours it, asking, "And what makes you think I'm one of 'them?'"

"Because I'm one of them, a different breed than you, but I'm one of them, and that's how I know you're one as well. Your sister was from the same place, and she couldn't find the frequency to activate us; even with the help of the government."

Bruiser tries to back out of the booth, saying, "That's not possible, she felt the same way about the government that I do."

David, pulling him back into the booth with his words, says, "You know how it is once the government gets involved, you have to play ball, or you get erased. She believed in creating a perfect being, strong enough to carry humanity into the future, and she did whatever it took to get us to this moment." David stares through Bruiser, thirsting for his reaction.

Bruiser sticks his face back in the pile, hoping to sublimate his stirring fury. "You're telling me, I'm out here creating a superior race for the fucking government!"

Addled by Bruiser's naivety, David asks him, "I'd be more concerned with who controls the government, but that's the part that haunts you? The government, not the stadium full of shadows that led you in here."

"Yeah."

"Why?"

Bruiser laughs nervously, saying, "Because, I'm responsible for … I've seen what they're … what you're capable of becoming."

David returns his laughter, saying, "Honestly, I don't think any of us can comprehend what we are."

Bruiser stares through Blaine, looking for ultimate truths, while he processes the concept of the words he just received. The questions spin through his head like motorcycles circling inside a steel sphere, and then one collides with the others, leaving only the one circling. "Do you know where she is?"

David leans back and asks, "Does it matter? She's gone."

"Yeah, dude, it matters. She was my—"

"Exactly, she was." David returns to his magic dust and then says, "There's so much more at play here, just assume that she's moved on to a new place, doing bigger things. You have to let go of the fear and stop worrying about everything. Do you remember what I told you on the roof?" Bruiser waits silently for his answer. "Embrace your demons. There's a necessary evil inside you, and you need to love it, or it will torment the weaker side of you until you give into it. We're moving into the fifth dimension, a place of unrefined light, but we must transcend Hell to get there. Open your eyes and ready yourself for your place in that movement. You're afraid of yourself and the relentless new power you've accessed, but you have no reason to be — you're protected, if anyone is."

Bruiser leans over, clears the table, and finds all his shadows on the other side of the mirrored tabletop, howling at him. David's phone lights up, and Bruiser gets up and finds himself surrounded by mirrors filled with shadows. He walks up to one of them and tries to compose himself. He braces himself, expecting to see his mother's reflection, instead, his head swells, his skin turns a chalky gray, and his eyes go from the brightest blue to the darkest black. Trying to avoid the truth in himself, he looks over his shoulder and finds an army of darkness behind him. The gathering of shadows howls at him with a subsonic growl he can feel in his gut, his vision blurs, and his ears start to ring.

When his vision clears, Bruiser finds himself back in the metal cell, but a voyeur this time around: as he can see himself sitting on the pulpit meditating, surrounded by the same cloud of darkness that was standing behind him in David's mirror, grinding their teeth. His shadows circle his meditative self with a parched thirst for the light emanating from his being. Bruiser steps into the circle of light that seems to be protecting his meditative self from the darkness, and unnoticed by the shadows, he walks closer to himself, almost as if he were doing the haunting. As he gets close enough to touch himself, he reaches out, and just as he's about to touch himself, the eyes of his meditative-self open.

"Bruiser!"

Bruiser steps back, asking, "Zealand?"

The being smiles and says, "Yes, your truest form. The original that existed before the simulation began." He stands up, confronting Bruiser, and there's a moment that passes where the two investigate one another, searching for an answer to a question they both never knew existed. Zealand puts both his hands together in front of his heart and says, "Please sit, we have a lot to talk about."

Bruiser looks around at the swarm of shadows circling them and says, "It's a pleasure to finally meet you, but I'd prefer to stand."

Zealand sits back down on the pulpit, saying, "I'm elated to see you as well." He pats the bench, asking him to join him again, and says, "I didn't think it was even possible. Where do we start?"

Bruiser hesitates, as anyone would when confronted by their best part, and then sits down, asking, "You were there that day?"

"Help me out here?" asks Zealand.

"When you told me your name, Zealand T. Dahl."

"That was a perfect moment. We went five for five."

Bruiser asks him in a childlike tone, "Where'd you go?"

"Bruiser, you've always been one of my favorite lives. I tried to stay with you and protect you, but there was a darkness I could not defeat. I only found myself returning to partake in your intoxicating lifestyle that always left me with a hangover filled with days of suffering."

"So, you abandoned me?"

Zealand stands up and starts walking around the cell while trying to compose his next words. He holds his light as he walks away, and Bruiser is forced to jump up and follow him, staying in his protective bubble. Zealand stops at the window, staring out into the void. He puts his hand on the window and says, "I'm sorry, I tried to be there for the moments that you truly needed me."

Bruiser watches himself, staring out of the perceived window, and asks, "You were on the four-o-five with me, weren't you?"

"I was, and I'm still surprised we pulled that off. Do you remember coming here while you were spinning around in the air?"

"Vaguely, but yeah. You showed me all these lives that I … we could go to, but—"

Zealand turns from the window, looking back at Bruiser, and says, "You chose to go back to your Earth. I never understood why, after all the darkness and suffering you endured, why you would choose to return to that place."

Bruiser catches Zealand's eyes as they examine the opening behind him. He turns to find a mob of beings, all with blonde hair, blue eyes, and a look of insufferable starvation, clawing at the invisible wall, trying to get in. He points to the opening and asks, "Who are they?"

Zealand walks Bruiser over to the opening and stops, standing next to him, saying, "They were all my family from home. We've been trapped on this ship, floating towards a new life in search of the winged planet, but we were pulled into a black hole and overtaken by a darkness that consumed their light one by one. Now my family is trapped inside of those monsters, and I'm trapped in here, waiting to be subjugated."

Bruiser watches their mindless battle as they push one another forcefully into the wall, trying to achieve their inimitable quest, and he says, "I'm sorry."

"It's okay. The only reason we're both here talking is because of that broken door you call your heart, refusing to open." He walks Bruiser back to the pulpit, saying, "I've been trapped in this cell for millenniums. The simulations do nothing to remove the suffering of confinement, and I want to be free.

"Simulations?"

"I can jump into other versions of myself, the same way I jump into you. It's just like a dream, but with a full immersion of the senses."

"So, you're saying I'm just the container for some alien consciousness that's stuck in a spaceship playing the video game that is my life."

"More like an iteration, a spiritual algorithm that's trying to pass a test in a virtual reality that's so real you have no memory of who you really are while you're playing it. It feels real, but still somewhat voyeuristic at the same time."

"How so?"

"Everything is so abstract and absurd, and you have no recollection of the life you came from, leaving you only aware of the moment. It's so far from this life, in this cell, where I do nothing, continually — forever, alone."

"I never understood where that feeling came from until I found this place."

"You know, you're the only iteration that was able to find me trapped here. It's like you started playing the game without me. If you can bounce around from life to life by adjusting your frequency, yet holding consciousness through the transition, we might be able to fix this relentless mess."

The two look one another in the eyes again, but this time with an unearthed awkwardness. Bruiser leans into Zealand and gives him a long overdue hug, asking, "How can I help?"

Zealand points at two pulpits, saying, "You're timing couldn't be more perfect. You're going to break me out of this solitude." He sits down on the pulpit, crosses his legs, and says, "Whenever you're ready."

Bruiser sits down across from him, mirroring him, and asks, "Is this going to hurt?"

Zealand smiles and says, "No more than anything you've endured already." He reaches out and puts his hand over Bruiser's sacrum, then over his temples, and he says in a penetrating voice, "You'll always be burdened with decision. It's the hardest part of this life. When you remove fear and start to make choices with your heart, knowing that there is no wrong or right, there only is, then you'll be free."

As he works on Bruiser, the shadows in the cell swarm around him, laughing, and start to peck away at his molecular structure. Zealand's hands light up, Bruiser's eyes open to a fragmenting vibration that blurs his perspective, and he returns to the bathroom where he is staring into the mirror, surrounded by the same darkness. Zealand puts his hand on Bruiser's chest, over his heart, and says, "Let the light fill you and take over like a virus." Bruiser's body starts to shake spasmodically, "Carry this light with you and beware of your conscious creation while transitioning back to the reality you call home."

Bruiser's eyes open, returning him to the metal cell, and then back to David's bathroom where the shadows overlap, and the two rooms become a hybrid. The shadows start to burrow into him, returning to their fleshy den, and he starts to shake vigorously with the fear of being consumed. He shuts his eyes and Zealand grabs him firmly, saying, "Let them eat. Feed them your light, knowing that there's nothing they can take from you that can't be replenished. You are stronger and more powerful than any of them, but only when you're anchored to me, your truest form. I will always be there with you, as long as you protect me."

Bruiser starts to smile, and the light permeates through his skin. There's a moment that passes as the two are connected, the rooms fill up with an unbearably white light and the shadows sizzle as they dissipate. The walls start to hum with a soothing, almost euphoric vibration.

Bruiser's eyes open in a panic and he finds himself alone. There's a rumbling outside of his cell, that he realizes he can hear for the first time. He turns around to find the door has opened and he is about to be overtaken by the hunger of this obscure place. "Why would you let them in?" There's a moment that spans time as the room freezes and Bruiser is overwhelmed by the complexity of what he feels is going to be his end. "Zealand," he asks himself, "what do we do?" There's no response, and he asks, "You want me to heal this endless mob, take over the ship, and fly you guys home?"

This time he gets a response, and it's, *I like your plan, but no. This ship is and has been hiding in a black hole. We're about to hit the nexus of that hole and the ship is going to be torn to atoms. We're all going back to Earth with you.*

Bruiser laughs and says, "I don't know if we've got enough room on the tour bus for everyone."

You're the tour bus, says Zealand.

"Wait, what?"

Do you remember the light that you felt pass through you when your mother passed?

"Yeah."

We're going to fill you with as much of that light as you can hold.

"You want me to kill them?"

Sometimes what you believe to be wrong is all that's left.

"What do you want me to do?"

Whatever you can do with what you've got at hand. As Zealand whispers those words, Bruiser's hand lights up, and time is released. The unruly mob falls to the ground on top of one another and the back rows start climbing over them. Bruiser feels the light permeating out of his hand and uses it to hold the crowd back like a shield as he hears, *When you believe it, you'll see it.*

While those words rifle through him, he looks down to the pulpit next to him and ponders the fluidity of the room. He puts his hand on the pulpit, and it forms a brilliant katana in his hand. "Let's go," Bruiser barks out as he releases the light from his hand and swings at the closest person to him, beheading it. The newly formed carcass hits the floor, and its head follows, rolling toward his foot. There's a light that bursts from the skull and crawls up his leg, entering his chest. "Oh, that's nice," he says to himself and feels his hand flicker with a new resilience. He starts swinging freely at anyone in his reach, slicing and dicing, all the while consuming the light of everyone he takes down until he is overwhelmed by the endless onslaught of golden penetrators.

They pile on top of him, pushing him to the ground, and start taking bites out of his person. The first bite he finds playful, but as they continue and he realizes he's about to lose, he hears, **Open your heart, and feed them.** He feels another one drooling on his neck, and in a thoughtless panic, releases a light from his core that pushes his workload off him and boldly into the walls, concussing them. He stands up and brushes himself off as his wounds begin to heal and his eyes twinkle with a strobe light of emotion. The light in his hands starts to glow eminently, so he grabs his sword with both hands, and runs through anyone in his path slicing away with a new vigor.

The line in the hallway has started to peter out and he feels as if there might be an end to it. He pushes his way forward, crossing over the threshold as he continues hacking through the on-comers until there are only a few stragglers. As the last being falls to the floor, the two plaid mustache dicks appear at the end of the well-lit hallway. The light that fills Bruiser now overpowers the light of the hallway, and it infects every molecule of their being as they approach him. "Kruder, Dorfmeister!"

The two slowly walk him down, honoring his win with a slow clap. "Trent Stedanko, and this is my comrade, Kirk Mcklusky."

Bruiser, holding his light, slowly steps back towards his cell, asking, "What are you two dicks doing here?"

They stare past him at the trail of bodies he left behind and they stop dead in their tracks, saying, "Impressive, Zealand, it's about time you opened up."

"You gonna' miss 'em?" asks Bruiser confidently.

"We're not here for them," says Stedanko.

Bruiser looks around as he realizes he's the only one left and playfully asks, "Who does that leave?"

They both start running toward him, saying, "You, Mr. Dahl."

Bruiser steps back through the opening and raises his sword, boldly placing it in front of him, directing it towards the two suits. They push forward at an accelerated speed, and Bruiser smiles overconfidently at their advance. As he feels he's about to be thwarted, he trips over himself, falling through the threshold of his cell and the invisible wall returns. Stedanko and Mcklusky run into it and end up on the floor, stammering at his presence.

At that moment he feels the heat of the sun on his back, followed by a cool breeze that pushes across his being. He turns around and is confronted by a blinding white light. A majestic form with wings three times its length emerges from it, saying, "Nothing about the future will be easy, but you've chosen your place. Accept it and move forward with three clear eyes, knowing that the only voice left that you need to listen to is yours."

"Fuck, I've missed you," he says and tries to hug her, but finds himself inside of the light.

When the light dissipates, he finds himself fully returned to the bathroom with David standing behind him, whispering, "Your sister's right, your voice is the only one that matters now."

Bruiser shakes his head egregiously and says, "Fuck, that's some good stuff. What the-absolute-fuck just happened?"

"From what I saw in the mirror, I believe they call it enlightenment."

"I can't say that I'm ready for that."

"I don't think you have a choice. It's time to own your shit, put your dick on the bar and show it to this world. You deserve to be happy, like the people you've touched. Just lay down your crucifix, the one you built, and free yourself to be whatever it is that you truly are. And Bruiser—"

"There's no more Bruiser."

"Sorry, Zealand," says David as he grabs Bruiser's arm, "what does the T stand for?"

"Thoth, David. It stands for Thoth." Bruiser smiles and walks out the bathroom, leaving David staring into the depths of the mirror he just jumped through.

Still lagging from his travels, Bruiser mindlessly walks past the bed full of prime specimens, and as his hand hits the door, he hears, "Bruiser, where do you think you're going, silly?" He looks up to find Angelora, tits out, leaning over the balcony, saying, "We want to be free. We have to be."

Bruiser climbs the stairs to the bed, saying, "My fault, it totally slipped my mind. I can't even start to explain where I just went with Dave."

Angelora pulls him into the den of buxom delights, saying, "Well, wherever you went, you came back with a glow about you."

As his presence is made, the girls shift around with a vivacious undulation and the room starts to vibrate like a metric ton of purring cats. Bruiser looks to Angelora and asks, "Who's first?"

"Take care of my friends. You'll have plenty of time to slap me around on the bus, right? You still need a masseuse?"

"Definitely," he says.

"Good," she says and takes his shirt off for him, pushing him towards the bed, saying, "I couldn't imagine being anywhere else."

Bruiser stands over the paragon in front of him and hears nothing but silent moans calling him. And without another moment of hesitation, he dives into the emotional conundrum and is immediately blanketed by pulsating bodies. Sung sits up abruptly and pulls Bruiser into her so that she can finish undressing him; and be the first. The blonde, Kaitlin, and the redhead, Morgan, follow Sung and start to molest Bruiser — in the nicest way possible. Sung grabs his gear and starts chewing on it like taffy while the other two nibble on his skin. His eyes roll back in his head, and he takes a moment to compose a plan of action.

Bruiser sits up and pushes Sung onto her back, penetrates her, and raises his left hand in the air, almost as if he were threatening her. Sung smiles and says, "Wait till I'm about to cum and then slap me as hard as you want." Bruiser starts pounding away at Sung with a passionate vigor, as if this moment were going to change the universe, or at least the immediate future. Sung starts moaning in a high pitched, Asian schoolgirl tone that throws Bruiser off his game. He retreats to avoid blowing the deal and embarrassing himself, and then slides face first between her legs, licking her in defense while he regroups.

After a moment of indulgence, she grabs a handful of his hair and pulls him back to eye contact, demanding, "I'm about to cum! Don't fuck this up, Bruiser. I want my fucking head to pop off!" Bruiser jumps in and closes his eyes, trying to remove himself from the moment, and as he hits his stride, Sung begins to hum with a high-frequency vibration that makes him think something in the room is about to shatter. Her hips start shaking, she closes her eyes, bites her lip, and Bruiser decides to hit her with a left hand as hard as he can, just to see if she might explode all over him. Sung lets out a bellowing, "FUCK YOU! AND FUCK ME FOR FUCKING YOU, YOU FUCKING FUCK!"

Bruiser rolls over on his back, looking down at his member, and says to it, "If you help me pull this off, I'll never hurt you again." Morgan mounts him as Kaitlin tries to find his uvula with her tongue but only finds a lack of compassion emanating from his being. Kaitlin backs off, gives him a peck on the face, and then mounts it. She leans into Morgan and starts making out with her as Bruiser fights for air, mumbling, "Blondes always were my weakness."

Sung pops up, twirling her hair with her finger, and asks, "What about blonde Asians?"

Bruiser, gasping for air, says, "Fifty points, Sung. Game over." He catches Sung's new look out of the corner of his eye, and with a nose full of model anus, he mumbles, "I hope this is how it ends."

Morgan grinds away at him egregiously as if she were trying to break him as Kaitlin finds her way off his face, on to his throat, and starts grinding away at his Adam's apple. He grabs Kaitlin's thighs and pushes her forward, right on top of Morgan. He slips out of Morgan, evading her arrhythmic beating, and as he gets to his knees, he pulls Kaitlin into his groin by her arms and pushes her face first into Morgan's freckled cunt. He pins Kaitlin's legs with his knees and retains her by her wrists, leaving her with only the control of her tongue. He pounds away at her with a relentless fervor until he feels her loins tense up and then let's go of her wrists, grabs her tightly by the top of her hips, digging his fingers around her hipbones for leverage, and pounds away until she bursts like a water balloon dropped ten stories onto hot pavement. He pushes her off into Morgan's arms, and as she lays there, dripping onto the exaggerated thread count, he reaches back, and slaps her full, firm ass with both hands: one on each cheek.

"Ohhnhuh!" she moans, releasing all her lung's contents and starts to melt into Morgan: who at this point is squirming around like a cat in heat, unaware of anything other than the insatiable itch that lies within her.

Morgan pushes Kaitlin off her into Sung's embrace, looks down at Bruiser's flaccid all-in-one tool, and asks, "Did you cum?"

"I'm not sure," he sighs.

She leans in, kisses him, and says, "It doesn't matter." She grabs his semi-erect member and rubs it on her face while caressing his alien dormitory. Bruiser lays back, staring at the ceiling, and then looks over at Angelora. She stops who she was doing and slithers over to him on her belly, hypnotizing him with her perfectly tan-lined butt cheeks. As she reaches him, she rests her supple handfuls on his arm and kisses him with a new respect. Bruiser fills Morgan's mouth uncomfortably fast, pushing her back, and she accepts his challenge, climbing back onto him with her mouth agape, dripping with fulfillment as the rest of the girls have formed a circle and are watching, waiting for the second coming.

Bruiser catches David, standing behind the girls, watching his sexual antics as he strips down, jumps into bed, and pulls at Angelora, finessing her off Bruiser and back to her friend.

"Adrianna, keep an eye on this one," he says and returns to watching Bruiser being ridden like a show pony by Morgan. "How weird do you want to get tonight, Zealand?"

Bruiser smiles and continues to entertain Morgan, asking, "How weird is weird for you?"

David crawls to Adrianna and Angelora, looks around, and says, "Vanessa's coming. I feel like that should do it."

"Who hasn't at this point?" asks Bruiser and then his eyes bulge. Angelora, who's being overtaken by Adrianna and David, raises her hand, catching Bruiser's attention. Morgan slaps Bruiser in the face as she watches him once again being distracted by Angelora. Bruiser rubs his face, saying, "Darling, I do the slapping."

Morgan doesn't acknowledge him and slaps him again, saying, "I can't wait to tell my sister I slapped Zealand T. Dahl. Are you going to enlighten me, lover?" Bruiser pushes Morgan off his dick, and as he is going to get on top of her and slap her, he sees David in his peripheral, shove his hand into Adrianna's chest.

Bruiser kicks Morgan out of the bed immediately, and realizing his vulnerability, he jumps up and puts his naked ass in the corner with his hand on his cock. He eyes his new cohort Janine, mounted on the wall behind his other new friend David Blaine, and barks, "What-the-actual-fuck, dude!"

David holds Adrianna's heart up in the air and blows a fireball across it, asking, "Sorry, was that too weird for you, Zealand? I couldn't resist. How do you like yours? Lightly seared?"

Bruiser jumps on top of Adrianna and slaps her in hopes of resuscitation as he watches David bite into her heart like it was a grass-fed, grain-free, late-night burger. He hovers over Adrianna, waiting for revival, but nothing appears to be happening. Morgan screams as she watches the magician eat her friend's core. Her scream demands all of David's attention, awakening him to the abundance of delights just lying around his room. He shoves the rest of Adrianna's crispy, black heart into his mouth and crawls towards Morgan curled up in the corner shaking. As Bruiser finds David distracted by his cannibalistic lust, he takes advantage, sprinting over to Janine. He grabs her, caresses her, strips her bare, and points her at David.

David hears the familiar noise, stands up, and walks slowly towards Bruiser, saying, "I just assumed with the blonde hair and blue eyes; you were one of us." Bruiser shakes his new friend, Janine, with a frightened quiver as David walks him down, saying, "I can taste the fear dripping off you, and it's not becoming. Let go of it, Zealand. You know there's no point to whatever it is you plan on doing with that ancient blade." He walks Bruiser down, blood dripping from his chin, and says, "I can't tell you how aroused I was when I saw that little girl eat your mother's heart." David puts his hand on Bruiser's chest, ignoring his empty threat, and says, "I had no understanding of the true delicacy that is humanity." He taps on Bruiser's chest, saying, "And now I understand why it's frowned upon."

324

Slaphappy

Bruiser points the sword at David's heart, asking, "Why's that?"

David, naked and covered in blood, pushes himself onto the sword, backing Bruiser into the wall, and as his blood cascades down the metal phallus, he says, "Because there'd be no one left." Morgan screams again, this time waking Sung and Kaitlin. Sung stands up with Kaitlin, they walk over to David, and perch their chins on his shoulders. David laughs and says, "I always wondered what you'd look like as a blonde. Fifty points. Game over, Sung."

Bruiser stands, naked, shaking Janine nervously inside David, and his hands start to sweat as he fights to hold onto her, saying, "Ha, that's what I said." He tightens his grip, straightens his spine, and embraces his new presence, saying firmly, "I can't let you continue like this, David."

David backs himself off the blade and asks, "Girls, can you give us a moment? My new friend just grew some nuts, and I feel like they need some breathing room."

Sung and Kaitlin walk over to Adrianna's body. Sung grabs Adrianna's arm and rips it off at the shoulder. She gnaws away at the shoulder bone, saying, "The marrow is completely to die for, Kaitlin." She rubs Adrianna's appendage on her friend's face, saying, "You have to try it."

Morgan jumps up and makes a run for it, shouting, "Zealand, do something!"

Bruiser thrusts his sword back into David and gets covered in more of the magician's blood. David cackles and says, "Kaitlin, can you please go after Morgan and contain her before she makes a complete sociopolitical mess out of this." Kaitlin runs off after Morgan, and David slides himself back down the blade, forcing himself on Bruiser once more, saying, "Zealand, you know it doesn't have to be like this. This is the whole binary thing. Is the glass half-full or half-empty? Even when you think it's empty, it's full – of air. You really have to look deeper into the gray and search for what's really going on."

Bruiser pushes David back and off Janine, saying, "It's not that."

David, looking deeply into him, challenging his existence with his gaze, and asks him, "You're still worried about the end? You're right, Bruiser. You are the catalyst that brings the end, but you will also bring the beginning of a new era. Where will you be? In front, leading us, or in front, running from us? Jump off the ledge with me and fly off into whatever life you choose. Or you can give into your fear and plummet down through every layer of hell, landing face first at the bottom. It's your decision."

Kaitlin returns holding on tightly to Morgan, saying, "Who's up for an Amuse Bouche?"

Bruiser grabs Janine's scabbard, sheaths it, and throws the sword over his shoulder, looks at his bare wrist, and says, "It's gotten plenty weird, Dave. I'm gonna' take off." He turns to shake David's hand, but David denies the embrace and shoves his hand in Morgan's chest, pulls her heart out, and presents it to Bruiser as her eyes roll back in her head and her lifeless form drops to the floor.

"Come on, Scott, have a heart."

"I'd love to, but I have this thing, and I feel like I've already overstayed my welcome. Apparently, Vanessa's on her way up here and if she sees this—" He grabs David's hand and shakes it with an agitated repetition as he watches Angelora cowering in the corner. He pulls David in close and whispers in his ear, "She's coming with me."

David pats Bruiser on the shoulder, saying, "I told you she was a gift." He pulls away from David's embrace, takes Angelora confidently by the hand, and starts to walk her out of the room. "Just the sword, Bruiser. That one's special," says David adamantly. Kaitlin and Sung put themselves between Bruiser and the stairs. He tries to pull Angelora past them, but David grabs Angelora by the wrist, saying, "She'll destroy you, Zealand. You have to trust me on this one."

David's free hand clenches and as he thrusts it forcefully towards Angelora's center. Bruiser removes Janine from her resting state and swipes swiftly through his wrist, turns and spins, beheading Sung and Kaitlin in one stroke, and as their carcasses drop to the floor, he continues his swing, lowering his blade, forcing it through David's midsection, cutting him clean in half. "And yet, for some odd reason, I don't." Bruiser surveys the room, drenched in more magicians' blood, looking for anyone else that wants a fast pass to their demise. He kicks David's torso, and a metallic looking mosquito flies out of it and lands in his lower half. He turns to Angelora, pushes her toward the stairs, and asks her, "You ready?"

Angelora, still shaking, grabs his hand and says, "You're definitely going to need another session; I don't think I got that crackling noise."

Vanessa enters David's penthouse expecting to be confronted by a room full of celebrity, yearning with ambiguous desires, but finds only the mediocre leftovers of a B-list gathering. The freshly adorned are all sitting silently with no animated signs of life, so she tiptoes through the remanent cautiously, hoping that her flaxen hair and azure eyes will sublimate their affections. Receiving only discerning looks from the room, she releases a pent-up breath and continues to walk softly through the penthouse, stopping at the bar, where she calms herself with a drink. As her heart returns to a pitter-patter, she gets on her phone and tries to text David, but once again receives only static. The remnants stare at one another, whispering with their eyes as they try to deduce her standings. Their heads all turn to her at the same time, leaving her petrified as they analyze her being, and then return to their silent conversation. Her confidence snowballs as she is ignored, and she skates effortlessly through the plausibly voracious crowd.

As she turns a corner towards the hallway, she is stopped by a tall, muscular, blonde man that catches her scent and approaches her. She shakes her phone with frustration and then looks down into it, hoping to avoid the inimitable hunger in his eyes and the awkward conversation that she assumes will come with it. The golden dude stalks her down, pushing her into a corner, saying in a sultry whisper, "Hey there." She puts away her phone, sets down her drink, and reaches behind her back, grabbing a hold of the nun chucks Bruiser gave her. She assesses the hallway behind him, looking for an out with the hopes of avoiding his misdirected affections. He runs his fingers through her hair, and then slowly across her neck, saying, "I'd love to spend some time inside of you."

She grabs his hand and pulls it from her neck, saying, "Barf."

He drops to the ground, limp and lifeless, and Bruiser appears in his absence, wearing only gray jeans, his new friend Janine, and a lot more of the magician's blood, saying, "Nice moves, boss, but I really would've liked to watch you use those things."

Vanessa pauses and imbibes his presence, trying to gauge his fleeting levels of temperance, and says, "You might just."

"I could go another round, for sure." Bruiser stares down at the inept beauty and then at the room full of golden stragglers.

Vanessa analyzes the blood covering her talent, laughs and says with a sliver of jealousy, "I bet you could. Looks like the orgy went well."

Bruiser tries to wipe off the blood, saying, "Those things get so messy." Deterring her from the thought, he asks, "What was that thing you did with dude's finger; pressure points?"

"I'm not sure, but I feel like it's related to why nothing digital works when it's in my hands and the nanotechnology that you mentioned they're infused with."

Angelora emerges from the shadows behind Bruiser, and he reintroduces her, saying, "You remember Angelora."

Vanessa responds, "Oh yeah, rubdown. She's coming with us?"

Bruiser takes Vanessa's drink from her, sniffs it, finishes it, throws the empty glass over his shoulder, and says, "Definitely, let's smoke this burger joint."

Vanessa, with a minuscule amount of entertainment in her voice, asks him, "How high are you?"

Bruiser puts his hand over his head, looks up, and says, "As giraffe pussy. He made me do some magic dust with him."

Vanessa stares at him with that twinkle in her eye that she wishes she could have removed and says, "Made you. I assume that's why you're covered in more blood?"

"I'm starting to think there's a correlation," he says as the golden-haired stragglers stand up simultaneously and gather behind Vanessa. He looks around, judging the crowd, trying to decide if they want an autograph, or some sort of physical donation, and says, "So, I'm starting to get a Children of the Cornish vibe. If everybody could take two steps back, we'll be on our way."

There's no response from the viking-esque gathering, only the sound of a communal stirring hunger. The wall of perfection that now surrounds them parts and Mcklusky and Stedanko present themselves, saying, "You're not going anywhere; not with her."

Bruiser unsheathes Janine, shakes her at the wall of mindless followers as they drool with a guided hunger, and says, "Sorry boys, she's coming with us."

"You can hand her over, or we'll take her from you."

"I'd like to see that," laughs Bruiser.

"Zealand, just let them have her," begs Vanessa.

Angelora grabs Bruiser and shakes him, saying, "She's right, your life's too important to risk," and starts to walk off.

Bruiser grabs Angelora, saying, "Fuck that, what are these two cumshoes going to do anyway?"

With those words, Stedanko pulls out a tablet and starts to tap away vigorously on it. The room pushes in on the threesome with a distant look in their eyes, almost dead, showing no emotion. One of the perfect beings reaches for Angelora and Bruiser decides to shove Janine inside of it. Vanessa shrieks at the penetration, draws her nun chucks, separates them, puts them boldly in front of her face, and steps into Bruiser's flank. She looks at him cocked and ready for hell, and yelps, "I swear if you hit me with that thing."

The threesome now back-to-back-to-back, surrounded by the 'chosen ones,' spins slowly as they watch their eyes turn to pure darkness. "He's actually pretty good with it, he split David in half," says Angelora dauntingly as David appears behind Mcklusky and Stedanko blowing a fireball.

"Looks like that went well," laughs Vanessa.

"It doesn't have to be like this, Scott," states David.

"Like what, Dave?"

"A fight. We can work together like your sister would've wanted. We can change this world … for the better."

"I don't know if you're using that word right: better. And on paper I'm with you, but I can't back the whole cannibalistic lust and consumption of humanity. I'm just kind of over the class system and would love to fight for equality and balance, rather than jump into bed with the government and whatever alien species controls them."

"It's your choice: With us, or against us, but I have a feeling you're going to submit gracelessly by the end of this night," he says and nods his head across the room.

Bruiser turns to address David's nod and finds David's other half waving back, and groans, "Fart sandwiches!"

Stedanko taps away at his tablet and one of the girls pushes Vanessa into Bruiser. He feels her weight on him and turns to find Vanessa's aggressor on the ground unconscious and forces Janine inside the girl's heart repeatedly, hoping that it matters, but it doesn't. As her chest heals, he swings Janine blindly at the gathering, asking Vanessa, "Can you do more of that?"

Vanessa raises her hand as if she's about to start speaking tongues shaking it vigorously and says, "Follow me!" She jumps into the crowd slapping and poking her way through it as Bruiser swings freely with a tight grip on his new friend Janine, slicing, dicing, scattering, smothering, and chunking his way through the mindless fucks, stopping only when the floor has become a hash of flesh.

As Bruiser is catching his breath, there's a scream and he searches the room, finding other David grabbed Angelora while he was distracted and is trying to abscond with her. Stedanko taps away agitatedly on his tablet, the floor starts to grumble, and slowly the beings start to reform. Bruiser looks back at Stedanko tapping away grotesquely on his tablet and two larger model-esque dudes jump him. Vanessa lets out a vengeful scream and charges into them headfirst. They drop to the floor as she touches them, and Bruiser slips away from their embrace as they lose their exuberance. He goes to stick it in them before they have a chance to regroup, but hears, **Close your eyes, breathe deep, and think about anything that warms your heart. Connect with Urantia and to the sky from wherever you came, and when you truly are free from pain and life flows through you, you'll have your companions back.** The whisper gifts a momentary lapse of blind aggression and unearths a spiritual vicissitude that pushes him to his knees. He puts his hands on his aggressor's hearts, closes his eyes, and smiles.

"Zealand, what are you doing?" asks Vanessa.

"Embracing my demons." There's a transference of light and their eyes open, but the distant look has been replaced with a vibrant serenity. He stands up, holding his composure with a resilient light in his eyes, and confronts the rest of his failures as they stare at him like a freshly fried turkey. "Fuck me, this is going to be a long night," groans Bruiser, staring across the room at both Davids. And as he's formulating his next move, the two larger dudes step forward and grab him, but with a loving touch. They wrap their arms around him and start licking his face.

Vanessa pokes them in the jugulars, dropping them to the floor.

"What are you doing?" asks Bruiser.

"What ARE you doing?" asks Vanessa with a sideways look.

"I think I connected with them."

"Yeah, looked like it," says Vanessa with a sneer.

He leans into her ear and whispers, "No, I think I can control them. Can you just keep knocking them out and push towards Angelora."

Vanessa raises the nun chucks above her head as she realizes the mob has reformed fully and once again surrounds them. Standing her ground behind him, she swings her nun chucks furiously, hoping to buy some breathing room, and says, "Can we just get the fuck out of here!"

"I'm done running from this dream, Vanessa. If this is how we go, this is how we goes." He walks up to the snarling mob and puts his hands over their hearts. As the others attack, Vanessa continues dropping them to the floor, and Bruiser follows, putting his hands on their chests to the same resolve. They continue this process, stunting their hunger and transforming them into docile, malleable specimens of perfection until they reach the two Davids and Angelora.

"What will you do, Zealand?" asks David.

"It looks more like, what will you do, Dave? I am that I am, and would that I could, but who really cares? If I'm lucky I wake up from this dream bartending at a Ruby Tuesdays with rent being the only thing I can afford to worry about. No matter what happens here tonight: I'll fuck it up, you'll fuck it up, inevitably someone will fuck it up, and we'll keep doing this until we get it right."

David's hand twitches. "Man is truly doomed to perfection."

Bruiser looks at David's hand twitching and says, "Stick it in me, bub. Feast on my fleshy motor. I hope you choke on my entrails and that my essence burns its way through your being, sears your innards, and kisses your lips with a fire right before it returns to its home. I know there's better places then here and that this life is just a chaotic collision of molecules where strength has nothing to do with survival, only purpose and the guiding hand of an anonymous force. So, if the only path to true love is a direct flight to the kingdom of light; take me there." Bruiser stretches his arms out and presents his heart, looks back at Vanessa, and says, "Please forgive me."

David licks his lips and says, "Thank you," and pushes his hand forward toward Bruiser's center, saying, "I'm sorry."

Bruiser puts his hand over David's heart as his chest is being penetrated, and he says, "I love you!" He releases a smile that beholds no fear in it, and as David grabs a hold of his cockles, a blinding white light is released that erases all of it.

Fool's Gold

Six perfect blondes, three male and three female, walk into the green room of the Jerry Springer show, carrying our once again unconscious friend, Bruiser. They set him down ever so gently onto a massage table and then all sit down silently in unison. Angelora stands over Bruiser, takes a deep breath, warms her hands, releases her breath, and puts her hands over him palms down. She closes her eyes as her hands start to shake vehemently. The closer she gets to touching him the harder they shake. "Does this happen often, Less?" she asks with a tremble in her voice.

Less pulls his gaze away from his laptop, saying, "Yeah, seems to be a reoccurring theme. Last time Leslie and I had to dreamscape him back from the future pre-apocalypse."

"Dreamscape?"

"It's like Inception, but cute and furry like the eighties. Do you think he'll be okay?"

"Yeah, just have to jumpstart him. It's like a rolling brown out from what I can tell. He seems to have left his body for more vibrant pastures of light."

"Do you think you could get me next? I've had this funky crick in my neck ever since I got caught up in those two sister witches."

"It's not a crick, it's an alien implant you picked up on the transcendental byways, and I think you should keep it, you're going to need it. How was that by the way?"

"I've never been in a more comfortable position. Bruiser slapped this … these conjoined twins and they ran off into the woods. I ran after them and found them screaming like banshees while they were grotesquely separating. They were in so much pain, I just wanted to stop their suffering, but when I got close to them, they pulled me into this esoteric reality where they were releasing lifetimes of pain. It was this place where they were truly from, this universe where magic not only existed, but was taught and worshiped, and there was a balance there that came from respecting it. I believe they were evil witches that were being punished for their acts of acquiring power. They took me inside of a glowing rock that changed me exponentially. It was a pure green light that evaluated my being and released my third dimensional chains, along with Leslie's as she is the other half of my soul — so I was told."

"You saw that while you were inside the twins?" she asks.

"No, I went there with them, and when we came back it was this fuck-ball of energy that we shared and manipulated by pounding our simple machines together," says Less with an awkwardly egregious smile.

"That tops my first threesome for sure," says Bruiser as his eyes open and he returns to this realm of confusion. Angelora stutters energetically and her knees buckle as the room fills up with a lucid new vibration. Less stumbles verbally as the eyes of the six pack light up a brilliant neon blue with their leaders return. "Two big girls on a pull-out couch. It might have been rape, but that was before rape was so serious."

"Who'd you rape?" asks Vanessa, walking into the green room.

"Two fat girls," says Less in a defensive tone.

"Big girls need love, too," says Vanessa.

"In this scenario, they needed it really bad, so they got me drunk and took it," says Bruiser, smiling with a distant, pensive gaze.

"Your first threesome was a rape scenario?" asks Vanessa.

"Yeah, technically speaking," he says.

"Beats my first threesome," says Vanessa.

"Joie de beaver?" asks Bruiser.

"Menage a twat?" asks Less.

"More like two meats and a vag, but nowhere near as exciting." Vanessa looks at the six-pack of golden ones and asks, "Can you do something with them? They creep out the gnarliest bone in my body."

Less shuts his laptop and asks, "You want me to put a sheet over 'em, boss?"

"Have you told him yet, Less?" asks Vanessa.

"No, he just returned."

Bruiser sits up and scratches his head as it flooded with visions from his most recent journey. There are five holes in his chest from the night prior where Blaine reached into his breast and toyed with his core. The five finger holes in his chest fill and the scars start to dissolve as Less, Angelora, and Vanessa stare at him speechlessly while they witness his regeneration. He slides off the table and walks through the silence over to the bathroom, saying, "Less, you really think that Jerry Springer is working with the federal government to discredit me as a healer on TV, in front of the whole world, to stop me from healing people, because they have what they want from me, which is: I woke the sleeper cells and started a chain reaction that is their 'cannibal slaves.' And you saw that last night, because you and Leslie have psychic powers you obtained when I slapped you with my right hand. And then the girls amplified that sight after you split them in half and had a threesome with them."

"Not the government, but, yeah," says Less. "You saw it too?"

"Just now as I returned, but it's just a fear-based dream," laughs Bruiser.

Stunted, Vanessa says, "They lock the doors when the crowd turns, and everybody dies. And you still want to go out there?"

Bruiser pops his head out of the changing room, so that he can see Less, and says, "Clearly, they could have ended us last night if they wanted to, but they didn't. Instead, they protected us and carried me out of Blaine's place after he tried to eat my heart, because I reprogrammed them – with love." He returns to the room wearing his go to, gray jeans and a black T-shirt, and finds Less, acting like he's regurgitating his words.

When Less finishes his dramatization, he sits down on the couch and says, "Let's just say these nano-technologically advanced cannibals can be controlled, and the government or whoever, knows how. What do you think they plan on doing with an army of perfect soldiers?"

Angelora laughs aloud as she puts her table back into its case and says, "Streamline capitalism."

"Bruiser, you can't create another one of those nannibals."

Bruiser looks at her sideways and says, "I've got total control over these 'Nano-cannibals.'"

Less laughs and says, "I think it's a genetic cleansing!"

Bruiser sits down next to Less and says, "That's exactly what they're doing." He points to his six new friends from the party that are sitting quietly in the corner and says, "Look at them, they're absolutely perfect in every facet."

Angelora throws her table over her shoulder and scoffs at the six-pack, saying, "I mean, there's no such thing as perfection." Less and Zealand stare at Angelora's disgust for their new friends and laugh at her blatantly apparent jealous bone that's now poking through the flesh. She walks over to Bruiser, kisses him on the cheek, and asks, "Do you need anything else, Zealand?"

"I'm good. Thanks for bringing me back," says Bruiser.

She smiles, releasing two childlike dimples, and says endearingly, "Anytime, love."

Less stares at the six-pack, asking, "You really trust them?"

Zealand walks over to the silent group and plays with their hair as he walks by them, inspecting their docility, poking at their restraint, and says, "Yeah. I don't believe it myself, but yeah. It's weird, I'm connected to them like Bluetooth. I can feel each of them on the deepest level as if they were a part of me; or at least an extension."

"But they attacked you and tried to kill…" murmurs Vanessa.

333

Bruiser interrupts her, pointing at Angelora as she walks out the door, saying, "That wasn't about me; they were programmed to detain her for Blaine." He sits down on one of the more stunning girls' laps, pets her face and strokes her hair.

"And instead of gouging away at their perfect forms, sending them back to whatever mall shaped hell they came from, you touched their hearts and reprogrammed them?" asks Less.

"Less, you ever see any video games where people walk around loving people?" asks Bruiser.

Less scratches his chin as he joins Bruiser in the analyzation of one of the chosen ones, sitting in one of their laps, saying, "No. Well, Leisure Suit Larry."

Bruiser continues to pet the face of the girl whose lap he's sitting on and says, "Yeah, but he was running around fucking chicks with dildos he'd whittled out of driftwood. Titties – the only reason we're here; the true source of nourishment are shunned from eyesight. Meanwhile, violence is worshipped, and destruction rewarded as a quality program. Welcome back to your regularly scheduled programming … you ever heard that before? They don't want us loving, Less. Those games, TV, movies, and the news all program fear and breed aggression because that's what they want. That's where their power lies. They program us with fear, using the airwaves, and separate us with language, color, and religion. All the while, they do whatever they can to keep us docile and submissive. I realized we can't kill them, and I heard a whisper from beyond say, 'Close your eyes, breathe deep, and think about anything that warms your heart. Connect with Urantia and to the sky from wherever you came, and when you truly are free from pain and life flows through you, you'll have your companions back.' So, I decided to try something different."

Less feels something shift in the pants of the gentlemen's lap he's been sitting on and jumps up, returning to the couch. "When you say companions, you mean you were placing alien souls in them, that you rescued from a spaceship, that was hiding in a black hole, that you visited in a PCP induced dream where you stole your soul."

Bruiser sits down next to Less on the couch and says, "I never told you that, Less."

"I saw it in the same vision as the RumSpringa Break."

"Anyway, I saved my soul, but I don't expect you to get it. I don't get it, and I was there in some way, shape, or energetic presence. I just want to know why they would want to crucify me in front of the whole world."

Less laughs and says, "It worked with Jesus. We based our whole time-structure on his birth, and they crucified him for saying he had superpowers that involved love. They nailed him to a cross and rewrote the Bible to induce a fear that breeds slavery."

At that moment, Bruiser's following stands up silently and walks out of the door. "Can you see what that's all about, Less?" asks Vanessa, shaking her head. She locks the door behind them and turns to Bruiser, shouting, "You can't seriously tell me you're going to walk out there, knowing that it's a set up!"

Bruiser looks at her with puppy eyes and says, "As long as you're there to protect me, Bitté."

"What level of stupid are you?" she asks, leaning into him.

"All of them," he says confidently.

"Why would you want to put us in that situation if you know you can avoid it?" she asks with a passionate frustration in her voice, staring down at him with her hands on her hips as if to break his blind confidence.

He gets lost in her furious concern for him, lays down on the couch as if he were about to be emotionally interrogated, and sarcastically asks, "What else is there to do in Chicago on a Monday? I'm tired of running from my mistakes. I'm bored with the drivel I continue to create to entertain myself, and I know there's better places than here. Honestly, I don't feel like there's any other option, Vanessa. You saw how the room shifted after we touched them."

Vanessa sits down on the couch, slides under his head, and runs her fingers through his hair without words. Bruiser leans into her, begging silently for a reprise from the truth in the moment, and she stops him, places her hand on his heart, saying, "They want to eat us, and we can't kill them."

He nestles his head in her lap, begging for more affection, saying, "Not you, you're a beast, my protector. Together we have the power to control them, so there's nothing to fear."

She smiles at his wavering ego and says, "That's absurd. How do you expect this to end? Did you see the lack of presence in their eyes when they walked out of the room, Bruiser? There's something else controlling them."

Bruiser sits all the way up and leans back on the other arm of the couch, saying, "That's why we have to get to them first; and I told you, no more Bruiser. It's Zealand and only Zealand. He's just a voice in my head at this point. Look, I'm not afraid of the chaos, I don't expect it to end, and I believe that it's going to go the way it's meant to go. All fear does is redirect us from our purpose. I want to walk out there with my heart pure and wide-the-fuck open, standing next to you, in front of the world, knowing that I'm safe and loved no matter what happens."

"Zealand, what Less said makes sense, and you of all people should know they don't want you healing more people. Assuming that these perfect beings are going to go viral, they don't need you anymore," she says.

Zealand looks at her, asking as he points to his heart, "So you think I'm the enemy now, and the Romans are just going to crucify me on TV, in front of the whole world?"

Vanessa scoots over to Zealand, bridging the gap, and says in a delicate tone, "I'm saying, why play a losing hand. We can just go, run away, we've … you've got millions. We can be safe and loved together."

Zealand laughs and says, "You want **me** to roll over? I started this, and if I run … I'm a pussy."

She slaps his leg, demanding, "You're an imbecile if you go out there tonight and conjure up one more of those creatures for them."

"What if they really are the future?" he asks. "The next step in the evolution of man."

"Where does that leave our friends and family? In pens like cattle for the upper crustaceans to feed on?" she asks.

"That's exactly why I have to go out there tonight," he says.

She cringes on the inside as she asks, "How? By going out there and creating an army of your bastard children to fight the powers that be. You don't have to fight to be right!"

"There's no more right, only what's *left*. They're my demons, and I have to embrace them. Blaine kept saying it last night, and I thought he was trying to turn me to the dark side, like he wanted me to be the leader of the new regime and own my pure evilness."

"So, what does it mean then?"

"I can't run from them, and I can't kill them, I have to—"

She looks at him sideways and says, "Love them."

Bruiser leans into her, saying, "Because we're connected. They're a part of me, and the more I fight them, the more I fight the person I am."

Frustrated, she looks away from him, asking, "And you think creating more of these beautiful bastards is your path?"

He pulls at her attention, saying, "Clearly, or we wouldn't be here. Who's to say that these creatures aren't supposed to exist. If I can control them, we're safe."

She refuses to look back at him, saying, "You can't control anything in this life, and you want me to feed them my friends, my family, my heart. Just so that in the next Bible, you'll be mentioned as the creator."

Zealand pushes Vanessa over on her back and gazes into her as he says, "That's not fair. This isn't about my ego, my dick size, or infamy."

"What's it about then?" she asks, realizing she's lost him.

"Vanessa, I'm the only one that can help. No one's ever wanted me, and now the whole world needs me. And I need you … on stage next to me, fixing this world, loving it all," he says, staring at her as his eyes light up.

Vanessa stumbles in his gaze nervously, as if threatened, and looking for the best way out of the incomprehensible situation, she covers her face and says, "I would but—"

"But you're afraid," he says.

"That's not fair."

"Why'd you come back to Blaine's last night, if you were so sure it was going to be a massacre?" he asks, leans in, and kisses her on the forehead.

She struggles to wipe him off her forehead, saying, "Because, I didn't have a choice."

Zealand leans back, setting her free, saying, "That's exactly how I feel. We're the only ones equipped to deal with this."

"What if dealing with it means running away?" she asks.

"That doesn't compute. Do you want to run? Take a mill, you can dip and never look back. Tell Less and Leslie they have the same offer. I'm not forcing anyone," he says. She doesn't respond and he pounds his hand with his fist, saying, "Fuck it. You and Dick can go play, while I figure this out."

"You don't think he's coming back, do you?" she asks.

"Fuck Dick, he'll be back when the money runs out, with some cool shit, and a lukewarm story about it. Dick has his own path, and it's probably with better people. He's just as scared as the rest of us. He said nothing changed when I slapped him, but I came to realize he has a different path. He just didn't seem to care, all he wanted was superpowers."

Vanessa, still lying there, watching his retreat, asks him, "You're scared, aren't you?" She sits up and walks him down slowly this time, watching his energy sway.

"Shitless, how could I be anything otherwise, but I'm tired of running from myself, avoiding any uncomfortable feelings, all the while creating more messes." Vanessa climbs on top of Zealand as she realizes he might be evolving on some level for the better, and he continues, saying, "I'm going to stick my dick in this mess and fuck it into something I love. At the heart of it all, I've never cared about any of it. I feel like this life was meant to tear you apart; and this is what's left."

He plays with Vanessa's shirt and then starts to lift it off her slowly. She doesn't stop him, but says, "Now the world that tormented you, needs you, but they don't need the exalted you; they need the humble lover you."

He takes her shirt off and is caught off-guard by three dainty moles placed in a triangle, resting in her cleavage. He caresses the moles with his pointer finger, saying, "I never noticed these before." She pushes his hand away and covers them, but he pulls it away, saying, "No, I like them. They have meaning."

She shakes her boobs at him, asking, "And what would that be?"

Zealand caresses them lovingly and says, "It means I'm in the right place, or the left place, I guess. I've been seeing them lately everywhere I travel, and I believe they're a sign.

Vanessa undoes his belt, unzips his pants, and overtakes him with a newfound affection, forcing herself in his mouth. The two entertain one another, distracting themselves from the gravity of the moment. She slowly makes her way to his dick with her hand, and he grabs it, stopping her. Hurt, she retracts from the moment, saying, "I know I'm not a bed full of models, but after you fell asleep inside of me the other night, I realized that I'll never be enough for you." She lifts her skirt, slides her thong over, and climbs onto him unprotected. She looks him in the eyes as he settles in and waits for him to destroy the moment.

Zealand bites his lip and says, "There's no place I'd rather be than inside of you, Vanessa. I fell asleep because I was comfortable. It was like being in the home I've always wanted."

"But you're afraid of that," she says, waiting for him to run.

Instead, he continues to let her ride him comfortably without trying to buck her off, saying, "So, this is the part where I tell you whatever it is you think you want to hear in hopes of alleviating your current level of suffering. Vanessa, I don't know how to do love. I've always felt that love was like Santa Claus."

"How so?"

"It's fable for children that keeps their world magical until it takes its course and starts to tear them apart. Something to hold onto, a fairy tale; something to prolong the inevitable darkness that will change them. I have no idea what it is or if it even exists between two people at this point. Last night I was in a pile up of models worshiping me, and I tamed every one of them, but there was nothing there, and that's what's comfortable for me. This, what we have, *IS* my biggest fear, and it turns me into a sniveling child that wants to run away and hide from the inevitable pain lurking in my heart."

Vanessa slaps his face egregiously, shouting, "And fuck you by the way! Not that you owe me any sort of conciliation. And I can't say that I would have done any better at saying no to that prime selection. Honestly, I would have jumped right in, had it not ended so abruptly."

Zealand rubs his face, winks at her, and says, "See, that's what I'm looking for in forever — sexual tenacity." He watches her face as it turns to a full disdain for him regarding his toxic masculinity and waits. She pushes down on him, stroking him with her loins, and unable to fight the moment, he asks her, "So, what do you want to do, boss?"

Vanessa dismounts him and pushes him back into the couch. She rests her head in his lap, staring at his fallacy, saying, "Look, if you want to go out there and end the world on live television, I support you, but I'm sure as fuck not locking myself in that sound stage with you and them on live TV."

Zealand stutters, saying, "There's no way they'd show a massacre on live TV?"

"Why not? What if that's what they want? To induce panic and start some fucked up cleansing by the Fourth Reich."

"You think it's the Nazis?" he asks.

"I don't think Springer would help them if that was a thing, but the blonde hair, blue eyed thing is just too weird. What if dealing with it, embracing your demons, is running away with me, and loving me, your biggest fear: being trapped with a crazy woman — forever. Let's get out of here and we can watch the world end from the beach. We can go to Costa Rica, start a family, live in a treehouse, get stoned, and surf all day."

Bruiser smiles sincerely and asks her, "That's what you want: mangos and avocados in the backyard, a treehouse in the canopy, and getting high with the monkeys?"

"Sounds awesome," she says.

"What about your girlfriend?" he asks.

"We can pick her up in LA, on the way down there."

"You're serious?" he asks.

"Dead," she says and leans back against the opposing arm rest. "Shut down that voice in your head that says fight. All that matters is us, and our love will heal the world around us. We have enough to walk away, and you can heal people on your terms along the way."

He crawls to her and hovers over her, saying, "God, I want to climb all the way inside that fat little cheeseburger of yours."

"You think it's fat?"

"No, it's perfect, but it's just as inviting as the greasiest burger I've ever thought about sticking my dick in," he says and collapses on top of her, grabbing her in hopes of returning to her.

She pushes at him, saying, "We don't have time for that. We need to leave now, before this starts."

He tries again to enter her relentlessly, saying, "I don't need much time."

Zealand leans in to kiss her and she pushes his face away, saying, "We can fuck on the bus, but we have to leave now!"

"I can't."

"You can. You just have to love yourself enough to walk away from the fight, knowing it's not yours, and that it'll work itself out. But we have to leave now before it starts."

"Fine, let's go somewhere better, brighter, where the stars sparkle for us," he says.

"Really?" she asks.

Zealand grabs her hand and says, "Whatever you want."

"Seriously?" she asks.

"Yeah, let's get out of here. I couldn't imagine anything better than watching the world end with you on the beach." Zealand zips his pants, grabs her hand, and pulls her to the door, asking, "Costa Rica, though? What are your thoughts as far as Panama?"

Gleaming deeply into his soul, Vanessa says, "Anywhere on the beach with you, Zealand."

Zealand opens the door and is confronted by Mcklusky and Stedanko as they are about to knock on it. He shuts the door in their faces, turns to Vanessa, and asks, "What the fuck?" He puts his hand on the doorknob, saying, "When I open the door, make a run for the bus."

Vanessa holds her ground, saying, "I'm not leaving you."

There's another knock at the door. Zealand opens it, puts his finger up, and says, "Could you give us some space?" He shuts the door in their faces again. There's another knock at the door. He opens it to find two pistols pointed at them and he hears, "Space is what we're known for," says Trent, drooling over Zealand's presence.

"What's up, Kruder, Dorfmeister?"

"Zealand, you weren't planning on leaving, were you?" asks Stedanko as Mcklusky puts his palm over Zealand's third eye.

Zealand slaps Mcklusky's hand away and forces his way out the door, past Mcklusky and Stedanko, pulling Vanessa along with him. Stedanko grabs her by the arm, stopping Zealand where he stands. He looks down the hallway and finds Less and Leslie, just kicking it with his six-pack of golden champions. He thinks to himself, *Could you guys be dolls, and detain these dicks so we can get out of here?*

They don't react to his thought and Kirk says, "Nice try, Zealand, but we reprogrammed them, just in case you were thinking about leaving before the show."

The six pack walks up behind Kirk and Trent instead and stare blankly at Zealand. With a hint of cock, he asks, "Reprogrammed them? Like you've got an app to control these things?"

"Basically. Alice was just a test run. We couldn't find the right frequency until the party at David's," says Trent.

"That explains why you guys were on your phone the whole time in Charlotte." Zealand turns to Kirk and Trent, asking, "Am I supposed to die tonight?"

Kirk looks at him and says, "Many times, in many different lives, but it's your choice, Zealand. Death is the only path to true love, so smile and know that the kingdom of light comes swiftly."

"Don't you need me to create your army?"

"Not really, they have the frequency and your DNA," says Kirk as he puts his hand back on Zealand's third eye.

Zealand is overwhelmed by a vision of the metal cell at the moment when Ü penetrates him, but this time he's overtaken by a vision of Kirk and Trent standing outside of his cell watching. He returns, saying, "Where were we? An underground bunker?"

Kirk looks to the sky and says, "That was a simulation, like the one you've been hiding in here. In the deepest reality, you're locked in a room with a head full of star charts that we needed. Star charts with the location to the place where all life is detained in darkness begging to be set free."

Zealand steps back, asking, "Needed?"

"I just pulled them out of your third eye," says Kirk.

Zealand pauses while he tries to digest the obscure thought. He looks at his hands curiously and finds he must ask, "This isn't real?"

Trent steps forward and says, "As real as any other dream you hide in, but the whole concept of awareness is a circuitous venture."

Zealand pulls away from Kirk's grasp, saying, "If this is a dream, then let's have some fun." Two of his golden bastards grab Trent and Kirk, Zealand's eyes light up a lurid delphinium blue, his hands light up with a pure white light and he places them on their hearts, asking, "What do you two really want?"

Kirk drops his gun, as does Trent, and says, "We told you, we just want you to love us. Your sister sent us to make sure you make it to this show. I'm surprised she didn't mention it when you saw her last night."

"That **was** her; she was pure light," he says.

"She's evolved into something beyond your comprehension."

"So, you guys have been working with my sister the whole time … and the government?"

"We had no choice. You know how it is once they get involved. She was trying to heal this world, and she needs your help. That's why she injected you with the nanotechnology."

"I'm one of them."

"No, you're different. You're not one of these mindless plebes," Trent says, staring at his statuesque bodyguards. "Your programming can't be compromised. How do you not know that Zealand? You're the only one that can finish starting this."

"Starting what?" asks Zealand as his hands drop to his side.

"The end," says Kirk. "She sent us to escort you to the live broadcast of the dawn of a new day. The end of an error, humanity as we know it will be a bygone species like the Neanderthals. It's time to evolve past the present and into the future. They need a voice to strengthen them, and it's yours."

"Strengthen them for what?" asks Zealand.

Trent looks into Zealand, hoping to spark an undeniable light inside of him, and says, "To fight a well-deserved battle against a program of controlling darkness that's been hiding in the shadows since the beginning of time."

Kirk joins him, saying, "A revolution. So, would you like to stand here in the mud, stuck in this repetitive cycle, or are you ready to lead them into a future where this repressive force of evil no longer exists?"

Zealand turns to Vanessa and says, "If you want to go, go now. I'd love to have you at my side, but all I know right now is that I'm the only one that can clean up this mess!"

"You're serious?" she asks.

Zealand stares into Vanessa, saying, "Dead. I'm tired of watching while they take everything from us. My heart's wide-the-fuck open, and I'm going to show the world that the only power they have over us is imposing an imaginary fear of leaving this bastardized realm of suffering."

Vanessa drops his hand, saying, "What about us? Aren't you afraid of dying?"

"It sounds like my consolation prize is the kingdom of light, and that sounds like a win-win." He grabs her hand and says, "Honestly, Vanessa, I don't even think I can. I'm a souped-up, alien scumbag, and I'd love to get some serious sleep, so why not go down trying. I have to do this. These guys work … for my sister and I feel like I have to … for her and every other soul that this life of indentured servitude has broken. So, I'm going to walk out there and make a contentrance that changes the world forever."

"A what?" she asks.

"I'm going to make a content entrance, entrance them with my content, and have some fucking fun with this life. I feel like a baby dick for taking this strange dream so seriously. I've been crying my whole life, and I missed out on the whole thing while I was busy paying rent. I just woke up. I can't go back to sleep, and even if I could, I'd probably end up somewhere worse than here, so let's go burn this motherfucker down to the foundation. We can play house in the next life, Ness. I just found you, but I'm not worried about losing you again, because I don't think I can. You're my heart, and I want to thank you, tell you I'm sorry, and that I hope you'll forgive me for this."

"Sounds more like you're going to make a cunt entrance," she says and laughs. She tries to process the depths of their conversation, asking, "You're really buying their shit? You're going to submissively walk straight to your death."

"If they work with my sister, I have to trust them, but with only one condition," he says, staring into Trent and Kirk.

"What's that?" they ask together.

"You work for me now," he says without flinching.

"That's been the plan, Zealand," says Trent.

You can release them, he thinks and the golden ones release
Trent and Kirk. Zeal and puts his hand out to Vanessa and asks the
only question that really matters to him, "Are you coming?"

She puts her hand out shakily, grabbing his, and says, "I can't,
Zealand. I can't."

He looks at Vanessa and smiles, saying, "You can. You just don't
want to, because you're scared, and that's okay. I'll love you either
way, even if it's only for this passing moment, or forever,
throughout every life we live. It's nice to have found you — again."
He leans in, kisses her on the lips, and says, "I'm not looking for
someone to run from or someone to run to, I'm looking for someone to
run with, and I'm pretty sure that's you. Open your heart to this
moment, and there's truly nothing to fear."

She returns his affections, saying, "Fuck it. What else is there
to do in Chicago on a Monday?"

Zealand grabs Vanessa's hand and pulls her towards the stage
with Mcklusky, Stedanko, Less, Leslie, and his six golden children in
his slipstream.

Less catches up to Zealand, asking, "You all right, boss?"

Zealand stops, grabs Less by the shoulders, and shakes him,
saying, "All left, buddy. Never been better. Can you turn that thing
on and film this debacle."

Less laughs and says, "I've been filming the whole time, I
wasn't sure how that interaction was going to end." He lifts his
camera and points it at Zealand.

"Hello people of the 'free' world. It's Zealand T. Dahl, and I'm
about to go on live TV to film a mass healing or maybe just a good
ole fashion massacre. Either way, we're going to answer a lot of
questions. Today, they plan on ending my life, and when they do,
they're going to spin it so that it looks like I was the monster, and
that my demise was by my own hand, but I want you to know that none
of it matters. We're meandering into a new period in time, and
there's a shift coming that's going to clear the debt. There's a
darkness here that we've come to call home, and we must confront it
now. It's become so comforting that we're afraid to abandon it as we
fear there is nowhere better or brighter. Maybe you can feel it, or
maybe it's taken over your being and you've fully conformed to its
arrhythmic crackling.

"No matter what happens here tonight, know that this this life
has become a game of losses for us, and I'm no longer afraid to walk
away from it. Every time I die, I come back to a more twisted place
that shimmers the same way, except when you turn the lights off the
howl lasts longer, and the stench penetrates deeper. I woke up to
this life tacked to the floor, pressed hard to it by the fear of
continuing to let it win. Pinned by the silence, playing with the
exact same thought I had last time they stood with their loafer atop

my head, pressing it into the failing linoleum; I realized we deserve better, but no one's ever cared enough to tell us because they were too busy feeding off our light in the name of survival.

"There's only one thing that can save us now: look up to the sky and ask yourselves where you're truly from, because it's not this dilapidated theme park. If you think they're coming back to save you, the gods that came from the sky, you're sadly mistaken, because they're the ones that have enslaved you for their own entertainment. We're just the help, and if you're sitting there thinking you're not, you definitely are. Someone owns you, someone owns them, and they're owned by the undefined shadows that pull the strings from the darkest corners. What do you plan to do when this rock crumbles and you find yourselves chained to it because you sold yourself to them?

"Now is when we have to wake up and fight. We have to fight ourselves and the fear they've instilled in us since the beginning of time. The fear that keeps us trembling in front of our dream boxes. The only way to find freedom today is by trying, by hoping, and by believing in the goodness that's trapped inside the fleshy slave quarters you call home. Our only strength to fight this darkness will come from forgiving the person we've become, believing that love is a strength, and releasing our light with no concern for reciprocity. Let that child out and unleash the pure love we were sent here with; the love that's meant to disintegrate all darkness. The only way to do that is by letting go of the fear of losing this miserable existence that we've deemed life.

"This is our chance to fix something that was never meant to work, but we have to do it together, with our hearts open. Anyway, it's been a blast, and I just want you to know that … I love you."

Zealand looks to Less and says, "Post that, now. I want as many people watching this as possible before they erase me from the archives."

They arrive backstage, and as they wait for direction, Zealand looks over at Vanessa, grabs her hand, and smiles as he thinks, *Hey*.

She looks at him as if she just might have heard him and thinks to herself, *Hey*. He hears her thoughts for the first time and giggles as she continues, saying, *If you make it back home, know that I've got a big beef patty waiting for that microwave ass.* She slaps him in the face playfully and starts to say, "I—"

Zealand puts his fingers over her lips, mushes them around, and says aloud, "We don't need words!" He removes his fingers and kisses her deeply, with all his love, as if it might be the last time that he has the chance.

"Thank you for letting me in, Zealand," she says, slaps him on the ass, and pushes him onto the stage. "Now, go change the world… for the better!" She looks down at the floor, and completely exacerbated, says, "Fuck, dude!"

Slaphappy

Zealand steps onto the stage and he's hit by three stage lights in a triangle. They burn through him and the crowds' screaming turns into a high-pitched buzzing that pushes him to his knees and all he hears as he's blinded by pure white light is, "Welcome to a special edition of the Jerry Springer Show. Today we've got a special treat for you. I brought in the freshly acclaimed Second Coming, if you believe in that sort of thing, Zealand T. Dahl. If you haven't heard, he's been traveling the country, healing people of all sorts of ailments. With no religious background or secular claiming, he's been working miracles to the point of amputees growing back their limbs, removing chromosomes from children with Down's syndrome, and even bringing people back from the dead. I brought him here today because, well, in all my years, I've wondered, would I even have a show if someone like this existed? I try to bring some sort of clarity to our guests, but I can honestly say this … it seems pointless. They come on the show for a new dress, a hot meal, and a night in Chicago. Does anything change? Fifteen years later, and you'd think I would've run out of guests. So, with no further ado, I offer you the relentless messiah of the new millennium, Zealand T. Dahl."